The DEVIL'S HORIZON

Matt Tomerlin

"The Devil's Horizon"
Copyright © 2013 Matt Tomerlin
All rights reserved

This is a work of fiction. Names, characters, places and incidents either are products of the author's imagination or are used fictitiously.

No part of this publication may be reproduced or transmitted, in any form or by any means, without the author's prior written permission.

Cover art by Brendon Mroz.

ISBN-13: 978-0615930497
ISBN-10: 0615930492

www.TheDevilsFire.com

This one is for Karen,
the best aunt a nephew could hope to have.

PROLOGUE

September, 1717

At the pinnacle of *Harbinger's* mainmast, an enormous black flag thrashed violently in the wind, embroidered with a bone-white cutlass that was impaling a succulent crimson heart. Just beyond the fluttering cloth, the sun beamed down from a brilliant sapphire sky, but the clarity of the day did little to purge the chill from the North Atlantic air.

"You might have obliged our first cannon fire," Captain Jonathan Griffith said, standing tall on the main deck of *Lady Katherine*, a merchant ship that did not belong to him. He gestured to the frightening flag atop his sleek brigantine, which was running parallel to its prey. "I have a reputation to preserve, you understand."

"But sir, you promised you wouldn't harm anyone else," protested Thomas Lindsay. The normally distinguished captain looked haggard now, forced to his knees on the deck of his own ship. The sun glanced off his shiny scalp through thinning blonde hair.

Captain Lindsay's pretty young wife, Katherine, writhed ineffectually in the clutches of her captors, her eyes consumed with mad desperation. She seemed to know what was coming, even if her husband did not.

The wind swept Griffith's shoulder-length black hair past his ruggedly handsome face, which betrayed no emotion. He wore a long blue coat, white shirt, and a thick black belt with a gold-accented pistol tucked into a red sash. "I promised I wouldn't harm any of the *crew*, beyond that unfortunate young man over there."

The desecrated corpse of Arnold Johnson was starting to stink in the midday sun. Arnold's head had nearly been hacked off, dangling from the neck by nothing more than a few strands of muscle. His blood had formed a red lake around him, swishing back and forth with the motion of the ship, leaching into the seams of the planking. The pirates had murdered him the night prior, as an example of what would happen to anyone else who disobeyed. No one had given them any trouble after that.

"I will uphold that end of the bargain," Griffith continued. "However, I said nothing of sparing the ship's *captain*."

Griffith's bald quartermaster, who had introduced himself as Edward Livingston, grinned sadistically.

Terrence Baldwin could no longer stand by and watch. He had served under Captain Lindsay for two years now, and he considered the man a friend as well as his captain. Lindsay had employed him when Terrence was on the verge of starvation, begging for scraps in London. Terrence's father had died a poor man, leaving him with nothing at a young age. Terrence would have probably died before he reached eighteen had he not happened upon Thomas Lindsay near the docks. Lindsay recognized a young man in need and employed him without hesitation. It was not the sort of decency Terrence had come to expect of the wealthy, as that sort of decency did not come naturally to those who had not earned their fortune. The Lindsays were a prominent, powerful family who had made their fortune in the merchant shipping business long before Thomas had been born. There was no reason for someone like him to be concerned with a poor man.

Terrence started forward without thinking. He couldn't just stand by and watch a pirate murder the man who had saved his life. But before he got very far, he was jerked to a halt.

His best friend, Jeremy, had seized his arm. Jeremy was sporting a swollen purple eye where one of the pirates had punched him. "You'll only get yourself killed," Jeremy hissed sharply in Terrence's ear. "Maybe the rest of us, too."

Terrence struggled to free himself. "We've got to do something!"

"It's too late," Jeremy said.

Griffith grasped the jeweled hilt of his cutlass and drew it. The polished steel flashed blindingly as it ensnared the sun. He plunged the blade into Captain Lindsay's chest. Blood bubbled from Lindsay's mouth, and his face turned pink as he grasped at the pirate captain. Griffith slapped Lindsay's hand away and wrenched the blade from his chest, sheathing it. Lindsay tilted his head toward his wife. The life left his eyes, and he fell to the deck.

Katherine's shriek was the most chilling sound Terrence had ever heard. She attempted to thrust herself at her husband's corpse, but two pirates locked her firmly in place. Her legs moved, but she didn't. She managed to free her right arm and smash one of her captors in the nose with an elbow. She aimed a fist at the man on her left, but he easily evaded it and punched her in the stomach.

The other pirate laughed despite his bleeding nose. "Watch

yourselves, mates. This lass has spirit."

Terrence knew he wasn't alone in admiring Katherine. She was hardly the most beautiful woman he had ever laid eyes on, but women were few and far between for a sailor. She was too skinny, her skin was too pale, and her breasts were too small, but she had an elegant, youthful face, and her fiery mane of curly red hair made up for anything she lacked. Whenever she strolled into his peripheral vision, it was impossible to keep his eyes from shifting her way. He knew she had been uncomfortable around so many men, with no other women in sight, but Terrence thought himself far more polite than his peers. He had approached her only once. She had been leaning against the bulwark, as usual, with a thick black book tucked under her arm. She glanced apprehensively at him as he neared. He asked her what she was reading, and she replied in a jittery voice, "The Odyssey. Do you know it? No, of course you don't. None of you can read." Before he could correct her mistake, she scurried off. Ever since that awkward encounter, he had tried to avoid her whenever possible.

Whatever disdain Terrence had forged for Katherine poured out of him as he watched Captain Griffith gather a handful of her red hair and drag her kicking and screaming toward the planks connecting the two ships.

Terrence looked at Jeremy, who was still holding his arm. "We're just going to stand here?"

Jeremy nodded stiffly, the lid of his inflamed eye lining with water. "If we don't, we're all dead. No sense in that."

"Do you have any idea what's going to happen to that woman?"

Jeremy set his jaw. "Yes."

Katherine stretched her arms to the crew, her eyes fraught with terror. "Help me!" she pleaded. The muscles strained in her thin neck, and a purple vein threatened to pop from her forehead. "Help me, you cowards!"

Terrence recoiled at the word, warmth flooding his cheeks. He wanted to scream back at her, "I tried to be nice to you!"

Instead, he blinked his anger away. This wasn't the time. It didn't matter that she had mistreated him. All that mattered was that she was a young woman. She didn't deserve this.

"Anyone got something they want to say?" asked Edward Livingston, who was scanning the crew with a challenging glower. His fearsome eyes locked with Terrence's. "What about you, boy? You got words?"

Terrence's eyes flickered away involuntarily. He hissed a curse through his teeth.

Livingston cackled. "Strange, no one ever wants to talk to me."

"You bloody cowards!" Katherine went on, her voice breaking. Her saffron dress tore on a splinter as Griffith dragged her across the plank. She looked down, and for a moment Terrence thought she might jump into the water below, where she would most likely drown or be crushed between the two ships. He wondered if that wouldn't be a kinder fate.

Griffith finally hefted her onto the deck of his ship. She scrambled away from him, running to the rail and gazing desperately at her dead husband's crew. Terrence was certain she was looking right at him. He pulled his eyes away in shame.

And then Griffith reacquired her and dragged her to his cabin, hurling her inside and slamming the door. He stood outside staring at the door with a contemplative look on his face, as though he wasn't entirely convinced this was the best course of action.

It wasn't long before *Harbinger* started to pull away. Its black flag seemed to be waving goodbye. None of the pirate crew spared a final glance at the ship they had just plundered.

Terrence's gaze fell on Thomas Lindsay, facedown in a pool of his own blood.

The crew glanced at one another, wondering what they should do next. No one said anything for a long time.

Jeremy's hand fell on Terrence's shoulder. "There's nothing anybody could have done."

"We could have done *something*."

Another voice chimed in. "Not without meeting our makers!"

Terrence glared at the crew, but he wasn't sure who had said it. Could have been anyone. Might as well have been all of them. "Dying would have been something," he shouted at them, and he stomped off.

"Didn't see you do anything!" taunted one of them.

He didn't stop walking until he was inside Lindsay's cabin. He wasn't sure why his feet had carried him here. It was lonely and dark; a stark contrast to the bright blue out on deck. At least there was no blood.

The Lindsays kept their quarters very clean, save for the unmade bed. Terrence pictured the two of them frolicking beneath the sheets. He had to admit he had envied Thomas Lindsay, even after he had forged a dislike of Katherine. The captain got to have her anytime he wanted.

Now he felt only pity and sadness for the both of them.

Something on the bedside table caught his eye, and he was inexorably drawn toward it. He picked up the book, turning it over. "The Odyssey" was engraved in the leather cover.

A hand fell on Terrence's shoulder, and he cried out in alarm, dropping the book. He spun, snatching the wrist that the hand belonged to. Jeremy stared at him. "It's only me. The pirates have gone, remember?"

Terrence released Jeremy's hand and bent down to retrieve the book. He examined it, making sure it hadn't been dented in the fall. The book had opened to a folded page two thirds of the way through.

"What's that?" asked Jeremy, who couldn't read.

"It's called a book," Terrence drawled.

"I know what it is," Jeremy sighed. "What book is it?"

"A good one," Terrence replied. "I wonder if she finished it. I hope she did." Despite the folded page, this might have been her second or third time through. There hadn't been much else for a girl like Katherine to do at sea but read.

"What's it matter, anyways?" Jeremy prodded.

"It matters," Terrence huffed, tucking the book under his arm and exiting the cabin. He heard Jeremy following him, probably with a dumb, worried expression.

Terrence approached the port bulwark, where Katherine Lindsay so often looked out to sea, dreaming of whatever it was she dreamt of. He placed his hands in the same spot she always placed hers. The wood was cold under his palms.

Jeremy appeared at his side, and Terrence felt his eyes on him. "If she keeps her wits," Jeremy said, "she'll make it."

Terrence smirked bitterly as he stared off into the horizon, where the pirate ship was nothing more than a tiny speck that would soon vanish entirely. "Nay," he replied flatly. "That woman is already dead."

1

LANCASTER

February, 1719

An impenetrable black plume lifted from the center of *Ranger's* deck into the clear morning sky. The pirate ship had come to rest in a yawning inlet carved in the center of an island shaped like a horseshoe. The lake sat just beyond a tapered channel flanked by treacherous rocky hills sloping in an uneven V into the water. Apart from a white beach and the scattered palm trees that lined the outer rim, the island was mostly just a semicircle of barren rock.

Captain James Lancaster surmised his wounded prey from the quarterdeck of *HMS Advance*, the tails of his standard issue blue coat flapping in the wind. He lifted his tricorn hat long enough to adjust the stubborn white wig beneath it, and then fitted the hat back in place. The curled locks were heavy with sweat, nudging his powdered cheeks every time he turned his head. The sun was particularly merciless today, especially for early February, and it was just three hours after dawn.

Lancaster had never developed a taste for the Caribbean. He had arrived a month after Woodes Rogers in order to aid him in putting an end to the pirate menace. He had been promised a tropical paradise, but no one had mentioned the relentless humidity. Port Nassau was gradually becoming more habitable, but there was nothing the new governor could do to quell the stifling wet heat. Lancaster had originally intended to build an estate just outside of town and send for his wife, Meredith, but now he just wanted to return to England. Meredith had lived in England all her life, and the Caribbean sun would not be kind to her pale skin. She was a delicate woman who had miscarried twice. Lancaster wasn't sure she'd survive crossing the Atlantic.

He glared at the ship ahead, bobbing gently in the water, with smoke still pouring out of its center. He prayed this would be over swiftly. The sooner he had Charles Vane in custody, the sooner he could retreat to the shelter of his cabin.

Vane was one of the last real pirate threats in the Caribbean, assuming Captain Dillahunt wasn't lying about the death of Edward Teach. Guy Dillahunt, reputed as a highly successful privateer, claimed Teach had perished right in front of him, but he hadn't returned with a corpse. Dillahunt was prone to queer behavior. He was impossible to carry on a conversation with, as he would too often halt midsentence to fixate on an inconsequential detail. He was courting an obscenely young strumpet. He had the gall to bring her to a dinner hosted by Rogers, who was, for whatever reason, fond of Dillahunt. The girl asked embarrassing questions of each of the captains, displaying an alarming fascination with violence. It was clear that Rogers' wife, Sarah, didn't care for her. Some of the men seemed charmed by her, though Lancaster attributed that to her fetching looks rather than her unrefined charisma.

Lancaster supposed he should allow Dillahunt the benefit of

the doubt, given that Rogers trusted the man. *Just as he trusted Benjamin Hornigold,* he reminded himself. That friendship hadn't ended well, with Hornigold running off to pursue some phantom treasure, and discovering his death instead. Employing former pirates to hunt down their own kind never sat well with Lancaster, but he was not one to question the king's wisdom.

Lancaster's first mate, Aaron Roberts, approached with his hands locked behind his back. As always, Roberts was a picture of propriety, with one eyebrow elevated above the other, a lofty nose aimed skyward, and pursed lips that rarely surrendered a smile. He was several years older than Lancaster, and his real hair was starting to match the color of his wig. "Captain, I'm not convinced we can slip through that gap."

Roberts indicated a spot ahead where the rocky walls that flanked the estuary narrowed like the midsection of an hourglass. *Ranger* waited in the wide oval of water just beyond that gap. Lancaster shrugged. "We approach handsomely."

"Our hull is broader than *Ranger's*," Roberts reminded him. *Ranger* was a brigantine, and *HMS Advance* was a fifth-rate warship with forty guns. She was small compared to the large ships of the line, but she was fast, maneuverable, and armed well enough to frighten her prey.

Lancaster allowed himself a smile. "I'm willing to risk a few scrapes on the hull to catch that man. Mr. Arrow and Mr. Daveys heave the lead as we speak. I doubt men as diligent as they will see us run aground without a word of warning." Two leadsmen stood on slim platforms on either side of the ship, swinging ropes with lead plummets at the end, gauging the depth of the channel.

Roberts turned to the helmsman. "Mind your rudder, Mr. Parish."

"Aye, sir," Parish stiffly replied, knuckles white as he

gripped the helm.

Above decks and below, gunners stood at their posts, ready for battle.

Roberts moved close to Lancaster and spoke low. "Captain, we can't be certain Vane is aboard."

"Where else would he go?" Lancaster wondered, sweeping his arm to indicate the barren slopes on either side. The rocky hills were ascending as *Advance* delved further in, and the highest ridge on the starboard side would soon be higher than the mainmast. The early sun in the east would be blocked from their view, and Lancaster was looking forward to the shade's relief.

"This island makes for a rather clever hiding spot," Roberts said.

"Indeed," replied Lancaster. Vane had apparently spent much of his time discovering volcanic islands that were natural hideaways, though the location of his impressive base, Pirate Town, had been compromised after Dillahunt and his crew escaped Vane's clutches. Governor Rogers sent scout ships shortly after Dillahunt reported back, but there was nothing left except a labyrinth of tunnels littered with corpses.

"We have him cornered," Lancaster concluded.

Roberts considered that with a pinched brow. "It is entirely possible he's leading us into some sort of diversion. These pirates are desperate types, after all. A certain mad ingenuity occasionally arises of desperation."

Lancaster focused on the starboard ridge, angling his hat upward. For an instant, he thought he saw a shadow atop the ridge. He squinted, but he saw nothing more. He chuckled lightly, brushing off the odd feeling. "There's nothing clever about Vane's actions. He runs like a dog with its tail tucked between its legs."

"It's strange," Roberts persisted, adjusting the frill of one of his sleeves. "His ship is much faster, yet he went out of his way to broadside us before retreating."

Indeed it was strange, given that *Advance's* return fire had all but devastated *Ranger*, forcing her to limp away to the sanctuary of this little island. "It is my understanding that Charles Vane is a bold man," Lancaster said. "He is not, however, particularly wise."

Lancaster recalled the story Woodes Rogers had told him about Vane burning a ship in the harbor upon Rogers' arrival in Nassau. Despite that rebellious display, Vane had been forced to flee, just like any other common pirate. When it came to authority, pirates were all bark and no bite.

"There's nowhere left to run now," Lancaster assured his first mate. After he delivered Vane into Rogers' hands, perhaps Rogers would grant Lancaster's request to return home. There would be no better time to ask.

Roberts nodded uncertainly. "Aye, Captain."

The first mate didn't sound convinced, but Lancaster didn't care. Roberts would see for himself soon enough.

Advance easily made the narrow gap, and Lancaster smiled confidently. There was at least twenty feet of space on either side at the slimmest point. It was close, but the steep hills plunged much deeper into the water than the ship's hull. Roberts inclined his head. "Apologies, captain."

"None required, my friend," Lancaster replied with a hand on Roberts' shoulder. "It was guesswork on both our parts, and there was half a chance I'd be apologizing to you right now." Roberts' keen advice had benefited Lancaster more than once. It was good to have a man like him onboard, even if he *was* a tad overcautious. They had served together for five years, and survived many battles. Lancaster would invite him to his cabin for a celebratory dinner tonight, where they would toast the end of piracy and contemplate their futures. He knew Roberts would happily follow him back to England, but he would give the man a choice nonetheless.

"Captain!"

Lancaster frowned down at the main deck. The crew was gathering at the bulwark, staring upward. Master Stevenson was pointing starboard. "On the ridge, captain!" he shouted. "Men on the ridge!"

Lancaster's eyes scaled the hill on the starboard side, all the way to the ridge above the ship's highest mast. Nearly three dozen pirates were silhouetted up there, moving fast. Some of them were crouching, nudging the ground with sticks.

No, not sticks, Lancaster realized in horror. *Torches.* A thin trail of fire was spreading along the ridge.

"Oh my God," said Roberts.

"Muskets!" Lancaster cried, but it was too late.

The slope erupted in a tremendous fireball that was five times as large as *Advance*. Bits of rock and dust billowed into the air in a giant brown cloud that blotted out the sun. The slope rumbled violently, dark fissures split the surface, and massive chunks of hillside shook free. A slab of rock the size of a longboat tumbled down the hill and impacted the water, sending a rolling wave against *Advance's* hull, rocking her. The slab started to sink as huge boulders piled on top of it, nudging it toward *Advance*.

Lancaster turned around and saw more shadows appearing on the opposite ridge, and several of them had torches as well. "Fire!" he called, pointing at the other ridge. Even as he gave the order, he knew a musket shot would never hit anything from this range without a miracle. "Don't let them light—"

The port slope exploded. The fireball wasn't quite as large as the first, but it was enough. Huge chunks of the hillside crumbled toward the water. Boulders bounced down, cutting through the dust.

Lancaster looked from one slope to the next in disbelief. The hills on both sides were crumbling toward *Advance*. Rocks piled up in the water, coming closer and closer to the hull. An impossibly large boulder impacted the rubble on the starboard side, and it kept rolling. It smashed into the hull, shuddering the ship and nudging her closer to the opposite slope. And then another boulder hit from the opposite slope. The ship rocked violently, throwing Roberts off his feet. His wig flew from his head. Thick clouds of dust swept over the deck from either side.

Half of the crew rushed to the starboard bulwark while the other half fell to the port bulwark, crouching low. Many of them aimed muskets. Shots cracked off the close walls. Three shadowy figures went tumbling down the starboard slope. Two of them caught outcroppings, but the third rolled all the way into the water, disappearing somewhere below *Advance's* hull.

On the port side, another boulder was projected into the air from a curved ledge. It touched down on the bow, splintering the deck and propelling a man skyward. He hit the foremast like a ragdoll, back bending the wrong way, and tumbled to the deck.

More rubble hit the port side. The leadsman on that side was suddenly pitched over the rail. He slid along the hull and landed feet-first on the rocks that had collected below. His legs buckled on impact. A huge boulder came rolling over the rubble just then, splattering the leadsman's torso like a bug under a boot.

The last boulder collected in the rubble, the hull groaned a mournful protest, and the ship was firmly wedged in place. Lancaster looked to the lake ahead, just beyond the gap, where *Ranger* taunted him, just out of reach. "This can't be happening," he muttered.

Gunshots cracked from above. Pirates bellowed battle cries

as they zigzagged down the diminished hillsides, vanishing into the lingering clouds of dust.

"Fire cannons!" Lancaster instructed.

Advance unleashed a volley of cannonballs at both slopes. Each impact was thunderous, kicking up even more dust, spotted by an occasional spray of red as a man was perforated.

"We're aiding their attack," Roberts said as he got to his feet, sweeping a hand over his matted silver hair. "Can't see where they—"

A shot zipped past Lancaster's cheek. "That was close," he gasped.

Roberts said nothing.

"Roberts?"

Roberts didn't answer. A stream of blood ran down his open mouth, dribbling off of his chin and collecting on his chest. His eyes rolled up in their sockets, until they were nothing but white. As the first mate collapsed, Lancaster glimpsed a gaping hole in the back of his mouth.

Lancaster turned to the main deck. "Hold fire! HOLD FIRE!"

Gunshots and cannon blasts gradually petered out, except from the enemy. The crew looked to Lancaster questioningly. "We will not fire blindly," he said. "We'll wait until they show themselves."

The men did as commanded, waiting patiently despite the enemy musket balls shooting from the dust. Six men were hit. Three of them died instantly, while the other three fell to the deck and clutched their wounds. They were each dragged away from the bulwark, and the doctor, Gilkerson, went to work on the first man.

"Hold!" Lancaster urged, sensing the crew's eagerness to fire. If one man pulled the trigger, they all would.

After a moment, he realized the gunshots from the dust had

ceased. There was a long silence that was somehow worse than gunfire. "What are they doing?" he asked Roberts, and then he remembered the corpse a few feet behind him. He refused to look. He would mourn his friend later.

A three-pronged grapple flew out of the dust, sailing toward the mainmast, with a thick rope trailing behind it. It hooked a yardarm. Two dozen more grapples followed. Pirates swung out of the dust toward the main deck.

"FIRE!" Lancaster ordered.

The crew opened fire. Several pirates crashed to the deck. Others fell before they reached the ship, their bones cracking on the rubble below, leaving smears of blood as they slid into the cracks between the rocks.

A pirate came swinging through the haze toward Lancaster. Lancaster drew his pistol and fired into the man's chest, dropping him from the rope. The pirate's back hit the port rail of the quarterdeck with a sickening *snap*, and he glanced off and spiraled into the water below. Lancaster threw the smoking pistol aside and unsheathed a polished small sword, descending the stairs to the main deck. It was a dress sword given to him by his late commodore father, who had received the weapon along with his commission. At fifty, Lancaster's father had unexpectedly taken ill and died in his sleep. Lancaster was beginning to suspect he would not be afforded the same luxury.

Several more grapples flew forward to claw the yardarms and ratlines. Too many pirates were getting through, dropping to the deck and engaging Lancaster's crew with pistols and cutlasses. They were also scaling the hull. Some of them met with a pistol shot or sword to the face the instant they peeked their heads over the rails.

It wasn't enough.

Lancaster joined his men on the main deck. He would not let his crew fight for their lives while their captain was safely removed from battle. Gilkerson had often berated him for that while tending to his wounds after a fight. "I should have served on a ship with a captain sensible enough to stay out of the path of a sword," the doctor would gripe. "What good is a ship without its leader?" Lancaster prayed his men would never have to discover the answer to that question, but his presence was a boon to their resolve, so it was a risk he was willing to take.

His sword pierced the shoulder blades of a pirate who had left his flank unguarded. Lancaster wrapped a muscular arm around his victim's neck and yanked him into the blade, until the man's back hit the hilt, and then he kicked him away. The pirate crumpled to his knees, managed a stunned look over his shoulder, and then fell on his face.

Lancaster moved to the next. The pirates were everywhere now, and there were already too many corpses to count, on both sides. However, a quick glance was enough to tell him that *Advance* was losing. More pirates kept swinging onto the deck and climbing over the bulwark, as if their numbers were endless.

Gilkerson was seeing to a man's wounds when a pirate grabbed a handful of the doctor's hair, drew his head back and sliced his neck, spilling his blood all over the man he'd been attending.

"Doctor!" Lancaster screamed after the fact.

He looked to the starboard slope and saw another horde of men charging down through the thinning dust, swords pointed at the ship. A smaller group was charging down the opposite slope.

Rollins, the master at arms, stepped beside Lancaster, his gaunt face as white as the sails above. He had a perpetually grim expression that was somehow a shade grimmer than usual. "This is impossible," he said as he stared at the men flooding toward the ship like a river unleashed from a ruptured dam.

"Evidently not," Lancaster replied through clenched teeth.

"What do we do, captain?"

Lancaster stared at him. "We fight to the very last. I will not see this ship fall into the hands of Charles Vane, is that understood?"

Rollins nodded and returned to battle, thrusting his sword into the nearest pirate's throat. "You heard the captain, men!" he yelled. "No quarter!"

Lancaster saw a particularly large pirate trying to get over the starboard bulwark. The captain rushed forward and brought his blade down on the man's knuckles. The large pirate shrieked and involuntarily relinquished his grip. A few bloody fingers remained on the rail.

Lancaster kneeled beside the corpse of a dead deckhand and retrieved his gun, which hadn't been fired. He returned to the bulwark, aiming down at the next pirate ascending the hull. He pulled the trigger, and the pirate's right eye disintegrated.

A hand shot up from his left, grasping Lancaster's wrist. He saw an evil dark face beneath a red bandana. The pirate must have been flattening himself against the hull, hidden in shadow. Lancaster flipped the discharged pistol over, letting the hot barrel slap into his palm, and beat the man repeatedly over the head with the pommel, until his skull caved in. The evil face went strangely innocent and childlike.

Lancaster returned his attention to the main deck. His heart sank. There were far more corpses and wounded men than just a few moments ago. Those that stood were difficult to see through the pirates that swarmed around them.

Lancaster couldn't believe this was happening. They had lost in but a few minutes. *This is the last mistake I'll ever make,* he realized grimly.

He found Rollins near the mainmast, engaged in a duel with a much taller pirate. Rollins finished his combatant off by swiping his blade across the man's knees. The pirate collapsed, and Rollins sank his blade into his skull. When the master at arms turned to greet Lancaster, his face was doused in blood. "Captain," he greeted.

"We're not done," Lancaster said.

Rollins shrugged. "I didn't say we were."

"The powder magazine," Lancaster said, setting a hand on Rollins' shoulder. "I want you to ignite the powder magazine. We'll take all of these bastards with us."

Rollins ran his arm over his mouth, smearing the blood. He sniffed and nodded. "Aye, captain." Without another word, Rollins made for the hold.

Lancaster didn't pause to watch him go. He joined the dozen or so of his crew that were still standing. "To the very last!" he reminded them. They nodded, all proud to die beside their captain.

They formed a circle as the pirates swept in around them. The clash of steel was deafening. Ten pirates died before the enemy tried a new tactic. A stout pirate with a yellow and black striped bandana threw a granado. "Move!" Lancaster shouted, and the circle was broken. The deck ruptured where they had been standing, splinters raining down. Two of Lancaster's crew fell dead instantly, with bits of wood lodged in vital areas. Lancaster got to his feet and scanned the advancing pirates until he glimpsed yellow. He lunged for the man, thrusting his sword. Two pirates leapt out of the way, and the tip of the blade found its target.

Before Lancaster could locate his next victim, a sharp pain pinched his abdomen. He glanced down to see a blade wedged in his right side, just beneath his ribs. The pirate who held it was older, with grey hair and a surprisingly distinguished face. He almost looked apologetic, even as he twisted the hilt.

The pain buckled Lancaster's knees. The older pirate eased

the blade free, placing a heel on Lancaster's back and shoving him onto his belly.

"That's it, then!" whooped a very young pirate with mussed hair painted blue, yellow, and red. "We done it! We caught ourselves a frigate!"

"Shut your hole, Keet," growled the older pirate as he wiped Lancaster's blood from his blade with a soiled handkerchief.

Lancaster kept his head down and waited. Any minute now they'd all be in for an explosive surprise. He couldn't help but chuckle, despite the pain shearing through his torso. The wound was fatal, he knew. He had been wounded many times, but none had ever felt like this. It was difficult to keep his eyes open. His fingers tingled, his lips felt numb, his head light and distant. Despite the heat, he was suddenly freezing.

"What's so funny, captain?" wondered the old man who had felled him.

"He thinks he knows something we don't," said an authoritatively powerful voice, tinged with a mocking flourish. "But I, too, know something, captain."

A boot slipped under Lancaster's belly and rolled him onto his back. He cried out, clutching his ribs. He hacked violently, and a gooey blob ejected into his mouth, tasting of rusty metal . . . or what he imagined rusty metal must taste like.

"Did this go as you expected?" said the amused, imposing voice.

Lancaster squinted as the sun peeked over the eastern ridge. The thinning dust swirled around a tall man with curly auburn hair. He was illuminated on one side, shadowed on the other. His strong jaw was shrouded in stubble, his mouth angled in a smirk. His eyes gleamed of an impossibly vibrant emerald. He wore a long forest green coat with buttons that glinted gold.

"Vane," Lancaster wheezed.

Vane's smirk widened. "I see I require no introduction. I'm

deeply flattered." He frowned. "That said, I'm afraid I haven't the murkiest fuck of a notion who you are."

"Captain James Lancaster, his majesty's royal navy."

Vane scoffed. "His majesty's royal arsehole, more like."

Lancaster spat blood, but it didn't go very far, arcing only two feet in the air and splattering the deck. A pirate moved his foot before it could touch his toes. "I am but the first of many."

Vane made a show of false fear, clutching his breast. "I tremble."

"You will in a few moments," Lancaster promised through chattering teeth. He was so damned cold. He felt the life seeping out of the hole in his side, but he knew he had just long enough to feel the heat beneath him before it consumed the deck. He would savor Vane's final surprised expression, even as the flames claimed them both.

For some reason, Vane was laughing. "Let's not get ahead of ourselves, captain. I wouldn't want you making a mockery of yourself so near the end of your life. What we do in our final moments is all anybody will remember of us." He snapped his fingers at one of his men. "Bring me that."

One of Vane's crew stepped forward, blocking the sun, and handed something the size of a large cannonball to Vane. It was difficult to make out the details with the sun just beyond it. Vane shook the round object, and fluids oozed from it in thin tendrils, splashing the deck. Vane kneeled beside Lancaster and brought the object into view. "Has your vision faded yet? I hope not."

The gaunt face was instantly recognizable, though Lancaster had never seen it so contorted. Rollins' jaw was hanging open, twisted to one side. His bloodshot eyes were raised to the sky. Blood dribbled out of his nose and ears. Strands of muscle and skin and a few notches of severed spine dangled from the wet mess underneath.

"When you want something done . . . " Vane said, and tossed the head aside. Lancaster didn't see where it landed, but he heard it thumping across the deck, until it hit the bulwark with a *squelch*. Some of Vane's men laughed.

Lancaster let his head fall back as his body convulsed with shivers. "You're every bit the monster they say you are."

Vane's smirk faded for an instant, and a disturbing sincerity crept into his eyes. "You should have listened to them before you followed me blindly into this channel. I've been waiting a long time for a fly to fall into this trap. I must say, you're a bold man, captain. Foolish, but bold. I thought you'd send in longboats. I might have only picked off a few of your men if you'd held back and tested my defenses. But not you, brave sir. You sailed in with your entire ship." His delighted giggle would have suited a ten year old boy. "This went better than I could have imagined."

"Your luck will run out," Lancaster promised.

"Eventually," Vane replied carelessly. "Everyone's does, as you can now attest."

"Get on with it, then."

"Oh, I'll happily end your suffering in a moment," Vane assured him. He leaned closer, setting a hand on Lancaster's chest and pressing down. It took everything Lancaster had left not to shriek. "But first, you must answer a simple question."

Lancaster cackled bitterly through his teeth. "I will not compromise my station to spare myself a few scant moments of agony."

"I'll wager you will, captain," Vane persisted. He slid a hand around the back of Lancaster's head, drawing him closer, as a lover would. He whispered softly into Lancaster's ear. "You've more life in you than you give yourself credit for. We can give you another hour or two, with proper attention. My surgeon is highly skilled. He knows how to keep a dying man alive. Your fingers, on the other hand, aren't vital. Or your toes. Or your balls."

"Do what you will," Lancaster growled.

"Fetch the clippers," Vane called over his shoulder to the man with painted hair.

Keet started off, then halted and turned slowly, scratching his chin. "Which ones, captain?"

Vane withered. "The ones that cut through bone."

Lancaster squirmed beneath Vane's hand. "Cut away," he said. It didn't matter what Vane did to him now, nothing would stop him from dying. Even if he did survive another hour, there was only so much pain a man could withstand before he went into shock.

"You haven't even heard the question yet," Vane said. "It's an easy one, I promise. It doesn't even concern you. All you have to do is tell me where I might find Katherine Lindsay."

The name was familiar, but Lancaster couldn't place it. "I have no idea who you're speaking of."

"A redhead with a rather large reward on her head," Vane offered helpfully, rolling his finger in a progressive motion, as if that would encourage Lancaster's thought process. "Dillahunt brought her in, last I heard. I imagine she's rather furious about that. She's a feisty one. Tell me, was she shipped off to England?"

Lancaster remembered the woman now. He had met her only once, but her fiery hair was impossible to forget. She had somehow survived being kidnapped by Jonathan Griffith and an encounter with Blackbeard . . . the very same encounter that Dillahunt claimed had ended with Blackbeard's demise. Rogers had been keeping Lindsay safely tucked away in his mansion, waiting for her dead husband's family to arrive and provide Dillahunt with a reward before returning her to London. But

Lancaster didn't see how that could be of any interest to Vane. "What could you possibly want with her?" He choked on the question, hacking another thick glob of blood into his mouth.

Vane smiled courteously, lightly patting Lancaster's chest. "That's the part that doesn't concern you."

2

KATE

Three bolts of lightning flashed silently in rapid succession, illuminating the drab white walls of the oversized dining room and the dour figure in the huge painting above the mantle. A crackling fireplace provided most of the light, along with two candelabra flickering at either end of the long table, branching three tapers each. A large brass chandelier hung above the center of the table, but the candles were not lit.

A prolonged tremor of thunder arrived several moments later, and the silverware rattled on the table and empty soup bowls jittered atop their plates. Kate Lindsay couldn't resist a shudder, and Sarah Rogers let out a mousey squeak of alarm, but Governor Woodes Rogers did not raise his head to acknowledge the disturbance. "It's going to rain, I think," he said absently, and forked a large bite of poached egg into his mouth.

The blue drapes had been pulled away from the windows

lining the side of the room opposite the fireplace, but the outside world was dull and colorless. The clouds had swept in earlier that afternoon, blanketing Nassau in premature darkness. Kate looked forward to the storm. The pattering of rain against her window always put her right to sleep, and sleep did not come easily of late. She tried too hard to dream about ships and blistering sunlight and rolling waves, but the anticipation of such dreams made it all the more difficult to reach them. And whenever she did dream those wonderful dreams, she would wake to the tight walls of her dark little room, huddled in expensive sheets so snugly tucked that she could barely remove herself from them.

Sarah Rogers, sitting close to her husband at the head of the table, with straight and proper posture, took another nibble of her first poached egg. Kate, seated far from the couple at the foot of the table, was long done. The eggs had been delicious, the yolks spiced with paprika, and she wished there had been more than just three. Woodes finished his last egg, washing it down with a glass of brandy and orange juice, which he claimed would "stifle a cold before it can muster." Upon hearing that, Kate quickly adopted a sniffle and requested a glass of the same, which she was halfway done with and already feeling pleasantly lightheaded. The brandy was silky smooth and the juice was invigoratingly fresh and pulpy.

Sarah ate so slowly that Kate could hardly stand it. It made these dinners, rare though they were, all the more unbearable. Every Wednesday she was summoned from her room, where she had spent the better part of a month waiting for Thomas's family to arrive in port and withdraw her back to London. Woodes had provided a dark blue dress for dinner occasions, which looked black in anything except direct light. She told him she would have preferred green, and he promptly alerted her to the garment's extreme value, as if that should mean something to her. The exquisite floral patterns were difficult to see, especially with her fiery red hair to divert the eye. The dress was a size too large for her, and the neckline didn't show as much of her breasts as she would have preferred.

Sarah was ever a stark contrast, with straight brown hair and a plain beige dress. She was painfully skinny and pale, with bony cheeks and big brown eyes. She was very pretty when she smiled, but she rarely did. When she spoke, her voice was so slight that Kate had to lean forward to hear what she was saying, and sometimes Kate just pretended she had understood her when she hadn't the foggiest clue. She had grown accustomed to nodding and smiling politely at anything Sarah said. She liked Sarah, in spite of their diminished communication. She had learned that Sarah's maiden name was Whetstone, and that she was the daughter of Sir William Whetstone, a distinguished rear admiral in the Royal Navy who had also been a friend to the Lindsay family, before his death in 1711. Kate remembered Thomas talking about Sir William in grand detail. "The further you go, the smaller the world gets," Kate had told Sarah on the night they had discovered their connection. Sarah responded with a knowing smile and a tiny, unintelligible retort that Kate took for consensus.

Kate looked again at the painting above the fireplace, with a tall man silhouetted against the horizon, his back to the viewer, one foot set upon the railing of a ship. He wore a long coat and a tricorn hat, with the locks of a curly brown wig tumbling down his back. "Is that meant to be you?" she asked Woodes, drawing out her words so as not to slur them. The brandy was working too fast. She had hoped to finish it quickly and ask for another, but now she wasn't sure she would even be able to finish this one.

Woodes glanced at the painting. "I suppose it is." He was indeed tall, but his belly was considerably larger than the man above the fireplace, and he wore a white Governor's wig in place of a brown one. Kate wondered what his hair looked like beneath it, assuming he retained any at all. Perhaps he had once been a dashing young man, but she was put off by his sloping chin and bushy eyebrows. His most interesting feature was a scar cratered in his left cheek. His jaw was distorted on that side, as if it had been shattered. His skin was irrevocably dark and leathery, from all his time spent at sea.

"What are you thinking about?" Kate asked. "In the painting, I mean."

Woodes looked at the painting and frowned dubiously, as though considering it for the first time. "I'm probably thinking about the future. That is what all young men think about, isn't it? Not where they are presently, but where they might be. Where they want to be."

"And is this where you want to be?"

Sarah looked to her husband expectantly.

The governor's bushy eyebrows bunched closely. "Yes. But the queer thing about reaching a goal is that once you've reached it, you fondly recall the path that led you there, and wish you had thought to pause and enjoy it."

Sarah murmured something and then looked down at her remaining eggs.

Kate smirked. "If you had paused to enjoy it, you might never have reached your goal."

The governor's distorted jaw prevented an even smile, but it was something of a smile nonetheless, and for a moment Kate glimpsed a younger man. "And what goal do you strive for, Mrs. Lindsay?"

"I am enjoying the path," Kate replied with a smile of her own.

Woodes gulped the last of his brandy and set it down, regarding the empty glass. "Expulsis piratis, restitua commercia," he stated portentously, raising his eyes. "Do you know what that means?"

"No."

"It's Latin. It means, 'Piracy expelled, commerce restored.'" He stared at her. "All paths must come to an end. That is the only certainty in this life."

Another bolt of lightning flashed in the distance.

"I am not a pirate."

Woodes' tongue worked the inside of his scarred cheek, pushing it outward. "You might have fooled me."

The thunder finally arrived, rolling over the house like a wave.

"I must have," she noted, "seeing as you've treated me to luxury instead of the gallows."

"Your husband's family is influential," Woodes grated, visibly flustered. "Believe me, I had a mind to string you up for corrupting my good friend."

Kate's scoff echoed loudly off the plain white walls. "I assure you, Benjamin Hornigold required no incentive. The mere mention of treasure set a fire in his eyes."

"And you were quick to fuel the flames, weren't you?"

She shrugged. "I did very little. In fact, he came to resent me, despite his part in the deed. I was little more than a guide. It was clear he lamented his betrayal, especially when things started going ill. I fear he died a coward. I don't think he was as fond of you as you as you are of him. If everything had gone to plan, I doubt his thoughts would have turned to regret."

"Yes, well, as far as England knows, the man died a hero, pursuing pirates through a storm."

Kate couldn't believe what she was hearing. "So you lied."

"I have preserved Benjamin's integrity, even though he could not. History will recall a better man. A man who successfully conquered his base instincts."

"You just don't want the king to know that one of your best men returned to piracy. History won't know that you failed." She saw an opportunity and seized it quickly. "I will not be silent about the matter, should you return me to London."

Woodes was unmoved. "Say whatever you like. No one will believe the ravings of a widow who mistook herself for a pirate."

"I never claimed to be a pirate," she objected. "Nor do I claim to be otherwise, unlike you."

"You're fortunate your reward is high," Woodes muttered through his teeth. "Guy Dillahunt is a good man and I would not deprive him of his prize. That is the only reason you are still alive."

Kate bristled at the name of the man who had betrayed her. She had tried to think about Dillahunt as little as possible. In exchange for saving his life, he had promised he wouldn't turn her in. Instead, he had swiftly handed her to Rogers and claimed credit for her heroism. "Dillahunt is as much a traitor as Benjamin Hornigold. His word means nothing. He will turn from you just as readily, if it serves his purpose."

"I could still throw you in a dungeon cell until your in-laws arrive," Woodes snarled, cheeks trembling. The brandy was affecting him as well. He was generally not so easily rattled. Kate had prodded him before and failed to rile him. This excited her.

"But you won't do that," she said, "because you wouldn't want them to find me in a condition of disarray. I needn't remind you of their influence."

"And I needn't remind you of your scars," Woodes returned, aiming a finger at her face. "Already you are in a ghastly state of disarray."

The thin line that slanted down her left cheek was only plain in certain light. She had two other gashes along her scalp, hidden by her thick hair. But the worst injury was her missing right ear, bitten off by Edward Livingston. Nothing remained but shiny garbled flesh and a small black hole. She took care to make sure it was concealed, but she could not always keep her hair in place, and she would often note a flash of revulsion from anyone she was talking to as they caught glimpse of it. Despite the scars, she was far happier with her appearance now. She was curvy where she had once been bony, and her muscles were much stronger. Her skin had been darkened by the sun, although after a month in Rogers' mansion it was not quite as dark as it had been when she first arrived. Still, she was a far cry from the timid, skinny, pale girl that Griffith had taken from *Lady Katherine*. That seemed so long ago now, although it was barely a year and a half.

"You plant seeds of doubt," Woodes prattled on, "with no regard for the consequences unless they directly affect you. Benjamin Hornigold is dead because of your meddling."

Kate enjoyed seeing him so flustered while she remained calm. "Hornigold is dead because of Hornigold. He has no one to blame but himself, though I doubt that thought occurred to him in his final moments."

Woodes took several breaths, trying to calm himself. "In spite of his flaws, Benjamin was a good man. You exploited his weakness. Had you never existed, I'm certain his path would not have turned to treachery."

"You surround yourself with wolves and are shocked to find feathers in place of hens. Hornigold was always a pirate, and now he's dead." She smiled confidently. "Another step towards restoration of commerce, yes?"

Woodes slammed a fist on the table, rattling his plate and giving Sarah a start. Kate felt the vibration of the wood all the way down at her end of the table. "You're a conniving little—"

"Woodes!" Sarah pleaded, her voice uncharacteristically

loud and clear. Her slender fingers gripped the frill of his sleeve and tugged on it. "Insults do not become you," she said, her voice lowering toward its normal decibel.

Woodes blinked and quickly composed himself. He took his wife's hand in his and smiled apologetically "Of course, you're right. Mrs. Lindsay is skilled at raising a man's blood, and this brandy has stolen some of my senses."

"Mine as well," Kate said. She didn't want to be dismissed before dinner and have to return to her room with a growling stomach.

Woodes smiled at her, but there was no mirth in his eyes.

In the silence that followed, Sarah finally finished her first poached egg and then set her hands on her lap. Kate wondered how long it would take her to get to the second. An elderly butler with a large nose and half-closed eyes entered the room, approaching Woodes at the far end of the table. "We're ready for the main course," Woodes told him, a tad briskly.

"Are you finished, Mrs. Rogers?" the butler asked Sarah. She nodded and smiled, and he took her plate of leftover poached eggs and stacked it atop Kate's. Kate stared lustfully at Sarah's eggs until the butler took them from the room. She prayed the main course would be something substantive.

"Why does your family want you back?" Woodes asked. "I'm curious."

Martha cannot let me go, Kate might have said, but she didn't feel he deserved an answer. She had thought about Martha Lindsay's sweet, loving face more and more over the past month, for she had nothing but time to dwell on the past. Martha was her husband Thomas's mother, and Martha had doted on Kate as if she were her own daughter. And since her real mother was dead, Kate readily accepted Martha's warmth. Martha had birthed four boys, and Kate suspected she regretted not having a daughter. She had taken a liking to Kate instantly.

Thomas had been her favored son, and with him lost, Kate was her only link. The Lindsay merchant trade was immensely profitable, so they had money to spare.

It wouldn't be so bad to see her again, Kate realized. But then she looked at the painting of the man who was supposed to be Woodes Rogers, looking to the horizon from the deck of his ship. And then she looked at Sarah Rogers, skinny and polite, confined to a big, dark, mostly empty house. *I'm sorry, Martha. That is not me. Not anymore.* She doubted Martha would even recognize her now. What would they talk about? That time she put a shot through One-Eyed Henry's knee and left him to die on a burning ship? Or maybe that time she roused Hornigold's crew into stealing the sails from a merchant ship that was merely trying to help?

"I see," Woodes said when he realized he wasn't going to get an answer.

The big-nosed butler returned with a pretty maid named Emma, both carrying large platters, each with a very large grilled fish, steamed potatoes, and a side of butter. The butler placed a platter before Woodes. "Refill this, would you?" Woodes said, handing the butler his empty glass. "No juice this time. Just brandy."

Emma set a platter before Sarah and another before Kate, winking conspiratorially. Emma sometimes snuck into her room at night, when the house was asleep, so they could talk about things improper for ladies to talk about. Emma was a few years older, but she had lived her entire life in servitude, was illiterate, and knew very little about the world. She had made the crossing to the Caribbean with Woodes Rogers, who her mother had worked for until she died, and she knew very little about the Caribbean from the confines of the mansion grounds. Kate would sometimes comb Emma's long, wavy black hair, which was always tied up in a bun for her house chores. Kate would tell her stories of her adventures at sea, and Emma always listened intently with wide eyes and a smile. If not for Emma's company, Kate might have lost her mind.

The butler swiftly returned with a new glass of brandy for Woodes. Sarah nibbled at a bite of her fish and murmured that she wasn't feeling very well. She never was. Woodes ate half of his, and then nursed his second brandy. Kate cleaned her plate in five minutes, except for the head of the fish, with its big round eye staring up at her accusingly. She drained the last of her brandy and juice, wincing at its sharp tartness.

When the butler and Emma returned to retrieve the plates, Woodes said, "Emma, please see Mrs. Lindsay to her room." He did not make eye contact with Kate again. Something told her this would be her last dinner with the Rogers family.

"Yes, sir," Emma said with a little bow.

"Good night, Katherine," Sarah murmured, offering the meekest of smiles.

"Good night, Sarah," Kate genuinely returned, and said nothing to the governor.

Emma escorted her up the half-circle grand staircase in the foyer and down the long hall on the second floor to her room. "I'll come visit as soon as I can, miss," Emma promised as they reached the door.

Kate had told her a dozen times to call her by name, but there were some formalities Emma would never relent. "I look forward to it," Kate replied, giving the pretty maid's hand a tender squeeze.

Once inside the dark room, Kate heard Emma latch the door behind her. She was not allowed to roam freely after six o'clock. Kate crossed the room to the window and opened the drapes. Rain drizzled softly against the warbled glass. The clouds had covered the jungle beyond the grounds of the house. On a clear day she could see the ocean stretching out over the tops of the trees, blue and shimmering. Nassau was mostly obscured beneath the hills of the jungle, but she could see the tops of some of the taller buildings. Sometimes in the morning she heard the reports of the cannons around the harbor and fort, and she liked to imagine pirates were sacking the port, and that they would storm the governor's mansion and whisk her off to her next adventure. But she knew the soldiers were simply running drills.

She wasn't sure which was worse; the thought of being sent back to London, or being trapped in a condensed piece of London with the Caribbean just outside, taunting her with its beauty, in plain sight, but well out of reach.

She swung the shutters wide. The wind swept in, snapping the drapes and tugging at her hair. Light rain speckled her face, soft and cold on her cheeks. She closed her eyes and filled her nostrils with the wet tropical air, which was laced with brine and a tinge of seaweed. She couldn't see the ocean through the grey, but she knew it was there.

3

CALLOWAY

"It was him!" the strumpet shrieked as she scurried naked down the hallway. Calloway was struck by how unsightly the female form could be when running nude. The strumpet's thighs reverberated with each impact of her heels, like too much pudding on a quivering spoon. Tears streamed from her huge round eyes, irises darting madly through white pools. "It was Blackbeard!" she cried. "He killed Elise! He killed your mum! Oh God! Oh God!"

The words were meaningless.

Calloway covered her mouth, but a laugh spewed from her nostrils in snorts. *Doesn't she realize how silly she looks?* "You should find your clothes," she informed the silly girl. *I think her name is Polly.* "Polly?"

Polly's head swiveled as she ran past. "He's killed your mum! Oh God!"

"Alright, Polly," Calloway said, withdrawing her laughter.

Something was seriously wrong with the poor girl. "You watch your step, Polly. You'll go straight down those—"

"Didn't you hear me?" Polly's long head was tilted all the way around like a duck's. She wasn't watching where she was headed. "It was Blackbeard," she said again.

Calloway raised a hand. "Polly! The stairs!"

Polly didn't stop.

Polly never listened to anybody.

Polly dropped into the dark round hole in the floor, and a rickety scream trailed off as she rolled down the spiraled staircase all the way to the bottom.

Calloway sighed. *Oh, Polly. You silly girl.*

Polly's overweight patron wandered out into the hallway after her. He at least had the good sense to cover his waist with a sheet. He approached Calloway with a dazed look, two fingers pressed against his forehead in distress. Above a bushy red beard, his cheeks were pale and damp. "That's a sight I'll not soon forget," he muttered with a quivering lip. When he noticed Calloway, he thrust out his palms. "You'd best not go in there, miss. You'd best leave that to someone else."

"I'll go where I please," Calloway huffed. Why was everyone suddenly telling her what to do? It was infuriating!

The man's fat cheeks trembled as he ardently shook his head. "Going in there won't please you, miss."

Calloway had no idea what he was talking about. "Shove off," she said, slapping his hands away. He reached for her again, and she plunged her fist into his considerable gut, which reverberated outward in waves, like ripples in a pond. His cheeks ballooned, and a puff of hot breath popped from his lips and blasted her face. The sheet fell away, and she saw more of him than she cared to.

"That wasn't nice," the man groaned, bending over to retrieve his sheet.

"You should be more concerned with Polly," Calloway haughtily informed him. "She went and took a spill down the steps. I hope she's alright. Never looks where she's going, the silly girl."

The patron quickly refastened his sheet around his waist, gasping for breath. "Did you not hear what happened, miss?" he wheezed.

"Polly said something about my mother. It didn't make any sense. Polly never makes any sense."

The bearded man continued down the hallway towards the stairs. He looked down the hole to the spiral staircase. "Oh, Polly."

"I'm alright," came a tiny voice from below. "I hurt me bum, is all."

At the opposite end of the hallway, three strumpets were gathered outside Calloway's mother's doorway, staring in with their hands clasped over their mouths. A brunette named Alice noticed Calloway and hurried over. Alice's pretty face spasmed as she wrestled against tears. "It's your mother, dearie. She's gone away."

"Gone away? Where's she gone?"

"She's passed."

"Passed?"

Alice put a hand on Calloway's shoulder. Calloway was distracted by the fine black hairs on Alice's arm. "How'd she pass?" She didn't know what she was asking. No one was making any sense.

"Someone took a knife to her," Alice said, removing her hand from Calloway's shoulder. Alice's chin started to tremble. She sniffed frenetically. "It's dreadful bloody in there, dearie. You'd best not go in."

"Not someone," a hefty blonde named Bonny interjected, turning angrily from Elise's doorway. "It was Teach. You all know it. You all saw him leave, same as I did. He was the last one saw her. Who else could it be?"

"Her wrists are open," said the third girl, another blonde, five feet tall and skinny, save for her big round butt. Calloway had never bothered talking to this one. She had a high-pitched, scornful voice that Calloway didn't care for. "She's done herself in."

"I don't think so," said Bonny, whirling on the squat little blonde and pointing a finger. "That's what Blackbeard wanted us to think, is all. He's a keen one."

"Why would Blackbeard care what anyone thinks?" asked Alice. "Especially a bunch of whores?"

Calloway tried to get past Alice, but Alice wasn't having it. "You'd best not go in there, dearie."

Calloway had had enough of people telling her what she'd best not do. "Get out of my way," she ordered, and when Alice didn't move, Calloway shoved her aside and marched toward her mother's room. She would get to the bottom of this, whatever this was. Bonny and the little blonde pressed their backs to a curtained wall to let her pass, but the little blonde pressed too hard and the curtain gave out behind her, and she went tumbling into the room beyond, and a skinny man in the bed pulled the sheets up to hide his manhood. Calloway found that hilarious, and let out a little giggle. Bonny curled her lip. "Jacqueline, don't you understand what's happened? This is no laughing matter, dearie."

"No, I'm afraid I don't understand," Calloway replied. "None of you are making any sense." She left Bonny standing there with a dumb look on her face, and continued to her mother's room, shaking her head at all these foolish women. She pushed the curtain aside.

Beside the small bed, her mother was facedown in a pool of red, her head tilted sideways, eyes open but staring at nothing.

The ringlets of her beautiful black hair were scattered wildly about her head, dipped in blood. She wore a thin red robe that was a shade brighter than the pool beneath her. The candle atop the round bedside table flared violently.

Calloway heard the strumpets whispering behind her. Their whispers sounded like the hissing of snakes, if snakes could converse with one another. They were as subtle as a wave crashing over a beach.

"What's wrong with her?"

"Is she laughing?"

"She's gone nutty, she has."

"Quiet! It's her mum."

"She's laughing."

"She's gone nutty, she has."

"Will you just shut it!"

"She's scaring me."

"I told you she was off. Look at her face."

"It's her mother. How would you be?"

"I wouldn't be laughing, I'll tell you that."

"Me mum's dead. I didn't laugh."

"My mother's still alive, but I'll laugh when the bitch dies."

"Quiet girls."

"She's scaring me."

"Everything scares you."

"I don't like the way she's—"

"Shuttup."

"What?"

"I said shuttup, you silly whores! Shuttup!! Shuttup!!! SHUTTUUUUUUUUUUUUUUP!!!!" It wasn't until Calloway turned to face them and saw their stunned faces that she realized the words had come out of her mouth.

And then the strumpets stretched taller before her, and her knees cracked against the hard floor. Her stomach hollowed out as a torrent ascended to her chest, bubbled into her throat, and shuddered from her mouth in a tremendous wail.

Invisible hands clutched her wrists, and she thrashed terribly against them, but their grip was too firm. When she became infuriated, she opened her eyes, and she was shocked to see Bastion staring down at her with an unsettled look, the whites of his eyes a stark contrast to his dark skin. He released her.

"Are you not well?" he asked.

She rubbed her eyes and blinked until everything became clear, and she remembered where she was. She was in Guy Dillahunt's bed, in the cabin they shared aboard *Crusader*. It was dark, with faint rays of moonlight falling through the aft windows. It must have been early morning, for there was a bracing chill in the air.

She had cast aside the sheets in her sleep, and she was stark naked. When Bastion realized she wasn't injured, he sheepishly turned away from the bed. She didn't bother covering herself; more men had seen her naked than she could count.

"What are you doing in here, Bastion? You're not on a pirate ship anymore, remember?" Bastion had been a member of Benjamin Hornigold's crew, before joining Guy Dillahunt. Pirates were free to share the captain's cabin, but *Crusader* was no pirate ship.

"You were talking in your sleep," Bastion informed her in his thick islander accent.

"I was having a dream," she replied, sitting up. "What of it?"

He shrugged. "You were shouting. I thought something was wrong, so I come and see. I thought maybe someone come to kill you."

"I was dreaming about my mother," she said as she stared into the darkness.

"A bad dream?" he asked, gradually turning to face her. She

caught his eyes descending toward her breasts. She knew he fancied her, and she didn't mind. He had a handsome, youthful face and thick brown hair that was only a touch darker than his skin. He was very short, but he had stringy muscles and a rippled stomach that she had stolen glances at when he was shirtless on deck. There wasn't a hint of fat on him. He looked a third younger than his thirty years. She appreciated his unassuming manner, which was refreshing considering most sailors loved nothing more than the sound of their own voices.

"The dream changes from time to time," she told him. "I'm not sure how much of it is real anymore."

The strumpets claimed Edward Teach had murdered her mother, but that wasn't true. Or was it? Calloway didn't know anymore. Teach had insisted her mother had committed suicide. And why would a man like him, who thrived on a reputation for murder, bother to lie? But Teach had been her mother's last visitor. What had he come to tell her? Calloway supposed she would never know. It was pointless and maddening to think about it, but her dreams would not succumb to logic so easily. Elise spoke wistfully of past suitors, so dashing and wonderful. Most of all she spoke of the tall rogue who had gotten her with child. Calloway had never known her father. He was a shadow without features. "He is coming back for you and me one day," her mother always said. "And on that day he will take us both in his arms, and it will be like he never left. You'll see. He'll come back. He'll come back with gold and jewels, and he'll shower us in them, and things will be good again."

After her mother's death, she spent the following months trying to convince herself that it didn't really matter, that sorrow could do nothing for her. She focused on her clients, eager to please them in every possible way, out-strumpeting every strumpet at The Strapped Bodice. They soon became jealous of her. She was the youngest of them, a child in their eyes, but her body had already developed into a woman's, and she swiftly grew to be the most desired among clientele. The strumpets threw her nasty looks and hissed whispers just loud enough for her to hear. When it became more than she could stand, and she realized she could seek out clients on her own, she took leave of the whorehouse, becoming an independent strumpet. It was unheard of, but it worked.

That was the best any woman could hope for, was it not? She had been given no reason to think otherwise. Her mother had shown her nothing else. Hideous men fondling and probing every inch of her with their sweaty fingers and other unmentionables had not seemed so terrible when she knew nothing better, so long as they left the proper coin. They weren't *all* horrible looking, of course, but the men whose looks she fancied straight away were sometimes more perverse in the bedroom than timid ugly men.

And then she met Captain Guy Dillahunt.

She fell immediately in love, or so she had thought. She wasn't sure what love was, but the overwhelming affection she felt for him must have been something very much like it. Her first adventure with him was nearly her last, but even the bracing taste of death was finer than the life she had known. And when she returned to Nassau with Dillahunt, their love was already waning, but fleeting moments of happiness within a growing pool of awkward silence was preferable to entertaining strangers night after night, until one of those strangers inevitably decided to stick a knife in her belly because she didn't smile at him just right. That was the life her mother had shown her, and she would never go back to it, no matter what fate had in store for her. She would die first.

"Your mother," Bastion said. "She was beautiful too?"

Calloway had heard that compliment so many times it no

longer made her blush, but Bastion probably meant it. She forced herself to smile. "She was."

Bastion seemed to remember himself, blinking rapidly. "Captain Dillahunt should be here. Not me. I will go fetch him."

"Good luck finding him," she laughed sardonically.

Bastion frowned as if he didn't understand, but he must have seen Dillahunt leaving every other night. "Guy tends to avoid our bed of late," she sighed. The last time she succeeded in arousing Dillahunt, he had woken with a start and pushed her from the bed. She hadn't tried since. It was as if he was afraid of her, although she couldn't imagine what he had to fear. He hadn't been the same since the battle with Blackbeard, and it was clear to her now that the man she had fallen for was not coming back. She was sick to death of his wary looks and stilted dialogue. She wanted to leave him, but her options were nonexistent until she received her share of Kate's bounty. *Just a little longer,* she kept telling herself. *Just put up with him a little longer, until the money is in your hands, and then you can do whatever you want, go wherever you like.*

"I am sorry," Bastion said. He seemed genuinely pained that he had nothing to offer. That didn't stop him from trying. "Is there anything I can do?"

She tried not to laugh. *Surely he doesn't mean that the way it sounds.* She looked up into his eyes. His irises were brown by day, but black and unreadable in the gloom. He stared right back, and silence fell between them for longer than was proper.

"I'm fine," she assured him at last, while oh-so-casually reaching out to touch his rippled stomach, which was nearly as hard as rock. She affected a look of surprise and let out a little gasp, as though she hadn't meant to do that. If he did not respond, she would pull her hand away and offer a sheepish smile. But the whites of his eyes were greater than ever, and he clasped a warm hand over hers.

Men are too easy, she mused.

His slim chest lifted as his breath increased. The moonlight glanced off his dark pecs. She slowly slid her hand downward and clutched his crotch. He was larger than she expected. *Larger than Dillahunt.* She slid forward, opening her legs to let him see the dark hairs between them.

"I cannot do this," Bastion said with little conviction.

She gave him a squeeze. "You're lying."

He shuddered pleasurably, but his face was twisted in distress. "No. This is not right."

She wrapped her long legs around him, locking her ankles behind his legs, and drew him closer to the bed. His fingers curled around her hand and struggled to remove it from his crotch. "I cannot do this," he repeated.

Bastion was known—and often mocked—for his unquestionable loyalty to whomever he served. That only made her want him more. She could think of no greater retaliation than taking Dillahunt's most trusted man into their bed. Not that she planned on telling the captain that his man had betrayed him. Private knowledge of the encounter would be enough. Every time she looked at Dillahunt she would think of her night with Bastion, and she would smile, and Dillahunt would ask her what she was so happy about, and she'd say, "Oh, nothing."

"I cannot do this."

"Don't be afraid," she replied in a soothing voice as she massaged him. He was so hard. She wanted to free him of his breeches and take him in her mouth. Then he would be hers. No man had ever resisted her tongue. "Guy will never know."

"He will know when he looks at me. He is smart."

"He's not as smart as he lets on," Calloway said as she slipped her fingers over the waistline of his breeches.

"I will not do this!" he insisted, baring the whites of his teeth. He clutched her hand, preventing her from delving any further. His grip tightened until it sent a jolt of pain through her hand. She recoiled with a hiss and rubbed her throbbing hand, glaring sourly at him.

"Fine," she spat. "Next time you hear me screaming in my sleep, don't bother to look in on me. It's not like you can be of any help!"

"I . . . I am sorry," he stammered. He turned and abruptly fled the cabin, leaving Calloway alone and naked in the dark.

4

DILLAHUNT

Swirls of a dense white fog sifted through the open doorway into a dim, dank little tavern far removed from the harbor, on the outskirts of Nassau's eastern quarter. Large holes riddled the thatched roof, with palm fronds poking through. Water was dripping into strategically placed wooden buckets, spilling over at the moldy brim. A few ghostly beams of moonlight pierced the fronds, illuminating the fog as it steadily infiltrated the room. A wave crashed over the beach just outside.

It was maybe three hours before dawn, although Captain Guy Dillahunt couldn't be sure. The only other man that remained in the tavern was snoring at his table, one hand still gripping an empty tankard. The dark-skinned owner, who had an incomprehensible island accent that Dillahunt pretended to understand, had vanished an hour ago, leaving only a few candles burning. Apparently he trusted Dillahunt to leave the appropriate coin should he decide to pour himself another drink.

Out front, a disgraced sailor who had taken refuge on the thin porch was singing a mournful tune about a woman named Mary. He slowly trailed off into humming, and then the tune faded entirely, presumably as he fell asleep. Suddenly, he loosed a tremendous *belch* and started murmuring to himself. "Is that you, Mary?" he called desperately. "Leave me be already, you frightful wench. I'll kill you." A few moments later his loud snores dwarfed the snoring of the man in the tavern.

Dillahunt had finished his ale an hour ago, but he couldn't bring himself to stand. He faded in and out of a light sleep. He didn't want to go back to . . . *her*. The tavern was about as far from her as he could get without marching blindly into the jungle, which was starting to sound more appealing every day. He couldn't look into her glacial blue eyes without recalling Blackbeard's final riddle. He had tried for a month to pretend it didn't matter. For a week, after returning to Nassau, it had nearly worked. And then Blackbeard returned to him in his sleep, posing that riddle again and again, night after night, and Dillahunt would wake covered in sweat, with Calloway nestled against him, sleeping soundly as a babe.

"Have you not yet realized who shares your bed?" Blackbeard had asked in that final instant, grinning like a devil. And before he could elaborate, the evil pirate was claimed by the fire that ate away at *Queen Anne's Revenge*.

Dillahunt dreamt about their duel many times over, with the two of them scrambling through roaring fires, dodging falling yardarms, and occasionally pausing to engage one another's crew. In the most recent dream, Dillahunt found himself enjoying the battle, even though he hadn't taken a moment's pleasure from the actual event. As their blades clashed, Dillahunt was surprised and embarrassed to find himself sexually aroused. Blackbeard glanced downward and grinned hideously. Dillahunt then woke to Calloway working away at him with her mouth. His hands instantly moved in revolt. He shoved her so hard that she tumbled out of the bed, taking the blankets with her. She landed hard on her back and stared up at him questioningly, wincing through the pain. Before he realized where he was and who he was talking to, he screamed, "Away with you, devil!" She made an injured face and retreated to the chair behind his desk, where she slept for the rest of the night. The next morning, he insisted it had been nothing more than a nightmare. She didn't seem convinced.

Why didn't you kill her, Teach? Dillahunt wondered for the thousandth time. Calloway had been in Blackbeard's clutches long enough for him to slaughter her and toss her over the side, but he'd kept her alive for some reason. It didn't make sense. *Why didn't you kill her? Why didn't you kill her?*

He shivered in his uncomfortable wooden chair. The mist carried with it a slight chill. It had rained earlier in the night. The moon was just now peeking through the breaking clouds. Perhaps the morning would bring a clear, hot day, but in this dark, damp tavern, with no more than a few small candles for light, the morning seemed so very far away.

Dillahunt kept his weary eyes on the door. He worked for the governor, and Woodes Rogers was hated by pirates, and by association Dillahunt was a potential target. Charles Vane had spies everywhere, or so he had heard.

As he drifted toward what might have been a heavier sleep than before, he thought he glimpsed movement in the fog; a shadow, vague through the narrowing slits of his eyelids. His eyes shot open and he slapped a palm to the black pistol at his belt. The fog was swirling to fill a gap, as though it had been displaced. He thought he heard a soft creaking. One of the five steps leading up to the tavern was loose, always groaning underfoot.

Dillahunt stood at once, taking off his hat and setting it gently atop the head of the dozing patron. The man was too far gone to notice. Dillahunt moved to a dark corner on the right side of the door and waited, aiming his gun at the entrance.

He waited what seemed ten minutes before he heard that distinctive *creeeeeeeaaaaak* again. He steadied the gun and held his breath. A fresh wisp of fog rolled in, as though urged forward by a presence. A barrel appeared in the doorway, steadily aimed at the dozing patron wearing Dillahunt's hat. A dark-haired man with a muscular frame in a long leather coat stepped into the tavern, face shadowed. "Captain Dillahunt?" the intruder called in an easy, young voice.

Dillahunt quietly moved behind him and announced his presence by cocking his gun. The would-be assassin stiffened. "Set the pistol on the table," Dillahunt instructed.

The intruder did as he was told, placing his weapon beside the sleeping man. "What if he takes it?" he asked.

"He's out cold," Dillahunt assured him. "Turn around."

The intruder turned, and his features were revealed in the low light. He was a strapping young man with a pinched brow and a strong, clean-shaven jaw. His raven hair was full and curly, framing his face in shadow. He wore all black, save for a blue sash. His long leather coat was well worn, with a broad collar, huge folds at the cuffs, and plain black buttons running down both sides, unbuttoned. He raised his hands in a non-threatening manner. There was no sign of a cutlass at his waist.

"*You!*" Dillahunt exclaimed in shock, clenching the grip of his gun. This man had been a member of his crew not so long ago.

"You've forgotten my name," the young man replied. "Or did you ever know it?"

Before the mutiny, Dillahunt had never bothered getting to know the younger members of the crew. His first mate, Phillip

Candler, generally relayed his orders. Candler was dead now, and he had proven himself no better than the others before the end. After Dillahunt had regained command of his ship, Calloway had naturally fallen into the duties of first mate. The new crew liked her, but Dillahunt made a point to familiarize himself with everyone this time. He would not risk losing *Crusader* again. Rogers had provided him with a stiff officer named Wincott, whose lone goal was to keep Dillahunt in check, questioning every little thing he did, no matter how trivial. "If you insist on pirates for a crew," Rogers had scornfully warned him, "you will find yourself with pirates for a crew." Dillahunt was one of the few privateers who had not submitted to traditional royal hierarchy aboard his vessel. Until the mutiny, Rogers had turned a blind eye. Dillahunt still refused to wear stifling navy uniforms, preferring his usual white shirt and black breeches. He dressed the part for dinners with Rogers, but that was all.

"I don't know your name," Dillahunt told the young man before him, "but I have not forgotten your mutiny."

The young man did not remove his eyes from Dillahunt's. "My name is Gabriel Jenkins. Everyone calls me 'Gabe.'"

"Waste of breath," Dillahunt spat. "I will not remember your name after I've put a shot between your eyes."

Gabe Jenkins chuckled. "I would deserve no less, captain. However, you deserve to hear my proposition."

"I'll decide what either of us deserves."

Jenkins broadened his smile. "If you kill me before hearing my proposition, your decision will be tragically ill-informed."

An icy breeze swept in, dispersing the tufts of mist that had settled between the tables. Dillahunt managed not to shiver. "You're here to kill me," he said, jerking his gun temporarily at the sleeping man wearing his hat, "yet now you claim to win my favor with a proposition?"

Jenkins laughed. "You are not dead, therefore I have not come here to kill you."

Dillahunt laughed loudly enough to dwarf Jenkins' laugh. "Says the man I've outwitted and disarmed. I suppose you're here to pledge your loyalty to me? How many masters have you gone through, not including me? From that dullard Nathan Adams to that horrid strumpet . . . I forget her name . . . to Edward Teach . . . to . . . who is it now? Davy Jones?" He chortled at his own jest, impressed with himself for coming up with it so quickly.

"Charles Vane," Jenkins answered.

That didn't surprise Dillahunt. "You're a shadow in all that black, happy to linger behind whatever master suits you. Even your hair eats the light. It's no wonder I forget your name so easily. Shadows do not have names. I should kill you."

"Maybe you should," the young man coolly replied.

Dillahunt's arm was starting to tremble under the weight of the pistol. He was suddenly aware of how exhausted he was from lack of sleep. He should have been on his ship, in his cabin with Calloway, rather than lingering sleepless in a seedy tavern, fending off assassins in the night. He was wasting time letting Jenkins talk, but there was something in the young man's eyes that held his interest, a kind of sincere desperation masked behind an easy smile.

"After you did away with Blackbeard," Jenkins went on, "I quickly pledged myself to Vane. Apparently he was aware of my loyalty to Teach, which was never in question, not even when I served under you, Captain Dillahunt."

"Is this meant to lessen my resolve?" Dillahunt wondered, tightening his finger on the trigger.

"Blackbeard is dead, and I assure you my loyalty died with him." He looked past the gun, to the door. His careless demeanor hardened for a fleeting moment. "And so did my debt."

"And I'm to believe you owe Vane nothing, *boy*?" Jenkins was hardly a boy, but Dillahunt was hoping to get under his skin.

The edges of Jenkins' jaw tightened below his ears. "I came here under threat of death, captain. Why else would I sail into Nassau disguised as a merchant, under false papers, with constant worry of discovery?"

"I can think of many reasons."

Jenkins widened his eyes and grinned irreverently as he said, "I am a pirate, and this is no place for the likes of me! Not since Rogers occupied the island, anyway. Vane would have killed me had I refused his orders. He's rather ill-tempered, you know. I have no wish for another master, but I also prefer my bowels in my belly, where they rightly belong. I did as I was told, with every intention of betraying Vane to you. I'm sick of scheming pirates."

"And here you are," Dillahunt said with a wave of his gun, "a pirate hatching a scheme."

"A final scheme that would see the end of Vane," Jenkins replied with a correcting finger.

"I should strike off your cock with my cutlass," Dillahunt hissed. "I imagine a strapping youth such as yourself values his cock."

The young man embellished a look of mock horror. "I do, captain."

Dillahunt let his gun hang in the air a moment longer, the muscles in his arm burning. He lowered it at last. He slid out a chair for Jenkins and nodded to it. "Sit."

Jenkins sat. He ran a hand through his hair. A stubborn curl sprang free, dangling over his forehead. Dillahunt took a seat opposite the young man, trying not to stare at the wayward lock of hair. His mind was too easily distracted by trivial details. The more he tried to suppress this fact, the harder it became to ignore.

"Are you alright, captain?"

"I hate your hair. That stupid curl. I want to snip it off and hide it somewhere you won't find it."

Jenkins frowned. "I see."

Dillahunt set his gun on the table, making sure the barrel faced Jenkins. He could snatch it up quickly and shoot him between the eyes, should the need arise. "Tell me why Vane wishes me dead."

Jenkins blinked. "I'm sorry?"

"He sent you here to kill me, obviously."

"I wasn't sent here to kill you, captain. I wasn't sent here to kill anyone. Well, unless someone gets in my way. No, I'm only here to kidnap Katherine Lindsay."

Dillahunt was growing tired of that woman's name. The Caribbean seemed to revolve around her. The sooner her reward was in his hands and she was on a ship back to London, the better. A part of him wished he had never betrayed her in the first place. She had saved him from a prison cell during Blackbeard's assault on Pirate Town. If not for her, he surely would have died at Blackbeard's hands, just as Benjamin Hornigold had. Kate had given Dillahunt the opportunity to escape to his ship and face Blackbeard on equal footing. He owed her everything, and he had promised not to turn her in. Yet he had done just that, at the behest of Jacqueline Calloway. Kate was now under the care of Woodes Rogers, imprisoned comfortably in his mansion, probably cursing Dillahunt's name, without the faintest notion that Calloway was the one who had put the idea of betraying her into his head.

"I am circumscribed by evil schemes," Dillahunt hissed.

Jenkins frowned. "Circum-what?"

"It means surrounded. I apologize. I often forget to dull my vocabulary in the presence of the less cultivated."

"No apology required," Jenkins assured him as he adjusted the fold of one of his coat's cuffs. "I've learned a new word."

Dillahunt looked away, refusing to acknowledge the young man's humor. "Now Vane seeks to steal Lindsay's bounty from me? After letting her slip through his grasp? Why would he change his mind?"

"I didn't ask," Jenkins replied. "But knowing Vane, there's a good reason."

"Tame that fucking curl!" Dillahunt snapped, fixating.

Jenkins jerked his shoulders in alarm, and then ran a hand through his hair, pushing the loose curl into place.

"That money belongs to *me*," Dillahunt grated.

Jenkins inclined his head, and the stubborn lock fell over his forehead again. "And I mean to keep it that way. But if I'm to lead you to Vane, I will need to carry out my plan. The man who captains the ship I came in on is fiercely loyal to Vane. If this is going to work, I must get Lindsay on that ship, or we'll never leave port."

"You think I'm an idiot?"

Jenkins shook his head firmly, but Dillahunt thought he glimpsed a smile trying to break loose. "No, captain. As you pointed out, your vocabulary far outweighs my own."

"Find some redheaded whore. Your captain won't know the difference."

"He will," Jenkins insisted. "His name is Jack Rackham. Calico Jack. I'm sure you've heard of him."

"Of course I have." Everyone had heard of Calico Jack.

"Well, Calico Jack met Lindsay in Pirate Town. He will know if I bring any woman but her. She does make quite an impression, after all."

Dillahunt let his hand fall to the grip of his pistol. He made sure the gesture appeared casual. He ran a finger over the silver sloop set in the grip, rubbing away a smudge. "Convenient."

Jenkins' eyes fell to the gun. "I disagree. I'm to sneak into the Governor's mansion and steal Lindsay right out from under him. I'm told she's on the second floor. Nothing 'convenient' about that."

"That sounds impossible," Dillahunt remarked with a skeptical smirk.

Jenkins smiled, sweeping a hand through his hair. The stubborn lock held for only a few seconds before it dropped to its former position over his brow. "Difficult, yes. But not impossible. I have a way in."

"Magic?"

"A woman."

"Of course," Dillahunt said, sitting back in his chair and thumbing a rather large scar on his forehead. One of many. He could no longer stand his reflection. A scarred, sour, puffy face always glowered back at him. He wasn't sure how anyone else tolerated looking at him. He had never been as good looking as Gabe Jenkins, not even at twenty, but he had been a lot better looking than he was now.

"After I've taken Lindsay to Calico Jack," Jenkins said, "you need only follow."

"Follow you to my death?"

Jenkins laughed. "Vane is desperate. He commands but two ships, one of them crippled. The other is a sloop docked in the harbor now. You probably didn't notice it. It's very small, in *Crusader's* shadow."

"Yes, you would know all about shadows, wouldn't you?"

The mist continued to swirl in through the doorway, urged by the occasional breeze. A large wave crashed over the shore, causing the sailor outside to snort in his sleep. "Get off me, wench," the man muttered.

"It occurs to me," Dillahunt announced in a renewed tone,

"that I should simply turn you in to Woodes Rogers, warn him of Vane's sudden interest in Lindsay, capture Jack Rackham, and save myself the trouble altogether."

"You could do that," Jenkins casually agreed. "Or you could follow me and bring Charles Vane to justice. A much bigger prize than Rackham, wouldn't you say?"

Dillahunt felt his teeth grinding.

Jenkins studied him closely. "It must be difficult for you. You felled the scourge of the Caribbean, yet have nothing to show for it. I doubt there will ever be another whose name inspires such terror as Blackbeard."

Dillahunt recalled the doubting face of James Lancaster, scowling at him from across an extravagant dinner table. Woodes Rogers had asked Dillahunt to recount the death of Blackbeard to a dinner party. Dillahunt had done so with flourish, and they all smiled and laughed at his tale. All of them except Lancaster, whose eyes seemed to penetrate his. *He thinks me a liar,* Dillahunt had realized then, and his voice began to break before the story was done. He barely made it through the end, choking on his own words. The laughter slowly died, and the guests started to exchange uncomfortable glances. He hated Lancaster in that moment. He barely knew the man, but he wanted to lunge across the table and clench Lancaster's throat until his face turned pink and his eyes popped from his skull.

"How did Edward Teach die?" Jenkins asked suddenly.

"He was consumed by fire," Dillahunt answered bitterly. "In truth, I did nothing. I merely defended myself until he fell."

Jenkins' smirk was annoyingly confident. "You didn't tell Rogers that last bit, did you?"

Dillahunt stared down at a large crack running across the surface of the little table, from Jenkins to him. Water had collected within. He looked up at the mysterious young man.

"We are not friends, Gabriel Jenkins. Do not mistake us as such."

"Friends, nay," Jenkins agreed. "Partners?"

Dillahunt nodded slowly.

Jenkins set his palms flat on the table and pushed himself up, briskly straightening his long coat. He adopted a serious expression and thrust out a hand. "Then we have an accord, Captain Dillahunt?"

"We are accorded," Dillahunt replied, ignoring Jenkins' outstretched hand.

Jenkins lowered his hand and pretended as though the formality wasn't important. "Calico Jack's sloop is docked directly across from your ship."

Dillahunt nodded. He had glimpsed the ship on its way in yesterday. "I will pursue at a discreet distance."

"If I think you've lost our trail, I will leave crumbs. Mind your sails on the horizon. Rackham is a keen man."

Dillahunt folded his arms. "I will not lose your trail."

Jenkins nodded his understanding. "I'll be on my way, then. We depart on the morrow, at midnight. Keep a weather eye out." He started for the door.

"Jenkins," Dillahunt called, throwing an arm over the back of his chair.

Jenkins halted at the doorway, tilting his head. "Yes?"

"How old are you?"

"I am twenty, captain."

Dillahunt frowned, wondering how a man so young had accumulated so great a debt. "Your loyalty to Teach wasn't so fickle. What precisely did you owe him?"

Wisps of fog curled around Gabe Jenkins' legs like smoky fingers. His features were difficult to see so far removed from the light. "That is a long tale," he said in a voice faintly strained. "One that I don't care to recount just now."

"Or maybe you simply don't care to recount it to *me*."

Jenkins lowered his head, but his eyes soon lifted. "It's nothing personal, captain. I've never told anyone."

"Because Teach would have had you murdered?"

Jenkins' silence was answer enough.

"The man is dead," Dillahunt said. He glanced around the tavern. "I see no ghosts here."

"Well, that's the trouble about ghosts," Jenkins said with a chuckle. "They're good at not being seen when they don't want to be." After a brief silence, he smiled. "Goodnight, captain."

"You play a treacherous game, Jenkins." Dillahunt aimed a steady finger. "If you are lying to me, I will personally ensure that you do not live to see twenty-one."

Jenkins snickered softly. "I didn't expect to see *twenty*." The young man disappeared into the vapor, a shadow returning to the darkness. The fog closed behind him, filling the void left in his wake.

Dillahunt lingered in his seat a while longer, staring out the door. It wasn't too late to turn Jenkins in and have Rackham's ship seized. Rackham was a notable prize as well, though not nearly as hefty a prize as Charles Vane, as Jenkins had keenly observed.

"What be this?" a foreign voice suddenly cried in alarm. Dillahunt shifted in the direction of the outburst. The other patron had woken up and was cautiously feeling his new headwear. After he seemed to conclude the hat wasn't an animal that had fallen asleep on his head, he took it off and appraised it, lifting an eyebrow. "I did not come in with this," he concluded.

"That's mine," Dillahunt said, raising a finger.

"Oh? 'Splain why it be perched atop my head in place o' yourn?"

Dillahunt shrugged. "Because I put it there."

"Well thank ye kindly," the man said, putting that hat back on. He stood and wobbled toward the door. "I pray it be sunny tomorrow," he said on his way out.

As the drunken man stumbled outside with his new hat, Dillahunt noticed the haze was taking on a purple ambience. It must have been closer to dawn than he realized. He had spent the entire night in this dark place without realizing it. Had Gabe Jenkins really just visited him, or had the young man been nothing more than a dream?

Dillahunt forced himself to his feet, fighting against the numbness that stiffened his legs. He stuffed his gun in his belt and walked to the door. As he stepped out onto the little porch, something seized his leg. He fumbled for his gun.

"Have ye seen me Mary?" the disgraced sailor asked, clutching his leg with an outstretched hand. Dillahunt pulled away, and the sailor spilled onto his belly. "Tell her I want me turtle back!"

"I'll do no such thing," Dillahunt replied.

"She'll burn for taking my turtle," the man said. "She'll burn. She'll burn. She'll burn."

"There are far worse crimes than taking a man's turtle."

"You'll burn too," the sailor replied casually. "You'll burn. You'll burn. You'll . . . " His forehead thunked the porch as he passed out.

Dillahunt turned away, stepping down the little stairway and into the soft radiance of the mist. He walked down a thin path between the town and the beach. He could hear waves crashing over the shore nearby, but he couldn't see more than five feet in any direction. A cool breeze tugged at his shirt. The path finally opened to a wide beach, and he trudged through the soft sands. A wave broke over the shore, water creeping toward his feet. He shuffled away to keep his boots from getting soaked. Eventually he came to the dock, and he climbed the crooked steps to a long pier. He followed the pier down to the end, until he saw the long bowsprit of *Crusader* emerging from the fog. The beautiful mermaid that once decorated the bow was gone now, lost in the battle with Blackbeard, after Dillahunt had rammed the ship into *Queen Anne's Revenge*. The bow had since been repaired, but Dillahunt hadn't the heart to fit a new masthead.

On the opposite side of the pier was another ship, much smaller than *Crusader*. This ship had a single mast and was short of hull. Dillahunt couldn't see her flag, but he assumed it was the ship Jenkins spoke of. The infamous Jack Rackham was probably in there now, sleeping comfortably in his cabin. *And I'm not going to do anything about that,* Dillahunt realized. A bigger fish was waiting. *A bigger risk.*

He found the ramp leading up to *Crusader* and ascended to the main deck. Three of the crew were playing dice near the capstan, barely visible in the dim flicker of the only lantern that was lit on deck.

Not in the mood for banter, he quickly made for his cabin, passing Lieutenant Wincott, who stood watch in his silly white wig and blue coat. Wincott saluted him, and Dillahunt half-heartedly saluted back. He heard Wincott mutter something derogatory to himself, probably about Dillahunt's lack of navy attire, or the late hour at which he was returning. Dillahunt thought it ironic that this official man, underneath his dutiful salutes, was the least respectful of his crew. He would humor Rogers for now and wait for Wincott to make a mistake so he could dismiss him.

Once inside his cabin, he was surprised to find the bed empty.

Jacqueline Calloway was reclining in his chair, her long legs crossed atop his desk. When she saw him, she put her feet to the deck and sat up. She was very tall, even sitting down. The dull purple light fell through the aft windows onto bare skin. Her short black hair had grown past her cheeks, curving a little at the ends. Even in the low light, the freckles were prominent around her nose. Her broad shoulders were now riddled with spots as well, darkened by constant sun.

"You should be asleep," he said.

"And you shouldn't?" she countered in an acidic tone. "I thought maybe someone killed you. I thought maybe you were drawn into some dark alley, caution clouded by drunkenness, only to have your throat opened."

"The specificity of your imagination alarms me."

She leaned back. "You are careless, wandering around at night." The subtle traces of a French accent slipped through, as it always did when she was angry. Calloway's mother, Elise, had been a prostitute who had made the crossing from France. Or so Calloway had told Dillahunt.

And her father . . .

Dillahunt pushed the thought out of his mind. "My thoughts gnaw at me," he returned, "as you well know. I've had trouble finding sleep."

"You're so stupid," she spat.

"Insults do not become you," he protested with a sigh.

"Doubtless Blackbeard still has allies looking for retribution."

He didn't like hearing that name from her lips. "Pirates have no allies. Not for long, anyway. And certainly not after they're dead."

"You're willing to bet your life on that?"

"Risk of death is preferable to insanity. This cabin stifles me."

"Maybe it's *me* who stifles you."

He sighed again, louder this time. "You put thoughts in my head otherwise unconsidered, and you keenly divert attention from yourself. It is I who should be alarmed. After all, you don't appear relieved to see me unkilled."

Her laugh was musical. "If you'd strolled in two hours ago, when I was beside myself with worry, entertaining all manner of gruesome notions, you would have seen relief." She folded her arms over her small breasts, placing each hand on the opposite shoulder in a tight self-embrace. "I've since come to terms with your death."

5

OGLE

Ogle swayed in his hammock, drifting in and out of consciousness.

It had been a month since they found him collared to a double-sided chair deep beneath Pirate Town, where Charles Vane had left him to die. When he closed his eyes he could still smell the putrid stench of the rotting corpses piled in the pit at the back of the cave, and the stink of feces from the dead man behind him, in the opposite chair. It was a simple torture device. Two collars were attached to the necks of two men, with a chain stretching through a hole, allowing each man a few inches to avoid the rusty iron spikes set into both backrests. Both men would live longer if they managed to work together and remain perfectly upright, but someone always pulled first. Before Vane left, he strapped one of his lackeys to the chair. Ten minutes later, Ogle summoned all his strength and leaned forward, pulling the smaller man against the spikes.

He didn't like competition.

Three days passed in the dark.

Vane's torturer, Mr. Tanner, had been kind enough to extinguish all the torches before he took his leave. He propped himself forward in the chair, with the collar trying to strangle him, while the spikes prickled him painfully whenever he leaned back. He wanted nothing more than to sit back and have a rest, and sometimes he would get so tired that he would forget about the spikes, but they quickly reminded him.

His mouth throbbed. Five of his teeth had been knocked out during the interrogation. His left arm was on fire where Mr. Tanner had carved to the bone. Rivulets of blood had dried on his face, stiff and caked, running from three vertical slices in his scalp.

It wasn't long before Ogle heard voices whispering amid the maddening droplets of water that constantly pattered the floor. He shook his head and pretended it was just a trick of the water echoing off the walls. But the voices grew louder, until they were impossible to ignore. He heard voices from his past, friends and enemies. Men he had killed asked him why he'd killed them.

Edward Teach's strumpet, Annabelle, who had led Ogle to this torment, taunted him. "Why'd you listen to me?" she asked. "You knew I was false. You should have killed me. You should have killed me, you fat, bald, ugly pirate. Why would you let a woman get the better of you? You don't even like women, do you? Oh, you pretend to, but I know when a man is trying too hard." He wrestled to break free of his restraints so he might find her hiding in the dark and strangle the life out of her, but all he did was choke on his collar and scrape his back against the spikes.

He heard his little sister, long dead, teasing him about his affinity for playing with her dolls. "I'm going to tell Father," she said, giggling from the darkness. "And you know what he'll do when he finds out."

He heard his own voice, much younger, desperately crying, "No! Don't tell Father, please!"

"A boy shouldn't play with girl's dolls," came another voice, this one masculine and frightening. He heard the crack of a belt echoing through the cave. The belt made sure he wouldn't forget what a boy shouldn't do. The belt continued to crack in the dark, until a warm stream flooded down his inner thighs and collected in the hard seat of the chair, and he pleaded, "No more, no more."

And that's how they found him: sitting in a puddle of his own piss, with a dead man behind him stinking of shit and decay.

He heard their footsteps first, louder and louder with their approach. When they entered, their torches were as bright as the sun to his dark-adapted eyes, and he could not see their faces beyond the glare. "It's Ogle," said a man whose voice sounded vaguely familiar.

"Who is that? Who's there?" he demanded.

"Did you tell Vane anything, Ogle?"

"Didn't tell that bastard nothing," Ogle muttered, squinting to see the man's face, but the torchlight was blinding. He squeezed his eyes shut and saw a big glob of white stamped on the back of his eyelids. "Who are you?"

"We're your family, Ogle," said a new voice. This one was throaty with age, but he sounded friendly enough.

"Family dead," Ogle replied with a croak of a laugh. This man couldn't be real. He was just another trick of the darkness. When Ogle was fourteen, his mother and sister had died in a fire, and his father followed two years later, thrown from his horse on the way to town. Ogle had no other family.

"Family be more than blood."

"I don't know what that means," said Ogle. "Leave me be. I am dying."

"Nay. Vane did a number on you, but you're not dying."

"Head hurts."

"We'll stitch you up, my friend," said the familiar voice.

"Do I know you?"

"Aye."

"All of you?"

"Nay," said the unfamiliar, older voice. "But we know you."

"Aye, we do," chimed in another, somewhere further back in the cave.

The familiar-voiced man helped him from the chair, slicing through the straps with a dagger. He was very careful not to nick Ogle's neck as he cut through his collar. The older man and the familiar man lifted him up, slung his arms around them, and carried him through the long, twisty tunnels. It seemed to take forever, and he wondered when he would come to and find himself still strapped to the chair.

But that didn't happen.

When they reached the surface, daylight greeted his eyes with an explosion of blinding color, and Ogle clasped his hands over his eyes and screamed. They dropped him, surprised by his outburst, and his body slapped the cold rocky ground.

When next he woke, he was on the main deck of a ship, swaying in a hammock, with a great white canvas whipping above his head. The sky was a deep sapphire, not a cloud in sight. The salty air smelled so fresh and clean, and the breeze caressed his skin. He had never felt anything so wonderful.

His left arm was bandaged up, and the searing pain running through the bone had been reduced to a dull ache. Something was tight around his skull, but he was too weak to lift his hands and feel it. He wondered how bad his wounds looked. It wasn't as if he could grow his hair out and hide the scars. He had started balding before he was seventeen, and he had lost all his hair by twenty-two.

When he woke again, a huge old man with blank milky white eyes was feeding him chicken broth with a spoon. "Ash, be my name," said the old man. His throaty voice was that of the man who had found him in the cave. Ash had a great round head, bald and spotted on top, bushy eyebrows, and a shaggy silver beard.

"Where am I?" Ogle asked between sips of the wonderful salty broth.

"Eat." The old man dipped the spoon and fed him a large sliver of pale meat, heavily saturated in broth. The meat tasted as though it had gone foul, but Ogle knew he had to eat. The broth made it go down easier.

"What ship is this?" he asked.

"Don't you worry about that," said Ash.

"Just tell me already," Ogle insisted, giving to frustration. He tried to sit up in the hammock, but his arms wouldn't muster.

Ash lightly patted Ogle's chest. "Don't tax yourself with queries. A troubled mind slows mending wounds."

Ogle let Ash finish feeding him, and promptly passed out.

When he was stirred into consciousness again, he was being carried in his hammock by four men, two on either side of him. Sunlight flashed through a dense jungle canopy overhead. The air was thick with humidity, and Ogle's clothes were wet with perspiration. One of the men on his right looked down at him and smiled. He was six feet tall and broad of shoulder, with a clean-shaven jaw and a single braid of thick black hair that reached to his waist, fastened at the end by a knot of hemp. He wore a stained shirt and a necklace of shriveled ears. "Almost there," he said.

"Almost where?"

"Carrying you is easier than I expected, Ogle. You've lost a lot of weight since last I saw you. I wager a few days starving in a cave was good for you."

"Marcus? Is that you?" This was one of Edward Teach's men. They had both served as gunners, until Teach ordered Ogle to join Guy Dillahunt's crew and await further orders, which had arrived in the form of Annabelle. Ogle couldn't claim many friends, but he had always enjoyed Marcus's belligerence. They had shared many a bottle of rum on the deck of *Queen Anne's Revenge*.

"Aye, that's my name," Marcus replied with a broadening grin. "Nice of you to remember. You just get back to sleep, and when you wake up, we'll get to work on fattening you up again."

His eyes started to close just as the canopy thinned above. When he opened them again, he was tucked in a little boat, with a man sitting by his head and another at his feet, both of them rowing dutifully. Massive beetles hovered overhead. The boat rocked gently, and he heard frogs croaking and monkeys shrieking in the distance.

The world faded again, and when he woke, it was nighttime, with a canvas of impossibly bright starlight twinkling overhead. The night air was cold, but his entire right side was warm. When he turned his head, he saw the edges of his hammock once again. He looked up and then down, and saw that his hammock was secured between two trees. He looked right, and twenty feet away was a raging bonfire, crackling and lifting into the heavens. The fire sat at the edge of a sharp cliff, which jutted outward like the bow of a ship. Men were sitting around it, drinking and laughing. One of them looked over and stood when he noticed Ogle was awake. It was Marcus. He sauntered over, dipping his head in a greeting. "Look who's up."

"Where in the hell am I?"

Marcus offered Ogle his bottle of rum. Ogle lifted his right arm and flexed his fingers. He was regaining his strength. He grabbed the bottle and took a swig. The rum burned his throat. He handed it back and wiped his lips. He touched the top of his head. The bandage was gone, and he felt stitches running down three long lines. "How bad is it?" he asked Marcus.

"Vane is a sick bastard," Marcus said, looking away and clenching his jaw. "The scars will last. If it helps, they make you look fiercely."

"I already looked fiercely."

Marcus laughed. "True."

Ogle glanced at his left arm. The bandage was still there, colored rusty with dried blood. He didn't want to think about what was under there. "Vane didn't do this. It was Tanner."

"Tanner?" Marcus frowned and looked up for a moment. "Oh, aye. Met him in Nassau, before Vane recruited him. He sewed up my leg. Terrible bedside manner. He stuck that needle awful deep. I would have killed him, had I not passed out."

Ogle shivered as he recalled Tanner's gaunt face and bulging eyes, which seemed to see straight through him. He remembered Tanner introducing each of his knives, one by one. He had given them names. Female names. "I will kill that wretch, if fortune sets him in my path."

Marcus smiled. "I've lost count of people I want to kill."

Ogle was struck by a sudden thought. "What of the whore? Annabelle?"

Marcus shook his head. "Vane did her in. We found her corpse strung up, guts on the outside. She was all beat up, bones all broken up inside her. Looked like she'd taken a long fall."

"Good," said Ogle. "The bitch betrayed us all. That just leaves Vane."

"Don't fret," Marcus said. He took a swig of rum and belched. "We'll find him."

"Who's your captain? Where are we? Where's the old blind man who tended to me? Ash. I haven't seen him since the ship."

Marcus merely smiled. "Get some sleep, Ogle."

"I feel I've slept a year."

"You may yet."

The next week was a blur of dreams permeated with more fleeting bouts of consciousness. He usually woke in the middle of the night, with the bonfire burning low and the pirates sleeping around it.

Marcus would wake him with plates of greyish meat, overcooked and dry. Ogle's teeth hurt as he chewed, but he was ravenous. It wasn't particularly good, but it wasn't awful. The more he ate of it, the better it tasted. "What is this?" he asked Marcus. "Hog?"

Marcus smirked. "You don't want to know."

Perfect, thought Ogle. *Now I know what monkey tastes like.*

One night Marcus returned very late with a pretty strumpet. She had long dark hair and big hazel eyes, and she didn't flinch when she smiled her pretty smile at Ogle, though he must have been a horror to look upon. "I gave her a go last night," said Marcus, winking. "You can thank me later." He left, and the girl wasted no time stripping naked. She was small and lithe, with tiny breasts and little dark nipples. She crawled on top of him and kissed him. He didn't really like kissing, so he let her lips do all the work. She tried to slip her tongue into his mouth, but he kept his jaw clamped, and she prodded the holes where teeth had been knocked out. After a while she gave up. She slipped a hand into his pants and fumbled around, but he was limp as the day he'd been born. He closed his eyes and tried to concentrate, but that only made it worse. "My strength has not returned," he said, although he was actually feeling much better.

"You don't have to apologize," she said. Her voice was shrill and irritating.

"I wasn't," he snapped.

He'd never been comfortable around women. He liked the curly hair between their legs, but if he looked too low, he would lose his desire and have great difficulty recovering it. Marcus had always bragged about licking women down there and making them squeal with delight, but the very notion of slipping his tongue in that pink oyster of flesh turned Ogle's stomach. Sometimes when he was plowing a strumpet, he would turn her around and close his eyes and pretend she was a boy, and he would find himself harder than ever. *Maybe if you pretend she's Marcus,* suggested a distant voice. Her hair was the same color. But Marcus was so tall and strong, and she was so very small.

When she failed to arouse him, she covered her mouth and giggled. He shoved her out of the hammock with his good arm and barked, "Get off me, bitch."

She hopped off of him, retrieving her clothes. "Should I come back later?"

"If you do, I'll open your throat."

Her eyes widened with fright and she scampered off. Ogle stared up at the stars for a long while, until the sky started to turn violet. He realized he wasn't the least bit tired. He sat up in his hammock, careful not to place any pressure on his left arm. He swung his legs out and set his heels on the ground. It was strange to sit upright, and he struggled through a bout of dizziness. He cautiously exited the hammock. His legs wobbled. When he was certain he wasn't going to fall on his face, he started walking toward the bonfire. He stepped around several snoring pirates and continued to the point of the sharp cliff, which stretched hundreds of feet above the ocean. He saw a sloop moored below, but no flag. He looked west, and in the dim predawn light loomed the mound of another island, very close, with patches of soft orange lights scattered here and there. Perhaps the island was an extension of the one he was on, but he couldn't tell from here.

"Watch your step," Marcus blurted as he approached the ledge, giving Ogle a start. "Poor Hopkins got too drunk and took a stroll right off the edge. Found him washed up on some rocks, his bones turned to mush."

"Where's Teach?" Ogle asked suddenly. "Did he bring me here?"

A grim look passed over Marcus's face. "You've been out of the world for a spell. Teach . . . " he hesitated, shook his head. "*Queen Anne's Revenge* went down outside Pirate Town. Guy Dillahunt sunk her. I was on *Adventure* when Dillahunt took out our mast with a chainshot. Longest chain I ever saw. Sliced Peg Leg Dave's head off right in front of me. Took us a while to repair the mast. That's her down there." He pointed at the sloop far below the cliff. "She's the one we brought you in on. We found you three days later. Ash sniffed you out. Had no idea where he was taking us, but he insisted we follow. Glad we did. Kept saying he smelled death and life. Didn't know what that meant till we got down there."

Ogle chuckled. "You followed a blind man through that maze? Vane swore no one would find me."

Marcus scratched the back of his head. "Most wouldn't have."

6

GABE

Astrid was a pretty thing, as long as she smiled with her mouth closed. Her big crooked teeth marred an otherwise youthful, slender face, framed in full golden locks that curled without any incentive and rested on porcelain shoulders. She had big brown eyes and full red lips, ripe for kissing. Her bosom didn't exactly fill his hands, and her hips were too narrow, but her lovemaking was always so energetic that Gabe was willing to forgive her physical scarcities. When it was his turn to take control, he grabbed her by the waist and flipped her over. She shrieked with delight as he gathered a handful of her hair and pulled her head back. He exhaled into her ear. "Do you want me to stop?"

"No," she gasped, reaching back to rake her nails along his thigh.

He thrust violently, pressing her face against the pillow. She loosed a muffled wail of pleasure. Her back curved outward, revealing just how skinny she was as the notches of her spine jutted from her skin.

When he was spent, he collapsed beside her. She grinned at him, lips parting to reveal awkward teeth.

"What should we do now?" she asked cheerily.

"Get married, I suppose," he answered.

"Very funny," she said, lightly slapping his broad chest.

"I should get some rest," he said. "Wake me at dusk, would you?"

It was midday, but it might as well have been midnight in Astrid's little room on the second floor of The Hellbound Strumpet. It was a new establishment owned by a wealthy privateer named Nedly. According to gossip, Nedly enforced a strict hiring policy, sampling each whore for himself before deciding whether to employ them. Gabe had pressed Astrid for the truth of this rumor, but she remained coy, which he took as a confirmation. The exterior resembled every other new building on Nassau, lacking the former island charm. The lower floor had been refurnished with cushioned chairs and soft carpets. Candles lined the walls, and the thatched windows didn't let a single beam of outside light in. The second floor was partitioned into six rooms separated by thick red drapes with gold accents that glimmered in the candlelight. It was impossible to see through the drapes, but the pleasurable moans of strumpets and their patrons formed an unending chorus.

Despite the constant noise, Gabe's eyelids grew heavy.

"Sleep's going to cost you, dearie," Astrid said, tickling one of his nipples.

"Count your coin again," he said, turning away from her. "I gave you enough for the whole day."

"The extra was for the key," she reminded him sourly.

He let one arm fall over the bed, fingers brushing his black leather coat crumpled on the floor. He felt about until his hand closed around the hard object in the inner pocket: the key that Astrid had given him before passion took priority.

She leaned against him. "I don't think the chef ever realized where he lost it."

"'Lost' would be the wrong word."

She smiled coyly behind a raised shoulder. "Lost is still lost, even when it's stolen."

"Wouldn't be the first thing lost in here."

Her smile widened into a toothy grin. "Won't be the last. Anyway, he didn't come back looking for it. I hope he wasn't fired."

"If he wasn't, he will be."

"That's too bad," she sighed sadly.

"You knew there'd be consequences. Feeling bad about what you did isn't going to change what you did."

"My point is, I done a lot for you. Don't wager you could get into the governor's house without a key."

He grunted. "I'd find another way."

She moved her fingers toward his crotch yet again. "A much *harder* way."

He snatched up her hand and set it on her hip. "The task is greatly eased, thanks to you. That what you want to hear?"

She rolled onto her back with a sigh. "Not really."

"Should I spend the next few hours pondering a suitable answer?"

"Ponder whatever you like," she haughtily replied, fidgeting with her nails. "All this for a silly redhead. What's so special about that wench, anyways?"

"That wench is worth a lot of money," he answered.

"You fancy her?" The question appeared casual, but her voice was pitched noticeably higher than usual. Her eyes shifted his way for an instant.

"I don't even know her." His encounter with Katherine had been brief, but he hadn't forgotten her wild red hair and forward demeanor. There was something undeniably alluring about her, but he hadn't had enough time to discover what that was. He would have liked to get to know her a little better, but his mind had been on other things. *You'll have plenty of time to get to know her soon enough.*

"Do you *want* to know her?" Astrid asked nonchalantly.

"Enough with the questions," he snapped. A whore feigning jealousy would normally amuse him, but he was tired and irritable. "I need sleep."

"You're no fun," she pouted.

He closed his eyes. A line of soft orange light filtered through the seam of his lids. "Not when I'm sleeping."

He felt her groping him. "Oh, I bet I could have some fun with you when you're asleep."

"If something comes up, you're welcome to it. I'll be none the wiser."

She giggled. "You'll have sweeter dreams, I wager."

I doubt it. His dreams were rarely sweet.

Five minutes later, he was asleep and dreaming of a different whorehouse on the other side of Nassau. The Strapped Bodice was a two-story building that had been constructed around twin palm trees ascending through a spired roof that was shrouded in tattered sails. Inside, candles were set in small circular patterns on the floor, with a strumpet lounging in each circle, in varying degrees of undress, beckoning with a hooked finger and a fetching smile.

His gaze fell on a Spanish girl with a deceptively shy grin. She had thick black hair, copper skin, large lips, and a full bosom trying to burst out of a loose-fitting bodice with straps that drooped over copper shoulders. Her name was Annabelle. She was very beautiful, but he knew better than to go to her.

Distantly he knew she had been dead a long time, but that didn't lessen his trepidation. "Come over here, handsome," she said.

"Not tonight," he curtly replied. "I'm here for another."

"You don't know what you're missing."

He scoffed. "Yes, I do."

She wrinkled her pretty face. For an absurd instant, he felt sorry for her.

He ascended the spiral staircase to the second floor. The hemp drapes were much thinner than those of The Hellbound Strumpet, with the silhouettes of groaning men and women projected against them. Gabe moved through the thin hallway, flanked by writhing shadows, until he reached the last partition on the right. He cast a glance over his shoulder to make sure no one had followed him, and then he dove in.

He froze.

"Hello, Mr. Jenkins," Blackbeard said, standing tall in the middle of the room in a long dark coat, with rows of pistols running down his broad chest. Smoke rolled up over his face from the glowing fuses lodged in his great beard. Cobalt eyes gleamed through the haze. Rows of white teeth split his beard. His leathery cheeks shriveled and blackened as he grinned, the skin flaked away like burnt paper, and tiny orange flames lapped at the cracks from within. "It be time to wake up."

Gabe woke to Astrid shaking his shoulder, her face close to his. "It's time to wake up," she urged.

He cast a groggy glance around the room, as if that would help him determine the time. It looked exactly the same as before. "It's dusk?"

"Well that's what it means when the sun goes down, don't it?"

He sat up. How could it be dusk already? The dream had seemed no longer than a minute. Yet his limbs felt stiff, as if he hadn't used them in hours. He tilted his head and heard a crack in his neck. It took him longer than usual to get his breeches, shirt, and boots on. He tied his blue sash around his waist and slipped into his coat. He glanced at his pistol, but decided it wouldn't be much use. He would need to be quiet. The report of a gunshot would draw every guard in the house down on him. Instead, he tucked his favorite weapon into his sash: a Turkish Ottoman dagger with a curved, double-edged blade. The ribbed horn hilt was mounted in silver, with four round turquoise stones. The blade, which he kept dangerously sharp, fit snugly into a steel scabbard. It was a perfect weapon for opening a man's throat or belly.

Astrid's hands slid around his sides. He pulled away. The time for distraction was over. He reached into his coat pocket, closing his fingers over the key once again, cold against his palm.

"Be careful," she told him.

He didn't turn to face her. "If I'm not, will you attend my hanging?"

"As long as it's in the morning."

"They always are."

He swept back the thick curls of his black hair and ducked out of the room. He had never been very good at farewells, so he tended to avoid them altogether. Just as his father, Henry, had when he left for New York on business in 1714 and never returned, leaving a fifteen year old Gabe and his mother, Moll, to care for the family's tobacco farm in Virginia. The tobacco act, passed by Governor Spotswood in 1713, had seriously hindered the farm's exports. Henry had been in a constant state of panic thanks to strict regulations that would eventually require all leaf exports to be inspected. Henry took on more slaves and supplies, struggling to raise the quality of the farm's tobacco. Perhaps the increased burden had simply driven him to escape and start a new life.

Gabe's mother had been a graceful woman with a kind face and the same curly black hair. He couldn't fathom why any man in his right mind would abandon her. He wasn't sure exactly when his mother stopped referring to Henry as her husband. At some point or another Henry simply became, "Your father."

"I can't remember his face," Gabe had told his mother once, over dinner, a year after his father had departed. That wasn't entirely true, but he wanted to talk about it, since his mother rarely broached the subject. And maybe he wanted a reaction out of her. Anything would have comforted him. He needed to know she still cared.

"I remember it," she said, not looking at him, knuckles white as she gripped a fork and mashed it into a potato. She seemed to be pretending that the potato was his father's face. And then he knew that she *did* care, but not in the fashion that he had hoped.

He pushed a bit further. "Sometimes I wonder if he truly existed at all."

He would never forget the shadow that passed over her face as her eyes lifted to meet his. All traces of kindness faded for a terrible and thankfully fleeting moment. "You're living proof that he did," she had said.

That was the worst of it. The next day and every day since, Moll was exceedingly motherly to him. It was as if she had made a resolution to never treat him ill again. He loved her for that, even if he never found the appropriate moment to tell her.

Gabe was an only child with no friends, and the farm's many acres separated it from other settlements, so he looked to the younger slaves for camaraderie. It took some time to earn their friendship, as Henry had flogged several newly hired slaves for slaughtering a fat hog. Henry had made it clear he didn't like Gabe "fraternizing with negroes." When the slaves finally realized Henry wasn't coming back, they warmed up to Gabe.

Following his father's disappearance, Gabe increased his duties on the farm, planting seeds in the beginning of the year, moving young plants to larger fields, removing pesky tobacco worms, topping the plants, harvesting, and hanging and curing the tobacco. After a full year of this, he was an expert. Tobacco prices were steadily rising towards a staggering two cents per pound. Gabe's future was looking bright, even without his father.

Unfortunately, everything changed on a particularly dry summer day when the house and ninety percent of the crops were lost in a terrible fire. The fire had burned too quickly and too successfully, as though aided by unnatural forces. Moll was forced to sell off the slaves, including Gabe's closest friends, and she and Gabe moved to live with Moll's sister, Lilly, in Barnstable, Massachusetts. Lilly ran a very profitable fishing company. Gabe's mother soon accepted the deed to an inn that catered to fishermen, and she supervised it personally. From then on, her attention was thoroughly diverted from Gabe, who spent much of his time exploring the docks, memorizing every inch of every type of ship, and befriending salty fishermen. They liked him, and they favored him with tales of pirates and adventure on the high seas.

At seventeen, Gabe got it in his head that he could find his father and bring him back home. A crusty fisherman named Hawkins claimed he knew a Henry Jenkins, who had chartered a ship to England. Confused and curious, Gabe enlisted with a ship bound for England, but it was raided by none other than Edward Teach in the Atlantic. He was given the choice between a slow death and joining Teach's crew. He chose life. He still wasn't sure he had made the right decision.

Whenever Teach's pirates took a British merchant ship, Gabe questioned the crew about their employers, but none of them knew a Henry Jenkins. After a while, Gabe decided Hawkins' gossip had been false, and he gave up hope of ever finding his father.

Over the past year he dwelled less on his father and more on his mother. He often wondered if she had sent anyone to find him, but he concluded that she hadn't. She probably saw Gabe's departure as confirmation that he was so very much like his father. She had been so busy with the inn, he doubted she had much time to dwell on the absent men in her life. Still, something told him he could always go back and she would not turn him away. But he knew she would not welcome him with open arms and a loving smile, not after leaving her without so much as a goodbye. She had probably taken a new husband by now. He liked to think she had. It absolved him of the burden.

I have been out here too long, he realized as he departed The Hellbound Strumpet and started up the main street, putting the harbor to his back. Too much had happened over the past three years. He couldn't go back to a simple life. *Murderers don't deserve simple lives.*

The sun had vanished, leaving a salmon-pink horizon beyond the western exit of the channel between Providence and Hog Island. He strolled through the deserted bazaar as the vibrant tarps, curtains, and red roofs gradually surrendered their colors to the bluish-greys of twilight. All of the merchants had closed shop for the evening. The windows of double-storied buildings on either side of the street flickered orange, and shadows moved within. Stars dotted the darkening sky; too many to count, like sea-salt scattered over a black table. The clouds had fled, and the moon would be up soon. A woman's giggles drifted out of one of the windows, interrupted by a man's boisterous laugh, and then she shrieked joyously. "You'll have to catch me," she teased. "Oooh, slow down, you brute! Stop it! Stop it!" She burst into another fit of giggles.

Gabe pushed up the street, his legs already burning. He hadn't been sleeping very well over the past week. He knew he needed to be alert, but that had only made sleep more difficult. And when he did sleep, his dreams allowed him no peace.

Twilight had nearly faded to the prosaic black of night by the time he made it to the top of the street, which tapered into a winding road that cut through the thick jungle. He followed the road for about a mile, wary of the dark trees on either side. He didn't care for jungles. He preferred to see what was ahead of him. He heard birds chirping and monkeys screaming. The monkeys' voices were particularly eerie. At times it seemed they were calling his name, hoping to draw him into the wilds.

He stuck to the road, knowing he would have to dive into the trees if a carriage or a patrol approached. Fortunately his journey was uneventful. Eventually the road opened upon the grounds of the governor's estate. The two-story white mansion stood proudly atop a grassy hill, surrounded by lush gardens, which were no doubt colorful by day. The mansion had been constructed within the last few months, and its pristine white walls seemed to glow in the night. The portico covering the grand entrance consisted of four pillars supporting a triangular roof with a small pentagonal hollow in the middle, which looked to Gabe as though it was missing something.

Only two of the windows were illuminated, both on the second floor. One was large, near the center of the house—probably Rogers in his study—and the other was on the far eastern side, with a slender shadow moving back and forth. This room looked smaller, designed for a guest. And the maids' quarters would likely all be downstairs. *That has to be Katherine*

Lindsay, he decided.

A ten foot white wall bordered the base of the hill in a square of ten acres, with a giant arched gate at the front, which opened to a pebbled road that led right up to the front porch. Two sentries were posted outside the gate in long coats, deep maroon in the night, carrying muskets. Gabe skirted the jungle, which had been cleared twenty paces from the gate on all sides, so no one could use the foliage to get over the wall. He made his way around to the eastern wall.

It took him a few uncertain moments searching in the dark before he rediscovered the spot where he'd buried his grapple and rope. He had visited the grounds last night, before meeting with Dillahunt early that morning. He found the little mound beneath a notably tall palm tree at the edge of the jungle. He dug fast, until his fingers brushed metal. He pulled the three-pronged grapple and the attached rope out of the hole and shook the dirt off. He glanced around to make sure no sentries were patrolling this side. They weren't. He scurried over to the wall, pressing himself flat against it. He looked around again. No one was coming. He let the grapple hang two feet from the rope, and started to swing. He released, and the grapple sailed over the top of the wall. It struck the other side with a *thunk* that echoed off the house. Gabe lowered his head, mouthing a silent prayer. When he was certain no one had heard, he gave the rope a firm tug to make sure it was secure. He took off his coat and his shirt. He tore two strips of fabric from the shirt and wrapped them around each hand. He bunched up what was left of the shirt and tossed it into the jungle. He put his coat back on, leaving it unbuttoned and his chest bare. He hefted himself up the rope, placing his feet against the wall. He quickly reached the top and threw his arms over. As he crawled up, he saw the moon rising over the jungle. The grapple, freed of his weight, slipped off the wall and fell within the grounds, landing quietly in a patch of grass. The rope whipped past Gabe's face, singing his cheek, and he snatched it. He started over the top, and the hilt of his dagger let out a teeth-chattering screech as it scraped along the wall. He hunched low, straddling the top of the wall.

A spot of red was moving toward him. "'Ello? Is someone there?"

Gabe smacked his forehead lightly on the top of the wall, hissing through his teeth. "So close," he whispered to himself.

"Oy! Oy, there! What're you doing up there? Stop that!" the sentry barked, running up to the wall and fumbling to aim his musket. The man stepped on a prong of the grapple and yelped, hopping on one foot. "What in the bloody hell?"

Gabe realized he was still holding the rope, stretched taut to the grapple. He jerked hard, swinging his arm over his head, propelling the grapple into the air. The sentry gawked downward as the grapple shot toward his face. One of the prongs entered his mouth, lifting him off his feet, and his head twisted until his neck gave with a sickening *snap*. Gabe released the rope and let the man crumple to the grass. He rolled off the wall, landing on his feet beside the corpse. He didn't see anyone else. "Lucky," he muttered. He grabbed the sentry by the ankles and dragged him behind a hedge. "Well, maybe not for you."

He made his way to the north side of the house, which overlooked a large garden. Carefully trimmed hedges and red-pebbled walkways swirled elegantly around an unfinished stone fountain. The top rim of the fountain was resting to one side, waiting to be set in place.

Gabe continued on until he found a dark stairway cut into the ground, flanked by stacked empty crates that smelled of poultry and fruit. At the foot of the stairs was an unpainted door set in the foundation of the house. Gabe reached into his coat pocket, feeling for the key. Panic swelled in his throat. *It's gone!* Had he dropped the key somewhere along the way?

And then he checked the opposite pocket, and cold metal greeted his fingers. He sighed, shaking his head at his stupidity. He stuck the key in the lock, closing his eyes before turning it. The bolt released. He carefully opened the door and moved inside.

"May I help you, sir?"

Gabe nearly leapt out of his breeches.

An archaic face with a hooked nose stared at him from beneath a white wig. The old man wore a long blue butler's coat.

Gabe glanced around the kitchen. "I'm . . . I'm the chef's apprentice."

"The chef has been sacked for losing his key."

Gabe presented the key. "Then I'm the *new* chef!"

"Your timely arrival is most coincidental," the butler drawled, blinking slowly.

"I assure you this is not what it looks like."

"And what does it look like?"

Gabe hesitated. "Whatever it is *not* . . . is what it looks like. Which it isn't."

"That makes no sense, sir." The butler's half-lidded eyes fell to Gabe's shirtless chest. "And a chef without a shirt is a poor chef. You'll get chest hairs in the soup. Not that you have many chest hairs."

Gabe sighed. "You make a fine point." He kneed the butler in the groin, doubling him over his leg, then brought his elbow down on the back of the old man's head. He took off his coat and set it on a counter, with every intention of coming back for it; he liked this coat. He stripped the unconscious butler of his coat and slipped into it. He started for the exit, then halted. He plucked the wig off the butler's head and fit it snugly over his own, tucking his thick curls in as best he could. He imagined he looked ridiculous. It was hardly a foolproof disguise, but it would hopefully be enough in the dark, from a distance.

He ascended a slim stairway to a long gloomy hallway with doors on either side. It smelled of fresh paint. Indistinct faces stared at him from large paintings lining the walls between the many doors. He moved down the hallway as quietly as possible, until it opened to the foyer. The large front door was on his left, and a grand staircase on his right. He heard two female voices whispering and saw a faint orange glow coming from the hallway on the opposite side of the foyer. He darted for the staircase, moving quietly up the wide steps, curving around in a half-circle to the second floor. An extravagant chandelier was hanging in the center of the half-circle.

As he reached the top, a butler passed by carrying a silver tray of fruit toward the west wing. Luckily, Gabe didn't need to go that way. He clutched his wig and hurried down the eastern hallway, glancing over his shoulder repeatedly. He reached a door at the end with a strip of light in the crease beneath it. The door was bolted twice from the outside. *Are they holding a woman in here, or a dragon?*

He slid both bolts back and opened the door, glancing one last time down the hall. He clutched the hilt of his dagger, knowing that Katherine might require some encouragement. He didn't like the idea of threatening a woman with a blade, but he would do what he had to do. He plunged into the room, closing the door behind him.

A brass lamp flickered gently on a little bedside table. Propped against a plethora of luxurious pillows, with one leg raised, Katherine Lindsay lifted an eyebrow over the thick tome she was reading. She let the book fall into her lap. The left half of her face was lit, with that side of her mouth curling into a curious smirk. Her red lips were far less chapped than the last time he'd seen her. Her intelligent eyes narrowed. The light revealed thin scars; one ran in a slant down an otherwise smooth cheek and another pervaded her eyebrow. The curls of her red tresses rolled over her shoulders, like fire tumbling from her scalp, highlighted with orange strands. She wore a short-sleeved, white chemise with a low neckline that bared the top of her breasts. The skirt of the gown had fallen back from her raised leg, revealing creamy skin.

She slammed the book shut, tucked it under her arm and hopped out of the bed. The skirt dropped to cover her leg. Gabe glimpsed a voracious curiosity in her flaring pupils, like a cat that has caught sight of a loose twine of yarn and will not look away for fear of losing it. "You're not a butler," she said. Her voice was husky, and her neck muscles strained when she spoke, as though words pained her.

Gabe removed his wig and ran a hand through his hair, which was damp with sweat. He hadn't realized how much energy he'd been exerting. "My name is Gabe Jenkins. I'm here to . . . " he paused before he could say, "rescue you," because that wasn't exactly true.

"Kill me?" she suggested.

"What? No."

The curves of her hips swayed through the thin fabric as she casually stepped before the lamp. "I know you, don't I? Yes, I remember you from *Crusader*. You were there. You took part in the mutiny. That dreadful whore had a hold over you, if I recall."

He was tired of being reminded of that sad affair, though he knew he had no one to blame but himself. "Annabelle had no hold over me."

Blackbeard, on the other hand . . .

"Did she not take you into her bed?" Katherine wondered.

"She tried," Gabe replied.

Annabelle's final request of Gabe had been born of jealousy

and desperation. She had instructed him to murder Katherine after she realized her mistake in bringing Katherine before Charles Vane. Gabe refused, for it was clear Annabelle no longer served Blackbeard. She had hoped her beauty would be enough to coax Gabe into murder, with the not-so-subtle promise of the fruit between her legs. Their parting had not been pleasant. It was the last time he saw her, before Vane tossed her to her death.

"Are you certain you aren't here to kill me?" Katherine asked. She might have been asking him to pass the salt, for all the concern she showed. "All I need do is scream and the entire house will rush to my aid."

"Why would I kill you?" he asked.

She shrugged. "Retribution for Blackbeard."

He frowned. "Retribution? It's not like *you* killed him."

"Really?" She cocked her head. "Who do you think killed him?"

"Why, Captain Dillahunt, of course."

Her face bunched with irritation, mouth shrinking as she pursed her lips, elegant nose wrinkling around flaring nostrils. Her words were quick and sharp. "Oh, I'm sure that's what he tells everyone. In point of fact, I blew up *Queen Anne's Revenge*. The fire killed Blackbeard. Thus, I killed Blackbeard."

Something about her vehemence convinced him she was telling the truth, as unbelievable as it was. "I didn't know that. Regardless, I'm not here to harm you. I have no loyalty to a dead man."

She clutched the large book to her stomach, muscles straining visibly in her arms. He wondered if she intended on using it to bludgeon him over the head. It was certainly heavy enough. "So what are you doing in my bedroom? I hope you're not expecting to rape me. That would end poorly . . . for you."

"I'm only here to kidnap you," he answered, flashing a grin.

"I'd appreciate if you didn't put up much of a fuss."

To his surprise, she looked distinctly relieved. "It's about goddamned time," she said, carelessly tossing the large book to the floor. Gabe cringed as it landed with a *thump*. She moved to the window, unlatching it and swinging the shutters open. A cool breeze wafted in, pressing her gown against the smooth contours of her body. "Rogers confined me to this room for a reason. Unless you've brought rope, we probably can't escape out this window. There's no ledge. Believe me, I've tried. Have a look for yourself." She moved aside, gesturing to the window.

He allowed himself a shrewd smile and stayed right where he was. "I'll take your word for it."

After a moment she smiled in turn. "Good. I would have been disappointed if you'd gone for it."

But that wouldn't have stopped you from giving me a shove. He kept his eyes on her as he reached for the door handle behind him. "We'll go back the way I came in, through the kitchen."

"I'm sure there's an easier way."

He shook his head. "I'm not leaving without my coat."

"Fine. After you."

He drew his curved dagger. Her eyes widened. He gestured at her with the blade. "It's only a precaution, should you decide to alert anyone."

The edges of her lips turned downward. "And I took you for the chivalrous sort."

"Oh, I am." Gabe opened the door. "Ladies first. I insist."

7

KATE

"What were you reading?" Jenkins asked as he ushered her into a gap between a long hedge and the high wall on the eastern side of the mansion.

"What?" She had no idea what he was talking about. Adrenaline was still surging through her from their escape through the hallways. Sweat was cool on her chest and arms, glistening in the moonlight, and the thin gown clung to her skin. They had eluded a maid and a butler, sneaking through the kitchen—so Jenkins could retrieve his black coat—and out the back. She was ecstatic to be quit of the house, though there was still the matter of getting over the wall. She wasn't worried. If Jenkins could get in, he could get out. He seemed to know what he was doing. *And he isn't exactly sore on the eyes,* she mused as she watched him.

"That tome," he said. "It was bigger than you."

"Oh, that," she gasped, placing a hand on her chest as she

caught her breath. The book already seemed inconsequential. "The life and times of my captor, Woodes Rogers. He has little else by way of reading material, and he's frightfully self-absorbed."

Jenkins made a face. "Sounds terrible."

"It wasn't so bad," she said with a shrug. "He was quite the adventurer, before all this. Bit of a pirate, too. There were times when I was able to fantasize I was him. It was momentarily diverting, before I remembered I was imprisoned in a stuffy mansion. I've been inescapably bored."

"Not so inescapable, it would seem," he reminded her with a boyish grin.

His youthful charm put an irritating flutter in her belly. *Yes, I remember you well enough, Gabe Jenkins.* They had only talked once, and she hadn't seen him since *Crusader* docked at Pirate Town, but he had left an impression. She had assumed he had been killed in the battle between Vane and Blackbeard's men. She was pleased to see he had made it out alive. She probably didn't want to know what deal he had struck. *Maybe I'm part of that deal.*

"Not sure I would call this an escape," she said.

"From one captor to the next," he agreed.

She let out a sigh of resignation. "It's what I do."

Jenkins blew a loose curl of hair out of his eyes. It fell right back into his vision. "Don't you want to know the name of my employer?"

"Seeing as Blackbeard's dead, I can only assume Charles Vane has need of me. Possibly something to do with my reward, which I'm told is considerable. He was a fool to let me go in the first place."

Jenkins looked impressed, though he was doing his best to hide it. "Some would call that a kindness."

"Kindness does not befit a pirate. He should have kept me

as a bargaining piece."

"I wager he realized that too late."

She studied Jenkins intently, hoping to make him uncomfortable with a hard gaze. She had been uncharacteristically bashful the first time she met him, and she wished to return the favor. He frowned at her. "Is there something wrong with my face?"

She worked her jaw irritably. "Not yet."

"Funny."

"How long have you been in the business of kidnapping women?"

"You're the first." He grabbed the neckline of her gown and pulled her down low behind the hedge. Her cheeks flushed with warmth as his fingers brushed her breasts. She slapped his hand away and adjusted the top of her gown.

"Explains why you're so bad at it," she said.

He threw her a withering look. "You can educate me later, since you're far more experienced at being kidnapped than I am at kidnapping."

She rolled her eyes. "Does your wit know no end?"

"It's known many ends," he replied suggestively.

She scoffed. *You won't be so funny when I put a rock through that pretty face.*

"Stay low," he said as he peered over the top of the hedge. A bead of sweat emerged from his thicket of curly hair, trickling down his forehead.

"Oh dear, there's a dead man here," she said, pointing to a corpse that had been discarded behind the bush. It was one of the guards. Something metal was protruding from his mouth with a rope attached. It was one of the sentries. She spent a few seconds trying to remember which guard he was, and then she recalled that he had made an obscene comment about her rear during her first week under Rogers' care.

Jenkins had the good grace to feign concern. "I trust he wasn't a friend?"

"Hardly," she answered. "I might have killed him myself, had I the means."

"Good," he said. He might even have meant it. "I've got enough on my conscience already."

"Do tell."

He smiled politely. "Now isn't the best time."

She scowled as a dreadful thought occurred to her. "You didn't murder any of the maids did you? I'm quite fond of two of them. One of them, not so much, but not enough to want her killed. I'll admit I entertained ill thoughts, but nothing I would act on."

"No maids," he replied.

Good, she thought. *Emma is alright.* She would miss her.

"What about Rogers? Did you kill him?" She tried not to sound too hopeful. Rogers would be furious when he learned she had slipped from his grasp. The man seemed to despise anything he could not control. *He's punished me long enough.* No matter what happened tonight, she would not let anyone take her back to that house.

"As you've no doubt already guessed," Jenkins said, "I'm not here for Rogers."

"I'm shocked," she said. "I would think assassinating the governor would be at the top of any pirate's list."

"Wouldn't do much good, would it? Another man would just replace him. The king is determined to take back the Caribbean. One man's death will hardly put an end to it. It's like to make things worse."

"Yes, well, pirates aren't exactly the most prudent lot, are they?" She opened her hands at him, wiggling her fingers. "I mean, here you are, scuttling about the governor's gardens."

He ignored the insult. "Most aren't. But Rogers arrived

with pardons. Truth be told, pirates admire him as much as they hate him. Maybe they're even a bit jealous."

He crawled up to the corpse and wrenched the metallic thing from his mouth, and Kate realized it was a grappling hook. She winced as blood poured out of the dead man's mouth. It seemed an age since she'd last seen blood.

"We're going over the wall?" she asked.

"That's right."

"Fine, but you're going first."

"I'm afraid not," he replied in an even tone. "I won't have you dashing off to alert the guards once I'm over the top."

"Then we have a problem," she said, sitting on her feet and folding her arms. "I won't have you stealing a glance at my private bits."

He pinched the bridge of his nose and closed his eyes. "I promise not to look up your gown."

She kept her arms folded and smirked. "And I should take my kidnapper at his word?"

He opened his coat, baring his chest, and tapped the hilt of the exotic dagger sheathed in his sash. "As your kidnapper, I'm not giving you any choice in the matter. Besides, I've already seen everything there is to see of you."

She opened her mouth to disagree, but was halted by the unpleasant memory of Annabelle stripping her naked and parading her before *Crusader's* mutinous crew. Gabe Jenkins was the only one who had looked away in shame. "There's more to a woman than skin," she stubbornly replied.

"Of course," he agreed. "There are organs and bones and a heart and maybe even a brain, if you look very hard."

She raised a dubious eyebrow. "You're not particularly skilled at pretending to be a chauvinistic dullard, are you?"

"I need practice."

"Three words a woman never hopes to hear."

He withered. "That's not what I—"

She stopped him with a shrewd smirk, letting him know it was merely a jest.

He cleared his throat. "Alright, enough stalling." He looked around to make sure none of the guards were near. Kate looked with him, but only saw a small shape patrolling near the gate. Jenkins hurled the grapple upward, and it hooked the top of the wall. He gave the rope a few good tugs, his considerable biceps bulging beneath his coat, which was two sizes too small. He handed her the rope, then lowered his hands and interlocked his fingers, offering a step. "Up with you. Go on."

She eyed him skeptically.

"I already promised not to look," he said. "Besides, it's dark."

"Moonlight," she reminded him.

He tossed his hair back in frustration. "Unless the moon's shining out your arse, I'm not going to see anything."

"Only sunshine," she replied.

She set her heel in his hand and started climbing up the rope. She looked down and saw his cheeks flush red just before his eyes flickered away. She set a bare foot on his face and mashed his nose. He muffled a protest as she pushed off of him. "Oops," she cheerily quipped.

She quickly reached the top and threw a leg over the other side. She glanced down. Jenkins was busy watching for guards. She took hold of the grapple, wrenched it loose of the wall, and tossed it over the opposite side. Jenkins snapped to attention too late, leaping for the rope as it whipped up the wall. His fingers barely grazed it, and then the rope went up and over, joining the grapple on the other side, well out of his reach. "Thank you for letting me go first," she said.

"You're a bitch," he concluded.

She waved a hand. "Oh, stop it. Something tells me you'll

find another way. I need a little head start, is all. I've business with Captain Dillahunt. If you're still keen on kidnapping me, you'll find me at the dock."

"Maybe I can help," he offered, adopting a transparent smile.

"Lovely of you to offer, but this is something I have to do on my own."

"I need that rope," he insisted, abandoning his smile. "The only other way out is through that gate, and it's guarded."

"You'll think of something. You're a clever boy."

His face darkened. "Boy? We're the same age."

"It's just a figure of speech," she assured him, surprised by his temper. She suddenly wasn't certain she wanted to leave him down there, looking so angry and nervous. *And so very fetching.*

The moment passed. She leapt off the wall to the opposite side, buckling her knees as she landed. She immediately darted for the thick jungle. She skirted the edge, keeping to the trees, so that the sentries guarding the front gate wouldn't see her. When she was far enough from the grounds, she set upon the road.

When she reached the town, she kept to the shadow of the buildings on the left side of the main street. Most of the candles had gone out all over town, but the moon was nearing the middle of the sky. Halfway down, she ducked into an alley and found a line of clothes stretching from the small window of one building to the roof of another. She quietly stole a pair of dark brown breeches and a stained, long-sleeved shirt that might have been white. She wouldn't bother searching for any boots, because the leathery soles of her feet were impenetrably tough after so much time spent walking barefoot about the decks of ships. She glanced around before stripping off her thin gown and discarding it. The pants were too large and the shirt was frumpy, but that was exactly what she needed right now. She didn't want anyone noticing her womanly figure. Soon Rogers would have the whole town looking for her. She stole a black shirt as well, tearing off a small strip and one of the sleeves. She bound her hair in a ponytail with the strip and fashioned a bandana over her head with the sleeve.

As she tightened the knot of the bandana, her breath caught in her throat. Two large green irises materialized from the darkness. A silver sheen ran along a lithe little body as the moonlight struck its slick black fur. It was just a cat, slinking down the alley, searching for scraps. Kate recalled the tortoise shell kitten Jonathan Griffith had hoped to placate her with; one of many friendships that had been violently severed before given a chance to blossom. She winced at the memory of Edward Livingston dashing her kitten against a rail and tossing its broken body over the side.

"I don't have any food, my furry friend," she told the black cat. It approached her anyway, purring at the sound of her voice. She lowered a hand and let the cat nudge its face against her fingers. She felt its stiff whiskers and wet, rubbery gums along her knuckles. "I wish I could take you with me, little one, but I don't know where I'm going. You'd probably get hurt, or worse." The cat opened its mouth and sank its fangs into her hand with surprisingly forceful jaws. Kate hissed through her teeth and jerked away. The cat bolted into the darkness, back the way it had come, and Kate was left rubbing a red welt along the stretch of skin between her thumb and forefinger. "Little shit," she muttered sullenly.

It felt like midnight by the time she reached the dock. The moon brightened the surface of the calm water that stretched to the long shadow of Hog Island. At the foot of the harbor's western channel, a large HMS warship was ominously silhouetted, guarding the exit to open sea. The eastern channel was unblocked, however. Kate wondered if another warship was lurking somewhere out of view.

At the dock, *Crusader's* familiar hull stood out from the rest, even without the mermaid. The sails were as clean as ever, and the polished decks gleamed in the moonlight. If she hadn't witnessed the battle firsthand, she would never have known what the ship had endured.

She ignored the dozen or so other ships and hurried down the long pier. A single lantern lit *Crusader's* deck, just below the forecastle, and she smiled to herself, in spite of her dire intent. Sure enough, as she ascended the ramp to the main deck, she saw Fat Farley, Jeremy Clemens, and Bastion playing dice near the capstan. It was as though nothing had changed.

Not for them, anyway.

A tall, skinny officer in a white wig suddenly blocked her path. He frowned dubiously, with a nose that protruded like a toucan's beak. "What's this, then?" he asked stiffly.

"This is a woman," she answered.

"I know what you are," he said, blinking through sudden frustration. "What is your business here?"

"I would have words with Captain Dillahunt."

The officer considered her request for all of a second, his rigid expression never faltering. "No."

"Why not?"

"I smell foul intent."

I don't have time for this fool. Kate stuck out a hand and flicked the tip of the officer's nose with her middle finger. "With a beak like that, I'm sure you smell bird shit before it hits your crown."

The man recoiled in horror, shielding his nose from further abuse with a cupped hand. "Insults will earn you no favor with me, young miss! And if you touch me again, I shall be forced to restrain you!"

"Kate!" Farley had spotted her, his huge belly jiggling as he lumbered over, waving to her excitedly. He signaled Jeremy and Bastion to follow. "It's Kate!" The other two stood at once, grinning ear to ear.

She suppressed a surge of warmth. Normally she would be overjoyed to see them, especially Bastion, who had saved her life with a "magic kiss" after she had drowned. She had never properly thanked him for that. But her time was running thin. Jenkins had probably escaped the Governor's grounds by now and was already on his way to retrieve her.

"You know this woman?" the officer asked.

"Aye, Lieutenant Winnie," Farley answered.

"Wincott," the lieutenant corrected with a fierce glare.

"Aye, of course," Farley muttered half-heartedly. "Anyway, this is Kate."

Wincott shrugged. "And that should mean what to me?"

"She's friend to Captain Dillahunt," Farley said, as Bastion and Jeremy rushed up to join him. "She's friend to all of us."

Kate wanted to kiss Farley for being so sweet, even though he was about to ruin her chances of getting to Dillahunt.

Wincott shifted his dubious gaze back to Kate. "It's obscene to even ponder what a 'friend' might need of the captain at this dark hour."

"The obscenity has already been committed, I'm afraid." The lie emerged before she had time to consider it. She looked down and placed tender hands on her belly. "I'm carrying Captain Dillahunt's child."

All the color fled Farley's face. "I feel sick."

"This is no good," Bastion sighed despondently.

Jeremy sputtered something unintelligible.

Concern softened Lieutenant Wincott's stern face. "Oh . . . oh, dear. Step aside, men!" Wincott stripped off his coat and put it around Kate's shoulders. She wrestled her lips against a budding smile. As Wincott hurried her toward Dillahunt's cabin, she looked over her shoulder and saw her old friends exchanging puzzled glances.

"I'll never eat again," Farley said.

Jeremy scoffed. "There's two improbables too many."

"This makes no sense," Bastion mumbled while shaking his head. "This makes no sense."

Wincott beat a fist on the cabin door. "Captain Dillahunt, your attention is required on deck. This woman is with child!"

There was a great deal of shuffling from inside the cabin. A soft glow filtered through the seams of the door. Eventually, the door opened, and Dillahunt's scarred, sleepy face appeared. He tossed his scraggly, brownish-blonde hair out of his eyes and squinted. "Who is that?"

Kate reached to Wincott's side, drew his pistol, and shoved him back. Wincott's coat fell away from her shoulders as she aimed the gun at Dillahunt's forehead, stepping through the doorway. Dillahunt, wearing half-laced breeches and no shirt, backed up quickly.

"She's out of her mind!" Wincott said.

Kate glanced back. "Shut this door behind me, lieutenant, or your carelessness will be the death of your captain."

"My *carelessness*?" Wincott guffawed.

"The word is perfectly apt," Dillahunt barked. "And we'll discuss this later."

Kate heard the door slam shut behind her. She smirked confidently over the barrel of the gun. "What makes you presume there will be a 'later'? I might just let that man off the hook."

Dillahunt continued to back toward the bed, his puffy face surrendering grogginess to desperation. "Last I looked, you're not a murderer, Katherine."

"I'm not?" said Kate.

"She's not?" said Calloway, just as surprised. The girl was

sitting against the headboard, clutching the sheets to her breasts. A candle flickered in a brass disc on the table beside her, with smoke trailing thinly from the flame.

"A killer, yes," Dillahunt corrected, "but not a murderer. There's a difference, you know."

Kate guffawed. "I'm sure you've worked the semantics out in your favor."

He lifted his hands, trying to look as innocent as possible. That made her all the more furious. "Let's not do anything rash, Kate," he urged. "You'd only regret it."

"My only real regret is letting you out of that cell in Pirate Town."

"What are you doing here, Kate?" Calloway asked.

"Hello, Jaq," Kate replied. "Lovely to see you."

"Hello. What are you doing here?"

"It doesn't concern you. This is between me and Guy." She glanced sideways to Dillahunt's desk, where he had left his two black pistols. They were well out of his reach.

"I would pose the same query," Dillahunt hazarded.

"You know why I'm here, Guy," Kate hissed, advancing. "Feign ignorance and you'll only make me angry. I was happy to let you steal the glory, but that wasn't enough for you. You had to take my freedom."

Calloway climbed out of the bed and kneeled to retrieve her clothes. Kate followed her with the barrel of the gun. "There had better not be a pistol under that pile."

Calloway's freckles bunched around her nose in annoyance. "There isn't."

Kate returned the gun to Dillahunt as Calloway dressed. "You gave me your *word*, Guy. I understood that to mean something. All my life I've heard men speak so earnestly of their word. 'A man is nothing without his word,' they all say."

Dillahunt lowered his hands and sighed helplessly, as

though the choice hadn't been his. "Teach's body was lost. I had to give Rogers *something*."

"I'd say so, since your word isn't worth half a shit." Kate's finger tightened on the trigger. She distantly wondered how much pressure was needed. Every gun was different. "I am not a thing to be given."

"Kate, don't do this," Calloway said as she tucked a black shirt into tan breeches.

"Why not? I saved your life too, Jaq. Remember? None of you would be here if not for me. This bloody ship wouldn't be here. How can you still sleep with this man after what he did to me?"

Calloway straightened to her full height. Kate had forgotten how tall the girl was. "It's a good thing he didn't murder your husband," she countered. "You would have slept with him yourself."

Kate blinked. She would not cry in front of these two. She hadn't cried since Nathan Adams had died. He had deserved her tears. Guy Dillahunt did not. Maybe Jacqueline Calloway didn't either.

"I don't believe you intend to shoot me," Dillahunt said.

She nodded. "Not if you apologize."

He tittered. "I fear an apology would seem insincere, given the circumstances."

"I'll decide its sincerity."

"Katherine," he pleaded, holding out his hand.

"My name is Kate."

"Enough of this farce, Kate. Give me that."

Kate sighed. She was no longer certain what she had hoped to achieve here. She should have been using this time to escape. Not that she had any idea where she could escape to. *Anywhere would have been better than here.*

"Hand me the weapon," Dillahunt persisted gently.

"Take it," she growled. She tossed the gun to the ground, a bit too forcefully. A blast rang out, deafening in the close quarters, and the cabin flashed white for an instant. Dillahunt's left foot was thrust out from under him, his big toe disintegrating in a spray of red. He landed on his side, curled into a fetal position, and clutched his mangled foot as blood squirted from the tiny stump. A pitiful moan escaped his lips.

"Jesus!" Calloway exclaimed, dropping to Dillahunt's side. She looked strangely excited at the sight of the wound, leaning in for a closer look. The tip of her tongue curled over her upper lip.

"Don't touch it!" Dillahunt snapped, shoving Calloway back, leaving a five-fingered stain on the thigh of her breeches.

"That wasn't supposed to happen," Kate muttered to herself. She swallowed an instinctive urge to apologize. She realized now that she had never intended to shoot him, but she wasn't about to feel sorry for him either.

"What was *supposed* to happen?" Dillahunt demanded, spit frothing from his trembling lips.

Kate placed a fist on one hip and said, "An apology."

"I have nothing to apologize for. My only real regret is lax security."

Kate's temples filled with blistering heat and darkened her vision. Her teeth scraped as her jaw tightened, pressure surging through her face. "I should have left you in the caves of Pirate Town. With Vane and all the rest of them."

Dillahunt's cheeks purpled and his eyes slowly rolled up in their sockets. "I'm losing myself a piece at a time."

"Well at least you still have your cock," Kate replied.

8

CALLOWAY

"I found it!" Calloway announced as she held up the red pulp of Dillahunt's toe. She squeezed it between two fingers and watched the blood ooze down her hand. A tiny white bone protruded from the shorn pink and purple flesh. She grinned as a shudder of excitement ran through her.

"Throw it out!" yelled Terry Bell. The elderly surgeon's hearing wasn't what it used to be, so he bellowed every sentence. The crew had nicknamed him "Terrible." They liked to sneak up on him, which wasn't hard to do. Calloway feared they would give the poor man a heart attack someday. A wild tuft of white hair circled his bald, pockmarked head. A loose flab of skin dangled beneath his trembling jaw. His right eye had gone milky white, though he claimed he could still see through it well enough. Dillahunt said the surgeon had come highly recommended by Woodes Rogers, but Calloway couldn't fathom why. Maybe the governor had more of a sense of humor than he liked to let on.

Dillahunt angled his sickly-pale face away from the toe. "Don't suppose it can be reattached."

"WHAH?!" shouted Terrible, putting a hand to his ear, as if that would make any difference.

"Nothing," Dillahunt said, shaking his head. He looked at Calloway. "Cast it over the side." And then he added under his breath, "And Terrible with it."

"WHAH?!"

Calloway clenched the toe in her fist. She walked across the cabin to the desk, where Kate was perched with her arms folded. Calloway offered her the toe. Kate made a sour face. "I had toe for breakfast."

"Still quick-witted, I see," Calloway replied, setting the toe on the desk, gore-side down. The toe fell to one side, and she quickly righted it again, pressing down hard so it stuck. It looked rather funny standing straight up.

"You mustn't leave port!" Terrible shouted into Dillahunt's face. "It's like to get infected!"

"Believe me, I've suffered much worse with no infection," Dillahunt said, wiping Terrible's spittle from his eye. "I won't be yielded by a careless accident." He glared at Kate.

"I took off the wrong piece," Kate whispered to Calloway. "I didn't want you to be angry with me."

Calloway let out a lavish sigh. "You might as well have. A cock that doesn't rise has no value to me."

Kate scowled curiously. "Really? But you were naked? I just figured . . . "

"I always sleep naked," Calloway answered with a shrug. "Guy seems not to notice."

Kate looked dumbfounded. Calloway wanted to take her aside and confide in her about the faltering relationship.

"This is hardly the time to discuss our private affairs,

Jacqueline," Dillahunt interjected. Apparently he could hear them just fine.

"There's nothing to discuss," Calloway returned loudly over her shoulder.

"You're insufferable," Dillahunt said. "I should—"

"Don't say something you can't withdraw," Kate barked at him.

Calloway bit back a hateful retort out of fear Dillahunt would reveal the truth about her part in Kate's capture. He was glaring hatefully through a purple, puffy face wrought in pain, and she knew he was on the verge of spilling everything to shift Kate's fury away from him. Kate still had no idea that it had been Calloway's idea to turn her in for her reward. Calloway had only done what was best for Kate, or so she kept telling herself. *Then why is it so hard to look into her eyes?*

Dillahunt collected himself, biting his lip. "I apologize. I am in pain. My uncouth words arise from that, nothing more." Yet he was rubbing his right thumb and forefinger. Calloway knew he only did that when he was lying.

She rolled her eyes toward Kate, but Kate's attention had been diverted toward the exit. She wasn't getting out that way. A shadow eclipsed the doorway, nearly filling it. Dumaka wore no shirt, proudly baring his gleaming black chest and all the scars that had been etched across it over the years. Powerful legs were concealed beneath frumpy brown hempen breeches, shredded beneath the knees, fastened at the waist by an inch-thick cord that was knotted beneath his navel. A horrendously rusty cutlass dangled from his hip, with a jagged edge and several holes where the blade had rotted through. Dumaka had never wiped the blood from his blade after a kill, letting it stain. Jeremy Clemens joked that if Dumaka's blade didn't kill you straight away, an infection would get you later.

Dillahunt loosed a puff of air before he spoke. "Where in

the bloody hell is Jenkins?"

Calloway frowned. "Jenkins?"

"Gabe Jenkins?" Kate said in disbelief, sliding off the desk onto her feet. "He was bringing me to you?"

"No," Dillahunt grunted, squirming on the deck. "Not to me."

"But you knew!" Kate protested.

"What's all this about, Guy?" Calloway asked. He hadn't said a word to her about Kate since turning her in. She suspected he resented her for putting the idea in his head in the first place. *As if the final decision hadn't been his.*

"It doesn't concern you," Dillahunt said.

Calloway felt her teeth grinding, pressure building behind her eyes with the promise of a headache. She took a deep breath, but it did not cool her. "Nothing is my concern."

"Jenkins waits on the dock," Dumaka interjected, baring his teeth in distaste. "He knows better than to set foot on this ship again."

Dillahunt was outraged. "He's been out there all this time and you didn't think to tell me?"

"You did not ask," Dumaka replied. "I had a mind to run my blade across his throat."

"Duty stayed your hand, I'm sure," said Dillahunt. "You are a pirate no more."

Calloway looked from Dillahunt to Dumaka. She knew Dumaka hadn't adjusted well to honorable work. He didn't like taking orders. He had mutinied against Hornigold after Hornigold turned from pirate to pirate hunter. As a pirate, Dumaka had been a member of a democracy, with a voice in every decision that was made.

"I am a pirate no more," Dumaka growled.

"You will kill him only when I say, and not a moment before. Is that understood?"

"This is understood."

"What's all this, then?" Lieutenant Wincott demanded. He was trying to squeeze through the slim gap between Dumaka and the doorway. Dumaka moved aside, and Wincott was propelled by his own momentum into the room, nearly toppling. He righted himself and adjusted his coat. He looked so very small and so very white in contrast to the black mass of Dumaka looming behind him, but he did his best to assume authority. "It stinks of treachery."

A strained pause followed, in which the creaking of wood was the only sound.

"I'm sure it's not your concern, Lieutenant," Calloway chimed in finally.

"My first mate speaks out of turn," Dillahunt said as he struggled to sit up. He propped himself against the bed.

Terrible, who was still inspecting his wound, gave him a nasty look. "Stop moving about!"

"Then stop prodding me and get on with it already!"

Terrible reached into his bag and produced a needle and thread. "Young people always in a rush! Don't regret it till it kills them!"

"A dead man regrets nothing," Dillahunt said.

"WHAH?!"

"Nothing. Just sew it up already."

"I'll have to fold the skin over the opening," said Terrible. "That will hurt."

"You think it doesn't already?" Dillahunt growled.

Terrible grunted and went to work.

"May I watch?" Calloway asked hopefully.

"You may not," said Dillahunt.

Wincott walked briskly over to Kate, and Calloway had to move out of his path before he barreled into her. He aimed a finger at Kate's nose. "You took advantage of my chivalry."

"I'm about to take advantage of your finger."

"I beg your pardon?"

Calloway snatched Kate's wrist before she could raise her hand. "Don't," she warned. "I have a feeling you're in enough trouble already."

"What's a little more?" Kate asked playfully.

Calloway let go of Kate's wrist and took in her pretty face. The slanted scar on her cheek stood out in the candlelight, which emphasized the thin swell of tissue. Her hair was mostly dark brown in the soft light, save for a red shimmer of curl here and there. "Do you take nothing seriously, Katherine?"

Kate looked at her, eyes blank, impossible to read. "You know I do, Jacqueline."

"Katherine?" Wincott whirled swiftly on his heels to face Dillahunt. "This is Katherine Lindsay? Why is she not in the Governor's mansion?" Wincott waited for an answer that did not come. Finally, he said, "You are scheming under the governor's nose. I will not stand for it. I will not."

"That's unfortunate," said Dillahunt, wincing as Terrible tightened a stitch. "You leave me no other course. Mr. Dumaka, escort Lieutenant Wincott to the brig, and see that he doesn't alert any guards along the dock. You may need to bind his mouth, as he can be rather vociferous when he wants to be."

Dumaka frowned. "Vocif—"

"It means loud."

Wincott's jaw was hanging open. It was a moment before he was able to form words. "This is an outrage! You'll all hang for treason!"

"You see what I mean?" Dillahunt said.

Dumaka advanced on Wincott. Wincott slapped at his waist for his pistol, but then it seemed to dawn on him that he no longer had it. He glared at Kate. "You've spent the last of your nine lives, Mrs. Lindsay."

"On you?" Kate chuckled. "I want a refund."

Calloway's snort was embarrassingly loud. She pinched her nose and glanced around sheepishly.

"The devil offers no recompense," Wincott proclaimed with a raised finger. And then he shuddered violently, his wig slid off his head, his eyes crossed, and he crumpled in a heap.

Dumaka stood over him, thumbing his temple in bewilderment. "I did not hit him very hard."

"You didn't kill him, did you?" Dillahunt asked, though he didn't sound too concerned.

Dumaka kneeled beside Wincott and placed a finger under his nose. "He draws breath."

"Take him to the brig. And send Jenkins in."

Dumaka's great brow descended, shadowing his eyes. "You wish that man in your cabin?"

"A pirate asks questions, Dumaka," Dillahunt said. "A sailor does not."

Dumaka liked that even less, but he nodded and scooped up Wincott in his massive arms. It looked like he was carrying a little boy. He disappeared outside with the unconscious lieutenant.

Calloway looked at Kate, whose eyes were darting back and forth as she searched for an escape route or something she could use. Calloway set a hand on her shoulder to calm her. "It's fine, Kate," she said. "I'm here."

Kate smiled warmly at that, but the worry hadn't left her eyes.

Again, Calloway felt shame tugging at her heart. *I must be stronger than this,* she told herself. Kate was the key to her freedom.

Gabe Jenkins entered the cabin. He was bleeding from a gash just below his scalp, and his muscular chest was covered in sweat beneath a long black coat. A loose wet curl clung to his forehead. He looked at Kate, then at Dillahunt, and spread his arms and grinned. "I look away for one second . . . "

"Spare me your jests, Jenkins," Dillahunt growled. "If not for your carelessness, I'd still have two big toes."

"I'm told they serve no purpose," Jenkins quipped with a shrug. He bit his lower lip, suddenly uncertain. "Or maybe that's just the little ones? I forget."

"Take your prize and get out!" Dillahunt ordered. Terrible looked up from his work to make sure the order hadn't been directed at him, the loose flap of skin wobbling under his chin.

"*His* prize?" Calloway blustered, stepping forward. "Guy, what in Hell are you playing at?"

"Fret not," Dillahunt replied with a raised hand. "The end result will be the same, if not for the better."

"Better for who?" Kate demanded angrily. She stuck close to Calloway's side. "You?"

Jenkins answered in Dillahunt's stead. "For everyone."

"Not for me, I think," Kate shot back.

Terrible finished his last stitch, clipping the extra thread. He wiped his wrinkled old hands on a dirty handkerchief and struggled to his feet. "I'll be back to bandage this up," he shouted. "No moving about, you hear?"

"The whales heard you," said Calloway.

"WHAH?!"

Dillahunt crawled up onto the bed, sitting on the edge, and crossed the leg with the wounded foot over one knee, inspecting it. "You will go back to London," he told Kate. "Nothing has changed."

"Nothing at all," Kate bitterly replied.

Jenkins cautiously stepped toward Kate, placing one hand on the hilt of his dagger while holding out the other. "It's time to go. No tricks or I'll have to restrain you."

Calloway stepped in front of Kate. She wasn't sure why. This was all wrong. She couldn't let it happen. "She's not going anywhere."

"Begging your pardon, miss," Jenkins said gently, "but you're not enough to stop me."

"It's Calloway," she snarled.

"Miss Calloway," Jenkins said, bowing his head respectfully. "I remember you. The girl who pretended to be a boy." His grin returned. "Most were fooled."

"I remember you too," she replied rigidly. "You're a traitor and a murderer."

"Aye," he admitted. "And you have set yourself between me and my goal."

Calloway held his gaze, breaking it only briefly to glance at the cutlass at his waist. She could draw it and plunge it into his belly before he realized what had happened. That's what Kate would do. "Strength is always within reach," Kate had told her not so long ago. Those words had already saved Calloway's life more than once.

"Miss Calloway is going with you," Dillahunt told Jenkins.

"What?" said Jenkins, tilting his head.

"What?" Calloway echoed.

"WHAH?!" said Terrible, who had wandered over to the door with his bag. When he realized no one was talking to him, he continued outside, mumbling irritably about young people and their lack of respect.

Dillahunt didn't bother to look up, he just kept massaging his foot, his face gradually releasing of tension as the pain eased. "She is my first mate," he said. "She'll make sure you don't try to give me the slip."

"I will?" Calloway balked, wondering what was going on.

Dillahunt ignored her and smirked up at Jenkins. "Did you think I'd let you go unwatched?"

Jenkins glanced nervously at Calloway. "It's not safe for her."

Dillahunt was unmoved. "Her hair is still short. She'll pass for a boy easily enough. She's done it before. You can tell your captain she's an old friend you met in port, in need of a job. I'm sure that sort of thing happens all the time."

"It makes things more complicated than they need to be," Jenkins said.

"Life is rarely uncomplicated," Dillahunt said as he prodded at the crudely-bound folds of skin where his big toe had been.

"I cannot be responsible for this girl's life," Jenkins pressed.

"I didn't say you were," Dillahunt replied carelessly.

Calloway's fingernails were digging into her palms. "I am not going with this man."

"You are," Dillahunt said, still refusing to look at her. "Or I'll leave you in port to tend to the rest of your life, minus your half of the reward. Would you like that? I'm sure you'll get along quite nicely. There are a few new whorehouses. I hear The Hellbound Strumpet is looking for a new girl."

"Her half of the reward?" Kate questioned. "Why would she get half?"

Calloway stomped toward Dillahunt, and then fell to her knees before him, placing her hands on his leg and squeezing. He hissed in pain, but she didn't let go. She struggled to look into his eyes, but he stubbornly looked away. "Don't do this, Guy."

"It is done." He looked at her finally, and she wished he hadn't. His gaze was cold, as if he were addressing some young deckhand whose name he couldn't recall. The scars on his face were suddenly harsh and distracting. Too many times she had overheard the crew gossiping about Dillahunt's ravaged face, and she had promptly jumped in to stand up for her captain. "Let's see how pretty your face looks with a bit of character," she told them. "Not so nice as his, I'll wager!" And they would titter as she walked away, because they knew she shared the captain's bed every night.

Now she felt silly for defending him.

"It's an order," Dillahunt said with finality, and looked away again.

"And if I die?"

He sniffed. "You've chosen a dangerous profession, but I'm confident you'll come out on top. Like Katherine, you possess a ruthless kind of cunning. I doubt there's any situation you can't think your way out of."

Calloway looked at Kate, who was shaking her head. "Pity you won't be there to take the credit for my ruthless cunning," said Kate.

"I'll be there, right behind you," Dillahunt reminded her.

Kate threw up a hand. "Of course you will."

"You have your orders," he told Calloway.

Whatever fondness remained flooded out of her in that moment, and she was left with a hollow pit in her core, cold and black. She felt no sadness, only clarity. She released the leg she had been clinging to and calmly stood, and he looked so small beneath her, sitting at the edge of a bed she was certain she would never share with him again.

"Aye, captain," she said.

9

GABE

The departure from Nassau's harbor was uneventful. They easily slipped out the eastern channel, which was unguarded. When Gabe asked Calico Jack Rackham where the warship had gone, the captain winked conspiratorially. "Off chasing after pirates, I expect," he said. Gabe didn't ask him to elaborate. Despite Governor Rogers' efforts against piracy, Calico Jack and Charles Vane still had many allies. Gabe wondered how much longer that would last.

Soon they were sailing through the night, with the island of Providence shrinking behind them. The pirates exchanged nondescript merchant clothing for more colorful garb, which seemed to free their flamboyant personalities as well. When they were certain they were far enough away, and free of pursuit, they started to celebrate.

But you're not free of pursuit, Gabe thought with a private smile. Pirates were at their most vulnerable when they had convinced themselves they were safe.

Gabe had a feeling he would not see Nassau again. After Kate's kidnapping, it was doubtful Rogers would let any ship slip away without thorough inspection. That suited him just fine. Nassau recalled too many memories best left forgotten. Outwardly, he masked his grief behind a smirk and a quick tongue. But his mind was young and sharp, and it rarely allowed him to forget anything for too long. Keeping busy helped, but the worst of his memories always returned in dreams, even after he managed an entire day without letting them intrude upon his thoughts.

Thankfully, the day's events had been far too strenuous and exciting, and his blood refused to cool. He wouldn't be able to sleep even if he wanted to. Kate had made things more difficult than he had anticipated. He had underestimated her, despite everything he had heard about her. Vane had specifically warned him. "She is offputtingly charming," he had said, while lamenting that he had allowed her to escape Pirate Town. "Do not let her get the better of you."

Spiriting her out of Rogers' mansion had been too easy. To his surprise, she had gone along willingly. Her movements were energetic and her eyes were alight, as if she enjoyed it. She had caught him off guard with her nonchalance. After Annabelle had ordered Gabe to kill a friend, he had promised himself he would never let a woman get the better of him again. They were just as treacherous as men, if not more so. Thanks to Kate, he had already broken that promise. Without his grappling hook, he had been forced to escape through the gate. The guards nearly spotted him twice. He distracted two of them away from his path with a well-aimed rock that cracked loudly off of a wall, and then he huffed back to town as quickly as possible, only to discover that Kate had tried to kill Dillahunt. It seemed any man who got on her bad side ended up dead eventually. Gabe wasn't sure if that intimidated or intrigued him.

Maybe a little of both.

He spent the remainder of the night on the forecastle, gazing into the calm water, with the stars glimmering in soft ripples that slid past the ship's hull. It felt as though the ship and sky were locked in place, and only the water moved.

The stillness brought him no peace.

He welcomed swelling waves and a swaying deck. Land seemed foreign to his feet, and this lifeless deck felt too much like land. He would find no slumber tonight. He had grown accustomed to waves rocking him to sleep, or the warm arms of a strumpet after a good thrash in the sheets. His life at sea had been nothing but excitement and danger, and he didn't know what to do with himself during these rare calm moments.

He wondered how well Calico Jack was sleeping. The captain had wasted little time ushering Kate to his cabin, disappearing inside with her for the night. Gabe didn't want to ponder what he was doing with her in there. He wasn't sure why he should be concerned for her, given that he barely knew her. And she could clearly take care of herself; it was Calico Jack he should have been worried about.

Sure enough, as the eastern sky purpled with the approach of dawn, the captain emerged with a red welt over his right eyebrow. When one of the crew asked what had happened, Calico Jack merely smiled and rubbed his brow. "A misunderstanding," he replied. "Fortunately for me, this journey is a short one."

After the sun came up, Gabe scanned the aft horizon whenever he could without drawing the captain's attention. Only once did he spot what might have been the top of a sail, but it was hard to tell without using a spyglass.

At midday, he found himself pacing about the main deck

impatiently, though there wasn't much room to move about. *Swift* was a small sloop with a single square-rigged mast, three lateen sails stretching across the bow, and a large spanker sail at the stern. The ship was armed with nine guns; four on each side, and one swivel gun at the bow. The constricted deck would have been cramped if they'd had more men, but *Swift* was only carrying twenty-five, to avoid rousing suspicion in port.

Gabe glimpsed Jacqueline Calloway at the forecastle among the many crates and barrels that had helped disguise the ship as a merchant vessel with a full hold. She blended easily enough with the small crew, adopting a gruff voice and speaking only when she needed to. She had fastened a blue bandana over her head and wore a frumpy dark brown shirt and black breeches, which she had taken from Dillahunt's wardrobe before leaving. Her hair was longer than the first time she had posed as a boy, but if anyone had noticed her gender, they hadn't said anything.

However, a tall burly man named Hennessey had been eyeing Calloway suspiciously. The right side of Hennessey's face had been horrifically burned in a fire, leaving a hole the size of a doubloon in his jaw, which showed through to his teeth. Whenever he drank, he had to slap his hand over the hole to keep the liquid from leaking out. He had stringy black hair that streamed down around his face like cords of wet seaweed. Sometimes a strand would get caught in his cheek-hole as he ate, and he'd have to fish it out. Gabe didn't know Hennessey that well, except that most steered clear of him due to the daunting combination of his size and his foul temperament. Well, except for his two friends, Bruiser and Bleeder. Bruiser was just as muscular as Hennessey, but a foot shorter and completely bald. Bleeder was Bruiser's brother, with a leather patch over his left eye, and close-cropped thick brown hair.

Gabe heard that he'd lost the eye in the very same battle that had ruined Hennessey's face. All three of them were shirtless, with matching red sashes and black pants.

He wandered to the stern for another casual look through the long, slender spyglass that was kept in a case next to the helm. He saw no sign of *Crusader*. He continued to scan the horizon, sweeping the scope from side to side.

"Are we being followed?" asked a forceful voice.

Gabe managed not to jump. He lowered the spyglass and smiled pleasantly at Calico Jack. Rackham was tall and athletically built, with a comely sleek face and long blonde hair that was always pulled into a ponytail. He wore a burgundy coat with silver buttons, a white shirt, black breeches, and black boots. His strict adherence to these three colors had earned him his nickname. A large gold earring dangled from his right ear, and he wore a big black tricorn hat with a bright red feather. He had a deep, regal voice that commanded his crew's respect. His sharp grey eyes could induce confidence as easily as fear. He was always coy about his age, but Gabe guessed him to be approaching forty, if he hadn't passed it already.

"Never hurts to be careful," Gabe said.

Calico Jack stared at him shrewdly. "You were never so careful before."

"We just left the lion's den," said Gabe, keeping his tone reasonable. "I only wanted to be certain one of Rogers' lackeys isn't following us." He managed not to laugh at the irony of his lie.

Calico Jack held out a hand. "You needn't fret, Mr. Jenkins. Our escape was guaranteed before we left. I saw to that."

"I see," said Gabe, setting the spyglass in Rackham's palm.

"You concern yourself with the wrong horizon." Calico Jack nodded forward. "What lies ahead is more dangerous by far."

"What does Vane intend to do with Lindsay?" Gabe figured

the captain owed him an answer, given that he'd risked his neck to deliver Kate.

Calico Jack looked down at the spyglass, turning it over. "The both of us will be compensated for our trouble, and that's the only thing that matters."

"So you didn't ask?"

"I asked," the captain said with a sad smile. "A very old man once told me a pirate is always chasing after the horizon, fooling himself into believing he can reach it. It might be gold, it might be freedom, it might even be a girl he's looking to impress. Always it beckons, beautiful and glorious, but no matter how hard a pirate pushes his ship, it remains just out of grasp. The woman who has stolen my cabin, I wager she was Jonathan Griffith's horizon."

"She's a feisty one," Gabe admitted. "Nearly got me killed."

Calico Jack rubbed a thumb against the bruise over his eye and winced. "I can see how she might steal a man's wits, but I've allowed her no more than my cabin. It's unwise to bring a woman to sea. Out here, a pirate might think her the only woman alive, forgetting that there are hundreds waiting in port."

None like her, thought Gabe as he recalled Kate standing before her window in a thin nightgown that left little to the imagination, fiery tresses tumbling down her back.

"Has she stolen something from you, lad?" Calico Jack asked, fixing Gabe with a sharp gaze.

Gabe scoffed. "Only my patience."

"A woman thrives on driving a man mad. And her power is fortified when we cannot easily fall into the arms of another. That is why they are best left on land."

The captain gave Gabe a little smile and took his leave.

The remainder of the day was uneventful. Gabe refrained from scanning the horizon again, ever wary of Calico Jack's watchful eyes. After night fell, he wandered aimlessly, again unable to find sleep. Instead, he found Calloway. He heard her squealing in her sleep on the forecastle. "Shuttup!" she said. "Shuttup! All of you!"

Gabe hurried over, snatching up a lantern near Hennessey, Bruiser, and Bleeder, who were seated before the mainmast. "That's ours!" Hennessey protested, but Gabe ignored him.

He crouched before Calloway, who was huddled uncomfortably between two barrels. "Shuttup!" she kept saying, twisting about. "Go away!" He shook her shoulder until her eyes opened. She blinked and looked around.

"You were talking in your sleep," he informed her.

"So?" she murmured, rubbing her eyes.

He threw a cautious glance over his shoulder, hoping she would catch on fast. "You were talking in a *womanly* voice," he whispered pointedly.

"Oh," she said. And then, much deeper, "OH."

Gabe smirked. "That's better."

"I was having a dream."

"A fierce one, from the sound of it. You were tossing about like some kind of sea serpent. What's a young woman doing having dreams like that, anyway?"

"Maybe I was fending off pirates," she said, glancing at her surroundings indicatively.

"You were telling them to shut up. Screaming for them to shut up."

He looked over his shoulder again. Hennessey was staring his way. "We want our light back, Jenkins."

"Find another." He set the lantern down between him and Calloway.

"How 'bout I kill you instead?" Hennessey challenged.

Gabe chuckled. "You're welcome to try, but you'll lose more than just a lantern."

Hennessey stood, puffing up his considerable chest. He angled the burned side of his face toward Gabe and started forward in a huff. Bruiser halted him with a calming hand. "I wouldn't do that, Henn. This one was Blackbeard's man. Now he's Vane's man."

"What's that mean?" Hennessey asked.

"It means if you kill me," Gabe answered, "Vane will have another excuse to let Mr. Tanner use his toys." Gabe shivered at the thought of Mr. Tanner and his many tools. "Gives me the chills just thinking about it."

Hennessey grumbled as he slowly sat down. "Vane won't be alive forever."

"Best not tell *him* that," said Bleeder.

Gabe smiled at Calloway.

"Are you leading Captain Dillahunt to his death?" she blurted suddenly.

He stared at her, surprised. "That's up to Dillahunt. He's lived this long. I trust him to live a bit longer. Are you truly concerned for him, even after he gave you to the wolves?"

"I'm curious, is all," she shot back defensively.

He snorted loudly enough to let her know he didn't believe her. "Sure."

"So you're not loyal to Vane?"

"Clearly not."

She shifted between the two barrels. She resembled an animal caught in a trap. "I don't believe you."

"That's because you're smart. Nevertheless, I'm telling the truth. I want Charles Vane dead just as much as I wanted Teach dead."

"Yet you did everything Teach asked of you."

"That was a long time ago."

"A long time ago?" she balked, forgetting to lower her voice. "It's been little more than a month."

"Exactly," he said, grinning. "You know why they call us 'dogs'?"

"I can think of several reasons."

"I like to think it's because a pirate's life is no lengthier than a dog's. Out here, a month might as well be a year."

"And you think Vane's death will lengthen your life, is that it?"

"No," he said. "I wager it will lengthen *many* lives."

She chewed on her lower lip for a moment. "How does Kate figure into all this?"

"You'll have to ask Vane."

"You're just going to hand her over without knowing his intent?"

"I'm not in the habit of questioning dangerous men."

"Yet you plot behind their backs?"

He shook his head. "I'm new to that one, but I'm a quick learner. That's why I'm still alive."

"You're alive, and many are dead because of you."

"Aye," he admitted. "But most would be dead by another's hand, if not mine."

"Does that make you feel better?"

He lowered those interesting eyes of his toward the lantern. She wondered what he was really seeing. "No."

"Is Vane going to kill her?"

"He wouldn't go to the trouble of kidnapping Katherine just to kill her. That wouldn't serve a purpose. He isn't Edward Teach."

"No one is Edward Teach."

"Aye," he agreed. "Teach is with Davy Jones now, where he belongs. If he'd focused on success rather than vengeance, who knows how long he would have lasted. You're lucky to have survived him."

She rolled her eyes. "He wasn't so terrifying."

"Tell that to Benjamin Hornigold, if you can find where Teach buried him. I don't know how the man died, but I can promise you it wasn't pleasant. Or slow."

She shrugged one shoulder. "Not my concern."

He stood and ran a hand through his hair, sweeping the stubborn lock back into place for the millionth time. "Sun's coming up soon," he said, gazing over the rail.

"No use going back to sleep," Calloway lamented.

He looked down at her, tilting his head inquisitively. "What were you before all this?"

"A strumpet."

He offered a hand. "You're awfully young for a strumpet."

She ignored his hand and helped herself up. "You're awfully young for a murderer."

10

FREDERICK

Frederick Lindsay grimaced as the longboat approached the thin beach outlining the nameless horseshoe-shaped island. He drew a handkerchief from his pocket and dabbed at his forehead before a bead of sweat could reach his brow. It wasn't the heat that bothered him; it was the humidity.

The island wasn't much to look at, but Charles Vane hadn't chosen it for aesthetic appeal. A thin white beach ran below the rocky outer rim, sprinkled with palm trees. A single square tent was waiting on the beach, its white walls flapping in the breeze. A few pirates were sitting casually atop a gathering of chests and barrels to the right side of the tent. Their raucous laughter trickled over the waves. Frederick had met Vane here once before, but this time he glimpsed no sign of Vane's brigantine, *Ranger*. He assumed it was docked in the lake at the center of the island, beyond the thin channel that cut through the rocky hills.

As the longboat neared the shore, bobbing in the waves, Frederick straightened the sleeves of his clean white shirt. He hadn't bothered with a coat in this heat. His long blonde hair was fastened into a ponytail with a dark red ribbon. He was thinning at the very top, and every day he noticed more and more heat filtering through. How many hairs would this meeting cost him?

He wondered if he would ever grow accustomed to dealing with Vane. He wasn't sure how much longer he wanted to. The pirate captain seemed to be constantly restraining himself from murderous impulses. Frederick feared every rendezvous with Vane would be his last. *This is the man I've chosen to conduct business with,* he reflected with a stiff shake of his head.

The longboat came to a shuddering halt as its keel slid into the stiff sand of the beach. Harrison and Desmond jumped out first. These two were the largest of his crew, and it was no coincidence that he had selected them to accompany him to shore. Harrison, Frederick's boatswain, had broad shoulders, and his thighs were near the size of cannons. The bangs of his shaggy blonde hair spilled over his eyes. It was a wonder that he could see, but his aim was always true when punishing slaves or disobedient crewmen. Desmond was the tallest of the crew, with wiry muscles and long black hair that trailed past his buttocks. His thin lips seemed incapable of mirth. Though he frequently laughed at jokes, he never smiled.

The two men helped Frederick into the shallow water as he gripped the rail of the longboat. Just then, a wave crashed over the beach, and Frederick lost his grip as the longboat raised up. The wave splashed over his back, doing its best to urge him forward, but Harrison held him in place. He clenched his teeth as water filled his boots. The water felt nice for an instant, but it was too warm to relieve him of the humidity.

Vane's three men snickered and elbowed each other as

Frederick approached with Harrison and Desmond flanking him, his boots squelching with every step as the water sloshed around. "Ol' Frederick brought his royal guard," said the biggest of them, shirtless and wearing bright red breeches with vertical black stripes, folded below his knees. His dirty blonde hair was short and curly, and he had a long, straight nose and a jaw that looked as if it had been carved of rock. His name was Roman, if Frederick remembered correctly.

"I hope he feels safe," squawked Keet. He was the smallest of the three, with spiky hair that was painted blue, yellow, and red. He looked and sounded the part of a parrot, bobbing his head this way and that.

"Wouldn't want him pissing hisself before his meeting," chuckled the third, whose name Frederick couldn't recall. This one was squat and muscular, with close-cropped black hair, a filthy yellow shirt, matching yellow sash, and black breeches.

All of them were wearing dual pistols, and rusty cutlasses dangled from their belts.

"He's even littler than I remember," said Roman.

Frederick had been taunted about his lack of stature all his life. He had heard two of his crew making fun of him behind his back once, and he promptly had them whipped for their jests. He hadn't heard anything from them since.

"Gentlemen," Frederick greeted curtly. "I am here to see your captain, not suffer your mockery."

Roman's cracked lips peeled from yellow teeth. "You don't know nothing of suffering, Lindsay. Might be one day I'll school you."

Frederick smirked. He knew everything of suffering. He captained a slave ship. On his most recent venture across the Atlantic, *Rampart* left Zanzibar with one-hundred and sixty-two slaves. Nineteen had perished in the crossing, mostly of dysentery. Five of his crewman died of the same. At sixteen,

John Dawson was the youngest crewmember he had lost yet. Deaths at sea were not uncommon, but it was difficult to make sense of losing someone so young. He vividly remembered the enthusiasm in the boy's eyes as he had signed on in Liverpool, just before sailing to Africa. Before the end, that enthusiasm was replaced by horror. Dawson was given far too much time to contemplate his certain death.

"I doubt your captain would like that," Frederick replied as coolly as possible. He sensed Harrison and Desmond tensing at his sides.

"Maybe I'll be quiet about it," Roman said, lowering his voice, "and my captain won't hear me kill you. Wouldn't be the first time."

"You'll have to get through us first," Harrison said, stepping forward and patting the sword at his hip.

Roman cackled. "That'll set me back a few seconds."

"Kill 'em quick, Roman," Keet prodded with a titter.

"Aye," agreed the squat pirate in yellow.

Frederick was considering retreating to the longboat when, thankfully, the tent flap opened and Charles Vane stepped out, silencing his men with a fierce glower. "What's all this?"

"Captain," screeched Keet, his head nervously bobbing up and down. "We was only looking out for you, just like you said we should do."

Vane's voice flowed like silk. "You were menacing my guest."

"Apologies, captain," said Keet and the squat man simultaneously.

Roman did not appear as remorseful as his companions. "Just making ol' Frederick feel at home, captain. I reckon he knows a good ribbing when he—" He returned his gaze to Frederick. "—*suffers* one."

Vane looked at Frederick, never squinting despite the sun

shining directly in his emerald eyes. "Hello, Frederick," he greeted with his customary smirk. "You're looking wet as a strumpet's slit."

"I can see why most of your lot neglects shoes," Frederick replied, frowning down at his waterlogged boots and damp breeches.

Vane glanced at his own gold-buckled shoes. As usual, he was keenly dressed. "Yes, well, some of us must maintain the illusion of civility." He tossed a hand at Frederick's ship, moored in the distance. The frill of his white shirt fluttered in the breeze, blooming from the sleeve of his green coat. "Even pirates and slavers."

Frederick smiled as politely as possible. "I prefer to think of myself as a trader."

Vane laughed. "That word can be mistaken for another."

"Traitor?" asked Keet, cocking his head.

Vane withered. "Yes, Keet. Thank you for the clarification. My subtlety was so obscure that even *I* didn't know what I was getting at."

"You're welcome, captain!"

"It was fucking sarcasm."

"Oh."

"Well," Vane said, snapping a finger at Frederick. "Let's not stand on ceremony. Step inside, and I'll reacquaint you with Katherine Lindsay, whom I'm sure you've met."

"What?" Frederick said, taking a step forward. He couldn't have heard that right. "Katherine Lindsay, you said?"

"I did."

"Last I'd heard, my dead brother's troublesome wife was in Nassau, under the care of Woodes Rogers."

"That was true when you heard it," Vane said. "True no longer. Step inside."

Frederick hastily followed Vane into the tent, leaving his

men outside.

"Where is she?" He cast a skeptical glance around the tent. Apart from a mahogany desk and two chairs on either side of it, there was no furniture for Katherine Lindsay to hide behind. The thin cloth of the walls was brightly illuminated, so it was hardly dark inside. There were no woman-sized lumps under the deep red carpet covering the sand.

Vane slapped a palm to his forehead. "Did I say I had her? I meant I *will* have her. A week from now, when you were meant to fucking arrive."

Frederick felt stupid for believing for a second that Vane was telling the truth. "I am a timely man, Charles."

"You are an early man, in fact," Vane said through a tight jaw, clearly losing his patience.

"Better to be early than late."

"I beg to differ." Vane circled the desk and took a seat behind it. "Being early is the same as being late, if not the greater offense. At least a late arrival greets a prepared party."

Frederick slid out the chair in front of the desk and sat down. He shifted uncomfortably in his damp breeches. "So I should have been late?"

"You should have arrived on the day we agreed upon."

Frederick leaned forward, setting a palm on the desk. "Charles, I just dropped off a shipment in Virginia. I should be well on my way back to Liverpool by now. This little meeting, lovely though it is, has veered me from my course."

Vane looked at Frederick's hand, and Frederick impulsively withdrew it, leaving a smudge. Vane stared at the smudge, which faded as it cooled, and then slowly lifted his eyes. "You should have brought your slaves my way first," he said, his tone dangerously cool. "Blacks are hard workers, I've found. They seem to appreciate a democratic environment." He smirked. "Even the illusion of one."

"That is not part of our arrangement," Frederick objected apprehensively. "I provide you shipping lanes and supplies, and you—"

"—allow a rich twit free rein of my ocean. And I provide you a bit of shine, now and again."

Frederick nodded. "It is the shine that concerns me. I am not as rich as you think, or I wouldn't accept your gold. And 'your ocean' will not be yours for long, if Woodes Rogers has his way."

Vane raised a finger. "Which brings us to my current predicament. I need cannons. A lot of cannons. Long range, top of the line. Not the rusty, short range smashers I find myself plagued with. You can procure them for me."

Frederick stifled a laugh. He didn't want to make Vane any angrier than he normally was. "My dear mother doesn't exactly trust me with that kind of shipment. And even if I could convince her, it wouldn't exactly go unnoticed if a shipment of cannons did not reach their intended destination."

Vane's laugh was unmistakably condescending. "Oh, no, no, no. You misunderstand me. I require considerably more than a single shipment. That's the problem with all these pirates. They think in such small terms. They think only about today, never tomorrow. And that is why they're losing."

"Losing? This isn't a war, Charles."

"It should be," Vane proclaimed, eyes glinting with manic enthusiasm. "I am proposing a long-term business arrangement. Your family deals in every kind of trade there is, not the least of which is weapons. I require continual shipments. Enough to arm a fleet. I want to send a message to that fat fuck, King George. The Caribbean does not belong to him. The Caribbean belongs to pirates. The Caribbean belongs to *me*."

Frederick shifted uncomfortably in his chair. He didn't like giving an insane man bad news. "If you truly intend to go through with such madness, you would need to strike a bargain with one of my brothers."

"Your brothers are not the sort who would strike a bargain with a man like me." Vane aimed a finger at him, with his thumb sticking up like the hammer of a pistol. "You are."

Frederick stared uncomfortably at Vane's finger until he lowered it. "That is precisely why Martha does not trust me with the family business."

"You're quite cavalier with your mother's name."

"She has made it painfully clear that I am no longer her son."

Vane smiled, intrigued. "Tell me, what did you do to earn her scorn? Did you put your cock in the family dog, or something?"

Frederick scowled distastefully. "You have a sick mind, Charles."

"Flattery will not divert my question. Come, tell me what you did."

"Many things," Frederick admitted. "Bedding my cousin, Margery, was the worst offense, I suppose."

Never mind that she came to me willingly.

Never mind my initial protests.

Never mind that we were both young and foolish.

"Ah," Vane said with a knowing smile. "So you *did* put your cock in the wrong place."

Frederick gave a woeful nod. The attraction had been undeniable, and he had fought against it for as long as his loins would allow, but her supple wet lips, hazel doe eyes, curly blonde locks, and perky breasts were impossible to resist.

After a few months, Margery could no longer conceal her swelling belly, and she confided the identity of the father under the extreme pressure of her parents. She miscarried a month later. Frederick had attempted to visit her after he heard the news, but he was turned away by her family's servants. Not long after that, Margery's mother arrived at the Lindsay household. Frederick heard her shouting at his mother. The sisters did not speak again after that, and Frederick's mother blamed him. "You've done it again, haven't you?" she berated him. "Not even sixteen, and you couldn't keep that little worm in your pants, where it belongs."

"I made a mistake," Frederick had insisted, hoping the tears he spilled would soften her.

"Margery fixed that mistake herself," his mother informed him. "The poor girl nearly did herself in, scraping around down there. She'll be lucky if she ever conceives again."

"I made a mistake," Frederick had blustered over and over, not knowing what else to say.

"And you will never stop. You are a liability."

Frederick would have fled his mother's foul temper and pleaded with his father, if the man had any wits to spare. After cracking his skull in the hold of a ship, his father couldn't maintain a memory past a few hours. Martha had quietly assumed management of the business. Father contributed his seal and a shaky signature, but nothing more than that.

Frederick watched as his older brothers each took their place in the business, shipping valuable goods across the Atlantic. With no shortage of begging, Martha finally allowed him a place of his own, shipping manufactured goods, textiles, and rum to Africa. It was a job none of his other brothers wanted. It wasn't long before Frederick was enticed by the greater value of the slave trade, after watching a slave auction in Zanzibar. He sold his ship and purchased *Rampart*, which was larger and specifically equipped to transport slaves, and was licensed through the Royal Africa Company in exchange for ten percent of the profits. Frederick filled the ship with as many slaves as it could carry and sailed to Virginia, where he sold the slaves, cleaned out his hold and loaded supplies of tobacco and hemp for the return voyage.

This angered his mother even more. There was no family rule against engaging in slave trade, but it was generally frowned upon by the Lindsays, despite its undeniable role in the British economy. "You should have thought twice about sending me to Africa," Frederick told his mother. "Did you honestly think I would stop there? Did you think I wouldn't complete the triangle?"

Her cold reply was impossible to misinterpret. "You've found your trade at last."

"You've allowed me no other," was all he could say.

"I suspect you'll be far too occupied for further visits, lovely though they are."

Those were her last words to him.

Frederick compensated his mother for the ship he had sold and cut ties with the family business, setting out on his own from then on. He hadn't seen her since, not even after he learned that his older brother, Thomas, had been killed at sea by pirates, and Thomas's pretty wife taken hostage.

Charles Vane's silky voice brought Frederick back to the present. "I never fucked a cousin, but that's probably because none of my cousins were particularly attractive. Was she worth it?"

Frederick had never forgotten the way Margery's lips had tasted, like fresh strawberries, and the soft sounds she made when he was inside her. "If I am prone to failure no matter what I do, then yes, she was worth it."

Vane's smirk grew. "I suppose I should be thanking your mother. If not for her, you and I would never have met."

Frederick nodded. *Yes, thank you for that, Mother.*

Rampart had been intercepted by Vane's ship about two

years ago, during its first run to the New World, and Frederick had bought his life by providing adjusted trade routes. Their dealings had blossomed from there.

"It baffles me," Vane went on, "that Martha could so easily neglect one of her own sons, when she has gone to so much trouble to retrieve a woman with whom she doesn't even share a blood relation. Why is that?"

Frederick had been asking himself that question ever since he received news of Thomas's death and Katherine's capture. Martha had wasted little time promising a reward for the woman's safe return. She had sent word along with Woodes Rogers as he arrived to govern the Bahamas. Frederick had met Katherine only once, very briefly, a few months before Thomas had married her. Frederick hadn't been spending much time with the family at that point, and he had failed to attend the wedding. She hadn't left much of an impression on him, other than her fiery red hair. He couldn't remember the specifics of her face, except that she was pretty in a boring sort of way.

"I suppose Martha was fond of Katherine," he answered at last. "She looked on her as she would a daughter." Frederick smiled bitterly. "Katherine's return would ease the loss of Thomas."

"That must be frustrating for you," Vane prodded with a smile. "Do you miss your brother?"

He's enjoying this, Frederick realized. "Not particularly."

"Why not? Was he a shit?"

"I thought so," Frederick conceded with a chuckle. "He never said he was better than me, not with words, but sometimes a downward look speaks louder than any slight."

Vane nodded. "I get it. He was taller. But then, who isn't?"

Frederick continued as if the jest didn't sting, as if he hadn't had two men whipped for such abuse. "It occurs to me that in a year, I will be as old as Thomas was at the time of his death."

"The dead do not age," Vane said, suddenly temperate. He waved a stiff hand, as if he would not permit himself to wax philosophical.

Frederick was tired of talking about family. "You said something about Katherine Lindsay?"

Vane nodded.

"Well, where is she?" He wasn't comfortable being forward with Vane, but he knew the man responded to nothing less. Vane had no respect or patience for equivocation. Then again, Vane had little respect for *anything*, aside from torture and death. Frederick did his best to shift that knowledge to the bottom of his overly stacked thoughts. He didn't want his voice to tremble.

"Your family has sent someone to retrieve Katherine from Nassau, yes?" Vane asked, though he certainly already knew.

"Yes." He wasn't sure who had been sent. Probably one of his two surviving brothers.

Vane's lids narrowed. "Not you, I take it?"

"Even if we were on speaking terms, Martha would never trust me with that task. I am no longer a part of the business or the family. I bear only the name."

"A malady I would happily remedy," Vane said. "Governor Rogers has no doubt discovered by now, to his great horror, that Katherine Lindsay has been stolen from his mansion."

"What?"

"She will be delivered to me within the week." Vane frowned to himself. "I would have had her sooner if I hadn't allowed her to escape Pirate Town. A mistake I intend to set right. That was foolish. I honestly don't know what I was thinking. It's as though I blacked out and a cock-less imbecile stole my place. Then again, I can't really be blamed. My home was being assaulted by Edward Teach's forces at the time, and I wasn't exactly at my best."

The rest of Vane's blathering barely registered. Frederick's heart was thumping rapidly against his ribs. "You are certain she will be delivered to you?"

Vane's right eye twitched. "I don't care to repeat myself."

Frederick raised his hands diplomatically. "It appears I have no choice but to believe you."

"Fuck you," Vane spat. "I will deliver Katherine Lindsay, and you will deliver her to your mother."

"No need for vulgarities, Charles. You'll have your weapons. Top of the line. As many as you like. Once Martha has that woman back in her hands, she will be inclined to trust me again, and I will easily secure your supplies. I must say, the plan is beautiful."

Vane nodded shrewdly. "You, the outcast son, will be the knight in shining armor who rescues Katherine from her villainous captors."

"Yes," Frederick said, unable to contain a grin. "Of course, she must never know my true role in this. She must think me her savior."

"Shall I stage an elaborate sword duel between us, with Katherine in attendance? I've always wanted to feign my own death."

"Nothing so theatrical," Frederick replied.

Vane withered, and Frederick realized that the captain was making fun of him. "With my sword at your heart," Vane growled, "I doubt I could restrain my hand from a quick thrust."

Frederick's stomach hollowed as he remembered who he was dealing with. "I'm on your side, Charles."

"Of course you are."

Frederick cleared his throat. "How long must I wait for her to arrive?"

"I'd advise against waiting here," Vane cautioned. "As soon

as Jack Rackham brings Katherine to me, I'm leaving this place. I've recently acquired a frigate that the Royal Navy will eventually come looking for."

Jesus, thought Frederick. *The man has truly lost his senses.*

"What's wrong, Frederick?" Vane asked, studying him. "You've gone white as bird shit."

"Me?" Frederick laughed lightly. "It's these damp clothes."

"A little water robs you of your wits? I was asking where we should meet. You know how much I love to repeat myself."

"Mariposa?" Frederick suggested as carelessly as possible. He had allies there, should he need them . . . but he wasn't about to tell Vane that. "I've heard it's one of the last ports a pirate can trade freely in."

"Yes," Vane said after a moment's deliberation. "Meet me at Keelhaul Tavern within the month."

"What guarantee do I have you will come?"

"I figured you might ask that," Vane said. "Before I retreated from Pirate Town, I acquired several treasure chests that once belonged to Jonathan Griffith. My men have instructions to see you off with two such chests. Think of it as a down payment."

Frederick swallowed. Vane wasn't giving him any excuses. "That is acceptable."

"It's a little more than fucking acceptable," Vane muttered. "When you arrive in Mariposa, you'll need to masquerade *Rampart* as a pirate ship, I should think, or you will be raided before you make it very far into the harbor."

"That won't be difficult," Frederick said. "She's ragged enough as it is. I need only lower our colors."

"Good." Vane slapped a hand on the table with finality. "I wouldn't want my benefactor murdered by pirates before our arrangement bears fruit."

"I've traded in pirate ports before, and as you can see, I am not dead."

Vane nodded proudly, as a father would to a son who has just conquered a bully at school. "A good businessman is not so easily vanquished."

"You don't have to butter me, Vane. Compliments do not suit you."

Vane's face reddened like a radish, and Frederick immediately regretted his quip. "I'm not buttering you, you stunted shit. I do not hand out compliments, merely truth. If it wasn't true, I wouldn't have fucking said it. The fact that I haven't spread your guts along the four corners of my tent proves you are skilled in your trade."

"Gutting me would not be in your best interests," Frederick reminded him carefully, doing his best to ignore the sudden surge of his heartbeat.

"We're saying the same fucking thing," Vane growled. "I needn't remind you of what will happen should you take Katherine and not uphold your end of our arrangement. Do not think for an instant to betray me. I will scour sea and land to find you, and your death will not be swift."

Frederick swallowed. "I am a man of my word, captain. Threats are hardly necessary."

Vane set his palms on the table and stood, tossing his hair. "I will see you in Mariposa, then."

"Aye, captain," Frederick said, standing in turn. He nodded politely, whirled on his heels and made for the exit, and only when he was outside on the beach did he let out the breath he had been holding in. He was greeted by insufferable humidity, and his armpits instantly felt sticky.

Vane's three men were helping Harrison and Desmond load the first of two chests onto the longboat. The pirates then returned to the beach and hefted the second chest. They glanced at Frederick on their way back to the boat, but they kept quiet this time. He could sense them barely withholding their mockery.

He stared out at *Rampart*, a hulking black shadow in the distance. It looked like an ugly chunk of rock jutting from the sea. Even from here he could see the thin silhouette of his first mate, Clarence, atop the forecastle, pacing anxiously, ever fretful. Clarence did not approve of Frederick's dealings with pirates.

"All finished," said Keet, clapping his hands. Both chests were in the boat now. The three pirates returned to the side of the tent, taking their seats.

"Not a word o' thanks," muttered Keet.

"Stunted shit," snarled Roman under his breath, just loud enough.

Frederick strolled toward the longboat as it bobbed in the large waves that crashed over the shore, which were increasing with every minute. The boat was much lower in the water now, thanks to the extra weight of the chests. Frederick looked to the island's rocky rim one last time, trying not to think about what was concealed beyond those walls. Vane had said something about a captured frigate. How many men had died in that venture?

The man is mad.

Yet Charles Vane appeared to be his only way back into Martha Lindsay's good graces. All Vane wanted in return was an arsenal. *But who is to say I must give it to him?* If Frederick returned Katherine, Martha would likely allow him to do whatever he liked. He would never need to travel anywhere near the Caribbean again.

But he knew that betraying Vane was no small offense. If he didn't uphold his end of the bargain, he would never be safe as long as Vane still roamed the sea.

He will find me. Just as he found Katherine, so easily. He

won't stop until he's dead.
Until he's dead.
Dead.

Frederick cocked his head, entertaining the thought. There were many in Mariposa he might sway with the riches Vane had just provided him. Putting a bounty on Charles Vane was a dangerous proposition, frightening to even consider, but the alternative was far worse. Frederick had no desire to look over his shoulder for the rest of his life.

He shivered, though he wasn't remotely cold. He knew he didn't have to make a decision just now, but the idea had already taken root. He found his pace quickening, and soon he was trudging through the water. A warm wave pummeled him, but he pushed through it. Harrison helped him into the longboat. "Take us back," Frederick told him. "Make haste."

11

KATE

It was late in the afternoon when Calico Jack opened the door and stepped into the room, eyeing Kate cautiously. Through the boxy aft windows the sky was turning violet, and the scattered clouds were tinged with a soft orange glow. Kate, who had made herself at home in the small cabin, leaned back in the captain's chair and set her legs atop his desk. She folded her arms. "Can I help you, captain?"

Calico Jack removed his red-feathered hat and tossed it on the bed, flashing a grin that had probably thrown countless women into uncontrollable fits of swooning. "Mayhap I should be calling *you* captain," he suggested. The welt on his forehead had lightened a bit since yesterday. He seemed unconcerned by it.

She glanced at the paperweight on his desk, a heavy silver skull that had fit perfectly into her hand when she bashed him with it as he advanced on her. After being struck, he had sourly insisted she had mistaken his intent. She wasn't convinced, and he graciously retreated from the cabin. He hadn't been back until now.

Calico Jack raised his hands. "Don't worry, I won't come any closer. I've learned my lesson. Nothing stimulates the memory like pain. A point my dear friend Charles is fond of demonstrating. However, I will be requiring my bed." He winced as he squeezed his lower back. "I slept in a hammock last night. I'd forgotten how unpleasant that is." He gestured to the bed, which was very small, with his pet spider-monkey sleeping soundly in the sheets. The monkey hadn't been much for company, as it was prone to leaping around the cabin and shrieking when it wasn't sleeping. "You're welcome to join, of course," he suggested offhandedly. "Mayhap I can fit a slab of wood between us."

Kate removed her legs from the desk and stood. "A thin slab that would splinter easily when rolled over, I imagine. No thank you, captain. I don't mind sleeping in a hammock. In fact, I rather like it. But I won't have your men trying to savage me in my sleep. I trust they know my importance?"

He blinked. "Your importance?"

"Vane's gone to all this trouble to kidnap me. I sincerely doubt he wants me ravaged and tossed over the side before I'm delivered to him."

He tried to reassure her with a smile, but she didn't care for the gleam in his eye. "You may roam about without worry."

"Roam about?" Kate laughed. "If I roam for more than a few steps, I'll be swimming back to Nassau. This is the tiniest ship I've ever seen. Your cabin is like a coffin."

He returned her laugh, unfazed. "Then you've been blessed. Small though it may be, no harm will befall you on my ship. Charles would have the head of any man who tried. And so would I." He raised a hand and thumbed the welt over his brow. "Although, something tells me you don't need any protecting."

"I don't," she said, "but it will be less of a strain on the neck if I don't have to look over my shoulder every second."

"Always keep a weather eye over your shoulder, I say. Most of all when you think yourself safe. It's the peaceful times that are the most deadly."

"Thank you for that." She didn't care to receive advice she hadn't asked for, especially when the advice was so obvious.

"Before you leave," he said, turning his back to her, "would you ease me out of this coat. It's a little snug."

Kate helped him out of the fine burgundy coat without hesitation . . . and quickly slipped it on herself, tossing her hair over the collar. It fit rather nicely. Calico Jack turned and stared at her, mildly amused. "I'll be needing that back."

"Find a new one. It might get cold tonight." The coat looked nice over her clean white shirt and brown breeches, which the captain had provided for her when she came aboard. He had given her a pair of boots as well, but she hadn't bothered with them.

She left the cabin.

The sun was dipping into the western sea as she stepped on deck. The thin clouds glowed in orange ripples, like a sea all their own, and the ocean dimly reflected their ambience. A breeze that was neither warm nor cold rolled over *Swift*. It would be a perfect night to sleep outside. She hadn't needed Calico Jack's coat after all, although she wasn't about to part with it.

The three crewmen who were topside stopped what they were doing and leered at her. The tallest, with a nasty burn that had eaten through his cheek, groped himself and winked at her. None of them did anything more than ogle.

She found Calloway sitting atop a crate with one arm hanging over the port rail. The girl was gazing out to sea, the tails of her blue bandana tossing in the breeze. Kate set a gentle hand on her shoulder, and Calloway jerked her head sharply around.

"It's just me," Kate said.

Calloway smiled in relief. "Oh. Hello, Kate. Nice coat."

"A gift from the generous Captain Rackham. You want it?"

"No thank you. It's not my color."

"I suppose not." Kate took a seat on a barrel opposite her.

"I thought you were one of *them*," Calloway said, casting a glance past Kate. "I think one or two have figured out I'm not a boy."

"Captain Rackham probably has," Kate said. "He's no fool. But I don't think he cares."

Calloway bit her lip. "I hope not. I'll see Dillahunt to Hell for putting me here."

Kate looked aft. "If Vane doesn't see him there first."

"Vane's in a bad way is what I heard."

"That's just what he wants his enemies to think," Kate scoffed. "I haven't a clue why Dillahunt trusts Gabe."

Calloway lifted an inquisitive eyebrow. "I thought you liked Gabe?"

Kate looked away. "Where'd you get that idea? He's clearly a loathsome scoundrel. Not to be trusted."

"Oh, I wouldn't go so far as to call him loathsome," the girl said with an impish grin. "But he's more your type than mine."

"And what's my type?" Kate wondered.

"A murderer."

"That's unkind." Kate had forgotten how cruel the girl could be, striking without warning. She had to remind herself that Calloway was only fifteen.

Calloway's gaze dropped to her lap. "You're right, of course. I don't know why I said that." Her right hand dove into her pocket and balled into a fist beneath the fabric, clenching something.

"What have you got there?"

"Nothing," she quickly replied, freeing her hand.

Kate reached over to lift Calloway's chin with her finger. "Dillahunt's a fool, Jaq."

"I'd say so," interjected a familiar male voice.

Kate caught movement out of the corner of her eye. A shadow detached itself from the darkness and stepped forward. Gabe's curly dark hair merged perfectly with his long black coat. He had found a new black shirt, tucked neatly into his blue sash. As he neared the light, Kate saw that he was carrying a large bottle of rum. He took a seat on one of the crates between the two women and uncorked the bottle, offering it first to Kate. She stared at the beautiful amber liquid, wanting nothing more than to take a massive swig. She shook her head. "I'd rather keep my wits about these pirates." *More importantly, I'd rather keep my wits about you, Gabe Jenkins.*

"You're safe here," he insisted, jiggling the bottle enticingly. "Charles Vane would—"

"—have the head of any man who tries to kill me," she finished for him. "Yes, I've heard that one already."

He rolled his eyes and tilted the bottle her way, until some of the rum trickled out and splashed the deck. "Go on."

"No thank you."

"I will," Calloway chirped, snatching the bottle out of his hand. She threw back her long neck and took several swallows. She lowered the bottle and coughed hoarsely, her face turning red. "That's just . . . that's just awful."

"The more you take, the less awful it gets," Gabe promised.

Calloway shrugged and allowed herself another swig. She squeezed one eye shut and wiped her lips. "Still awful."

"Well, I won't be left out," Kate decided, unable to resist any longer. She took the bottle from Calloway, wrapped her lips around the mouth and tilted the bottom skyward. The rum burned as it streamed down her throat.

The three of them drank until the last of the sun's light was gone. The clouds retreated to reveal twinkling stars dotting an inky black canvas. Calloway started slurring her words and giggling about how terrible Dillahunt could be in bed, and how small his manhood was compared to most men she'd been with. Her eyes were starting to close, and she lay back across two crates with her long legs dangling over the edge. She smiled up at the stars. "Who needs men when you have stars?" was the last thing she slurred before she started to lightly snore.

Something caught Kate's eye. A spider the size of a child's hand was crawling leisurely up Gabe's breeches, slowly making its way over his knee and casting a long, gangly shadow along his leg in the light of the lantern. Kate gasped, leaning back and nearly falling off the barrel. "Ohgodohgod!" she squealed, pointing frantically. "Spider! Big spider!"

Gabe looked at his leg and smirked. "You're surrounded by pirates and you're scared of this?" He cupped one hand beside his leg and nudged the spider into it with the other.

Kate shuddered. "You're touching it. You're actually touching it. That's lovely."

"It's harmless," he assured her, studying the spider closely. It encompassed his palm.

"What's it doing out here in the middle of the ocean?"

"Must have stowed away in Nassau," Gabe replied, running his index finger delicately over the spider's backside. It didn't seem afraid of him. "He's harmless. See?" He moved his hand toward Kate to give her a closer look. She had never seen a spider like this one before. Its body was covered with fair-colored hair and its legs were striped in gold.

"It's got fur!" Her voice had risen to a raspy screech. "It's got fuuuuuuuur!"

Gabe withdrew his hand, chuckling. "The bigger and furrier the spider, the less you need to worry about."

"Squash it, please. No! Toss it over the side!"

"No," he objected with a defensive scowl.

"Why not? It's horrible."

"Maybe so," he admitted. "But it's also rare."

She looked at him. "You won't kill it because it's rare?"

He shrugged. "It will fetch a high price."

She groaned. "Oh, so it's just another treasure."

He searched around until he found a small wooden box with a few mangos. He took out the fruit and set the spider inside. "Who says I'll sell it?" He reached into the box to stroke the spider's back again. "Maybe I'll keep it for a pet."

"You're drunk," she concluded.

"Aye," he replied. "But I know treasure when I see it."

The spider was already trying to crawl up the side of the box, thankfully without much success. Kate averted her eyes, unable to look at it for another second.

She downed more rum, and then looked at the bottle, which she and Gabe had drained by two thirds. She felt numb between her eyes. Rum sometimes gave her a headache. She handed the bottle to Gabe and watched him as he drank, his thick neck pulsating with every swallow. Her eyes descended to the loose laces of his black shirt, and the tan skin beneath.

A question escaped her lips without warning. "Would you kill me if Vane instructed you to?"

Gabe glanced at her over the bottle, a wayward curl of hair obscuring his right eye. "You're far too valuable for that."

Out of the corner of her eye, she saw the spider's legs working like fingers against the wall of the box, to no avail. That didn't stop it from trying. "What if I wasn't valuable?"

Gabe swallowed more rum, probably to give himself time to think of an answer. "It's pointless to consider. We wouldn't be talking right now if you weren't valuable."

She sighed, looking down at her coat and fingering one of the silver buttons. On closer inspection, each button was engraved with a grinning death's head. "You're avoiding the question."

He set the bottle down beside the spider's wooden box. "You're a woman."

"You've never killed a woman?"

He drew a long breath and looked away. "I didn't say that."

Kate leaned forward, intrigued. She had every reason to be wary of this man, but she couldn't help herself. "Who was she? Was it an accident?"

"It wasn't an accident," he replied firmly. "It's . . . it's a long and unfortunate tale."

"We've nothing if not time."

He turned his glassy eyes on her, and she realized he was drunker than he let on. "I've never told anyone."

"I like long and unfortunate tales."

"You asked for it." Jenkins' eyes settled on the lantern, and he began his long and unfortunate tale. He would occasionally look up at Kate, but not for very long before returning his gaze to the light. With his attention lost in the past, she was able to truly look at him for the first time, to study the details of his face. His skin was smooth and heavily sunned, but there were a few thin scars she hadn't noticed before. The vertical pinch between his eyebrows was permanently creased, whether he was scowling or not. The edges of his jaw constantly jutted between sentences, as if he clenched his teeth whenever his lips weren't moving.

"It was my first time in Nassau." He spoke slowly, as if in a dream, and occasionally slurred his words. "In those days, which weren't so terribly long ago, though sometimes it seems a lifetime, the harbor was more of a city than the city was. It was brimming with so many ships, you could scarcely see the water between them. Ships of every size and kind."

"I remember," said Kate. Gabe was right; it hadn't been long since she first looked on Nassau, but it felt like an age. "It was like that when I first arrived, before Rogers took it all away."

"It was a sight, no denying that," he said with a wistful grin. The grin slowly turned downward as he continued. "It's strange to think there was a time when I fancied that place. I went for the first whorehouse I could find, because that's what every young pirate does." He glanced uncertainly at her, as if he wasn't sure he should be telling her this. She nodded for him to continue. "Well, everyone I asked pointed me to The Strapped Bodice. I'm sure you've heard of it. I wasted no time getting there, but it scared the piss out of me when I first looked on it. The door reminded me of a mouth, glowing red from the inside. I didn't go in for fear I'd be swallowed up. I was feeling dizzy, so I went down the road and found a tavern. I got myself good and drunk, and later that night I stumbled back, and I didn't give myself any time to think about my prior fear. I walked right into the mouth of Hell without a care."

Kate couldn't stop a laugh from bubbling out of her. "I'm sorry," she said, instantly covering her mouth. "That was dramatic." She composed herself, because she knew that men didn't like being laughed at when they were trying to be serious. And then she wondered why she should care what Gabe Jenkins did or did not like.

To his credit, he chuckled a little, but it was clear he didn't truly share her mirth. "Maybe I should stop."

"No," she said, reaching out to touch his hand. He looked at her fingers, and she withdrew. "Keep going."

He cleared his throat. "Well, when I was inside, there were girls spread about with candles set around them in circles. They looked so beautiful. They were all naked and they were all calling me over with smiles that would melt an icy heart, saying nothing of a young, eager heart. In my drunken state, it was a task just to gather my wits and make a decision. But fortune was with me—or so I thought at the time—and I felt a woman's hands on my shoulders. I turned to look into the most beautiful blue eyes I ever saw. Her hair was full and brown. Her skin was white, but not unpleasantly so, and there were little freckles on her cheeks, when you looked real close. She was older than the others, but she was one of those women who holds her youth." He paused and looked at Kate. "I wager you'll be one of those women too. If scars can't diminish your face, I doubt age will do much damage."

She found herself again suppressing that irritating flutter that he had a habit of putting in her belly. "Finish the story."

"Well, the point is, she was a handsome sight."

"Aren't we all handsome when aided by spirits?"

"Not all," he replied warily. "Some get uglier and fatter. But she was just as handsome when my senses returned an hour later, after we had done the deed. Well, *many* deeds, if I'm being truthful."

He swallowed loud enough for Kate to hear it, and for a moment she thought he was embarrassed. But then she realized it was something else. "I've neglected the most important thing," he said. "The story is untellable without it. I was a deckhand aboard *Queen Anne's Revenge* at the time, captained under one Edward Teach."

Calloway stirred suddenly in her sleep, turning her back to them. Both Kate and Gabe looked at her. She didn't move again, and Gabe continued.

"Anyway, I had no way of knowing who this strumpet was, and she didn't know who I was when she picked me. After we had done our deed, we talked for a while. She got two glasses from her little dresser and a bottle of wine. I'm no wine lover, but it tasted fine to my lips. We drank and drank until the bottle was done and we were both giggling like children.

"Then she told me something that sobered me up right quick. She said she was going to let me in on a little secret. From the dangerous glint in her eye, I wasn't sure I wanted to know. But she told me anyway. She told me she was Edward Teach's mistress long ago. She was proud of this, probably told every man she bedded, after a few drinks. You can imagine my horror, but I managed to keep my features from deceiving me. I liked her a good deal, and I didn't want to scare her off so soon. And, if you want the truth of it, I was curious to hear a woman's notion of Teach. We all talked about him when he wasn't around, wondering about his proclivities. No one ever saw him with a woman. We had a bet he'd lost his member in a battle, and the fairer sex no longer interested him. Turns out we were wrong about that. Teach was a regular romantic, so this strumpet claimed, and I saw in her eyes and in her smile that she wasn't lying.

"She insisted the two of them were over. Well, even with my limited experience, I knew straight away that wasn't true. Even if she was done with Teach, Teach wasn't done with her. She said he told her he'd never take another woman to bed so long as she lived. I wager that made her feel good about herself, knowing there was a powerful man out there thinking about her day and night. Why else would she tell me if she didn't care?

"Any fancies I entertained about this strumpet falling in love with me in a night's length faded right there. We enjoyed each other a final time. I paid her more than fairly, and I was on my way, trying not to appear too hasty, though in the wake of this new gossip I was far more nervous than I dared let on.

"One of Teach's men, going by name of Jethro, was waiting

for me when I got downstairs."

"Jethro?" Kate interrupted. She remembered that name well enough.

"You've met the man?"

"He was on *Queen Anne's Revenge* when it went down."

"Did he live?"

"Only if he's immune to a shot between the eyes. He talked too much."

Gabe seemed relieved. "Well, Jethro was in the lobby, enjoying the company of a girl. When he spotted me coming down the stairs, he tossed that girl aside like she was a piece of trash, and he was on me faster than I thought him capable, sticking a gun in my ribs and hurrying me out of there. 'You'll be coming with me lad, one way or t'other,' he said.

"He led me outside and around the back and down a little path through the jungle, where we came to a small clearing. And there was Captain Teach standing in the moonlight like a monstrous shadow, his beard lit up and smoking. If you know Teach, you know he only fired his beard when he was going into battle, or about to kill someone. I didn't see or hear any sign of a battle, so I started counting down the seconds until my life was through. It was all I could do not to piss myself.

"'This is the one who had a go with your woman,' Jethro told him. 'Sorry it took so long to get him out, but he was in there a long time, he was.'

"When Teach looked at me with those blue eyes, sparkling in the fires of his beard, I fell to my knees before him and I begged his forgiveness. I slapped my palms together and I begged him to spare me. I told him I didn't know. I had no idea about them till she told me what was what, and I never would have done anything with her if I'd known. And that was the truth of it."

Gabe paused to shake his head shamefully. "I was a coward.

I wanted to live." He smiled sadly at Kate. "I had yet to learn that there are things worse than dying."

Kate nodded. She saw Jonathan Griffith's face in the light of the lantern, his hand outstretched, pleading with her to let go of the past and come with him.

"Teach asked what else she told me," Gabe went on. "He asked if she said anything about her daughter. I had no idea she had a daughter, and I told Teach as much. To my shock, he actually smiled. He gave me his hand and pulled me up off my knees, and then he patted my shoulders, real friendly-like. That scared me more than anything else, because I'd watched him warm to his victims right before he put that giant sword in their guts. He told me everything was alright, and that I needn't fret. But those words did nothing to slow my heart, because I knew there was more coming, or else why would he be hiding in the jungle behind a whorehouse, waiting for me?

"And then he gave me the rest of it. He told me, 'You're going back in there, and you're going to tell her you be far from done with her. You're going to ravish her again and again, until you both be spent, and when you're done, and she be slumbering away, you're going to take this vial and pour its solution into her ear.' He produced a little corked vial with a blue substance from his coat and handed it to me. 'When the last breath has taken leave of her lips, slice her wrists with a dagger to make it look like she did herself in. If you don't do this thing, I promise you'll suffer a death far slower than hers. And if you be thinking to run away with the task undone, Jethro will kill her anyway, and I'll find you, as I find every mortal who slights me.'"

Gabe continued to stare into the lantern, barely blinking despite its glare. "I summoned whatever scant courage I had at that time and I made myself look into his eyes as I asked him, 'Why don't you do it yourself, if you hate her so?'

"'Because I don't murder women,' he told me."

Kate snorted derisively. But then she remembered Calloway had somehow survived Teach long enough for Kate to rescue her. That had always puzzled her.

"So what did you do?" she asked.

"I wanted to live," Gabe said with a shrug. "The woman was going to die no matter what I did. I'd killed once before; a man a few years older than me, during a raid on a French ship. I stabbed him in the leg with a sword, and he went down on the deck. He crawled for his pistol, which had fallen a good deal away from him, and I told him to stop, but I guess he didn't understand me, because he kept on crawling. So I kept on stabbing until he stopped. That wasn't easy, and I thought about it afterward, dreamed about it for months.

"I'd never killed a woman, though. I knew it would be much worse, but I also knew I could live with a bit of guilt. There was no sense in both of us dying. If I didn't kill her, Teach would kill me and get someone else to do it. That's what I told myself, anyway. And I kept telling myself that as I walked back into the whorehouse. The strumpets were pawing at me, trying to get me to spend my coin on them, but I only had eyes for one. She hadn't come downstairs yet, so I went up the spiral stairs, grasping the knife hidden in my sash. I went down the hallway, and the shadows of strumpets and men were playing at the red drapes on either side of me. It felt like they were going to snatch me if I didn't hurry along. I dare not turn back. I sensed the devil on my tail, waiting for me to turn away from my task. When I reached her room at the end of the path, I looked back the way I'd come. There was no devil, but I knew he was there.

"She was glad to see me back so soon. Probably because she expected another generous tip. I let her seduce me a little. She was so soft and delicate in my arms, and I felt my resolve retreating as another urge traded its place. So I did as Blackbeard said, and I took her again. And when that urge was satiated and she was asleep in my arms, I drew her hair away from her ear, uncorked the vial and held it over her head. I held my wrist to stop my hand from trembling. I told myself, maybe this is just a test. Maybe it's just colored water. And before that notion could flee, I tilted the vial and spilled a few drops of the blue stuff into her ear.

"At first, nothing happened. I started to laugh, because I thought Teach had played a vulgar prank on me, to scare me, or something like that. Maybe she was in on it, and they would have a laugh about it later. Hell, Teach was probably outside laughing with Jethro about how stupid I was to believe water in a vial could actually kill a person.

"But that relief didn't last long. She started to quiver. It was small at first, like shivering from a chill breeze, but before long she was quaking so terribly that she tumbled right off the bed, and she took me with her. Her eyes opened and fluttered, then closed again, and all of a sudden she was quiet. It was over so fast. She didn't wake up. When I was certain she was truly gone, I took the dagger Teach had given me and I opened up her wrists. The lines weren't clean. I made a frightful mess of it with my shaky hands.

"I did what I could to gather my wits, and then I gathered my clothes. I was out of there like a shot loosed from a pistol. The whores pawed at me all over again when I got downstairs. I smiled as best I could, so as not to arouse their suspicions, and I went out the door. I found Teach and Jethro waiting where I'd left them in the jungle. Teach had this desperate look in his eye. 'Did you do it?' he demanded of me. I told him I did. That threw him into a rage. He started swinging his sword, nearly hacking a tree in half. Jethro dodged the blade before it took off his head. I'd always wondered if Teach's madness was some kind of an act, but I knew then that his mind was truly lost. 'No one must know of this,' he said, after he had cooled a bit. His voice was someone else's . . . a child's, maybe. I'd never heard that voice out of his mouth before, and I never heard it since. 'If you speak of it to anyone, I will kill you. And when I ask you to do something, no matter how terrible, you will do it.'"

"'I've proven as much,' I told him, as a gentle way of reminding him this was all according to his design. I wasn't sure he remembered that.

"But he was preoccupied with his insanity. He was pacing about, dragging his great sword along the sand, leaving a trail of circles. He told Jethro, 'I must see her one last time,' and Jethro told him he didn't think that was a good idea. But there was no stopping Teach once his mind was made up. He stormed into the tavern.

"His whole plan to make her death look like a suicide was undone, because he was the last person the other strumpets saw come out of the dead woman's room. In the end, he made me kill her for nothing, when he could have taken the satisfaction for himself."

Gabe fell silent, and Kate thought maybe he was finished. She wasn't sure what she should say. She knew that any normal woman would be horrified, and that she should probably never speak to him again, but his regret was palpable, and she was not a normal woman. "That's dreadful," she muttered at last, rather lamely.

"After that," he continued, "Teach knew I would do whatever he asked. I wouldn't dare cross him, not with the information I had. I expected he'd kill me any minute, but he never did. One day, he cut loose of me in Nassau and told me and a few others to join Dillahunt's crew, which is exactly what I did. He said I would prove useful there. I had no idea what it meant, but I knew it wouldn't mean anything good. For a short time, I forgot myself among Dillahunt's men. I made new friends."

Gabe's face twisted. "And then Annabelle arrived, and she brought Blackbeard's orders with her. She made me kill a friend, and I did it without pause. It was a small thing in the shadow of what I'd already done. What a horrible thing to say of murder, that it is 'small,' but that's exactly what it was to me. It was small. It was easy."

His features softened as he looked at Kate. "And then I met you on the boat. I knew you were a killer. I saw that in your eyes. But there was something different about you. You weren't haunted by what you had done. You had no cares, apart from a few scars. You wore those proudly."

"That isn't pride," she informed him. "I simply forget they're there. The luxury of not being able to see your own face."

He lowered his head, curly hair shrouding his eyes. The edges of his jaw protruded as he clenched his teeth. "I'm not a good person, Kate."

"I'm not sure I know what a good person is anymore," she replied.

He fell silent, frozen in that hunched position. The only sound was the gentle flutter of the sails. Kate wanted to say something. She wanted to make him feel better, even though she realized how ridiculous that impulse was. Why should she wish to comfort a murderer? *He only did what he had to, just as I have,* she told herself. But she knew this was different. She had only killed murderers. Gabe had murdered an innocent.

She looked to the lantern, and in the glare she saw a young and hopeful face smiling back at her. The face belonged to Nathan Adams. He had been a small thing to her as well, easily dismissed when acknowledgement would hinder her freedom.

He had been inconsequential, despite everything he had done for her, and he would have remained so had they not crossed paths again. Only when he was taken from her did she realize how selfish she had been.

The silence stretched on, and Kate knew she could not bear Gabe Jenkins' company for another minute. Not right now, anyway. "I have to—"

A young female voice interrupted her. "What was her name?"

Kate looked to Calloway, who was sitting up. Her face was pale, and she was grinding her fingers into her belly as if she was about to be sick. She glared hatefully at Gabe, head ducked low. "The woman you killed. The strumpet. You never said her name."

Gabe shrugged, not meeting her gaze. "Didn't know you were awake."

"I heard it all," Calloway hissed. "What was her name?"

"What does it matter?"

"Have you forgotten it?"

Kate looked from Calloway to Gabe, dread rising in her gut. *Oh no,* she thought. *It can't be . . .*

"I'll never forget," Gabe said.

"Tell me her name!" she shrieked.

Gabe flinched at her shrill demand. "Fine, if you really must know. Her name was Elise."

Calloway lunged at him with the speed of a cat pouncing on an unsuspecting mouse. Gabe stared at her in wide-eyed bewilderment as she barreled into him, knocking him off of the crate. Calloway sprawled him across the deck, straddling him and grasping his neck. Her fingernails traced red lines along his throat as she shook him, slamming the back of his head against the deck. Gabe seized her wrists and wrenched her hands from his bloodied throat, choking for air.

Kate wrapped her arms around Calloway, struggling to pull her off of him. "Jaq," she pleaded, glancing at the three crewmen who were taking notice of the scuffle. "They're watching!"

"I don't care!" Calloway snarled, writhing in Kate's arms. "He murdered my mother!"

12

GABE

Gabe's neck was on fire, inside and out. He coughed violently, fighting to regain his breath. A dull ache was spreading through the back of his head, clouding his peripheral vision with dancing particles of multicolored light. The girl had nearly killed him, and it was gradually dawning on him how appropriate a death that would have been.

He curled forward, straining to get up. Kate was doing her best to hold Calloway back, but the girl thrust out a bare foot and caught Gabe's jaw with her heel, snapping his head back. The ache in the back of his head was suddenly dwarfed by the pain that blossomed from his chin. "You killed my mother!" she kept screaming, forgetting to feign a masculine voice. "You killed her! You killed her!"

In her fury, the girl knocked the wooden box onto its side, and the golden spider scurried to safety, disappearing between two crates. *If only I were a spider,* thought Jenkins.

Hennessey and his two friends started wandering over with curious looks in their eyes. "She don't sound like a boy no more," said Bruiser.

"I told you she weren't," replied Hennessey with a sly grin. His molars gleamed through the hole in his cheek as he stepped into the light of the lantern. He grabbed a handful of Kate's hair and pulled her off of Calloway, thrusting her away. She crumpled over a crate, gasping. "No raping the redhead," Hennessey said. "Wouldn't want to sully Vane's precious booty." He turned to Calloway. "But no one said anything of this one."

"Get the fuck away from her!" Kate roared, throwing herself at Hennessey. Bleeder caught her, and she struggled in his rock-solid embrace. "Let go!"

"I don't think so," said Bleeder. "I like how you squirm."

"She's not on the menu," Bruiser reminded him warily.

"I just want to hold her for a while," Bleeder innocently replied.

"Alright, but I heard she killed Griffith's entire crew."

"Just those I didn't like," Kate hissed.

"Har!" Bleeder exclaimed. "I fancy a lass with a sense o' humor."

Hennessey lifted Calloway off the deck and bent her over a crate. He untucked her shirt from her breeches and felt around the front. "Aye, this be a girl, sure enough."

"Get off me!" Calloway squealed, twisting beneath him. He was far too strong for her. He pressed her face against the crate.

Gabe had seen enough. Despite the swirling dizziness from lack of oxygen, he got to his feet and drew his curved dagger. "Let go of her, Hennessey, or I'll carve you a third mouth."

Hennessey turned a dangerous glower on Gabe, molars clenched tightly through his cheek-hole. "What do you care, Jenkins? Not a moment ago she be trying to squeeze the life out of you."

Calloway lifted her head just long enough to flash Gabe a spiteful glare, before Hennessey shoved her back down. Gabe was chilled by the irony. *She's about to be savaged and she reserves her hatred for me.*

"We'll discuss this with Captain Rackham," Gabe said as diplomatically as possible, but the words came out harshly. Speaking pained his throat.

"Stay out of it, lad," Hennessey said. "I'll kill you, and then I'll fuck this lass until her ears bleed."

"That's not going to happen," said Kate. She jammed an elbow into Bleeder's ribs. He let out a puff of air, but his hold on her did not falter. "Kill him, Gabe!" she pleaded. "Kill him!"

Hennessey had the gall to look offended. "What did I ever do to you, missy?"

Gabe was doing everything he could to keep from falling over. His legs felt numb. "I will kill you," he promised. *If my legs don't give out first.*

"The lass really took the wind out of you," Hennessey scoffed. "Look at you. You can scarcely stand up."

"Do it!" Kate kept yelling.

"Shut that bitch up," Hennessey ordered.

Bruiser thrust a fist into Kate's gut while Bleeder held her. Her face turned red as she gasped for air, and a purple vein protruded from her forehead.

Gabe shook his head, but that only made him dizzier. He squinted, focusing on Hennessey's ugly face. Just one precise slice of his curved blade was all he would need to end this. Bruiser and Bleeder would close in on him after, but at least that would distract their attention from the women. In all likelihood, they would kill him. Maybe that wasn't such a bad thing.

"WHAT'S ALL THIS?" demanded an unmistakable voice. Gabe turned his head, nearly toppling in the process. Rackham had surfaced from his cabin, wearing his red-feathered hat. The blade of his cutlass screeched as he unsheathed it.

"This one, she be a lass!" Hennessey said, drawing Calloway close.

Calico Jack stepped forward, the tip of his sword trained on Hennessey. "What's her being a lass got to do with anything?"

Hennessey thought about that. "Seeing as we're pirates, we have the right to rape any woman fool enough to set her dainty heels on our deck."

"I hadn't heard that rule," said Calico Jack.

"Everyone knows that one," Bruiser put in.

"It's an unspoken accord," said Bleeder, his lone eye fixed on Calico Jack. "Woman comes aboard, she's signing her cunny up for rape."

"Aye, that be true," agreed Bruiser. "Can't have women running about a man's ship, getting funny notions in their heads. Have to put them in their place."

"Aye, put them in their place," Bleeder parroted. "With rape."

"Rape them before they rape you, I always say," Bruiser said.

Bleeder scowled at his brother. "What?"

"Didn't really think that one through," Bruiser admitted sheepishly. "It just popped out me lips."

"Nobody's raping anybody," boomed Calico Jack in his most commanding voice.

Bleeder reluctantly unhooked his arms from around Kate. She moved away and massaged her bruised stomach while glaring promises of vengeance.

Hennessey kept his arm around Calloway. "I don't like being duped," he said.

"No one duped you," Calico Jack replied, lowering his voice to a more negotiable decibel. "As I recall, she never said she *wasn't* a girl."

Bruiser rubbed his bald head and sourly muttered, "Suppose that be true."

"Strikes me as a cheat," said Bleeder.

Gabe's throat was throbbing. His legs were ready to buckle. He sat down hard on one of the crates, and the dagger slipped from his finger, landing near the lantern. Calico Jack glanced sideways at him. "What happened to you?"

"Nothing."

"This girl made a try for his life," Hennessey said. "Said he did in her mother or some such blather. I was only looking out for me fellow man."

Gabe choked out a hoarse laugh.

Calico Jack smirked skeptically. "It would seem Jenkins is out of danger. Release the girl. That's an order."

"An order?" Hennessey balked. "Mayhap I'll call me a vote and we'll elect ourselves a new captain." He glanced back at Bruiser and Bleeder for support, but the brothers did not seem to share in his confidence.

"I dunno, Henn," said Bruiser. "Best not cross Vane."

"Who's to say Vane needs to know what happened here?" Hennessey said, winking at Calico Jack. "Maybe our dear captain had hisself a little too much rum and took a saunter off the deck, eh?"

Calico Jack remained cool. "If you truly think you can get away with mutiny without Charles discovering it, you're welcome to make the attempt. But there will be no vote. I'd rather not wake the men sleeping below. They need their rest. We shall have a duel at dawn, just the pair of us. Cutlasses, not pistols."

Gabe would have smiled if he wasn't in so much pain. Jack

Rackham's skill with a blade preceded him.

Hennessey blinked uncertainly. "No. We vote."

"That would hardly be fair," Calico Jack chuckled. "I can assure you, with all the men present, a vote would not go in your favor. It is a duel or nothing. What say you?"

It was a long while before Hennessey responded. "Nay," he said at last. He shoved Calloway away so violently that she crumpled against the starboard rail. "I know trickery when I sees it, and this be trickery, clear as I ever seen it."

"That's settled then," Calico Jack declared, sheathing his sword. He started to turn away.

"Nothing's settled," protested Calloway, stepping forward.

"Pardon?" asked the captain, looking back.

Calloway jabbed a finger at Gabe's face, and he flinched away before she could skewer one of his eyes. "This man murdered my mother."

Calico Jack looked at Gabe. "Unfortunate, but unless the crime happened aboard my ship, it's hardly my problem."

He pivoted and started back toward his cabin.

Calloway lowered her finger. She bit her lip. Her eyes darted back and forth in desperation. And then a realization brightened her eyes. "He's conspiring against you with Captain Dillahunt!"

Calico Jack stopped and turned, his lower jaw jutting out as though he'd heard nearly all he could stand. He took a few deep breaths to calm himself. His eyes shifted toward Gabe. "Should I dignify that?"

"That's absurd," Gabe said at once. He forced a laugh. "Haven't seen Captain Dillahunt since—"

"Wait a minute," Bruiser interjected suddenly. He stepped closer to Calloway, inspecting her face while stroking his chin. "Aye. Aye! I thought she looked familiar."

"Enlighten us, please," Calico Jack pleaded with open arms.

Bruiser turned to the captain, smiling confidently. "This be Dillahunt's woman. Or girl. Or whatever you call her. Either way, she's one of the prisoners what came into Pirate Town with Dillahunt."

"That's ridiculous," Kate protested. She tried to stand up, but winced and clutched her stomach.

Bruiser swung around to face her with a challenging grin. "Shut your hole, missy, or I'll plug the one between your legs. I was there on the dock when they hauled her off. That be her, alright."

"He's telling the truth," Calloway said. "Dillahunt is following us as we speak. Keep a scope trained aft and soon enough you'll know it to be true. This man is leading Dillahunt straight to Vane."

"Explains why she's on my ship," Calico Jack concluded. He set a hand on Gabe's shoulder. "Unless you can offer a better reason, Mr. Jenkins?"

Gabe saw no use in further lies. He knew he deserved what he was about to get. It was fitting that the daughter of the woman he'd murdered would now seal his fate. He threw back his head, taking in the vibrant stars above, half-obscured by the billowing sails. He had never spent much time pondering the existence of a higher power, but being done in by the daughter of the woman he murdered seemed too great a coincidence.

"I asked you a question, Mr. Jenkins. And you'd do well to answer promptly, given that your life depends on it."

"I have nothing to say about it," Gabe evenly replied.

Calico Jack didn't like that. "Nobility does not become a pirate. If you are innocent, defend yourself, man!"

"What the girl says is true." He had to clutch his throat when he talked, because the words sliced like knives on their way out. He felt something wet and sticky on his hand, and when he looked at his palm it was striped with blood. The girl must have shredded his skin when she tried to strangle him. *That's the least of my troubles.*

Hennessey's eyes gleamed in the light of the lantern between him and Gabe. "You're shark food, mate. Only question be which piece we feed them first."

Calloway's irises had thinned, nearly encompassed by her pupils. "You're going to pay for what you did."

"That's not the answer, Jaq," breathed Kate in exasperation.

"Isn't it?" Calloway shot back, the tails of her bandana whipping as she snapped her head in Kate's direction.

"And what wrong must *Dillahunt* pay for?" Gabe asked her.

Calloway's jaw clenched and unclenched repeatedly. "He's a liar." She flung a hand, and her fingernails scraped the tip of his nose. "You're all liars!"

Gabe persisted. "What was his lie?"

"It doesn't matter."

"Can we kill them both now?" asked Bruiser. "This be a lot of talking without much doing."

"No," said Calico Jack. "Fortune smiles on us, gentlemen. Guy Dillahunt has no notion what he's walking into. And Charles may want to use the girl as leverage. She may no longer care for her captain, but he may yet harbor feelings for her."

"Then why did he put me here?" Calloway asked.

The captain looked aft, the feather of his hat fluttering in the breeze. "If he's truly pursuing us, you may soon be afforded the chance to ask him yourself."

"You want we should lock her up?" Bleeder asked, clearly hopeful.

"No." Calico Jack smiled at Calloway. "It's clear she has no love for Dillahunt. She is no threat to us."

"And Jenkins?" Hennessey growled.

The captain squeezed Gabe's shoulder. "Take him below and chain him up. Beat him, if you like. But do not kill him or remove anything. We'll leave that for Charles. I suspect he's starved for entertainment."

Bruiser and Bleeder quickly flanked Gabe and scooped him up by the armpits. Hennessey bent down to pick up the dagger Gabe had dropped. He tickled Gabe's stomach with the tip of the blade. The teeth parted within the hole in his cheek, and his tongue emerged to lick the pink rim. "I'm going to have fun with you."

13

OGLE

He slowly peeled the bloodstained rags from his arm, exposing the pink crevice carved in the top of his arm. At the deepest point, the bone was white and dry. The skin around the edges of the wound had started to fold inward, hardening as it healed, skirted by a green and yellow puss. Ogle rolled out of his hammock.

"I need another bandage," he croaked at Ash when the old blind man rushed over to check on him.

"It's not infected," said Ash, touching his arm and sniffing.

"How would you know, you withered fool? You wouldn't see a monkey flinging its shit until it splattered you in the face."

"Nay, but I would smell it before it hit me, and I'd have the good sense to duck."

"Fetch more bandages," Ogle commanded.

Ash made a face and left. He returned half an hour later

with clean bandages. Ogle refused to watch as the old man applied them. Ash gave his arm a painful squeeze when he was finished. "There. Keep it on this time, or a spider will lay eggs in your arm. Seen it happen, I have."

Ogle resisted a shudder. The old man was just trying to scare him. "Get out of my sight."

Ash shook his head. "You were nicer when you thought you were dying."

"Well I'm not dying, am I? Off with you, old man."

Ash shook his head and started back toward the jungle. "You're not my only patient, you know," he grumbled.

"Find me a surgeon with eyes," Ogle shot back.

He would have preferred Ash wander in the opposite direction, right off the ledge and hundreds of feet into the sea. The old man had been hounding him night and day, as if his life depended on keeping Ogle alive. But Ogle was well beyond the threat of death now. His energy had almost fully returned. He slept less and was eating heartily again. It would take a few weeks to restore his belly to its normal size, just the way he liked it, but he was on his way.

"I see you're back to your old spirits," said Marcus. He walked down from the bonfire, which was gaining in size as night fell over the sharp cliff that protruded over the ocean. "I like your new haircut."

Ogle reached up to feel the top of his head. The stitches were still in. The three vertical wounds were rough with flaking scabs. His scalp itched terribly every night. "I'll kill Tanner, I swear to Davy Jones."

"Have to find him first." Marcus handed him a full bottle of rum. He always brought rum. Ogle was starting to wonder if Marcus's only aim was to dull his senses so he wouldn't ask any questions. But what was Ogle supposed to do? Turn down rum? He took the bottle, popped the cork, and gulped. Marcus grinned.

Ogle leaned against one of the trees that supported his hammock, his head already swimming. "I need to murder someone," he said with a sigh. "I don't care who anymore. It's been too long." His injuries had given him too much time to dwell on uncertainties. Killing was easy. There was nothing confusing about it.

Marcus laughed. He set a shoulder against the opposite tree and fidgeted with the shriveled ears dangling from his necklace. He was up to thirty-three now. Ogle couldn't help but notice how bold Marcus looked without even trying, lazily poised and playing with his trinkets of war. "Soon enough, my friend," Marcus assured him. "Soon enough."

"What the fuck are we doing?" Ogle wondered, wrenching his eyes from Marcus's chest. "I'm tired of sitting around eating and drinking and sleeping and shitting. We should be out *there*." He gestured at the ocean, which was impossible to see beyond the bonfire. "We should be raiding ships and thieving and raping and killing, not sitting on our asses. I want to fire a cannon. I want to watch men die. That's what I was born to do. I am shit at anything else."

"No quarrel from me," said Marcus with a chuckle.

Ogle saw Skinny Benny and Smelly Joe, two pirates who were inseparable, sitting before the fire cooking red meat on sticks. "Where does all the meat come from?" he wondered suddenly.

"It's a big island," Marcus replied with a shrug. "A lot of animals." Ogle glimpsed a twinkle in his friend's dark eyes, as though he knew something he wasn't telling him.

"*Adventure* never leaves," he went on. All the questions that had been nagging at him since he was brought here were pouring out of him. "She's been moored down there for days. She just sits there, useless. Why'd you bother building a new mast if you weren't going to use her?"

"We don't need to use her right now."

"What does that mean? You're pirates."

"We're pirates with food," Marcus said. "What more do we need?"

"What are all these men doing here?" He had counted over fifty different pirates since being brought here, wherever 'here' was. "And why won't you tell me where we are?"

"You're on Isla de Mariposa."

That didn't make any sense. "I've been to Mariposa, and this looks nothing like it."

"That's because you're on the eastern isle. You've only been to the western isle."

"That's absurd." Mariposa was not one island, but two, connected by a slim ridge at the center. The western isle was frequented by pirates, but no one had been to the eastern isle and lived to talk about it.

"The rumors are true," Marcus added. "No one leaves the eastern isle. Not without Teach's say-so."

"Teach is dead."

Marcus looked to the fire. "Thus there is no one to tell these men they can leave."

The top of Ogle's head pained him when he laughed. "Now you sound like Teach. A puzzle of words meant to cloud the brain. I'm not so stupid as I look." He raised a finger and grinned craftily as the perfect retort occurred to him. "There's no one to tell them they *can't* leave either, now is there?"

"Not my words," Marcus said. His eyes burned with the reflection of the flames. "This is Teach's isle. It always was, and it always will be, even in death."

"That makes no bloody sense," Ogle said, curling his lip. "We are pirates. When our captain dies, we pick a new one."

"True of any captain, save for Blackbeard. You know his

influence, Ogle. He extended his hand across hundreds of leagues and took hold of you through the whore Annabelle, and you were made to mutiny. Was that your will?"

"Of course it was. Nathan Adams was an idiot. Who knows where he would have led us. And Teach would have paid me a lot of money for that mutiny, had he lived. Coin is my god, not Blackbeard."

"You feared him. That's why you obeyed."

Ogle spat. "I fear lack of coin."

"You will receive your share in due time."

"From who? A ghost?"

Marcus looked at him. "What is death to Blackbeard but another wave, easily crested?"

"You're mad, Marcus."

Marcus laughed. "I'm not the one who passed on that little black-haired beauty I brought you the other night. *That* is madness, my friend. There are times that I question your proclivities."

"Fuck off!" Ogle exploded, hurling the bottle of rum to the ground, where it burst into shards, dousing the dirt.

Marcus stared at the shattered bottle. "There was still rum in that."

Ogle aimed a finger. "Don't ever question my procliv . . . my procliv . . . that's a twist of the tongue, and I'm drunk."

Marcus burst into a fit of laughter. "That was fast."

Ogle couldn't help but laugh with him, in spite of himself. "I just need to do what it is I do."

Marcus pushed off the tree and snapped his fingers. "I have just the thing for you, Ogle. I wasn't going to show you right away, but I think you're ready."

Ogle frowned. "What thing?"

"Come with me, if you can walk."

"Course I can walk!" Ogle exclaimed, wobbling toward

him.

"So you can," Marcus observed with a grin. "Follow me, then."

Ogle followed Marcus away from the cliff and into a narrow path in the jungle. As much as he tried not to, his eyes constantly drifted to Marcus's rear.

Marcus led him to a small tent that was just big enough for two, and Ogle's heart started to flutter uncontrollably. Marcus ducked into the tent. Ogle waited a minute, looked around, and then bent down to follow Marcus inside. Marcus emerged, nearly head-butting Ogle, and then stared awkwardly at him. "What are you doing?"

Ogle stammered. "I . . . thought I was supposed to come inside."

"The tent's a little small," Marcus said. "I was just getting this." He held up a torch.

"I see."

Marcus set the torch on the stump of a tree and clacked flint and steel three times before igniting the rag. He lifted the flaring torch and motioned for Ogle to follow.

"Where are we going?" Ogle asked as they continued on. The huge wet leaves started to slap at his face as the jungle thickened with every step. He wasn't sure they were following any kind of path anymore.

"You weren't the only treasure we brought back from Pirate Town," Marcus said, smiling over his shoulder.

"Vane's stash!" Ogle realized. "You found his chests! I just assumed Vane took them with him."

"He did," Marcus said. "And good riddance, I say. That treasure was always cursed, ever since Jonathan Griffith took it from the Spaniards. Cunningham was promised a share, and look what happened to him. Griffith didn't last long. Adams got his hands on it, and then a bullet in the brain."

"And then it fell into Annabelle's clutches," Ogle added. "You're right. It *is* cursed."

"We don't need it," Marcus said. "What we found is far better."

Ogle struggled to imagine what it could possibly be, but he had never been particularly imaginative.

They came upon a yawning cave set in the base of a steep crag. It was wide and oval, not unlike a mouth, serrated along the top with little stalactites, and two particularly long ones that resembled fangs. Ogle rolled his eyes. "Nothing good comes of caves."

"True of most caves," said Marcus, "save for this one." He motioned for Ogle to go inside.

"You'll be right behind me, I expect."

Marcus shook his head. "Nay. Each man must go alone. I've had my turn."

Ogle folded his arms. "I'm not going down there."

"Surely you're not afraid of the dark, Ogle."

Ogle looked at the cave. It reminded him of the cave that he, Gabe Jenkins, Red Devil, and Peter Lively had met Annabelle in, where they plotted to mutiny against Nathan Adams. Peter Lively never left that cave.

"I'm not afraid," Ogle said. "I just don't want to break my leg, is all. I've had enough injuries. Give me your torch."

"Nay," Marcus stubbornly replied. "You will find light enough in the dark."

"I'm not one for riddles."

"It's not a riddle."

The cave was so very dark. "What am I meant to do in there?"

"Walk one hundred paces," Marcus answered.

"And then?"

Marcus smiled pleasantly. "It doesn't matter."

"Am I going to fall down a pit? Is that what this is? You're trying to kill me?"

"We haven't mended your wounds just to send you to your death, Ogle. But if you're afraid of a little cave, we can head back to the cliff."

Ogle raised a hand. "Nay. I'll go. Just stay here with the torch so I can find my way back."

"I'll be waiting."

Ogle set his jaw and walked into the cave. The ceiling was a foot taller than him. He didn't want to hit his head and reopen his wounds. He saw nothing but darkness ahead of him. He glanced over his shoulder as casually as possible. Marcus was standing at the mouth, holding the torch. He smiled and said, "A hundred paces, my friend."

"I heard you." Ogle continued onward. The cave was perfectly level, never inclining or declining. It narrowed like a funnel until he could touch either wall by spreading his arms. The distant light of Marcus's torch vanished behind a bend around thirty paces in. Ogle let his fingers craze the smooth rock, with nothing else to guide him.

About fifty paces in—he had already lost count—he started to cough. The air was thick and stifling, stinging his eyes. He thought he smelled smoke. Was there a fire somewhere down here?

A raspy sound, very faint, trickled past him, but he didn't feel a breeze.

He froze.

It sounded like . . . breathing.

"Who's there?"

A voice touched his ears on a sigh of breath. "Ogle," it wheezed.

Ogle would not scream. He was not a woman. He was a man, and men do not scream.

"Ogle."

Hot breath touched Ogle's cheeks. It reeked of decaying flesh, a stink he knew all too well. He heard a rustle of cloth and the unmistakable squeak of leather. Four tiny amber lights appeared out of nowhere, suspended like fireflies before him. A face was illuminated, only it was not a face; it was a volcanic ruin of blistered flesh that had been pieced together over a skull, flaked like the bed of a dried lake with a labyrinth of glistening red fissures. A single eye gleamed in the dark, so unbearably blue that it might have yielded the entire ocean.

The thing breathed his name. "Ogle."

Ogle shut his eyes and gasped frantic breaths. *I will not scream. I had too much rum, that's all. I was in that cave in Pirate Town too long. That's all this is. That's all this is. That's all this—*

Wet fingers touched his cheek.

Ogle screamed.

He spun on his heels and bolted for the mouth of the cave.

Marcus was still standing at the end of the tunnel, holding his torch. He seemed so very far, but even from this distance Ogle could see him smiling. *Why is he smiling? Can't he see what's after me?*

Guttural laughter echoed off of the walls, and he heard the thing shuffling behind him in the dark. Fingers grazed his neck, leaving cold wet trails. He looked back, and he saw its puzzle of a face not two feet behind him, with its horrible blue eye locked on his, and the four amber fireflies swaying this way and that.

His toes caught on a slab of rock, breaking it loose, and he collapsed to his knees. He quickly rolled onto his back and raised his arms as the thing fell on him. The weight of it was tremendous, punching the air from his gut. The eye stopped two inches from his face, never blinking.

Ogle looked up to see Marcus still standing at the entrance, not thirty paces off, smiling vacuously. "Marcus! Help me!"

Marcus just kept smiling.

Ogle looked at the thing on top of him. Black flesh parted, revealing rotting teeth, separated by huge gaps. Cracks in its lips split wide and seeped blood onto Ogle's face. "Do you not wish to live?" it asked.

"Oh god, I do," he exploded in a shuddering sob. "I do, I do, I do. God, I do."

"God?" the thing hissed mockingly. "You beg the wrong man."

It lifted its long arms. Ogle saw the slab of rock that he had kicked loose clutched in its huge hands, held above its head. And then it brought the rock down fast, and Ogle swiveled his head sideways at the last second. He heard a crack, and then a distant ringing. Half of his vision went black, as though his right eye was covered. Something white and slimy bounced a foot from his head, with twisty red vines stemming from the end. It rolled around until he saw an iris and a pupil staring back at him, and he realized that he was looking at his own eye.

14

VANE

He watched from outside his tent as *Swift* approached in the distance, the sails of her single mast a web of dancing light that reflected off of the rolling waves. She was a small ship, but the name was appropriate. Vane had not expected Jack Rackham to return so quickly. He had lied—or *thought* he had lied—to Frederick Lindsay about how soon he would have Katherine Lindsay in his possession. Then again, there was still the chance that Gabe Jenkins, the mysterious young man Edward Teach had put so much faith in for reasons unknown to Vane, had failed to retrieve her. He squinted in the glaring mid-morning sun, hoping for a glimpse of red hair on the deck, but it was impossible to make out fine details from this distance.

Everything depended on Kate being aboard that ship.

His jaw involuntarily tightened, and he hissed a curse as pain sliced up his right cheek. A vein pulsed in his temple, threatening to spawn a headache. After escaping Pirate Town, he'd enlisted Mr. Tanner to remove a rotten molar. Tanner was skilled at removing things from a man's mouth, though he was no dentist. Still, Vane had no one else to turn to. Tanner had a wide variety of tools at his disposal, including pincers for wrangling teeth. Vane told him to make it quick, and Tanner begrudgingly obliged; he was not accustomed to making his victims comfortable. The molar had shattered as Tanner tightened the pincers around it, and it took him a suspiciously long time to pick the pieces out of the gum while Vane writhed in agony.

His gum still throbbed, and Vane was beginning to suspect the rot had spread into his jaw. A tooth seemed insignificant in the grand scheme of things, but now he was starting to wonder if something so tiny could be the death of him. A silly notion, he knew, but he had nothing but time to dwell on silly notions. He'd been stuck on this island for a month now, and rarely did he find himself in one place for more than a few days.

Except Pirate Town.

His beloved hideout had been compromised with the escape of Guy Dillahunt, who no doubt revealed its location to Woodes Rogers. Vane couldn't go back there. Not yet, anyway. Not until the threat of Rogers was eliminated.

His hand dropped to the gilded hilt of his cutlass and clutched it firmly. It had been too long since he'd last used it. He had plunged the blade into Lancaster's chest after the captain told him everything he needed to know. As much as he enjoyed extending a dying man's pain, Vane respected Captain Lancaster for putting up a good fight, even if the battle was short-lived and futile. That respect earned Lancaster a quick, merciful death, if nothing else.

Vane ached to take a life. The ache had grown over the past month until it was greater than the hollow throb that echoed through his jaw. He glanced at the three belligerent men stationed outside his tent. Roman had menaced Frederick Lindsay. Was that reason enough to kill a man? Maybe not, but Vane could always craft a lie. He could not just murder a man without good reason. Most of the crew liked Roman, looked up to him. They would ask questions. If Vane wasn't cautious, his crew would elect a new captain.

His gaze settled on Keet's colorful hair. No one would miss Keet. *Except his friend, Roman.* Roman had enough allies among the crew to stir a mutiny, if he desired. Vane blinked through his frustration. Governing a crew was complicated business. He wished it could be simpler, less democratic. However, he wouldn't have been elected captain otherwise.

He returned his gaze to the sea and watched *Swift* draw near, excruciatingly slow in its approach now that it was so close. Again he squinted for a glimpse of red hair. *Patience,* he told himself. If Gabe Jenkins hadn't completed his task, at the very least Vane would get to bloody his sword.

Swift slowed to a halt and dropped anchor, bobbing in the waves. A few minutes later, Vane saw nine figures descending into a longboat, difficult to discern in the shadow of the ship's hull. When the longboat was halfway to shore, he caught a shimmer of red in the sunlight, and relief softened his muscles. Taking a chance on Jenkins had not been a mistake.

The longboat slid onto the beach, and Calico Jack hopped out first, never afraid to dampen his boots. He seemed naked without his burgundy coat, in only a white shirt and black breeches. At least he still wore his red-feathered hat. Jack reached up and helped Katherine Lindsay—*Kate,* Vane reminded himself—out of the boat. Vane noticed she was wearing Jack's coat, and he might have taken that for a scandal, except Lindsay seemed revolted by Jack as he lowered her into the water by her waist. She slapped at his hands all the way down. "I don't know how I've made it this far without a man to help me out of boats," she muttered sarcastically, tossing her wild red hair as she huffed toward Vane.

She was just as striking as he remembered. It pained his eyes to linger on her fiery mane for too long. Her delicate face, somewhat paler than he recalled, was a soothing respite from the vibrant flame that wreathed it. Beneath the coat, the V of her brown shirt plunged well beyond her breasts, exposing her cleavage, which she emphasized with a well-postured back. The heedless sway of her hips was hypnotic, and all Vane could do was stare at her slender legs as she shuffled barefoot through the sand, one foot stepping directly in front of the other. When she reached him, she traded an angry grimace for a playful smirk. "Hello, Charles," she greeted in that raspy voice he had not forgotten. "Don't suppose you brought that wonderful bathtub with you? I stink like a pirate."

"I'm afraid there wasn't time," Vane replied. "I was more concerned with prolonging my life."

"Shame," she sighed. "It's the only thing I missed about you." She placed a hand on her hip and looked away, allowing him a pleasing view of her elegant profile. The breeze whipped her hair away from her missing ear for a moment, revealing the garbled pink ruin underneath.

"I see an entire ocean just behind you," he replied with a sweeping gesture. "I would love to watch you bathe in it." He imagined a wave crashing against her back and rolling down her front, streaming off hardened nipples and darkening the patch of red hair between her legs. He casually shifted his weight as he stiffened against his breeches.

"I'm sure you would." She swiveled, nodding to the longboat. "Spot of drama on the journey from Nassau. Captain Rackham's miscreants are overly thirsty for blood."

"Aren't we all?" Vane said with a shrug.

He looked past her to the boat. Calico Jack was waiting at

the edge of the water. A hulk of a man with a hideously burned face leapt into the water. Vane didn't know him. Two brothers, who Vane recognized as Bleeder and Bruiser hefted Gabe Jenkins—whose hands were bound behind him in rope—into the air and tossed him overboard. He hit the water with a harsh *slap* and gurgled a scream. The man with the burned face seized Jenkins by his bindings and dragged him onto the beach so he wouldn't drown. Jenkins growled furiously as his bloodied face was mashed into the hot sand. He had been stripped of his shirt, and his back was striped with red lacerations.

This is curious, thought Vane with a tremendous flutter of excitement that prickled the hairs on the back of his neck. Perhaps his sword would find its use today after all.

Calico Jack clutched a handful of Jenkins' black hair and lifted his face out of the sand, setting him on his knees. "This wretched boy conspired to lead Captain Guy Dillahunt here," Rackham announced.

Jenkins' bloodied lips twitched into a smile. "Captain Rackham garnered this information from another. I remained silent as a mouse, even as they had at me."

Calico Jack dug the tip of his boot into Jenkins' thigh. "Your silence is of no import, dog."

"Who revealed him?" Vane demanded.

"Dillahunt's woman," said Calico Jack. "It seems Dillahunt ordered her aboard with Jenkins. She was none too pleased about that, and revealed this traitor for what he was."

"I'd like to speak with this girl," said Vane. "A spurned lover spills all manner of juicy secrets."

"She's still on the ship," Jack replied, nodding over his shoulder.

Vane crossed his arms and pretended to be taken by a most distressing thought. "I'm troubled that you stayed your course, knowing Dillahunt was on your trail."

"Only because I knew what was waiting for him," Jack barked defensively. "I did not think you would want me turning away with your prize."

"At ease, Jack," Vane replied with a titter. He gestured at Jenkins. "The young man did only as commanded."

Kate Lindsay hissed through her teeth. "I should have known."

Calico Jack loosened his grip on Jenkins' hair. He unfastened the rope around Jenkins' wrists and gave him a shove with the tip of his boot. Jenkins dropped his palms. Calico Jack's face contorted as disbelief, confusion, and rage fought for equal purchase. When the battle was over, all emotions appeared to retreat, and he was left desolated. "I am a fool," he concluded.

Vane reminded himself that this moment had been coming since their first meeting. "You always were too kind for this sort of work, Jack. That's why I didn't tell you."

Calico Jack's eyes darted along the beach, as if he were recovering pieces of a puzzle from the sand and assembling them one at a time. When the puzzle was complete, he looked at Vane. "You would have let me believe Dillahunt followed of his own accord. That I was simply careless. But no, he was strung along by this little shit." He aimed an accusatory finger at Jenkins. "I would have gone into battle with you and never been the wiser."

"Aye," said Vane. "I knew you wouldn't approve. You never do."

"How can I disapprove of something I was never aware of?"

"That's the beauty of it," said Vane.

Jack raised two fingers to his temple, closed his eyes and groaned. "You are hopeless, Charles."

"Fine," Vane sighed in exasperation. "Make me the villain if it makes you feel better. At least one of us still remembers what it means to be a pirate. When that shit who calls himself 'governor' strings you up by the neck, will you protest that you never murdered anyone you didn't have to? Do you think he'll fall to his knees, apologize for his mistake, and loosen the noose?"

Jack's hand fell away from his head, slapping his thigh. "I have no illusions about my fate, Charles. But it is not I who will have to face the dead when this life has ended."

"Oh, fuck you," Vane spat. "This *woman* is more a pirate than the great Calico Jack!" He turned to fling a hand at Kate, and she recoiled slightly, misinterpreting his gesture as a move to strike. "She's even stolen your coat! Did you forget your balls in one of the pockets?"

Calico Jack wasn't amused. "Ever the comedian, Charles."

Vane sighed. Insults rarely swayed Jack Rackham. He knew this, but insults came so easily to him that he couldn't resist. There was only one thing left to try. "You should know that I only meant to uphold our . . . "—he didn't want to say the word, but he said it anyway—"friendship."

"While scheming at my stern," Jack muttered darkly.

The tall burned man had the nerve to chuckle silently at that, his shoulders quaking before he remembered himself. Vane's face seared with heat. The tips of his fingers brushed the hilt of his sword. He couldn't remember the last time he had revealed his fondness for Rackham in front of another crewmember. He was always so careful about that, lest his image be diminished.

"What is your name?" Vane asked the burned man.

"Hennessey," he replied. His teeth glinted through the hole in his cheek. "Why?"

"I prefer to know the name of a man before I gut him. I'd normally hand you off to Tanner, but I'm pressed for time."

Hennessey's hand fell to his sword. He challenged Vane

with a grin. "You'll have to best me first."

Vane arched his back and roared laughter at the sky. "The fuck I will!"

He pointed at Bruiser and Bleeder. The brothers moved in instantly, seizing Hennessey by the arms and forcing him to his knees. Hennessey glanced frantically from one to the next. Bleeder removed Hennessey's cutlass and tossed it away. "You cunts!" Hennessey cried, thrashing violently. Their combined might was too much for him.

"No sense in us dying too, Henn," said Bruiser.

"Should have been kinder to Captain Rackham, Henn," said Bleeder, glancing respectfully at Calico Jack.

"Cretinous cunts, the both of you!"

A distressed look passed over Bruiser's face. "No need for language, Henn."

Vane drew his sword, relishing the shriek of the metal as it scraped the inside of the sheath on its way out. He looked to Jack. "Is this man important to you?"

"What does it matter?" Jack shrugged. "You will kill him either way."

"True," Vane admitted. "But I'd like to know if I should distress over it afterward."

"He attempted mutiny," Kate put in with a raised finger, like a child shyly offering the answer to a question in school.

The muscles in Vane's cheeks spasmed toward an uncontrollable grin as he looked at Jack. "Did he now?"

"No one asked you, bitch!" Hennessey frothed at Kate.

She gave him a little wave goodbye.

Calico Jack didn't appear angry, merely sad. Anger would have been kinder. Anger only amused Vane, revealing weakness in his enemies. Calico Jack knew that. "What she says is true," he said after a long pause. Rackham dodged confrontation whenever possible, especially if he knew it would lead to blood on his hands. "If you're looking for my approval, you shall not have it. It never seemed to matter anyway."

Not the answer Vane was hoping for, but hardly a plea for the man's life. "That will do," he decided. He plunged his blade into Hennessey's stomach, twisting the hilt. Hennessey's molars ground noisily through the hole in his cheek, until blood-laced saliva dribbled out of the wound and down his jaw in translucent bubbles. Vane continued to twist the blade until Hennessey's eyes went dull and his head slumped forward, stringy hair falling over his face.

Vane wrenched the sword free and whipped the excess blood from the blade in a thin red streak across the white sand. Kate's eyes flashed with excitement.

"I needed that," said Vane. Truthfully, it wasn't as refreshing as he had hoped, not with Calico Jack's wretched eyes weighing heavily upon him out of the corner of his vision. *Damn him. He thinks to threaten me with his absence? I'll be well rid of him and his judgment.*

"Can't say I'll miss him," said Gabe Jenkins as he looked on Hennessey's fresh corpse. He struggled to his feet and started toward Kate.

"Don't you come near me again," she warned him with a finger.

Jenkins obediently moved the opposite direction, sweeping his hair out of his bloodied face. He joined Roman and the other two, taking a seat on a barrel and folding his arms. "That's how it always ends," he told them with a laugh, but his levity seemed forced.

That's interesting, thought Vane as he sheathed his sword. What reason would she have to be so angry? Could it be she had succumbed to the dashing young man's charms? *Maybe even Kate Lindsay needs a good fuck now and again,* he mused with a giggle.

Calico Jack raised an eyebrow. "Well, I'm happy I could offer amusement one last time. I shall return to my ship and be on my way."

"Nay." Vane cleared his throat to recover his solemnity. "I need you here when Dillahunt arrives."

Calico Jack snorted a bitter laugh. "As bait? I think not. I spotted *Crusader's* sails not two hours before I arrived. He is already here, I assure you. I will round the island and depart. I have served my purpose, though my purpose was never known to me."

Vane rolled his eyes. "You don't have to keep whining about it. I said I was fucking sorry, didn't I?"

"Actually, you didn't. You've never regretted anything in your life, Charles. That is the difference between you and me. It always has been."

Vane glanced uncomfortably at Kate, who was watching intently. Bruiser and Bleeder turned to the sea, not wanting any part of this argument.

"I would prefer you stayed," Vane murmured. He would say no more than that.

"I would have preferred being left out of your deception," Calico Jack replied. "It seems we both want something we cannot have. Here our paths must divide." He favored Vane with a civil smile that lacked any semblance of their former friendship. "May the powers grant you fair winds and following seas." He turned to the longboat, and his ponytail swayed like a pendulum as he marched away.

Bruiser and Bleeder stepped in line with their captain, flanking him, but he held out his hands to both of them. "You're staying. Captain Vane will decide how best to employ you." Bruiser and Bleeder looked at each other in disbelief.

"Before you go," Vane called after his former friend, "send Dillahunt's girl to me. I promise not to kill her, if that nibbles at your conscience."

Rackham didn't look back. "You shall have her."

"And my effects?" Gabe Jenkins called. "A coat and dagger."

"And Mr. Jenkins' effects," Vane agreed.

Calico Jack was helped up into the boat by the men inside. He faced the beach. "The girl, Jenkins' effects, and you can keep the boat they arrive in. I'll waste no more time here than I must."

As two of Calico Jack's men rowed him back to *Swift*, Vane turned to Kate and shrugged. "Fuck him."

She smirked back at him. "You'll miss him."

"Miss who?" Vane quipped. "As I look on you, all other woes seem distant."

"Poetic," she drawled.

He nodded eagerly. "My cock is on fire."

She sighed. "Perhaps an ointment would set it right?"

"I'd much rather douse its flame in your arse. What say you?" He frowned. "Oh, wait, I don't care." He snatched her wrist and dragged her toward his tent. If he alarmed her, she wasn't showing it.

Roman giggled, nudging Keet, who giggled in turn.

"Shouldn't we be leaving, captain?" Jenkins asked.

"Won't be but five minutes, gentlemen," Vane announced with a grin.

"I'd only need one," said Roman.

Jenkins furiously worked his jaw and glared down at the sand.

Vane yanked Kate into the tent. To his surprise, she didn't put up much of a fuss. Maybe she had been dreaming of him as well. He dragged her over to the desk, knocking everything off of the surface with a sweep of his arm. A map, one of his pistols, and a quill and inkwell toppled to the ground, leaving nothing for her to use against him. He grasped her waist and perched her atop the desk. His hands opened her coat and slid down her hips, which curved so splendidly. She stared absently at him as he drew near her face, hungry for her lips. "In my haste, I've had no time for women," he said.

"Somehow, I don't believe you," she replied stolidly.

"My hand has been my only pleasure."

"I could have gone my entire life not knowing that and died a happy woman."

His lips brushed her cheek, and to his delight she did not recoil. "Your complexion is a tad ghostly," he said. "Has Rogers starved you of sun?"

She grimaced. "I was cooped up in a mansion for a month. It was dreadful."

He spread his fingers through the stubborn tangles of her hair, which smelled of brine. He twirled a finger around an orange lock, drawing it forth from the red thicket. "I haven't been able to get you out of my mind since we kissed. A fierce kiss without a fierce fuck to follow is maddening."

"I don't recall having much choice about the kiss."

"I'm a chivalrous man. I'll allow a woman her fictions." He wrapped his hand around the back of her head and tilted her mouth toward his. He seized her upper lip between his lips and sucked hard. She did not respond. He might as well have been pecking at a statue, albeit a soft, lovely statue. She required more stimulation. He squeezed a breast, which was small but firm. He probed her mouth, but his tongue mashed against her teeth, which were securely clenched. After a few seconds with no leeway, he pulled back in frustration. "I haven't got all day, woman!"

"I'm bleeding."

He pulled back and looked her over. He couldn't find any blood. "You're wounded? Who did this?"

She angled her head suggestively. "No, I'm *bleeding*."

"Oh!" he exclaimed, looking downward. He grinned and leaned forward. "No wonder my nostrils were flaring. That's splendid. Blood and fucking are two of my favorite things."

She set her palm against his chest, shoving him off. "Not so splendid for me. My belly is in knots."

He pointed at the brightly illuminated walls of the tent. "But it's such a sunny, warm day."

"My monthlies are fierce, regardless of weather."

"You haven't left a trail of blood behind you. You're not one of those queer women who plugs her cunny with a bunched cloth, are you?"

Her smile was icy. "Some things are better left to mystery."

"No matter," he assured her. "If it's a concern, you may take me in your mouth."

Her smile did not falter. "Anything you put in my mouth will not stop short of my stomach."

"No doubt," he boasted.

"You miss my meaning."

His fingers found her nipple through her shirt and pinched it, twirling slightly. Her right eyelid twitched. "I will have you," he promised. "One way or the other, rightways or wrongways. Whatever hole you turn away from me leaves another unguarded."

"You say such lovely things, Charles." She grabbed his hand and pulled it away from her breast. "Is that why you've gone to all this trouble? Seems a tremendous fuss over an urge so easily slaked."

"Well, no," he admitted. "But that shouldn't stop us from taking advantage of circumstance."

"Circumstance is about to take advantage of *you*," she reminded him. "Dillahunt is on his way, if he isn't here already. Whatever you're planning, you should probably snap to it instead of toying with my tits."

"You're stalling," he grated.

She arched her long neck and laughed at the roof. Her shirt tightened across her breasts and her nipples poked against the fabric, and Vane yearned to bury his face between them. He would have her, even if Dillahunt was storming the beach this very instant. He'd leave that battle to his men. He had a conquest all his own in the confines of the tent. He was throbbing so badly that he would only require a few hard thrusts. He would meet Dillahunt refreshed and ready to spill his enemy's blood. There was nothing greater.

"Fine," Kate sighed with resignation, her head still leaning back as if she was studying the fabric of the roof. A long vein pulsed in her neck. "Let's be quick about it."

He grinned and leaned in to kiss her neck. Her head suddenly snapped forward, hair tossing in a crimson blur, and her forehead collided with his. His vision exploded with blinding flashes of color as he stumbled backwards, clutching his face. Something warm and wet ran into his eyes and over his fingers. He blinked rapidly and wiped at his face until he could see again, though what he saw was blurry. His hands were covered in blood. Pain split his brow, and his eyes felt as though they were being drawn together, like magnets crushing through the flesh that partitioned them. "Damn your thick skull, woman!"

Still sitting atop the desk, Kate was in no better shape, pressing a palm to her forehead with blood trickling down the middle of her face in a thin line, dripping from the tip of her nose. She opened one eye. "I have this embarrassing spasm in my neck," she groaned apologetically. "Acts up at the worst of times. I hope I haven't spoiled the mood."

15

KATE

The bleeding had stopped, but the center of Kate's forehead refused to stop throbbing. Small price to pay to avoid being savaged, but she wasn't sure how much more abuse her poor skull could withstand.

It didn't help that the path across the steep slope was treacherously narrow and rocky. It had been carved into the hillside by Vane's men to provide a walkway from the beach to the lake at the center of the island. Kate was convinced every step would be her last. On the far opposite side was another slope. At the foot of both slopes, at least a hundred feet down, was a channel big enough to sail a ship through. Huge chunks of rock had broken free on either side and were piled up in the water along the banks of the river.

They walked single file, with Vane in the lead, followed by Gabe and the three pirates from the beach. Kate and Calloway followed next, with Bruiser and Bleeder in the rear, making sure the women could not flee, not that there was anywhere for them to flee to.

Vane and Gabe were engaged in conversation, but Kate couldn't make out what they were saying. Every once in a while Gabe would throw a glance her way. She would always glare back at him, and he would quickly look away.

She was relieved when the sun fell beyond the top of the opposite slope. A shadow ascended over the path, bringing with it a cool breeze. Between the heat and her throbbing head, she had feared she might pass out and go tumbling down the slope into the river below.

She glanced over her shoulder at Calloway, whose head was hanging low, eyes fixed on the ground. She hoped the girl was watching where she was going. "Jaq?" she gently called.

"He knew." The girl's voice was barely above a mouse's squeak.

"What?"

"He knew."

Kate slowed her pace a little. "Who knew?"

"Guy. He knew. That's why he started acting so queer after Teach's death. That's why he couldn't look at me the same way. He discovered who I am. He discovered *what* I am. He discovered that I am Blackbeard's daughter."

Kate's heart shuddered in her chest. It was jarring to hear the truth spoken aloud. "I'm sorry," she murmured. "I wondered why Blackbeard didn't kill you. Now I know."

Calloway's face twisted as she worked through her thoughts. Kate couldn't imagine what she was going through. "I'm not sure when Teach realized I was his daughter. But he must have said something to Guy, maybe to taunt him. And it worked. Guy never spoke a word of it, but he silently blamed me for something I never even knew."

"Is that the only thing he blamed you for?" Kate asked. She

didn't bother to soften her voice.

The girl frowned and looked up. "I don't know what you mean."

"I think you do. It wasn't Dillahunt's idea to turn me in, was it?" Kate scrutinized Calloway's eyes, which were darting every direction except hers, confirming what Kate had always known. "It was *your* idea."

"It was the best solution for everyone," Calloway said with a sigh of resignation, as if she had made her peace with the decision long ago. "I wanted to keep you safe."

"Ha!" Kate laughed bitterly. "Is that all you wanted?"

"Yes!"

"Maybe I don't want to be safe."

"You're so stubborn, Kate."

Kate could no longer restrain herself. "You may not look a girl of fifteen, but you certainly act the part. If Blackbeard told Guy who you are, then you confirmed it for him by plotting against a friend who risked her life to save yours. And you wonder why he fears you? He sees your father in you, and damned if I don't see it too. You did this to yourself, Jaq."

Calloway's eyes instantly lined with water. *Damn her,* Kate thought. *She will not temper me with tears.*

"I did what I did to save you from yourself!" the girl insisted desperately. "You're always trying to get yourself killed, and you won't stop! The first thing you did when you got away from Jenkins was try to kill Guy! You should have run! You knew Jenkins would catch you if you went to the harbor, but you didn't care! You let all this happen! You want this, Kate." She gestured at the thin pathway. "You're not happy unless you're inches from death. How much longer can you last?"

Kate tittered viciously. "Nice to know you care, Jaq, but something tells me coin was the greater influence."

"Don't tell me my motives," Calloway grated through a

hardening jaw, a tear rolling through a maze of light freckles.

"Someone must. You seem perplexed by them."

"Everywhere you go, death follows. You are as much a danger to yourself as you are to everyone around you."

Kate's laugh echoed off the rocky walls. "Yet everyone thinks me the answer to all their troubles. Are you really so concerned for me, or are you more interested in retiring early from your dingy career?"

"Is that so wrong? The end result favors us both. Must my hopes fade so yours can blossom? I would merely send you back to London, to live out the rest of your life in peace, free of danger."

Kate firmly shook her head. "That's no one's choice to make but mine."

Calloway seized Kate's shoulder, sunk her nails deep, and seethed hot breath in her ear. "Your choices always come at another's expense, don't they?"

Kate angrily shrugged Calloway's hand away. "I did not ask for any of this. You're all the same. All of you! Men and women alike, it makes no difference. You foolishly heap one hope after another upon my shoulders, and you would further weight me with blame when you are left hopeless."

"Must you be so selfish?"

Kate stopped and whirled on Calloway, aiming a finger at her nose. "I am not the answer to your troubles. You only think I am, but you won't realize that until after I am gone."

The anger fled Calloway's face as quickly as it had risen, replaced by despair. Kate buried her sympathy before it could arise. She turned from the girl.

"Kate—"

"Enough of this!" Vane leaned precariously over the slope to see past the entire party. "What the fuck are you squabbling about? Bruiser, Bleeder, do something useful, like keeping the women apart. Their bleating trails along the wall and into my ears, imploring me to throw myself to my fucking death."

Vane turned and marched forward, prompting the party to follow.

Bruiser slipped past Calloway and fell in line beside Kate. The two of them barely fit side by side on the pathway, but Bruiser seemed unconcerned about the precipice at his left. Kate's arm constantly brushed the rocky wall where the hillside had been cut away.

She looked back to see Bleeder step beside Calloway with an obscene grin. "I fancied you when I thought you was a boy."

Calloway screwed up her face. "What?"

Bleeder's cheeks flushed red as wine. "That came out all wrong. I meant it romantic-like. I don't fancy boys, but when I saw you, I thought I did. Put terrible thoughts in me brain. Spent a good deal o' time trying to figure what would fit where. Was relieved something fierce when it turned out you had teats."

"I see. That's nice."

Kate turned away in disgust, only to find Bruiser favoring her with a sadistic grin. "It's thanks to you we had to kill our friend, Hennessey. We shan't soon forget that, bitch."

"I can't make anyone do anything they don't want to." She was still feverish from her argument with Calloway. She wanted to hurt someone.

"You should have kept your hole shut."

"I'm always confused which hole I should close and which I should open."

Bruiser clutched her arm, giving it a sharp squeeze and a vigorous shake that let her know he wasn't playing around. "Me and me brother will show you what your holes are good for. We're going to have our way with you before this be finished. You'll see."

Kate's forehead was throbbing intensely. "Vane won't like that."

"Vane won't know no different. We won't bruise you up none. We'll keep your face nice and pretty. But what we do down there, inside you, Vane won't never see, now will he?"

"He might. He's keen on me."

Bruiser leaned close. "Might be he is, but I wager you're worth the risk. I promise to be gentle-like, if you don't put up a fuss."

"Tempting," said Kate, pulling away. Her shoulder hit the rocky wall on her right. There was nowhere to go. She glanced at Bleeder, whose attention was diverted as he fawned over Calloway. Kate smiled at Bruiser. "Regrettably, I must decline."

Bruiser's muscular shoulders trembled as he laughed. "There's no declining me, missy. Once I set me mind to a thing, there's no stopping it."

"I feel the same way." She kicked a heel against the wall and launched herself off, barreling into Bruiser. She bounded off of him with all the force of a pebble glancing off of a statue, but that was enough to tip his balance. He almost giggled at her audacity, before he realized that he was toppling. His arms suddenly flailed in wild spirals. His fingers brushed her hair, but she reared away just in time. He yelped a short and pathetic cry of alarm before he tumbled out of view. Kate leaned over the edge to see him rolling down the slope, leaving a trail of dust in his wake, until he smacked against an outcropping halfway down. The sound of his bones snapping arrived a moment later. He rolled limply off the outcropping and continued down, not stopping until he hit the water with an unceremonious *plop* and vanished beneath the surface.

"What in the bloody hell is going on?" Vane exclaimed, halting the group. "Have you simpletons forgotten how to walk? Is it really that hard to fix yourself to a path without meandering into the fucking clouds?"

Kate shrugged innocently. "I dunno what happened. He just fell."

"You pushed him!"

Kate turned to Bleeder, letting her mouth drop open. She hoped she looked suitably appalled. "Pardon?"

"You pushed him!"

"How did I manage that, I wonder? He was so very big and manly, and I am so very small and womanly."

"You redheaded bitch. You killed me brother! Fess to it!"

She laughed. "I cannot fess to something I did not do. Did you see me push your brother?"

"Well, no, but I know he wouldn't just fall! He's never taken a spill off a cliff his whole life!"

Kate smiled sheepishly. "First time tends to be the last."

"Bring her to me!" Vane called with a frantic gesture. "I leave you with one simple task and you FUCK IT TO HELL!" The last four words echoed repeatedly across the slopes.

"She killed me brother!" Bleeder repeated.

Vane took a deep breath, closing his eyes for a minute and composing himself. "Did she? It seems no one saw it. I can only surmise that one of three things happened: he lost his balance like a helpless babe yet learning to walk; he took a stroll right off the cliff while his mind was busying itself with the perfect pair of tits; or, as you claim, he was pushed off by a woman. A fucking *woman*! I'm not sure which scenario I like less. Whatever the cause, we're well rid of him. Now bring Lindsay to me at once, or you'll join your brother at the bottom of the fucking river."

Bleeder's fingers spastically opened and closed, and Kate knew he was considering giving her a shove off the path. Thankfully, self-preservation won out. He took her by the arm and moved her up the line toward Vane, squeezing past the others. When she was close enough to Vane to feel secure, she nudged Bleeder with her elbow. He glared at her, and she very clearly mouthed the words, "You're next."

Bleeder's eyes went so wide that his eyelids practically disappeared. His cheeks trembled violently. His fingers dug painfully into her arm. And then Gabe slapped a hand on his shoulder, smiling innocuously. "Wouldn't want to do anything rash, mate."

Bleeder shoved Kate away without a care. Her heels skittered on the gravel and the toes of her left foot slipped over the edge. She started to waver, but Gabe grabbed her by the shirt and jerked her toward him. She fell against him, hand on his chest. She felt his heart thumping rapidly. He stared at her. He had cleaned up his wounds. The bridge of his nose was sliced, and his left cheek was shiny and purple. His black coat was off, slung over one shoulder. "You alright?" he asked.

"Fine." She glanced at the dagger tucked in his blue sash.

"Don't even think about it," he warned.

"I'm thinking about it," she frigidly replied.

"Mr. Jenkins," Vane interjected, "you're in charge of her. I trust you'll keep your footing?"

Gabe teased Bleeder with a wink. "I know how to walk."

Bleeder puffed up his chest. "One day, Jenkins, you'll leave your flank unguarded, and you'll never know who killed you." He turned to Kate. "But you, missy . . . you'll know, right before I shove my cock down your—"

A shot cracked against the wall of the slope. The back of Bleeder's head exploded, spewing brains and white shards of skull into thin air. Blood spurted from a little red dot in his cheek. His entire body went rigid as a plank, and then he fell from the path. He hit the slope with the grace of a sack of meat and rolled all the way down to share his brother's watery grave in the channel. His body vanished within a dark red cloud that swelled just beneath the surface.

Vane holstered his pistol. He smirked at Gabe, who was blinking away a stunned expression. "I had meant to torture them both," Vane explained with a sigh. "Shame. Tanner's toys are neglected of late."

Vane motioned for everyone to get moving. They continued in silence for a while, Kate's shoulder repeatedly brushing Gabe's. She sensed his glances, but she refused to return them. She wobbled unsteadily at one point, and he took hold of her waist. She slapped his hands away. "Only trying to help," he innocently explained.

She snorted. "Tell that to Dillahunt's crew. My friends are on that ship, you know. They're all going to die."

"Dillahunt didn't have to follow." His voice was calm, as though he couldn't care less, but she knew he did. "He knew he might be sailing into a trap."

"He shouldn't have trusted you."

Gabe nodded grimly. "I agree."

"If he dies—"

He challenged her with a sudden glower. "What do you care, anyway? You saved his life and how did he repay you? He betrayed you."

He was not alone in that betrayal, thought Kate. She swiveled her head and leaned over the precipice to see past the group. Calloway was at the very end, trudging along with her head down.

"He may not call himself a pirate," Gabe went on, "but Guy Dillahunt is no better than the rest of us, and you know it."

"It is not just Dillahunt who will die. The men on his ship were your friends not so long ago."

"Dillahunt alone is responsible for his men.

"Whatever makes you feel better, Gabe."

The edges of his jaw bulged. "People die," he growled. "You just murdered a man in front of his brother and thought nothing of it."

"He slipped."

Both Vane and Gabe shared in a hearty laugh. Gabe's mirth was a bit less convincing than Vane's, however.

"And even if I did give him a push," Kate defensively rattled on, abandoning caution, "he was a horrible man. Dillahunt's men are innocents!"

"Why?" Gabe wondered. "Because they are employed by the crown? They were not always. Most of them were pirates once."

Kate opened her mouth but quickly realized she had no rebuke. He was right.

Vane tilted his head to smirk at Kate. "Glory gets the better of a man like Dillahunt, and it infects all who follow."

"You seem to know him as well as you know yourself," she retorted. "The two of you might make fast friends, if you weren't so keen on killing each other."

Vane shrugged. "We are what we are. Dillahunt is but one of many men I must remove from my path. Examples must be made. Woodes Rogers will understand the futility of his quest. My task is arduous, but I will destroy every man in my path until there is no one left but Rogers."

Kate laughed. "Seems a little more than arduous. It seems impossible."

"When I am nested in the Governor's mansion, having my way with Rogers' wife, I will remember you said that. I'm certain you will receive the news in London."

"London," she said with a conclusive nod. "So you mean to barter me. I should have guessed." She swallowed hard and winced as pain sliced through her throat. She hadn't realized how thirsty she was. Her head was still pounding, pressure sinking into her skull from her temples. *I am surrounded by enemies.*

"Yes," said Vane. "And I won't have you damaged."

"Beyond raping me."

"I would prefer you wet and willing."

She scoffed. "Your men don't care about such things."

He managed a sincere expression, for once. "Rest assured none of my crew will lay a finger on your woefully dry cunny. They would be far less delicate than I. Martha Lindsay wants you whole, I imagine."

She wondered where Vane had heard that name. Martha's management of the Lindsay business was unofficial. "In exchange for what? Weapons?"

"You're a wise woman, Kate."

She laughed. "And what will you do when the Caribbean is yours? Proclaim yourself king?"

"'King Vane,'" he announced with a wild flourish. "I do fancy the sound of that."

"You'll need a larger ship than *Ranger*, I should think." She remembered seeing *Ranger* docked at Pirate Town. It was roughly the same size as *Crusader*. If Vane meant to engage Dillahunt on the open sea, it would be an equal match. And Dillahunt was a cunning strategist in battle, when he needed to be.

Vane laughed. "*Ranger* has fallen to the bottom of the lake at the center of this isle, but her passing helped gain me a new ship."

Kate fixed Gabe with a hard, penetrating glare. "He has a new ship, and you knew all along?"

Gabe averted his eyes and provided no answer.

Half an hour later they rounded a bend where the hillside curved off as the channel below opened upon a massive lake that hollowed out the center of the island. Kate realized she was standing on the rim of a volcano, and wondered with a shudder how far down into the ocean it descended.

In the middle of the lake was a warship, similar to the two that guarded Nassau's harbor, except this one's hull had been painted black very recently. It had three masts, each with furled sails that were as black as midnight. At the top of the mainmast flew a massive flag embroidered with a grinning white skull above two crossed cutlasses. Three rows of guns ran along the hull, one on top of the other. Even from this distance, Kate could tell this ship's armament outmatched *Crusader's*.

"Lancaster called her *Advance*," said Vane. "I darkened her up a bit, as you can see, but decided to keep the name."

Lancaster. The name was familiar. Probably one of the many captains Governor Rogers had introduced her to.

Vane hooked his thumbs through his belt and beamed proudly. "And as Dillahunt will soon discover, she is aptly christened."

Kate turned to Gabe, clutching his arm. "Gabe, what have you done?"

16

DILLAHUNT

"After we've taken his ship," Dillahunt announced down at his crew from the quarterdeck, squinting as the sun touched the horizon beyond the port bow, "I want Charles Vane's cock removed!"

"Aye, captain," said Jeremy Clemens with an enthusiastic nod. "And where do you propose we shove it?"

Dillahunt frowned. "Pardon?"

Clemens glanced nervously at his mates. "Well, more often than not this sort of request is followed by a small hole of ill nature where we should forcefully insert said appendage."

"Aye, that's true," said another.

"Truthfully, I hadn't thought that far ahead," Dillahunt admitted. "My mind has been occupied by puzzles the likes of which would cause bleeding in a smaller brain."

He shifted his weight from his wounded left foot to the favored right. He had been limping ever since losing his big toe.

Every once in a while he would forget the injury, take a confident step and crumple to the ground, clutching his foot in agony. Fitting that foot into a boot each morning was an excruciating chore that sometimes took half an hour. Over the past two or three days—or maybe more, he couldn't quite remember—he had left the boot on when he went to sleep. Terry Bell had specifically advised against that, but Dillahunt didn't have the time to fiddle with it every morning.

A timid gunner named James Early was shoved by his mates to the front of the crowd. He was thirty, with sharp features and shiny blonde hair offset by a trim black beard. He had a slight build and small shoulders. "I have a suggestion, captain."

"I'll hear it."

"Maybe we could put his cock in a cannon, strap him to a mast and fire it at his face. That way the last thing that goes through his head is his own cock."

Clemens scowled at Early. "That's silly. The cock wouldn't really be the last thing, due to the cannonball what pushes it through."

Early stared blankly. "What?"

"The cannonball would go through his head *after* the cock. So the cock wouldn't be the last thing to go through his head, would it?"

"Oh, right," Early exclaimed as comprehension bloomed.

Dillahunt smiled sadly. "It was a fine suggestion, Mr. Early. Alas, it makes no sense."

Early humbly bowed his head and fell back into the crowd.

"It's the thought that counts," someone said.

Clemens raised a finger and grinned. "Maybe we should fire two cannonballs in a row, with the cock betwixt them, so as to complete the whole picture."

"That's ridiculous," Dillahunt balked. But then he started to think about it, and the image refused to leave his mind. "But strangely appropriate."

"I always thought cannons a bit cock-like in their build," offered an older deckhand named Surley. "Especially with the wheels on either side, like big round balls."

Dillahunt stared at one of the cannons along the starboard side. *My God! He's right!*

He blinked, clearing the image from his mind. "What's your point?"

"Only that it seems bizarre to fire a cock and balls from a bigger cock and balls," Surley explained.

Dillahunt gave a dubious nod. "Yes, well, that's how men are born."

He turned to the island on the starboard side, where *Swift* had led them and then vanished. They were nearing a thin channel, beyond which he knew Vane was hiding. He had circled the island two times now, and he was just waiting for Vane to show himself. He would not recklessly sail through that channel, as the sloped walls on either side could too easily provide vantage for an ambush.

"Return to your stations, men," Dillahunt instructed.

He limped about the quarterdeck impatiently while Dumaka, who was manning the helm, watched him. He hated waiting. The sea was growing restless along with him, tossing *Crusader* in huge waves that rolled over the thin white beach surrounding the island. The sun dipped below the horizon. Vane would wait for cover of night to venture from his den.

Dillahunt looked down at two cannons on the main deck, where he had instructed his men to saw away the bulwark and allow for a long chain to stretch unobstructed between the mouths of both cannons. His extended chainshot had worked splendidly during the escape from Pirate Town, cutting down *Adventure's* mast before she could pursue. He shuddered to think how the battle with *Queen Anne's Revenge* would have gone had *Adventure* come to the larger ship's aid.

Crusader circled the island one last time, and as she approached the channel again, a dark blue sky was littered with vibrant stars.

A shadow materialized from the channel, huge and terrible, crashing through the waves with unrelenting ferocity. Dillahunt's heart pounded against his ribs, as though it was trying to burst from his chest. A gasp caught in his throat, lingering there and swelling. He gripped the rail, doing everything within his mental power to suppress a surge of panic. This was not *Ranger*. This was a frigate. *Jenkins, you skullduggerous shit. You've led me to my death.*

"That is not Vane's ship," Dumaka redundantly remarked.

"No," muttered Dillahunt grimly. He knew this ship all too well. "That's *Advance*. Vane must have repainted her."

"We cannot survive this."

Dillahunt slapped a hand on Dumaka's bulky shoulder and squeezed. "We must be precise. No mistakes." He did not feel the certainty he hoped to convey. There was no winning this, unless Vane made nothing but mistakes. And Charles Vane did not make mistakes.

"It's madness, captain," said Dumaka with a hard grimace. The whites of his eyes were huge and round against the darkening night.

Dillahunt grabbed Dumaka by the arm. "I'll not suffer your oversized lip, Dumaka. Madness or no, I am still your captain." He let go of Dumaka's shoulder and looked down on the main deck. "Prepare for battle!"

"Won't be much of a battle," Surley protested as *Advance* exited the channel and came about.

"We should turn tail, captain," said Clemens.

"Yes, I am for the tail turning," said Bastion.

"Aye," said a very young sandy-haired deckhand named

Gerry. "There's no beating that."

"Steel yourselves!" Dillahunt replied. "She is a ship like any other, and she will sink like any other. We've come too far to turn away now."

"Can't win it," said Clemens.

"You are not pirates!" Dillahunt exploded. "You will do as I say without question unless I openly welcome your doubt, which I do not!"

He pointed at Surley and Clemens. "You two, man the chainshot. Adjust elevation of the barrels to account for that heightened deck. We'll draw Vane to our starboard. Aim for the mainmast, and do not miss." Surley and Clemens rushed to their two cannons and called over gunnery crews to help them angle the barrels upward. When they were done, they fired slow matches and stood ready to ignite the cannons. The gunnery crews moved away, afraid to be caught up in the chain should only one cannon fire.

Fifteen men with muskets filed up the stairs to the quarterdeck, hurrying around Dillahunt and leveling their guns on the rail. Dillahunt checked his black pistols to make sure they were loaded properly. He clutched the hilt of his sword to remind himself of its presence. He had a feeling they wouldn't get out of this without being boarded. He removed his tricorn hat and tossed it aside, as it would only serve as a target for an enemy sniper. He swept back his hair, which was woefully longer than usual. He wished he'd thought to have Calloway trim it before sending her off with Jenkins, but the thought of shears in her hands unnerved him.

Calloway, he remembered.

She would likely be on that vessel. He hoped she was wise enough to keep her head down when the fighting commenced, assuming she was still alive. *Jenkins might have done away with her as soon as he and Rackham left Nassau, the traitorous dog.*

Then again, Calloway had already shown a knack for surviving life-threatening scenarios. *She'll probably outlast me.*

Advance approached swiftly, a black monstrosity that swallowed all light, seemingly moved by a supernatural wind that simultaneously rendered *Crusader* sluggish and unwieldy, despite *Crusader's* smaller size and sleeker frame. The flashes of multiple chase guns illuminated *Advance's* bow. Intense booms sounded a moment later. A cannonball impacted the starboard bow, shattering the bulwark. Another tore through the spanker just above Dillahunt's head, and he ducked instinctively.

"The next volley will be closer," said Dumaka.

"So will ours," Dillahunt replied. And when *Advance* was almost parallel to the starboard side, he bellowed, "FIRE!!"

Cannon fire brightened both decks, and thick white trails of smoke extended across ships. Three of Dillahunt's crew were perforated. He heard a scream from the deck of the enemy ship, but he couldn't be certain if anybody had been hit.

"Fire chainshot!" he commanded. "Take out their mast!"

Surley and Clemens moved to light their cannons, but Surley's head snapped back and blood spurted from a hole in his forehead. In all the commotion, Clemens didn't see Surley fall, and he set the match to his cannon.

"NO!!!" Dillahunt screamed, flapping his arms madly to get Clemens' attention.

It was too late.

Clemens' cannon fired, but Surley's did not. The cannonball spiraled back toward the deck on a ten foot tether. Surley's unfired cannon shook in its carriage, but remained a steady anchor. The long chain whipped back around as Clemens stared at it with a vacuous expression, frozen in place. Comprehension showed in his widening eyes. The chain sliced through his waist, and his upper torso lifted into the air as the lower torso crumpled beneath him, legs buckling, with nothing above instructing them to remain straight. When his upper half landed, guts slithered out of him like snakes and splashed across the deck in a torrential red wave. As the crew ran about, many slipped in the gore and fell on their rears or bellies.

A roar of laughter went up from the enemy ship, which was swiftly followed by a merciless hail of gunfire. Three rows of cannons fired in near-perfect synchronization. A volley of cannonballs punched through *Crusader's* starboard bulwark, obliterating dozens of men in an instant. Three granados thumped the deck like stones, and everyone still standing scattered away, though many were too slow. The deck exploded in three places, and white clouds billowed toward the sails. Splinters rained back down. The deck ran red with a glistening layer of blood that sporadically reflected stars through dwindling gaps in the smoke.

Dillahunt saw Bastion duck as a cannonball zipped over his head, pulverizing the man behind him. Bastion turned around with wide eyes, staring at the man he'd inadvertently allowed to perish.

Farley scrambled to help the gunnery crews, which were growing lighter by the minute, but he was too cumbersome to be of much use. James Early shoved him away, yelling, "Get to safety, you fat fool!"

Both halves of poor Jeremy Clemens slid to the port side and collected between two cannons, leaving behind a trail of intestine and other bits Dillahunt couldn't identify.

Another cannonball bounded across the deck, catching young Gerry's left leg. The impact sent him flying into the port bulwark, and he flipped up and over the edge, spiraling end over end into the rolling sea while screaming, "Nooooooo!"

Several cannonballs shredded the sails of the fore and main masts. One end of the main staysail snapped free and whipped violently in the wind. "Secure that sail!" Dillahunt screamed, though it was unnecessary, as his men were already dutifully rushing to it. But each of them was shot down by musket fire before reaching the sail. "He hunts like an animal," Dillahunt observed in horrified awe. "Dividing the herd and picking off the weak."

"He hunts like a pirate," Dumaka said.

Two of the musketmen on the quarterdeck were struck. One of them was killed instantly, shot through the eye, while the other fell back and clutched his throat, blood spurting through his fingers. His terrified eyes locked on Dillahunt. The captain ignored the dying man in favor of the living, but when he returned his attention to the main deck, dying men filled his vision.

This battle could not be won. The first broadside had been devastating. A second would finish *Crusader*.

Dillahunt desperately scanned the enemy ship as it sailed past. *Advance* was sailing through the giant cloud of smoke that had collected from the cannons of both ships, already starting to turn, preparing to make another pass. *Crusader's* sails were in tatters. There was no way they could outrun Vane now. Dillahunt crushed his knuckles against the rail. If only they could slow *Advance* somehow. He needed to buy *Crusader* enough time to escape.

"Do we run, captain?" Dumaka asked.

Dillahunt shook his head. "She'll catch us."

The enemy ship came about, and *Crusader's* surviving crew diligently reloaded their guns and cannons. Dillahunt looked to *Advance's* hull, crashing through tremendous waves that rose like pyramids out of the water, and in the deep plunges between the waves he glimpsed the underbelly of the ship, which would not normally be exposed beneath a calm water line. He drew his cutlass and pointed it downward. "Train all fire betwixt wind and water!"

Gunnery crews went to work aiming their cannons downward.

Dillahunt turned to Dumaka. "After this next engagement, bring us as close to the island as possible. We're abandoning ship."

"Captain?!"

"It's our only chance. We're outmatched."

The dark shadow of *Advance* was nearing again, her bow slicing through the thick haze, her port to *Crusader's* starboard. *Vane is wise,* thought Dillahunt. *He exploits our already diminished starboard from a fresh angle.* Dillahunt looked downward again between the waves. He permitted himself a dour smile as he raised his arm to give perhaps the most crucial order of his life. At the very least, Vane wouldn't walk away from this battle without a limp. "FIRE!" he screamed.

Crusader's cannons bombarded *Advance's* lower hull with a satisfying harmony of concussive beats, splintering wood and sending tall plumes of water to splash against the curve of the upper hull. A fine mist arched away from *Advance* and sprayed Dillahunt's face. He glimpsed some confused faces staring downward over *Advance's* bulwark, probably wondering why he wasn't attacking their deck.

Advance unleashed another volley at *Crusader*, killing dozens more. A large chunk of the hull shattered. A cannon toppled through the crevice, taking two wailing gunners with it. Their shrill cries were silenced when they hit the water.

Four more musketmen went down beside Dillahunt, two of them fatally struck. The third was hit in the shoulder and the fourth grazed in the scalp, both bleeding profusely. Dillahunt did not react; he merely stepped forward to get a better look at *Advance's* lower hull. Water was pouring into several breaches. The damage had been done. Vane's crew were no doubt rushing to plug the leaks, but that would give Dillahunt and what was left of his crew just enough time to escape to the shore.

"Make for the beach," Dillahunt instructed Dumaka.

"Aye, captain."

"Reload the cannons! We're not done yet!" Dillahunt yelled down at the main deck. He hoped enough men were alive to carry out the order. Smoke washed over the ship like waves over a beach, and Dillahunt couldn't see who was alive and who was dead. The deck was an indistinct mass of rolling bodies and occasional movement. He could only guess at how many he had lost in just two broadsides.

The dark hulk of *Advance* started to diminish in the haze as *Crusader* pulled away, making for the island at a sluggish speed. The beach felt so very close yet so very far, and the ship seemed to be slowing to a stop. Dillahunt looked to the sails, which were flapping uselessly, with smoke pouring through the many holes. Men scaled the ratlines to adjust and repair them. Two were shot on their way up. One fell to the deck with an abrupt *thud*, while the other dangled limply by his feet, caught in a net, with blood draining from a hole in the center of his chest.

"She's coming back, captain."

Dillahunt squinted until he saw the bow of *Advance* pierce the mist like the muzzle of some great hound, ever persistent. "Keep them on our starboard," he told Dumaka.

"Our starboard is weak, captain. One more broadside will sink us."

"Yes, and Vane is tempted by an open wound." Dillahunt turned to the main deck. The smoke had cleared a bit, and he saw more movement than he expected as men prepared the cannons. The deck itself, however, was barely distinguishable through the heaping mounds of corpses. "Fire when ready!" Dillahunt instructed. "We will use the smoke to cover our escape into the longboats on the port side while Vane engages our starboard."

"What do we do once we're on the beach?" called Early.

"One predicament at a time," Dillahunt shouted back. "Fire!"

"But captain, at this range we won't—"

"We don't need to hit anything!"

Early angled his head doubtfully. "You heard the captain," he told the others. The gunners fired, and the ensuing smoke that poured from the barrels formed a massive white shroud that blanketed *Crusader*.

"That's it, men," Dillahunt called. "Abandon ship!"

Every last man raced to the port side, stumbling over bodies to get there. Dillahunt clapped Dumaka's shoulder, urging him to follow as he hobbled down the steps to the main deck. The thick cloud of gunpowder stung his eyes, but he refused to shut them. The men were lowering a longboat on cables into the water. Others were diving off and swimming toward the beach.

"Captain," gasped Farley as he approached, his cheeks red and glistening with sweat. "What about Lieutenant Winnie?"

"Wincott!" Dillahunt remembered, slapping a hand to his forehead. He had locked the lieutenant in the brig, down in the hold, to prevent him from raising an alarm when they left Nassau in pursuit of Jack Rackham's ship. He hadn't let Wincott out since.

"We could just leave him," Early suggested.

Dillahunt glanced starboard, but he couldn't see through the smoke. Still, he could sense *Advance* closing fast, preparing to unleash a final devastating bombardment. "Shit."

"Might be he's already dead," said Dumaka.

"That will not quiet my conscience should we survive this," Dillahunt sighed. "I do not expect a former pirate to understand."

"No one will think less of you, captain," Early insisted.

Dillahunt's mind was made up. "You men go ahead without me."

"But sir," Farley protested, "what about the boat?"

Dillahunt looked to the beach, which must have been eight hundred meters off. The tide had carried the ship closer to shore. Despite the heavy waves, some of his men were already halfway there. "It's a short swim," Dillahunt replied. "We'll meet you there."

"Short swim?" Farley sputtered.

"Don't fret, Farley," said Early. "You're going in the boat."

Dumaka stepped forward. "I will get Wincott, captain."

Dillahunt wondered how far into the hold Dumaka would get before he turned around and claimed Wincott was dead. "No. You go with the others. They'll need your sword if they meet pirates on the beach."

Dillahunt turned away from them, limping toward the main hatch. With all the smoke and dead bodies, it took him a moment to find the opening. He started down the stairs, taking caution not to slip in all the blood that had drained down the steps. He drew his sword and stuck it in every other step for leverage.

He reached the bottom and weaved through a maze of crates and barrels. Two chickens squawked as they fluttered around his feet, hysterically flapping their useless wings.

At the opposite end of the hold Dillahunt found one of the small iron cages that constituted the brig. He had occupied one of these cages himself once, and he wished such a poorly incarceration on no man, but he hadn't known what else to do with the stubborn lieutenant.

Wincott was sitting up, resting the back of his head against warped bars, as if he had violently impacted the metal. His body was perfectly intact, but his head hadn't been so fortunate. His skull had been punched in from the nose up, pulverized into a gooey soup of bone and flesh and tufts of a white wig. The left eyeball was missing, and the right was resting in brain matter. His tongue drooped over the teeth of his lower jaw, which jutted in a repulsive underbite. In his lap was a blood-soaked nine-pound cannonball that had probably fallen there after hitting his head.

Beyond the cage was a hole where the cannonball had penetrated the hull. Beyond the hole Dillahunt glimpsed the looming silhouette of *Advance* through the haze.

"Apologies, lieutenant," Dillahunt said, and hobbled for the stairs as fast as his injured foot would allow. There would be time enough for guilt later.

He hoped.

As he stepped out onto the main deck, a chain of deafening booms sounded from the starboard side. He wasted no time, bursting into a sprint and ignoring the pain that seared up his leg. He hopped over corpses, accidentally stepping on one of them. The cannonballs impacted the hull behind him, and the deck tilted precariously beneath his heels, increasing his pace as the port side slanted toward the water. Something erupted, impacting his eardrums. His coat flattened against his back, the tails whipping up around him. The world was suddenly washed in glorious amber light. The ship jolted sharply and hurtled him into the air like a catapult. His sword slipped out of his hand. Bodies tumbled along the deck, piling against the bulwark. The hull groaned. Leaning sails flanked Dillahunt's peripheral vision, but he hurtled past them. He aimed his good foot at the bulwark as he soared toward it. He set his heel squarely on the rail and bounded over it like a stepping stone in a pond. For a long, slow moment, he seemed to be suspended over the water, which roiled ferociously beneath his feet.

He didn't remember impacting the water.

One instant he was above the water, and the next he was under it, jerking his head this way and that to locate the surface. There was no sun to tell him which way was up, and his brain seemed to be twirling in his skull.

Thunder sounded somewhere behind him and a tremor shuddered through the water, pushing him further down. He looked up and saw the massive white canvas of a sail sinking toward him, little fish scattering beneath it. He thrashed in the water, fighting to gain momentum before the sail could envelop him. He kicked his legs and swung his arms, refusing to look up again. He felt something hard press down on the back of his right leg. Maybe a yardarm, but he wouldn't look to confirm. He withdrew his leg and kicked hard against whatever it was, using it to thrust himself forward. A moment later, his fingers brushed through ripples of soft sand. The water was shallower here than he realized. He felt along the bottom until his knuckles scraped a large rock outcropping. He grasped it and pulled himself along.

When he surmised he was far enough away, he swam in the direction he hoped was up. He saw tiny pinpoints of light twinkling beyond the rolling waves, and he knew he was going the right way. A few seconds later he was greeted with fresh air. He inhaled in an enormous, heaving gasp.

Once he had recovered his breath, he turned himself around and saw what was left of *Crusader*, resting on her side with both masts beneath the water. Flames chewed away at her exposed starboard, producing massive black columns of smoke.

Beyond that he could see *Advance* swinging past. The shadows of its crew huddled close to the rail, scanning the water. The frigate wouldn't be able to venture any further in without running aground in the shoals, but Vane's marksmen were not to be underestimated.

Dillahunt swam for the beach.

Early and Bastion splashed into the water when they saw him coming. Dillahunt was glad to see Bastion alive, as he had lost him in all the commotion. They helped him toward shore, passing the longboat, which Farley was still inside of. "Get out of there, Farley," Dillahunt snapped at him.

"Safer here," Farley gasped.

He drew one of his pistols and examined it. The powder was soaked. "The enemy may come for us any moment."

Farley peeked over the rim of the boat. "Really?"

"They'll want to finish us off, most like," nodded Early. "That's what I would do if I was Vane."

Farley scrambled over the edge and hit the water with a tremendous splash.

"Where's Dumaka?" Dillahunt asked, looking around.

Early and Bastion exchanged glances and shrugged.

Dillahunt looked up at the daunting rocky hills just beyond the little beach. There were plenty of outcroppings and boulders, but getting up to them would be a chore. "If the enemy comes for us, we'll have to take shelter in those rocks."

"The climb looks mean," said Early.

"A cutlass in the belly is meaner," said Dillahunt.

"Vane smart," Bastion said. "I don't think he'll finish us. Maybe just leave us here."

"That's a favorable way of looking at it."

Bastion frowned, missing Dillahunt's sarcasm. "Not really. Leave us here, we starve."

Dillahunt checked himself for wounds, but other than a few scratches, he was fine. Not all of the survivors would be so lucky, however. "Anyone see Terry Bell?"

"Terrible?" Bastion grimaced. "He go over the side. I look for him in the water, but he don't come back up."

"Where's Winnie?" Early asked.

Dillahunt turned a grimace toward the sand.

"Can't save them all," Early offered helpfully.

Dillahunt scanned the men on the beach. There were about

forty, maybe less. He felt ill. "I've saved less than a third, it would seem."

There was a concentrated orange flash from above, and then a crack, so distant and dull that it was nearly lost to the crashing of waves over the shore. One of Dillahunt's men, who he couldn't recognize in the dark, stiffened suddenly and fell into the sand. Several more flashes brightened the rocks above, and then a pattering of musket balls kicked up little puffs of sand. Three more dropped dead.

"They're in the hills!" Farley shrieked, shuffling clumsily back into the water. "They're in the hills! We're doomed!"

"Farley, get back here!" Dillahunt ordered. He pointed at the longboat. "Drag that ashore! We need cover!"

Farley ignored him and splashed into the water. Early and Bastion and three other men dragged the boat ashore and tipped it on its side, angling the keel so it faced the hillside. They took shelter in the hollow while Dillahunt watched the hillside. The gunfire had temporarily stopped.

"Get down here, captain!" Early insisted.

Dillahunt knelt beside one of his dead crew and retrieved the man's cutlass. Not as precise a weapon as his rapier, but it would have to do.

"Captain!" Bastion yelled.

"I counted ten shots," Dillahunt said. He joined his men behind the boat as they strained to keep it angled without letting it fall on top of them. "They're reloading, or on their way down."

"We've had it, captain," Early said. "It's no use."

"No guns, powder all wet," Bastion said. "Only cutlasses."

Six more men joined them behind the boat, hunching low. The rest had probably scattered along the beach, running separate directions. Dillahunt doubted he'd see them again.

"I count a dozen of us," he said, glancing over the group.

"We may outnumber them. If so, they will remain perched above rather than come to us."

"Farley!" Early exclaimed as Farley stumbled back onto the beach. "Get under here!"

Farley lumbered up and collapsed, coughing hoarsely.

"So what do we do?" Bastion wondered.

"We wait for the next round of fire," Dillahunt answered. "Then we make for the hillside, scaling it and taking shelter under the rocks. We'll taunt them from our hiding positions, draw their fire, and continue up until we've reached them."

"Engage them?" Farley sputtered.

Dillahunt nodded. "I don't think they expect an attack. Vane stationed them on the hill in anticipation of our arrival, hoping to keep us on the beach. He must have suspected we would flee here once he sunk . . . " He trailed off and bit down hard, unable to utter the name of his beloved ship. The loss was dwarfed by the amount of crew that had already perished. How would he explain this to Rogers? *One predicament at a time,* he reminded himself. He would be lucky enough to survive the next hour.

"I'd rather just stay here."

"Maybe Farley is right," Bastion said.

Dillahunt looked to the sea, where *Advance* had come to a stop beyond the flaming mound of *Crusader*, which was gradually sinking. "Either way, we're dead. If we attack the hill, we may at least retrieve their guns."

"How far up are they?" Early wondered.

"Near the top," said Bastion, letting out a heavy breath as he struggled under the weight of the boat. "Long climb."

"We can make it," Dillahunt assured them. "We must make it. Everyone, ready your cutlasses. If you've no blade, retrieve one from the dead on your way to the hill."

They waited.

After a long time, Dillahunt popped his head over the top of the boat. A flash illuminated the rock, casting rough shadows. A shot glanced off of the keel of the boat. Nine more flashes followed. Dillahunt ducked. "Now!" he said.

"I'm not going up there!" Farley blustered. "I can't go up there!"

"No one wants you to go anyway, Farley," Early shot back. "You're too broad a target." They released the boat and it landed upside down over Farley, encasing him within. He let out a muffled cry from underneath.

Before they got twenty paces, Dillahunt skidded to a halt in the sand. His heart seemed to drop into his stomach. He collapsed to his knees. Early, Bastion, and the others stopped beside him, gaping in disbelief.

What looked to be fifty dark figures cascaded down the hill like a human wave, the reflection of *Crusader's* flames glinting in their shiny cutlasses. Shots rang out, billowing the sand all around Dillahunt and his men in a thick perimeter.

"Back to the boat?" Bastion asked.

The thumping of his heart steadily slowed as he watched the enemy figures descend toward the beach. They moved as one, in a near-perfect pattern. They had planned this well in advance. "We cannot win this," Dillahunt said, letting his shoulders sag. "Throw down your arms, men."

The others did as instructed. "This is it, then," said Early, angrily tossing his blade into the sand.

The horde swept down onto the beach and quickly circled Dillahunt and what remained of his crew, aiming pistols and pointing cutlasses. Their faces were difficult to see in the night.

A pirate with short, curly blonde hair and red and black striped breeches approached with a big smile on his ugly face. "I'm Roman," he greeted, offering a little bow. The other pirates laughed boisterously at that. "You must be Dillahunt?"

"I am.

"Well fuck me if that isn't a stroke of fortune," Roman said. "Good to see you alive, captain."

"Soon to be remedied, I expect," Dillahunt returned.

"Nay. Captain Vane hoped by some scant chance you might elude a sword." Roman surmised the remainder of Dillahunt's men. "Can't say the same for the rest." He snapped a finger. "Kill them all."

A dozen blades lashed out before Dillahunt could react to Roman's order. He could only watch as his men were impaled, nearly all at once.

Early fled from one blade only to run right into another, which slid into his neck with the ease of a knife through warm butter.

Bastion was the only one smart enough to drop to the sand and scurry between two pirates' legs. Dillahunt lost him in the commotion.

When the pirates withdrew, Dillahunt's men lay dead in the sand.

"This one nearly got away," said a pirate with painted hair. He and another held a squirming Bastion between them.

Roman licked his lips and aimed a pistol at Bastion's chest. Bastion's eyes rolled toward Dillahunt, desperate for life. Dillahunt could only shake his head in silent apology. *I've failed you all.*

"Let's see how fast he can run," said Roman. "Release him."

The pirates moved away from Bastion, allowing him a clear line of escape.

Bastion didn't budge. He looked to Dillahunt again.

Run, Bastion.

But he didn't run.

Roman stepped forward, until the barrel of his gun was within arm's-length of Bastion. "Run, lad."

Bastion looked at Roman and lifted his chin. "I do not run."

"I'll give you to the count of ten."

"I do not run."

"Bastion," Dillahunt spoke up, unable to keep quiet any longer. "RUN! That's an order!"

A pained look perverted Bastion's brown face. He would not disobey an order. He was a good crewman. One of the best Dillahunt had ever known. He wondered if he'd ever told him that. He hoped so.

"Aye, captain," Bastion sighed. He turned and started up the gap the pirates had left for him.

"Ten," Roman said at once, and pulled the trigger. Blood sprayed from between Bastion's shoulder blades. He let out a yelp of alarm before collapsing into the sand. He didn't move again. Roman shoved the pistol into his belt and turned to Dillahunt with an apologetic smile. "Never was good with numbers."

Dillahunt's teeth ground so hard he thought they might shatter. He didn't care. It didn't matter anymore. He had lost everything. His ship. His crew. Even Calloway. He had willingly handed it all over to Vane. He had been so stupid, so impulsive, and now everyone around him had paid for it.

"Kill me," he told Roman. "Just get it over with."

"I'd love to," Roman replied. "But Vane would have my head." He drew something cylindrical and shiny from his striped breeches and offered it to Dillahunt. "Go on, take it."

Dillahunt opened his hand and Roman slapped the object into it. It was a spyglass. "What am I to do with this? Birdwatch?"

"Birdwatch," Roman laughed. "That's funny. He's funny, right mates? His crew is dead at his toes and he makes a jest."

"Aye, he's a riot," returned another stolidly.

"There's something Vane wants you to see at first light. We'll be well on our way to the ship by then, leaving you to your island paradise. You hold onto it for now, and just before the sun comes up, you train that glass on *Advance* over yonder." Roman flaunted a serrated grin, revealing yellow teeth. "A parting gift from Captain Vane to you."

"How thoughtful," Dillahunt murmured distantly as his gaze fell on the corpses of his crew.

"What's this?" one of the pirates called. Two of them had wandered over to the overturned boat and were presently lifting it up. They rolled it over, letting its keel land in the sand, and Farley was revealed, curled in a fetal position. "Looks like one of Dillahunt's hogs made the swim to shore. Didn't know hogs could swim!"

Farley raised trembling hands and sputtered something unintelligible.

"I think he went and pissed hisself," laughed Roman as he started toward Farley, drawing his cutlass.

"Wait!" Dillahunt protested. He had completely forgotten about Farley.

Roman turned to give Dillahunt a perplexed frown. "Wait for what? Is he someone important?" He looked down at Farley. "Are you someone important?"

"No, sir, I am not important, I swear on my mother's grave."

"There you go," Roman told Dillahunt. "From his own mouth."

He plunged his cutlass into Farley's belly.

17

CALLOWAY

The fire sizzled and steamed as waves lapped at what little of *Crusader's* keel remained above water. The sea around the ship churned and bubbled like a witch's cauldron as the last pockets of air escaped from within. Plumes of smoke rose from holes in the hull, merging into a single column that was giant and black against the purpling early dawn sky, blotting out the swiftly fading stars.

Calloway hadn't slept all night. Vane had forced her and Kate to watch the battle, commanding a lanky pirate with colored hair to make sure they didn't flee to the hold or the shelter of a cabin. Two cannonballs and more than a few musket balls had come dangerously close, and Calloway wondered if Dillahunt had considered that he might kill her. He must not have cared. Or maybe that was exactly what he wanted. Not that it mattered now. It was unlikely he had survived the massacre. If her life meant so little to him, she saw no reason why his death should concern her.

Though she couldn't muster much sorrow for Dillahunt, seeing the smoldering carcass of *Crusader* diminish into the sea tugged at her heart. Before sunrise, the ship would be gone, with no trace that it ever existed. She had called that ship home for over a month, and its crew had become an extended family of sorts. She had been through so much with them, including a prolonged stay in the brig. The best of Dillahunt's men had not so long ago crewed as pirates under Benjamin Hornigold, before various mutinies confused the ranks. It didn't matter where any of them had come from, no more than it mattered that she had come from a brothel. The important thing was they had found their rightful place for a time. Too short a time.

She fixated on a deep maroon cloud in the water, where one of Dillahunt's men had tried to swim for safety, but he went the wrong direction and was quickly taken apart by *Advance's* swivel guns. There were limb-sized chunks bobbing on the surface. She wondered who those body parts belonged to. One of her friends? Or maybe a random deckhand she had never bothered to get to know?

She was struck by a dreadful thought.

Was she looking at what remained of Bastion? *Please, no,* she silently prayed. But even if that wasn't Bastion, there was no way he had survived the bombardment. She hoped he had died fast and painlessly. That was all she could hope for now. Bastion was a good man, and she couldn't stay angry with him for spurning her advance. He was loyal to his captain to the end, for all the good it had done him.

Vane's crew crammed every inch of the deck, and the wretched stink of sweat and grime invaded Calloway's nostrils. They hungrily leered at the ruin of *Crusader*, licking their lips and twitching like starved animals. Their numbers had increased after longboats were sent to shore to retrieve the men Vane had stationed in the cliffs to ambush Dillahunt in the event that his men fled to the beach, which is exactly what they had done.

The last of these men were climbing aboard. Roman was the final pirate to step on deck, sporting a grin as wide and curved as a crescent moon. His curly blonde hair was shiny with sweat. "All dead," he informed Vane immediately. "Save for one."

"Dillahunt?" Vane barked hastily.

Roman nodded portentously. "Fortune smiles, captain."

"Fortune indeed," Vane agreed with a smug smirk.

So he is alive. Calloway wasn't sure how she should feel. She knew she should be relieved. She stuffed a hand in her pocket, closing her fingers around Dillahunt's toe, which she had stolen before leaving his cabin. The flesh was stiff now, and it smelled bad, but she hadn't been able to part with it. She had always been comforted by dead things, though she never told anyone, knowing they wouldn't understand. She didn't understand it herself. When she was five, growing up in Port Bayou St. Jean, before her mother whisked her to Nassau, she had captured a little frog in a swamp she liked playing in, and she kept it as a pet in a little wooden box. One morning, a month later, the frog died because she forgot to give it water. She didn't want her mother to see what had happened, so she hid the frog in her pocket until she could find a proper place to bury it. But for the rest of the day, she found herself clutching the tiny corpse. She kept it for another week, often running her fingers over the hardening skin, soothed by its texture. When her mother finally noticed Jacqueline's hand vanishing one too many times, she made her turn out her pocket, and promptly berated her.

Until recently, clutching Dillahunt's severed toe had calmed her nerves in much the same way her dead frog had. Now, it did nothing to soothe her. She had clutched it too tightly and too many times, draining it of all its sedative energy. Now it was just a dead thing in her pocket. It might as well have been a pebble.

Kate's hair infringed upon her peripheral vision, and she tried to ignore it, but she would have had better luck ignoring a fire spreading at her side. They hadn't spoken since their heated words on the hillside, and Calloway meant to keep it that way. There was nothing more for them to talk about. Kate was too stubbornly obsessed with running wild, no matter the cost to those around her. Calloway couldn't believe she had once looked up to this woman, who only helped others when it served her benefit. Of course Kate had rescued Dillahunt and his crew; Dillahunt had been her only way out of Pirate Town.

Calloway wished she had trusted her first instinct and kept Kate at a distance. She wouldn't make the same mistake again. She prayed London would be far enough away. However this ended, Kate was going back.

"Is this what you wanted, Jaq?" Kate asked, jutting her chin indicatively at *Crusader*.

Calloway kept her eyes fixed on what remained of the ship, but Kate's hair was impossibly luminous even in the gloom. Each lock that tossed in the breeze dared her not to look. "This is not my doing."

"As luck would have it, it's not," Kate granted. "But you had no idea Gabe was loyal to Charles Vane when you blurted Dillahunt's plan to Rackham. What were you thinking?"

"Hasty words born of anger," Calloway reminded her. "I wasn't thinking."

"No matter your intent, the blood of all those poor men could just as easily be on your hands."

"And you know all about bloodied hands, don't you, Kate?"

"Yes," she gently replied. "And I'd spare you the regret."

Calloway whirled on her. "Don't expect me to believe you regret a single choice you've ever made. You waltz about without a care." She savored the fleeting look of astonishment that passed over Kate's face, for it was a rare thing to glimpse.

"You think me inhuman?"

Calloway shifted her gaze past Kate's shoulder to indicate Charles Vane, merely one of many horrible people she had met in her relatively brief travels. "Not at all. You're perfectly human. And you're right where you belong."

Kate didn't follow Calloway's glance. Instead, her eyes fell to the hand that Calloway had stuffed deep in her pocket. Calloway realized somewhat sheepishly that she was still clutching the toe. She released it and withdrew her hand. Kate smiled shrewdly, as though she had stumbled upon some great secret that no one else knew. "It's convenient for you to despise me now, when you would use me for personal gain, but I don't think you hate me as much as you would like, Jaq. No more than you hate yourself."

Calloway's throat swelled with a fury that threatened to suffocate her. "Don't pretend we are alike."

Kate took a step forward, so confident, so sure of herself. "You want the same thing I want. There's only one person standing in your way. Just as Nathan stood in my way, before I left him behind. My freedom was too important. There were other ways, of course. There are *always* other ways. I took the path that was most convenient for me at the time." She aimed a finger at Calloway's nose. "Do not tell me I have no regret. I am forged of it, and I am stronger for it."

Calloway smirked. Something about Kate's anger calmed her, maybe because it was usually so difficult to muster. This felt like a small triumph. "And when another innocent person comes between you and your freedom, what then? Leaving a man to the gallows is easy when you don't have to watch him die. What if you had to do it with your own hands? Would you? Could you?"

"I do not shy from killing," Kate said.

"Oh, you've killed plenty of evil men. I killed a man in Pirate Town, did you know that? He was going to rape me. I stuck a torch in his belly and watched him burn. It was easier than I thought. But he was not innocent. I don't believe I could murder an innocent person. Could you? For something so trivial as freedom?"

Kate took another step forward. "Freedom is not trivial. I would do anything for it, as would you. An innocent person would not move to block my path." Her face softened regretfully. "But it needn't come to that, Jaq."

"It's too late to make a play for my sympathy," Calloway said with a sigh of finality. "You've made it clear where you stand."

Kate retracted her step. "I didn't realize I'd taken sides."

"Your own and no other."

"We needn't be adversaries."

"Only one of us can be free." Calloway angled her chin away in hopes of concluding the conversation.

Kate did not take the hint. "If that's how it must be, then may the best woman win."

Calloway was trying to think of a retort when she was distracted by Gabe Jenkins, who was approaching Vane. She wished her eyes could bore a hole through his pretty face. He hadn't so much as glanced at her since their confrontation aboard *Swift*. "Are we done here?" he asked Vane. "Dillahunt is defeated. There's nowhere for him to go. Starvation is the worse fate."

Vane's lips fumbled to preserve his smirk. "Thank you, Mr. Jenkins, but I had figured that out all by my fucking self."

Gabe humbly bowed his head, and a few loose curls of hair

dangled before his face. "Of course you had."

"So what are we waiting for?" a fat, bald pirate wondered, searching about for an answer to his rhetorical question.

Vane aimed a finger at Calloway. "Bring that bitch to me."

Roman stomped toward Calloway at once. Her legs hit the carriage of a cannon before she even realized she had been backing up. Roman raised both hands and slid huge leathery fingers around her throat. His breath was hot and rank upon her face.

"I said bring her to me!" Vane barked. "I didn't tell you to strangle her."

Roman looked disappointed.

"What are you going to do?" Kate asked, trying not to sound concerned.

But Calloway knew better. *She is so silly.* Only moments ago they had agreed to be enemies, and already Kate had forgotten. *Why does she care?*

"We're going to slice her throat and toss her over the side, of course," Vane replied, as though the answer should have been plain for all to see.

"You can't be serious!" Kate protested, her raspy voice breaking.

"Serious? Nay! I will *laugh* as I dispatch her." He drew his sword and elbowed Kate out of his way in a single motion.

"But she's not even important to him! Why else would he throw her to the wolves? This is pointless!"

"She's right!" Calloway gasped, prying at Roman's fingers.

Vane's smirk was fully renewed. His mind was made up. "Men like Dillahunt rarely know what they love until they've lost it. Give her over."

Roman jerked Calloway around and shoved her at Vane. She skidded to a halt just inches from the tip of his cutlass. Vane lowered the sword and reached for her. Her hair was just long enough to grab, and he clutched a handful, wrenching her toward him. His wet lips brushed her ear. "Mayhap Dillahunt will spend his final days fucking your waterlogged corpse. I do hope the tiny crabs that find their way into your hastily slackened cunny don't impede his desire. I would have a go myself, if only there was time."

Calloway's heart was thumping a league a minute. She couldn't believe this was happening. Dillahunt had forced her onboard this ship, and now Vane would murder her for it. Kate had embraced a perilous lifestyle, and her only punishment would be a return to London. *I'm only fifteen,* Calloway realized. She had barely had a chance to thrive outside the walls of a brothel. This wasn't fair.

"Let me do it," announced a low and carefully modulated voice.

Everyone looked at Gabe.

"Why you?" Vane asked.

Gabe shrugged. "She meant to murder me. I'd like to return the favor, if it's all the same."

"It is not," Vane growled. "Rarely am I afforded the opportunity to kill a woman. My pleasures are lessened of late. I must take them where I find them."

"You got to kill Annabelle," Gabe reminded him, "and I wager this death would be disappointing in comparison."

Vane lifted a wistful gaze to the sky, which was now violet and brightening by the minute. Most of the stars had faded. "That was a glorious demise, true enough. When I shut my eyes I can still see her bloody ruin sinking into the broken deck."

"This girl is nothing to you," Gabe went on. "I'll gladly forfeit my share for the pleasure."

Vane seemed positively stunned. "Will you, now?" He looked at Calloway. "This boy must really want you dead. Me?

I merely want Dillahunt to die slowly, his bones aching for vengeance he can never fulfill. Your speckled face *does* fill me with unquenchable, inexplicable loathing . . . but most faces do. I suppose the end result is all that really matters." He smiled at Jenkins. "Do as you please, Mr. Jenkins. Just make sure you toss her over the side after, so Dillahunt can see, and be quick about it. We have business in Mariposa."

"Mariposa?" said Roman. "I don't recall a vote."

"Fine, we'll call a fucking vote, if it makes you feel better. Who's for Isla de Mariposa?" Vane held up his hand and looked around. The majority of the crew raised their hands in turn. Vane looked at Roman. "Fucking satisfied?"

Roman scowled and reluctantly raised his hand as well. "Just wanted to stick to practice, is all."

"That's why you're the new quartermaster," Vane replied sullenly.

"Me, captain?"

"Shall we take another vote? I trust the odds will favor you."

Roman couldn't resist a grin. "Thank you, captain."

"Snap to it, Mr. Jenkins," Vane urged. He looked at the sky. "It should be bright enough now for Dillahunt to watch his beloved bitch plunge to her death."

"It's too far," protested the pirate with colored hair in his screechy birdlike voice. "How will he see it?"

Vane withered. "You may wish to sit down for this, Keet, but I've given Dillahunt means to see from a great distance; a mystical contraption called a spyglass."

"You don't have to do this," Kate said.

"Of course I don't," Vane snickered with delight. "That's what makes it so exceedingly cruel."

"Dillahunt is defeated!"

"Lindsay, if you don't tend to your mouth, I'll see it bound for the remainder of our journey."

Gabe smiled at Calloway as he approached. Her heart beat rapidly, but she maintained a level chin. "Only fitting," she said.

"What is?" Vane wondered.

"I killed her mother," Gabe answered easily.

Vane's eyes gleamed. "How fortuitous."

"Gabe, don't do this!" Kate pleaded.

Vane's arm moved like a bolt of lightning, the back of his hand dashing Kate across the jaw. She crumpled against the barrel of a cannon. "What did I tell you about that mouth?"

Kate glared at him. "I'll kill you for that."

Vane laughed. "I could do much worse, Kate. Don't forget that."

Kate looked past him. "Gabe, please!"

Gabe did not remove his eyes from Calloway. "I'm afraid I have no choice."

"You're right," Calloway hissed. "Because if you don't kill me, I promise you I will scour the seas until I've found you, and when I do, I will take from you the one thing you hold most dear."

"And what do I hold most dear?"

"The very thing that compelled you to kill my mother."

He chuckled softly as he drew his curved dagger from his sash. The blade glinted amber as it reflected the fires claiming *Crusader* in the distance. And then Calloway glimpsed a young woman's freckled face within, lips quivering as she struggled not to surrender defiance to fear. Even in that brief glimpse, defiance was clearly losing the battle. "Then for my sake," Gabe said, "I had better cut deep. Turn around."

"I will not." Her voice sounded so tiny and pathetic. She was about to die and she couldn't even muster a forceful protest.

Vane was grinning, enjoying the show. "I forgot how much

I missed the theater."

Kate, still hunched over the cannon, locked eyes with Calloway. "Jump!" she urged.

For some reason, escape hadn't even occurred to Calloway. But before she could spring into motion, Gabe lashed out and clutched her arm, spinning her around. She tried to keep her feet planted, but her heels spun in place.

"You can't do this, Gabe!" Kate rasped.

"I think you'll find that I can," Gabe replied. He shoved Calloway's belly against the bulwark. The blade descended past her face. The sharp edge bit into her neck. She pulled back, but Gabe pressed himself against her, pinning her. He breathed a whisper into her ear. "I'll make this quick. I promise."

"How kind," she seethed. "Did you promise my mother the same before you did her in?"

"She felt no pain." His voice was hollow.

"And what do *you* feel, Gabe?"

He did not answer. Did he truly feel nothing? He had sounded so penitent when he told the story to Kate. Was it all an act to win her over? *Of course it was,* Calloway realized. *He fancies her.*

"She'll hate you for this," Calloway whispered.

If that worried him, he didn't reveal it.

"May I ask you something?" she asked in a gentle, sweet voice.

The blade eased from her skin. "Ask."

"Do you believe in ghosts?"

He hesitated. "Never saw one."

"One day you will," she promised.

"Fair enough," he said.

The muscles of his arm tightened as he drew the dagger across her neck, and she felt an icy sting slicing into her skin. She was shocked by how little it hurt. She had expected far worse. But when she glanced down she saw blood lining the edge of the shiny blade as Gabe lowered the dagger. She held her breath, afraid to gasp, knowing that no air would pass through her throat.

A collective roar of laughter thundered the deck and clapped against the sails. Amid that, small and nearly lost, was a woman screaming in horror. *Kate,* she thought. *Will you miss me, despite all I've done?*

And then something slammed sharply into her back, her legs lifted up behind her, and she felt strong hands grasping her ankles. She slid over the bulwark, plunging headfirst toward the water. Her feet scraped the hull halfway down, and the world spiraled until she saw the sky, almost blue now. The sun would be up in minutes, but she would not see it. The last face she glimpsed was that of Gabe Jenkins. His expression was blank, one eye obscured behind a curl of hair, the other locked on her. His jaw was tight, his brow pinched. She would remember that face. She would take that face into the abyss, even if it meant forgetting all else.

He was lost from her sight as she continued to spiral, until she saw the water again, only inches from her face. She heard herself hit with a muffled *clap*. The impact stung her cheeks and set a fire in her neck. The pain didn't last long. She sank immediately, blood seeping from her wound into murky clouds that billowed like dark red smoke on either side of her face. She tumbled into the abyss, sliding through warm sheets of wet silk. A slow euphoria spread from her core, trailing through her limbs and into each finger and toe, until she was tingling all over.

This is a nice death, she mused.

18

FREDERICK

Mariposa, thought Frederick Lindsay with a shudder. *I hate this place.*

In the middle of the night, with only a slim crescent of a moon to provide illumination, Isla de Mariposa was little more than two great mounds ascending from the ocean, as though a giant, ample-bosomed woman rested just beneath the surface. Mariposa was roughly sixteen miles wide, and was actually two islands—which on a map resembled the elegant wings of a butterfly—connected by a thin bridge of rock that was nearly half a mile long. Both isles were shrouded in dense jungle. The bridge sloped steeply into the ocean on either side, and the natural pathway along the top was dangerously thin. Time had etched away at it, and one day the bridge would likely crumble and separate the isles entirely.

As he crossed the ship toward the bow, Frederick craned his neck to make sure their red and blue flag had been lowered from the mast. He had given the order well in advance, before the island had come into view on the horizon. Though Isla de Mariposa's shape was graceful, most of the seedy inhabitants were anything but. To approach under British colors was certain death. Mariposa was the only major pirate hub in the Caribbean that hadn't been compromised by Woodes Rogers. It had steadily increased in activity after Nassau fell, and was guarded by heavily armed pirate ships at all times. And despite *Rampart's* formidable compliment of cannons, she wouldn't last long against a fleet of converging ships.

As *Rampart* sailed closer, the dim amber halos of torches and bonfires came into view, peppering the western isle, which was heavily populated with huts and treehouses scattered along the mountainside. At the base of the isle, along the widest open beach, was a bright concentration of firelight.

Compared to the vibrant western isle, the eastern isle was dark and mysterious. There was an easily accessible beach, but Frederick had heard tales of a festering bog that swallowed anyone who ventured deeper into the jungle. On the island's southeast end, a long and sharp cliff jutted hundreds of feet over the sea like the bow of some colossal prehistoric ship. At the top of that cliff was a bonfire, small from this distance, but probably twenty feet tall up close. Far below the pointed cliff was the outline of a small sloop.

Few travelled to the eastern isle. Frederick had heard rumors of a vile pirate family that had lived there for over a century, increasing their numbers solely through inbreeding, and cannibalizing anyone fool enough to venture into their territory. It might have been wild gossip, but no one was willing to test the theory.

Rampart dropped anchor just offshore of the western isle's largest beach, amid fifty or so ships. Scouts had no doubt taken notice, but this was not *Rampart's* first visit, so she was allowed entrance without incident. Any ship fool enough to fire a cannon in this port would be sent to the depths before it could retreat.

On the beach, pirates were scattered about raging bonfires, laughing and singing and playing flutes, drums, and stringed instruments. The smell of roasting meat wafted over the waves.

The most obnoxious merriment, however, trailed from Keelhaul Tavern, which was located on the eastern end of the beach, suspended above the water on a short pier, glowing warm and golden in the night. Reflections of orange light from the many windows danced in the water just below the pier. On his most recent visit, Frederick had narrowly escaped death in that tavern, bargaining frantically at the point of a dagger, until the pirate who menaced him begrudgingly relented. The promise of no less than two dozen tankards of ale bought Frederick his life. And before he had left, he was forced to buy a hundred more for the disgruntled pirate's crew. That visit hadn't been as fruitful as he had hoped. He hadn't been looking forward to returning, but business was business, and this time he would not leave empty handed.

Frederick returned to the main deck, where his first mate, Clarence, was needlessly supervising as two young deckhands lowered a boat into the water. Clarence waved his arms, as though conducting their movements through some form of sorcery. He was tall and lanky, with a shiny bald head. Beneath a long nose he sported a well-groomed handlebar mustache. He wore a red and white striped shirt and black breeches fastened by a thick black belt with a huge brass buckle.

When he saw Frederick approaching, Clarence opened his mouth, then paused. *Fantastic,* thought Frederick. *He has something very important to say.*

"What is it, Clarence?"

"Shall I accompany you ashore, captain?" Clarence asked.

His breathy voice was pitched an octave higher than most men, with traces of a lisp. His extravagant mustache mostly concealed the etching of a harelip, but sometimes Frederick spied the cleft in his upper lip when he spoke.

"Not necessary," Frederick replied curtly. He didn't need his first mate questioning his every action. Going ashore was the only time he was free of the man's nagging.

The boat touched down in the water below with a splash, and the two deckhands rolled a ladder down to it. Frederick pointed at Harrison and Desmond. He would need strong bodyguards in case any fights broke out in the tavern. He had never been very skilled at fighting, and his punches yielded little force. "You two. I'll ask that you stay close at all times."

"Aye, captain," both men said at once.

A whisper caught Frederick's ear. "Ask him!" He turned to see Thomas Hobbs being nudged repeatedly by his friend, Jack. Hobbs was a timid young deckhand of small build and fair hair. He couldn't have been more than sixteen. "Ask him!" Jack urged. Hobbs jabbed an elbow in Jack's ribs, shutting him up.

"Ask me what?" Frederick wondered, strolling over with his hands locked behind a straightened back. With his limited stature, he couldn't afford to slouch.

Clarence adopted as strict a tone as his breathy voice would allow. "The captain has business, boys. Go play in the hold."

"It's fine," said Frederick. He smiled at Hobbs. "What is it you wish to ask?"

Hobbs glanced about and fidgeted with his hands, while his friend looked away.

"I haven't got all night," Frederick reminded the young man.

"Aye, captain. It's just, well, we've all heard rumors about Keelhaul Tavern, and I was wondering if I might have earned some shore leave."

"He ain't never been with a woman," Jack giggled.

Hobbs smiled sheepishly.

Clarence scowled and plucked at one of the handlebars of his mustache.

Hobbs was shorter than Frederick and just as lanky as Frederick had been at the boy's age. "You may come along," he replied at last. "You're too small to offer much aid in a fight. Stay out of the way if anything goes awry."

"That I will, captain," Hobbs replied, grinning broadly. "That I will."

Clarence threw Hobbs an angry glare as he stepped between the boy and Frederick. "Are you sure this is wise, captain?"

Frederick shrugged. "One more won't hurt."

Clarence's eyelids fluttered irritably.

Frederick and the others descended into the boat and crossed the choppy waves toward the beach, cutting between bobbing ships of various sizes, while pirates peered down from above. Harrison and Desmond rowed the boat directly between two galleons, and Frederick held his breath. The galleons were drifting so closely together that, for a horrifying instant, he was certain the little boat would be crushed between their massive hulls. But they slipped through un-squashed, and he remembered to breathe.

The boat came ashore within a hundred paces of the tavern. Desmond and Harrison helped Frederick over the front, taking care this time to not let his boots get wet. The walk to the tavern was slow and sluggish thanks to the soft sands, and Frederick nearly toppled twice. A group of pirates gathered around a bonfire started pointing and laughing. Frederick bit back an angry retort.

They started up a path of flattened stones that led up to the short pier Keelhaul Tavern was built upon, currently suspended ten feet above the water, though it neared twenty feet during a low tide. The structure was basically an upended ship, long and rectangular, modified into a building. It consumed the entire pier, with several boxy partitions that had been added onto the stern section. There were many rooms, but none of them saw much sleep, thanks to the fair compliment of exotic strumpets who escorted patrons to their rooms every night. Dozens of open windows had been carved in the walls, allowing the wicked giggles of strumpets and the drunken laughter of pirates to trail outside. The roof was the keel of a ship, with a jagged hole at the very top that glowed from within. A long mast protruded through the opening, like a harpoon through a whale, reaching fifty feet into the air, with a rope ladder scaling its length. The mast was topped with a little crow's nest and a massive black flag that had been left blank, as a message that all pirates were welcome. In the crow's nest Frederick glimpsed the silhouettes of a man and a strumpet, groping desperately at each other.

Thomas Hobbs' eyes yielded the eager and terrified gleam of a boy anticipating the loss of his virginity, amplified by the glint of the tavern's light. Harrison noticed it too and clapped Hobbs on the back with a massive hand. "Hobbs aims to make some memories. Plenty of willing girls here. Don't be scared. They'll take good care of you, they will."

Hobbs tried to shrug apathetically, but his bony shoulders twitched spastically. "If I see one I like."

Harrison cackled at the stars. "Take care with your coin, lad. Some of these girls are pricier than others. But don't go too cheap, or she'll reward your stinginess with a pestilence you won't soon be rid of, if ever."

"Harrison speaks from experience," Desmond said, without the faintest trace of a smile. Frederick was never sure when the man was joking.

They made their way around the stern of the upended ship, where most of the rooms had been sloppily added on, boxy partitions protruding beyond the keel above. It made for a very narrow walkway along the pier, no more than two feet wide at its slimmest point. Hobbs stood on his toes to steal glances through the windows as strumpets howled their pleasure and men grunted and growled like animals. Frederick snapped his fingers at the boy and said, "Keep moving, lad. We're almost inside."

They passed the stern and reached the main entrance near the middle of the long structure, flanked by two torches on tall poles. They entered beneath a crude awning made of a decrepit sail littered with holes. There was no door, for the tavern never closed, not even at this late hour. The entrance led directly into the main hall, which was a wide open room teeming with over a hundred pirates who were howling laughter, singing out of tune, and bellowing stories at the top of their lungs. All of them were trying to be heard over the next man. The pirates sat about dozens of round tables, guzzling ale from large pewter tankards and fondling beautiful strumpets of every shape and color. Torches burned brightly in metal sconces along the walls. Running down the middle of the room, a hearth was set in a long trench in the deck, piled with coals that smoldered orange. At the head of the hearth, the great mast that speared the roof had been fixed securely in the planking of the deck, surrounded at the base by barrels and crates and coils of rope. Atop one of the highest crates, a gangly pirate with ginger hair was playing a catchy tune on a wooden flute.

The convex roof was thatched with beams stretching from one side of the room to the other, and two pirates were sitting up there in the dark, drinking ale. Frederick had no idea how they had managed to get up there, and he didn't want to know how they were going to get back down.

A bar hugged the wall opposite the entrance, with several stacked kegs of ale and bottles of rum and wine. A huge barkeep with a frizzled, unkempt beard was pouring drinks as frantically as possible as pirates rapped their fists on the bar in a bombastic rhythm that was in accordance with the flutist's lively tune.

Toward the stern, a bulkhead separated the main hall from the rooms in the back, where strumpets were no doubt attending to their inebriated guests. A giant anchor was fixed in the middle of the bulkhead wall, pointing downward like an arrow.

In a darkened corner toward the bow, a naked strumpet was squealing as an equally naked pirate plowed her, his muscular buttocks clenching with every thrust. An audience of three pirates sat at the nearest table, sipping from their tankards as they watched the couple. Apart from those three, no one else seemed to care or even notice the open fornication.

Frederick strolled into the room as casually as possible, not wanting to attract attention. Many of the pirates were so colorfully dressed that Frederick's rather indistinct attire didn't stand out. He zigzagged through the tables. The air was thick with humidity and smoke, reeking of sweat and an overabundance of perfume. He scanned the tables, looking for familiar faces, pirates that he had conducted business with. A drunken man barreled into him and belched hot, horrid breath in his face, then continued on and crashed onto a table, toppling it and catapulting two empty tankards across the room. A roar of laughter went up from the former occupants of the table, and they all poured ale over the unconscious drunkard's head.

Frederick checked to make sure Harrison and Desmond were staying close. Hobbs was ogling a pretty strumpet with blonde hair, long and curly, glowing like gold in the firelight. Her shirt was unlaced and her medium-sized breasts were bare for the entire tavern to see. She must have spent most of her days in the sun, because her skin was nearly brown, though she had a distinctly Caucasian face. She giggled playfully at Hobbs, and his eyes lit up. He started toward her like a man in a trance. Frederick rolled his eyes. "Some use he is," he muttered to Harrison.

Harrison cackled. "Goldy's too expensive for the likes of him. I spent three month's pay on her last time we was here. It was worth it."

"You'll be spending no coin tonight," Frederick reminded him. The tavern was even busier than last time. A fight could break out any minute.

At a table situated in a corner between the bar and the aft bulkhead, he saw a familiar face. Trejean was a very dark-skinned Jamaican with long white hair that spilled over his huge shoulders, perfectly combed. He had a leathery face with heavy creases spreading from his eyes. A hemp necklace with the gleaming white skull of a small bird dangled from his thick neck. He wore a red shirt, wide open to bare his powerful chest, brown breeches, and tall boots. Last Frederick had heard, Trejean had taken over ownership of Keelhaul Tavern from Horace Reginald, under somewhat suspicious circumstances.

"Frederick Lindsay," Trejean greeted. His grin was interspersed with three gold teeth. "This be a surprise." He calmed his two young, mean-looking bodyguards by setting his hands on their shoulders as he stood. The bodyguards shared the exact same face and build. They were obviously identical twins. "Don't worry about this one," Trejean told them. "Him no harm a fly. He be family."

"Don't look like family," one of the bodyguards skeptically observed.

"He be what I say he be," Trejean barked. "This little man do me great service. That's more'n I can say about real family."

Frederick dipped his head in accord. *Then we have some-*

thing in common, Trejean. His prior dealings with Trejean had left him conflicted. He had divulged the trade route of British merchant vessels, knowing that the information might result in the deaths of innocent sailors. At the same time, he sold Trejean a large compliment of slaves, and Trejean assured him they would be put to good use as free men. That had eased Frederick's conscience somewhat, but Trejean had been trading with pirates such as Edward Teach at the time, and Teach had destroyed many innocent lives.

Trejean motioned to the empty chair across from his. "Have a seat, Lindsay. See your men attended to, on the house. Whatever they desire."

Frederick smiled shrewdly. "So long as they have the coin."

Trejean clapped his bodyguards on the back. "Off with you." But he stopped the one on his left. "Bring Lindsay a drink. Him look thirsty."

"Not necessary," Frederick said, sitting down. He discharged Harrison and Desmond with a nod. They started for the bar without delay.

"I do not drink alone," Trejean replied, tapping his tankard. The twins departed, and he sat down again.

"So Keelhaul is yours now?" Frederick asked.

"Aye, it be. Horace meet him maker. Unfortunate accident, that."

Frederick set his hands flat on the table. He knew that not being able to see a man's hands made Trejean nervous. The Jamaican had survived more than a few attempts on his life. "How did poor Horace die?"

Trejean shrugged, but the faintest hint of a smirk played at the edges of his lips. "Him take a nasty spill off the crow's nest atop the tavern. Fall through the hole, come crashing down in that firepit." He thrust a hand at the hearth. "Him body catch fire before we get him out."

"Horrific," Frederick muttered, trying not to envision it. One of the twins returned with a tankard of ale, filled to the brim, and set it before him. He stared at the foam spilling over the top. He had never cared for ale. It always gave him a pounding headache. "You and Horace are partners, yes?"

"Aye," said Trejean. "Full ownership come over to me when Horace die. Not the way I want it. I do what I can for me old friend." Trejean respectfully covered his heart and closed his eyes for a moment. And then he smiled. "But this be old, dark business. You come to talk about the future, yes? What can I do for you, little man?"

Frederick ignored the diminutive epithet, reminding himself that Trejean didn't intend it as an insult. This was no time to be thin-skinned. Vane was probably already on his way. "Dark business brings me here as well, I fear, but with the promise of a high reward. Captain Charles Vane is coming to Mariposa."

Trejean's lips peeled from his expensive teeth in disgust. "This Vane be no friend to me. Him sink one of me ships in the harbor last time he come. I do nothing to offend, and him sink it anyway."

"He is quite ill-tempered," Frederick agreed, though he suspected Trejean wasn't being entirely truthful. Surely he had done *something* to goad Vane into sinking his ship. Not that Frederick cared. In fact, this was exactly what he had hoped to hear. "I'm sure he has made many enemies, and his death would not go uncelebrated."

"Aye," Trejean agreed as a whimsical grin lit his weathered face. And then the grin faded, replaced by hard sobriety. "You want the man dead? Why?"

"Vane is a troublesome business partner. I worry for my life. Yet he has something I need."

"And if him be dead, you be free to take it."

"Precisely," Frederick said, inclining his head.

Trejean considered this for a moment, clasping a hand over the bird skull at his breast and stroking the little cranium with his thumb. New wrinkles formed along his brow as he privately deliberated. At last, he looked up. "Cannot help you with this, little man. Vane be too dangerous."

"I see," Frederick murmured, staring down at the grimy cracked wood of the little round table. It seemed as though his heart had plummeted into his stomach, and it wasn't about to stop there. He felt sick. If Trejean was too afraid to take on Vane, he'd have a hard time finding anyone else who wouldn't scoff at the offer.

"The boy you come in with must be brimming with coin," Trejean said, stretching his neck out to see over the crowd. "Look like Goldy take him in the back rooms. She not known for her generosity."

"What?" Frederick hardly cared what Hobbs was doing right now.

"I better be about me business." Trejean stood and offered his hand. "I do not like giving bad news."

Standing seemed a slow, sluggish affair. Frederick shook Trejean's much larger hand, looked him in the eyes, and even mustered a smile. "It was good to see you again."

"Likewise, little man," said Trejean, and then made his way toward the back, probably to make sure Hobbs could afford Goldy.

Frederick fell back to his chair, sighing heavily. The pirates laughed and fought and danced and sang all around him, oblivious to his misery. He supposed he had no choice but to deal with Vane, but there was no way he could go through with the rest of the plan. He had been double-dealing against England since his first jaunt through the Caribbean, but always in small ways that would never rouse suspicion. Merchant ships were set upon by pirates all the time, and it was always attributed to ill fortune. No one would suspect their coordinates had been compromised.

But Vane's plot was too bold.

Despite what Frederick had told Vane, the disappearance of so many weapons would not go unnoticed. Eventually, everything would be traced back to Frederick, and even if he escaped execution, which was the only conceivable punishment for such treachery, he would never be allowed to return home. Not even in the New World would he find sanctuary. His name and likeness would be spread to the far corners of the world, furthered by Martha Lindsay, who would do everything she could to absolve herself from her treacherous son by aiding diligently in his capture. Frederick would have to hide on some island somewhere, sweating away his life in the damp heat.

That was no kind of future.

All this for one stubborn woman who thinks herself a pirate, he realized, and not for the first time. He wished there was another way, but he knew there was not. Katherine was the only path into his mother's heart. By now, whoever Martha had sent to Nassau had likely arrived and been informed by an apologetic Woodes Rogers that Katherine had been kidnapped once again. Frederick would be a fool to turn away now.

Of course, the problem could simply solve itself. Vane was a pirate, and pirates were a dying breed. Vane knew this, and that's why he had turned to Frederick. Without Frederick's help, how much longer could Vane hope to survive?

He's lasted this long, a little voice reminded Frederick. *Maybe he'll last just long enough to find you.*

And give you to Mr. Tanner.

Frederick snatched up the full tankard of ale before him and gulped it down. Ale spilled down the sides of his mouth, and his eyes started to water. Before he knew it, he had drained the entire tankard. It was an awful brew that tasted coppery, although he wasn't sure what a good brew should taste like. No matter. It would numb his senses. He had always had a low tolerance for spirits. Thomas had introduced him to wine when Frederick was barely a teenager, and Frederick had passed out after a single glass.

He shifted in his chair and looked around. His head felt heavy and sluggish, his vision blurring in and out of focus. The ale was already taking effect. The waves of heat ascending from the hearth entranced him. The pirates and strumpets at the tables beyond the rippled transparent sheets were hellishly distorted, their laughter deep and ominous. The flutist's never-ending tune was no longer playful; now every note was low and protracted. Frederick blinked, pulling his gaze from the hearth.

Harrison and Desmond were enjoying the company of two fat whores at a table midway across the room, their backs to the hearth. Harrison raised his tankard in a toast to Frederick and beckoned for him to come over. When Frederick didn't budge, Harrison shrugged at Desmond. "I tried."

A curvaceous figure slinked into Frederick's vision. She wasn't old, but she wasn't young. Her skin was so pale that not even the soft glow of the hearth could warm it. Her thin, sandy blonde hair was pulled up in a bun, with only a few curls dangling strategically over her temples. Streaks of silver ran up the bun from her temples. Her prudish, pursed lips made her less attractive than she might have been if only she knew how to smile. But her figure curved pleasingly in all the right places, especially her hips. She moved toward him, never blinking, holding his gaze. Her hips swayed beneath the folds of a gaudy red dress. Milky white breasts jiggled as she approached.

She set a slender hand on his shoulder and winked mirthlessly as she circled him. Something about her stern demeanor excited him. A creamy leg emerged from the skirt of her dress and crossed over one of his. She nudged his crotch with her shin as she leaned into him, showing him the long line of her cleavage. A large red areola slipped over the top of her gown as her breasts slid up his chest, toward his face.

He took hold of her shoulders and pushed her off. "I'm in no mood," he told her.

"A man is always in the mood," she replied in a cold voice.

"I am in dour spirits."

"Let me raise them."

"Nothing will raise them."

She glanced downward. Her shin was still pressed against his crotch. Her hazel eyes lifted to meet his. "*Something* is rising."

He fixated on a thin vein running along her bosom. For a moment, he felt like he was going cross-eyed. He shook his head, but that only made it worse. "Are you well, love?" she asked in a flat tone that implied she didn't really care. It was just a formality. Or maybe she just didn't want him throwing up on her.

"I'm fine."

"Too much to drink?"

"Not enough." Maybe she was right. Maybe he needed something to take his mind off of the future, however long or short it would prove to be. He looked into her eyes. She had tiny crow's feet, difficult to see from afar, easy to spot up-close. She was on the verge of losing her stern beauty. In five years or less, only the stern would remain. Her breasts were still firm, but they were too large to stay aloft and supple for long. Soon they would deflate like sails without wind. He took them in his hands and thumbed a nipple through the thin cloth of her red gown. She slid into his lap.

"What's your name, love?" she asked. Another formality.

"Frederick."

"Pleased to meet you, Frederick. I'm Charlotte."

"You don't look like a Charlotte," he said. She looked like his earliest memories of his mother. A little prettier, but just as humorless.

She rolled her eyes and sighed. "I can be anybody you like."

He had never been with an older woman, and something about that excited him. He glanced over to the table in the dark corner on the opposite side of the room, where the muscular pirate was still ramming his strumpet while the three pirates watched. She had stopped squealing and was resting the back of her head against the table and looking at her nails, as though she had finished long ago and was dutifully waiting for him to follow suit. Her smallish breasts reverberated with every thrust, and Frederick was engrossed. But then something caught his eye; a small burn on her right hip in the shape of a T.

"What is that?" he asked Charlotte. "That burn on her hip?"

"That's a brand, love. Missy tried to run off, and Trejean gave her a reminder she couldn't forget even if she wanted to. She's not the only girl with a T. Not always easy working for a pirate. A girl has to be careful. Just the other day I heard tell of a highborn woman, by name of Lindsay, who got herself kidnapped a while back. Now she calls pirate ships her home. Can you imagine? A woman *choosing* to live with pirates? She must be daft."

Frederick angled his head in interest, pretending as though he didn't know who Katherine Lindsay was. "What else have you heard about this woman?"

"They say she killed Captain Griffith."

"Did she? She must be very brave."

"Or very wicked," Charlotte objected. "I liked Griffith."

"Had him, did you?"

"Twice," she said, almost smiling at the memory. But she

remembered herself and returned to her stern demeanor. "Neither here nor there, I suppose. What can I do for you, love?"

Frederick clutched her tightly, taken by a wild idea that he never would have suggested while sober. "What if I take you right here?"

She might have smiled, but it was gone before he could be sure. "In front of all these pirates? You're awfully sure of yourself."

"A room, then," he conceded too hastily.

"Follow me," she said, hopping off his lap and taking his hand and guiding him toward the back rooms. She was half an inch taller than him. Not that he was surprised. Almost everyone was taller than him. He craned his head to gawk at the massive anchor as he passed beneath it. Looking at it made him dizzy. If it fell off the wall, it would crash through the deck and keep going until it hit the water beneath the pier. He might have lingered to stare at it for the remainder of the night, but Charlotte tugged on his hand.

She took him through a slim passageway, with the curved upturned hull on one side and slim doorways draped with crude hemp tarps on the other. Flickering candlelight lined the edges of the tarps, and moans echoed into the passage. They passed five doors before Charlotte found her quarters and led Frederick inside. It was a small box of a room, with a little bed and a tiny square table with a baseless half-melted candle burning dimly at an angle, wax seeping into the wood. Next to the candle was a tankard of ale, half full. Frederick snatched it and drained it, setting the tankard back down.

Charlotte winced in disgust. "That's been there a while."

"I don't care." He didn't want to give his brain a chance to think right now.

She moved him to the bed and made him sit down while

she unlaced her dress. His eyes followed the dress to the floor, and then slowly scaled her body back up, from her petite feet to her somewhat stocky legs to her full hips to her slender waist to her large breasts. He reached out to cup her breasts, but she caught his wrists and set them at his sides.

She lifted the shirt over his head, obscuring his vision for a moment, and when he saw her again, her face had changed. She had more wrinkles than he remembered. The streaks of silver in her hair were more prominent. Her skin was mottled along her scalp. He stared into stony eyes, hoping for a glimmer of concern, but all he found was a hopeless little man reflected within her growing pupils, girdled by darkness. His vision blurred in and out of focus. Every time he blinked, her features were further diminished. She was aging before his eyes. He couldn't remember what he had found so attractive about her in the first place. What sort of spell had the ale played on his mind?

She kneeled and went to work unlacing his breeches, but he realized he was no longer aroused. He seized her hands. "No," he said.

She looked at his crotch and chuckled. It seemed she had found her sense of humor at last. "You drank too much, love."

"Stop calling me that." His mother had called him that. For a while. Before he became a teenager. Before he set his sights on his cousin and ruined everything.

"Oh, you're too serious," she said, folding her arms beneath her breasts.

When he looked at her face again, he shuddered. The woman who had brought him into this tiny room was gone, replaced by his mother. She stared at him disapprovingly, judging him. He squeezed his eyes shut for half a minute, focusing on the outline of the candle's flame, which had burned into the right side of his vision. And when he opened his eyes again, Martha remained. She was laughing. As always, her laughter bore no smile. She was one of the only women he had ever met who could laugh without smiling.

"Stop laughing," he said.

She shook her head. "You're hopeless, Frederick."

"How do you know my name?"

"You told me, remember? What are you, two oars short of a boat?"

"You can't talk to me that way. You're not my mother. You're just a whore."

He hoped she would shut up, but she kept on laughing without smiling, and her sagging, wrinkled breasts swayed unpleasantly. He suddenly wanted to throw up. He looked around, but all he found was the empty tankard. He went for it, hoping it would be large enough. He leaned over and clutched the cold pewter. The room tilted, and his head felt like it was going to topple off his shoulders.

She cackled. "There's no more ale in there, you stupid little—"

He swung the tankard toward her without thinking. He heard the impact of metal against flesh and felt the vibration shudder up his arm, but he didn't see it; he must have blinked. She crumpled to her side at the foot of the bed, clutching her head and whimpering. He dropped the tankard and stared, clarity returning to his vision in a sobering instant.

His mother was gone, and Charlotte had returned, her eyes squeezed shut and her mouth twisted in pain. The base of the tankard had carved a red crescent in her scalp, which was just starting to bleed. She touched the wound, then opened her eyes and looked at her hand, and after a moment of comprehension she loosed a horrible shriek at the sight of her own blood.

"Wait," Frederick said with raised hands. He started to get up. "I didn't mean to—"

She flashed him a look of terror, like a wounded animal caught in the sight of a much larger predator. No one had ever looked at him like that before. She scrambled to her feet and flew naked from the room, crashing through the hemp drape and tearing it from the doorframe. Three brass hooks fell to the deck with faint clinking sounds. Frederick stared at the empty doorway, wondering what he should do. Soon he heard footsteps thumping down the passageway, and he realized he'd waited too long.

Trejean appeared, with his twin bodyguards just behind him, peering over either shoulder. "Why have you bloodied Charlotte?"

"She was laughing . . . "

Trejean's bodyguards slipped past him and entered the room, converging on Frederick. They took either arm and dragged him out into the hallway while Trejean watched with a disappointed scowl. "Have to throw you out now, little man. Apologies. Can't have patrons uglying up me whores, you understand?"

"She was laughing at me!"

"You drink too much, little man."

"Stop calling me that!"

"Call you what I like in me place of business, little man. You come back when you sober."

"I won't ever come back!" Frederick spat over his shoulder. "Not ever!"

"I can live with this."

The twins dragged Frederick into the main hall, and all the pirates and strumpets turned to stare at him. The flutist finally stopped playing, lowering his flute. Charlotte was near the bar, getting her face attended to by two other strumpets. She briefly locked eyes with Frederick before shying away in fear.

Frederick frantically scanned the room for Harrison and

Desmond, but found no trace of them.

He squirmed in the twins' clutches as they dragged him to the exit. Before they got him outside, he twisted around and roared, "TWO CHESTS OF GOLD TO THE MAN WHO BRINGS ME CHARLES VANE'S HEAD!"

Several heads perked up. A low chorus of jittery whispers filled the tavern. After a moment, the flutist burst into a frenzied tune.

Trejean looked around and laughed nervously. "Him crazy. Him crazy!"

Most of the tavern burst into laughter, but Frederick noted several pirates staring at him contemplatively. And then he was dragged out the exit and hurled from the pier. His shirtless belly slapped the water first. He inhaled too late and swallowed salt water. He struggled to keep his head above the surface, hacking violently. When he recovered his breath, he paddled for shore. He crawled up the beach and collapsed in the sand. The waves that washed up alongside him did little to drown out the laughter that trailed from the tavern.

The wet sand felt nice on his cheek. Maybe he would fall asleep here. Maybe he would dream of a better life. Pleasant dreams were the best he could hope for now. When he woke, he would have no choice but to deal with Charles Vane. And he could only pray that his impulsive request in the tavern did not reach Vane's ears. But with his luck, it probably would.

Before his eyes had fully closed, a boot landed in the sand just before his face. He rolled onto his side and looked up, but all he could see was a tall silhouette. A long grey coat fluttered in the breeze. "I couldn't help but hear your offer. Two chests of gold, have ya?" The man loosed a painful wheeze of a laugh. "How quaint."

Frederick spit sand at the man's boots as struggled to his feet. "I won't suffer another pirate's mockery."

"Mockery? Nay. I bring an offer."

Frederick stood, brushing sand from his pants. When he looked up, he stared into milky white eyes devoid of irises or pupils. He might have yelped in alarm, but the stranger offered a disarmingly kind smile, though most of his teeth were missing. He had a silver beard and a big bald head littered with spots. "I can't see you, but I can hear you," the old man said.

Frederick wasn't in the mood to make a new friend, and those blank eyes unsettled him. They were like small bowls of creamy soup. "How could you possibly help me, old man?"

"Don't be hasty till you've heard my offer, shorty."

"Shorty?" Frederick balked. "You can't even see me!"

"Aye, that be true, but your voice be coming from down low."

Frederick's cheeks tingled with sudden heat. He'd had just about enough of people not taking him seriously. "Make your offer, old man, or get out of my sight. I am pressed for time."

The blind old man cackled. "Nay. You've all the time in the world, shorty. You'll listen to what I have to say, and you'll listen good."

Frederick rolled his eyes. "And why will I do that?"

"Because I know a man who will kill Charles Vane for free."

19

KATE

The day was overcast and intensely humid. The ship reeked of fresh paint and tar, subjugating the briny scent of the ocean air that she loved so much. Her hair was damp and hot, and matted strands clung to her forehead and cheeks. Beads of sweat trickled down her temples. Her clothes were saturated and cumbersome. The sea stretched grey in every direction, reflecting only the dense cloud cover.

She roamed the deck as would a ghost, unconcerned by the murderous men that surrounded her. She ran through her final argument with Calloway over and over again, analyzing their every word, hoping to convince herself that she had been right all along. She wasn't having much success. She felt so utterly justified at the time. Why couldn't the girl just see things her way? But she knew that Calloway had wondered the exact same thing about her.

Perhaps neither of them had been right. She knew it didn't

really matter. Calloway was gone, and no amount of internal debate was going to bring her back. They'd spent so little time together, but as frustrating as Calloway could be, Kate missed her already. Calloway had joined Nathan Adams and Douglas Thatcher and all the other friends she had lost.

Maybe Jaq was right, she thought. *How much longer can I expect to last out here?*

It felt as though she had spent a lifetime in the Caribbean. She had to remind herself that it had barely been a year and a half since Thomas's death. Since then, she hadn't dared to consider the future. The future that had been intended for her had been stolen by Jonathan Griffith in an instant. The future was no longer relevant. All that remained was the present. Thinking ahead was too frightening to consider. *Is this what it means to be a pirate?* she wondered as her gaze swept over a deck full of them.

But she had never truly been one of them. She was their treasure, not their equal. The meaning of her value differed from captor to captor. Griffith saw a wife. Hornigold saw a map to his fortune. Vane saw a hostage to be exchanged.

She had managed to hold off Vane's advances thus far, breaking his resolve with violent promises. He could have taken her by force if he wished, but he knew better than to damage his prize. And she had instilled him with no small amount of trepidation, backed by her undeniable knack for avoiding unwanted advances.

Immediately after departing the island, he had dragged her in his cabin and threatened to shoot her if she didn't take her clothes off. She laughed and said, "You won't throw away everything just for a quick bit of pleasure." She hoped she was right.

"Put out your tits," he had insisted.

"What?"

"Your tits. I want to see them. Tits make me happy."

"I will most certainly not 'put out my tits.'"

"Why not?" he whined. It was most unbecoming.

"For a start, you just murdered my friend."

"Friend? The way you bickered, I might have mistaken you for former lovers. And if memory serves, it was Mr. Jenkins who murdered your friend, not I."

"Because he wished the deed for himself," she reminded him. "And don't worry, I'll deal with Mr. Jenkins."

"Will you?" Vane laughed at that. "You are fierce for a woman, Kate, but the boy is more than your fucking equal. Take caution coming upon his back. He will know."

"We'll see."

He sighed. "We've strayed from the issue. Take off your clothes."

"I will not."

He then tossed the gun to the bed and drew his cutlass and said, "Fine, maybe I'll just cut you a little, where no one can see. A beautiful woman should not go unfucked."

She calmly explained that before he could overpower her, she would plunge her fingers into his eyes, sink her teeth into his throat, or take hold of his balls and twist until they tore free. All three in no particular order, if she could manage it.

She spied fear in his normally cavalier eyes, but he was quick to mask it with a smirk, as usual. "There are plenty of women in Mariposa," he casually replied, as though he hadn't really cared. But she knew better. The fact that she was so valuable made it all the harder for him to resist her.

Still, she was not as frightened of him as she should have been. She was far more afraid of the destination he was spiriting her toward. She had nothing but fond memories of Martha Lindsay, but as much as she would have liked to see her again, that part of her life was over. How would she return to a life of innocent monotony after all she had been through?

Martha hoped to fill the void left by Thomas, the son she had adored more than any other. And once Martha had Kate in her possession, she would never let her go. Kate would be confined to a mansion for the rest of her days, looking pretty and perfect while her color faded and her youthful vigor drained away, until she was nothing but a porcelain doll in an expensive dress. And all the while sweet servants who secretly resented her would attend to her every need.

Every need except one, she thought as she gazed skyward.

And now, in what were surely her final days of freedom, the clouds had conspired into a formless milky layer that denied her the sun. She might have laughed.

As she wandered the deck, the crew muttered quiet and not so quiet promises of what they would do to her when they got her alone. It was nothing new. She had heard it all. There was nothing they could say, no matter how vile or depraved, that would shock her. If their base impulses got the better of them and they converged on her, she would fight them furiously, defending herself with whatever she could find, using up whatever energy she had left. "Strength is always within reach," she had informed Calloway. That was true until it wasn't. She knew now that she had simply been fortunate. Strength had been within reach *so far*, but it wouldn't always be. She would maim and kill as many of them as possible before they overwhelmed her. That was the way of the Caribbean; a constant barrage of danger, until it stripped away all defenses and claimed whatever strength remained.

But the pirates did not converge. All they could do was leer, and leering never killed anyone. Her great value, which had turned so many friends into enemies, shielded her from death.

The only one who truly unnerved her was Mr. Tanner. He was tall and skinny, with ghostly skin. He had stringy blonde hair and eyes that seemed to take in everything yet see nothing. He rarely surfaced from the decks below. "The sun does not agree with Mr. Tanner," he had informed her when she asked why he stayed below so often. She had felt sorry for him, as he seemed to have no friends. "Mr. Tanner's skin peels and flakes."

"But aren't *you* Mr. Tanner?" she asked, confused.

"He is," Tanner replied.

"Oh, I think I understand." She didn't.

When she inquired what his business was with Vane, his thin lips formed a sadistic smile that sent chills up her spine. "Tanner makes men scream with his sharp, shiny, pretty girls. He has so many."

"Girls?"

"Aye. They carve smiles in places that should never smile." His vision seemed to pass right through her. "No man should have that many mouths."

She concluded she didn't want to make friends with Mr. Tanner after all.

When she caught sight of Gabe Jenkins descending below, she wasted no time. She made her way through hordes of pirates, brushing shoulders without a care, toward the main hatch. Before the hatch stood Keet, arms folded as if he had been waiting for her. She smirked down at him. He was much shorter, and his bony frame made her feel fat. She wondered if he had painted his hair to distract from the fact that there was nothing noteworthy about the rest of him. "Where you off to, missy?" he screeched in that high-pitched voice she hated so much.

"Wherever I like," she replied. "Get out of my way."

"Well, excuuuuuse me, princess," he squawked. But he didn't move.

"You heard me."

He furrowed his brow and bobbed his colorful head up and down. "I was only looking out for your well-being, missy. It's dark down there, it is."

She laughed. "If I was afraid of the dark, I'd find a bigger man to accompany me. Move aside." She easily pushed past him before he could object. He tried to stiffen himself in place, but she was stronger.

She descended to the hold. Keet was right; it wasn't smart to go down here. It was dark, and it was unlikely that anyone would hear her screams above. It was even less likely that anyone would rush to her aid, except Vane, who was tucked behind the sound-dulling walls of his cabin.

But Gabe was down here somewhere. He had eluded her thus far, sticking close to groups, as if he suspected what she intended for him.

She felt like an idiot for feeling sorry for him after he revealed what he had done to Calloway's mother. She had never considered herself a horrible judge of character, but Gabe was much harder to read than most men. Perhaps that's what had intrigued her about him. *Surely his pretty face had nothing to do with it,* a sarcastic voice teased from the back of her thoughts as she stepped cautiously down the stairs into the pitch darkness.

Her sleeves were unrolled, concealing the little rusty dagger she had stolen off of the corpse of a crewman killed in the battle with *Crusader*. It had a brittle wooden grip that seemed to have been left in the sun for too long. Such a crude weapon was no more than Gabe deserved. Even if someone managed to pull her away before she could finish, he would probably die of an infection. She grinned as she pictured him spending his final days writhing in agony, his face a twisted perversion of its once comely features.

She reached the lower deck and glanced around, seeing nothing but crates, barrels, and shadows. The expansive hold stretched into darkness. *Advance* was bigger than any ship she had been on. She preferred smaller ships. This one was too hard to get a handle on. No matter how much she explored, she couldn't remember where anything was.

She moved through the hold, winding through the mess that the pirates had made of everything. Many of the barrels had been tossed on their sides and emptied of their contents. Chickens fluttered about, and the hold reeked of their droppings. No doubt it had been much tidier under Captain Lancaster's command.

She looked over her shoulder repeatedly. The dim light of the hatchway receded behind her as she continued on.

He could be anywhere, she realized. *Maybe he drew me down here on purpose, hoping to ambush me, so he can slice my throat like he sliced Jaq's.*

She heard something shuffle behind her. She burst forward and squeezed between two crates that were taller than her. The crates slimmed inward. Her shoulders caught on the diminishing walls and she started to panic, thinking he might come upon her rear and she would have nowhere to go. But then she tilted sideways and slid forward, easily slipping through to the opening on the opposite side.

She chuckled at her silliness. *I'm probably running from a chicken.*

"Someone's in a good mood," came a familiar voice from her right, echoing off the bulkheads.

Kate nearly screamed, spinning in the dark and slashing at air with her stunted dagger.

"Not even close," he taunted, now from the left.

She turned in that direction. "Show yourself!"

"Look at you," he said, this time from somewhere behind. She spun in that direction, but she saw nothing except more crates and more shadows. "So eager to kill. Laughing in the dark. I think you like it here, Kate."

"Don't pretend to know me."

She heard him laugh. It was difficult to determine where he was with all the echoing, the waves hammering against the hull outside and feet stomping the deck above. "I knew you'd come for me when you saw the opportunity," he said. "Figured we should get this over with. I'm tired of you glaring at me all the time."

"Aww, I hope I didn't hurt your feelings," she replied through a tightening jaw.

"Maybe a little. I thought you fancied me."

She shuddered. "Come out of the dark and I'll show you just how much."

"No hurry, Kate. Everyone's up on deck. We have the hold to ourselves. All you have to do is find me."

"I'm not playing games!" she shouted at the dark.

"I didn't think you were." His voice was soft and calm, almost difficult to hear, as though he might have retreated to the opposite end of the hold. "Your choice of weapon gives me cause to doubt. Is that really the best you could find?"

"It will do the job," she hissed. "I want you to feel this."

"So this is the Kate Lindsay that Griffith suffered before his end."

"His death wasn't pretty," she said, jabbing the dagger in random places as she moved through the dark maze, "but it was quick. Yours won't be."

"So I'm worse than Griffith, am I?" He sounded slightly offended.

She laughed. "I killed him quickly because I didn't have the strength or courage to make it slow. I've since grown."

"And what would Griffith say if he could see what you've become?"

"The dead have no say in anything."

His reply was so low she scarcely heard it. "I wish I believed that."

She was descending further into the hold, but she began to make out shapes as her eyes adapted to the low light. She glimpsed a shadow, darker than the rest, darting in front of a nearby crate. She thrust her hand, sinking the rusty blade into wood with a *thunk*. She jerked the grip until the dagger came free.

Something brushed her side and she pirouetted, sweeping the air.

"That was close," he said, his voice trailing aft with a light scuffle of footsteps. He was so quiet. "Just so you know, I could have killed you just now."

"You'll come to regret that."

"You might ask yourself why I didn't."

"I don't care."

"You're not very good in the dark, are you?"

She laughed. "You'll never know."

"Haven't lost your sense of humor, at least."

"Nor you," she shot back, turning in the direction of his voice, which seemed to shift with every retort. "It's a rare man who can keep his humor after murdering a girl of fifteen. Why did you do it?"

"An apt question." His voice came from somewhere in the aft starboard corner.

She ducked low and shuffled in that direction, sliding a shoulder along several crates. The dagger was wet and clumsy in her sweating hand, and the loose splinters bit into her palm whenever she tightened her grip. She opened and closed her fingers, rolling the dagger for a more comfortable hold, but she felt splinters on all sides. Beads of sweat spilled down her temples, and her hair was a tremendous burden weighing heavily upon her head, tendrils thick, damp, and hot against her cheeks. As humid as it was on deck, it was worse down here. The center of her forehead, where she had head-butted Vane, started to pulsate.

"I'm surprised you haven't figured it out on your own," he said. He sure did like to talk. "You're a smart woman."

"And you're a sick boy." *Keep him talking. Make him angry. That's the only way you'll find him.* "Maybe you wanted to finish what you started. Maybe you get your jollies from murdering mothers and their daughters. Maybe you're no better than Edward Teach was. Prettier on the outside, but just as rotten on the inside. Maybe that's why he liked you. Maybe that's why he trusted you."

"Maybe you're right." His tone was distinct with remorse, as it had been during the unfortunate tale of his meeting with Calloway's mother.

An act to catch me off guard, Kate reminded herself. She would not fall for it.

By the time she reached the corner, he was gone. She passed under a sliver of light from a crease in the upper deck, which blinded her for an instant. She blinked. A malnourished chicken paced about, pecking at the deck. Kate heard a thumping from above and behind. At first she mistook it for the pirates on deck. And then something large dropped behind her, and she felt hot breath on the nape of her neck. She spun too late, her arm catching on Gabe's palm. He loomed before her, his curly hair shrouding his face and his long coat flowing behind him, a shadow that swallowed what little light there was. She kicked out a leg, digging it into his shin. He growled and fell back a step. She balled her other hand into a fist and shoved it into his belly, gnashing her knuckles against the hilt of the blade hidden in his blue sash. He snatched her wrist, clenching it firmly but not painfully. Her dagger hand was free. She flung it forward, bringing the blade to his throat. He fell through the sliver of light, which revealed for an instant a look of surprise, before his back cracked against a crate. She pinned him, pressing the rusty blade into the flesh of his neck. He winced. She grinned, but her satisfaction waned when his lips, so near to hers, curled into a lopsided smile. "I was wrong. You're incredible in the dark."

She pushed off of him in revulsion, but kept the blade at his neck. "And you're dead."

He held in a breath. His skin broke along the rusty edge, droplets of blood trickling over the blade, black and colorless in the gloom.

"How does this feel, Gabe?"

"Go on," he urged. He managed to keep his uneven smile. "I'm ready."

She looked down at his hands, which were now hanging limp at his sides. "Why didn't you draw your dagger?" she asked. "Did you think to kill me with your bare hands?"

"I did not think to kill you with anything."

She scoffed. "Then why lead me down here?"

His smile faded, and for an instant he looked sad and tired, and much older than his twenty years should have allowed. "Do what you must."

She tightened her grip, ignoring the little splinters gouging her hand. "Goodbye, Gabe Jenkins."

He closed his eyes, and then opened them suddenly as he seemed to recall something important. He tilted his head forward to look at her, resting his strong jaw on top of the blade. "Before you put me down like the treacherous dog I am, there's one thing you might want to take into consideration."

She was glad for the protest, for she hadn't expected him to die so willingly. It would be easier to kill him if he at least *tried* to get away. "Oh, I can't wait to hear this."

"Jaq's alive."

The words did not move her. His eyes were sincere, but she knew better than to trust them. "A lie," she decided quickly.

"No," he said, shaking his head. "She's alive. Assuming she knows how to swim, of course. It was early dawn and the water was dark. I don't believe anyone saw her swim to safety."

Kate somehow resisted grinding the dagger into his neck. Why was she even listening to this? It was absurd. "I saw you slice her throat!"

"You saw me slice her throat, yes . . . deep enough to bleed, not deep enough to sever her airway. It was a flesh wound, Kate, nothing more."

"You're lying!"

He sighed. "I understand why you would think so, but I assure you I am not. I took the deed upon myself because it was the only way I knew to spare her."

"Why would you care? You killed her mother!"

"You'll find the answer in the query."

She shook her head. She would not fall for his tricks again. "You'd say anything to save your neck."

That made him laugh. "If that were true, you'd be dead three times over. You're good, Kate, but I'm better." He lifted his chin off the blade and sniffed. "Do what you must. Slow or quick."

"I know what you're trying to do, Gabe. I'm not stupid."

"Then prove what you already know, and strike."

She held the blade at his throat, but her hand refused to budge. Something was stopping her. She leaned into the blade, but it remained in place, as though a phantom secured her wrist. This felt all wrong, but she had no idea why. Gabe had lied before. There was no reason for her to believe anything he said.

But what if he's not lying this time?

Again, she was questioning herself. She hated this newfound

doubt. Doubt was dangerous. Quick thinking was the only thing that had kept her alive this long. She couldn't afford to be indecisive. Why should she even care? It had never mattered to her before.

Jaq. Could you actually be alive?

After a moment, Gabe frowned at her inquisitively. "You're not going to do it, are you?" He sounded disappointed.

She studied his eyes, bright even in the dark. His irises swirled with two colors, green and brown. She had never noticed before. "You want this," she concluded.

His hand shot up as fast as lightning, slapping her wrist and whipping the dagger away from his neck. It landed somewhere far away, well out of her reach. He plunged the other hand into his sash. The curved blade shrieked as he drew it from the concealed sheath. He raised it high above his head. It happened so fast, she hadn't even time to gasp.

This is it. She had hesitated too long. She let those pretty eyes get the better of her. *What a silly way to die.*

He barreled into her, his shoulder impacting her chest and tossing her aside. She collapsed to the deck, clutching her chest and gasping for air. Gabe continued on with the dagger held high. The blade flashed as he passed through the sliver of light. She looked to the spot he was charging and saw stripes of blue, yellow, and red, dulled by the dark. A thin body was pressed flat against the bulkhead. She knew that face. It was Keet. "Wait!" he screeched, pleading with a raised hand while reaching for the pistol at his hip with the other.

Gabe was too fast.

He drove the dagger downward in a powerful arc, kicking out one leg behind him to propel himself forward with the greatest possible force. The dagger cleaved Keet's skull right down the center, stopping midway down his forehead. Blood curtained from either side of the blade, dousing Gabe in a red spray before his feet returned to the ground. Keet's eyes went crossed, his mouth dropped open, and his tongue lolled. He fell to his knees. Gabe set a foot on Keet's shoulder and wrenched the dagger from his head. Keet slumped forward, hitting the deck, and brain matter spilled from the wedge in his colorful hair.

When Gabe turned to Kate, his features were washed in red beneath a shroud of sodden black curls. He ran a hand over his face, smearing stripes across his cheeks. His chest heaved as he attempted to catch his breath. "He would have reported everything I said to Vane," he explained between gasps. "I had to do it."

She blinked away her stupefied awe. He offered his hand, but it was covered in blood. She got to her feet on her own. "Thought you weren't concerned with your neck," she said.

Through the gore that dirtied his face, his eyes locked with hers. "I'm not, but this might put *you* in a spot of trouble. Not even Vane would be able to save you from Roman if he found out you had anything to do with this. Roman and Keet are— *were*—the very best of mates."

She snorted incredulously and looked away, rubbing the sore spot in the center of her chest where he had collided with her. "This doesn't change anything," she assured him. "I'm still going to kill you."

Gabe gestured at the corpse with his blood-coated dagger. "Fine, but you might want to hold off until *after* I've disposed of the body."

She set her hands on her waist. "And how do you plan to do that?"

His shrug implied that the solution couldn't have been more evident. "We'll stuff him in an empty barrel and I'll toss him overboard after dark, when everyone's asleep."

"You're just stalling," she said.

"Not at all." He flashed a smile, and clean white teeth gleamed through a crimson mask. "Tomorrow, you'll have the whole day to figure out how best to do me in."

20

DILLAHUNT

He was still clinging to the spyglass that Roman had given him. It was all he had left. Roman and his men had stripped the corpses of their weapons, to ensure that he could not kill himself. Vane hadn't left anything to chance.

Through the spyglass Dillahunt had watched Calloway tumble from the ship into the water. *A parting gift from Vane,* he realized. Afterward, he scanned the water for an hour as the rising sun brightened the eastern horizon, but he knew she would not emerge. He thought he saw a head break the surface, but he lost sight of it in the rolling waves. And when the waves calmed, he could find no trace of her.

So he spent the rest of the day aimlessly wandering the beach, running through the names of his crew over and over. Those that he could recall, anyway. Some came quicker than others. "Bastion," he said aloud. "Farley. Dumaka. Early. Clemens. Surley. Gerry. Terry Bell. Wincott. Jacqueline." The final name was always the most difficult.

He knew he would be joining them eventually, but his death would be far slower. Many years ago he had heard a sailor talk of nearly dying of thirst on a ship that had run out of water before reaching port. "Worst headache of me life," the sailor claimed. "Felt like me brain were cut in half and trying to pop out me eyes. Me tongue was dry as sand and puffed up to the size of a lemon, and that's no lie. And then I got the shaking. Not a gentle shaking, mind you; this were a fiercely tremor that tossed me about like a crazy man. I had no control over meself." And then he paused, and a smile came to his weathered face. "After that, it weren't so bad. I got so dizzy that I fell over, and I didn't wake for a day. When I came to, we was in port, and me mate was splashing water all over me face."

There would be no one to splash water in Dillahunt's face. There would be no port. But, at the very least, there was the chance he simply wouldn't wake up. That didn't sound so bad.

But that fate was still days away.

His entire left foot ached, from the missing toe upward. He had nothing to fashion a crutch out of, and the longer he walked, the more it hurt. He had kicked off his heavy, soggy boots to find a foul-smelling milky pus oozing from the wound, which had split open again. Half his foot was purple and swollen. He tried to remember the last time he had looked at it. How long had he left his boots on? He couldn't recall. Everything seemed so distant now.

It didn't matter.

His ship was lost.

His crew was dead.

Jacqueline was dead.

"Bastion," he said again. "Farley. Dumaka. Early. Clemens. Surley. Gerry. Terry Bell. Wincott." He didn't add her to the list this time. He couldn't.

The pain in his foot grew and grew until it was nearly unbearable. *In a few days you'll feel nothing at all,* he reminded himself. So he let the pain burn through him, savoring every agonizing throb that pulsed up his ankle. He would walk until he could walk no more. It didn't matter where he died. Everything here looked the same. The beach never changed. Every once in a while he would happen upon a tree, but it bore no fruit. He would rest against the thin trunk in what little shade the gently fluttering branches above provided. He would stare at the sharp leaves, attempting to count them until a wayward thought distracted him. And when he lost count one too many times and became infuriated, he moved on.

He couldn't wait for the sun to go down. He was sweating terribly, and the breeze was too warm to offer any relief. There was no water in sight, other than the ocean, of course, taunting him with its refreshing beauty. More than once he considered walking into the waves and not stopping. Drowning in water would be quicker than dying from a lack of it. The realization gave him an ironic chuckle, but little else. He would not allow himself so easy a death. He had not earned it.

"Bastion. Farley. Dumaka. Early. Clemens. Surley. Gerry. Terry Bell. Wincott." He spoke the names again to the sea, and the sea replied with the sound of gentle waves, but that did nothing to soothe him. He opened his mouth to say the final name. Why was it so hard? "Jaq . . . quel . . ."

He froze.

A long and slender body was sprawled facedown at the end of a long sandbank that stretched away from the beach at the mouth of the estuary from which Vane's ship had materialized. Her black hair and equally black clothes were easy to spot against the white sand. He sprinted toward the body without thinking.

It's her.

It has to be.

As he neared, he saw that she was moving. He quickened his pace. But then he realized her body was just swaying lifelessly in the thin waves that slid over the end of the bank.

Dread gradually slowed his step, until he stopped ten paces from her and could progress no further. He urged himself to do something more than just stand there, but his heels had taken root in the soft wet sand.

I must not dawdle, he told himself. *I am no coward.*

He owed her a proper burial. She deserved more than the fishes. *And she deserves more than a burial on some cursed, uncharted island.* But it was the only thing he could give her now. He hadn't the energy to bury the others, but he would bury Calloway, if it was the last thing he ever did.

And it would be.

He tossed the spyglass into an oncoming wave and thrust his left foot forward. The missing toe screamed in pain, but he pressed on, and he did not stop until he was standing over her. Her soaked clothes were covered in strands of seaweed. Her arms and feet were pale. Her short black hair mostly concealed the side of her face that wasn't pressed to the sand. He crouched and plucked the seaweed from her, one tendril at a time. When that was done, he tenderly took hold of her and started to turn her over as slowly as possible, but his grip slipped on her wet clothes and she flopped gracelessly onto her back. Her eyes were closed and her lips were white and flaked, running with ghastly red fissures. Her freckles barely showed. Despite all that, she actually looked peaceful.

Dillahunt sighed. "I should never have let you go," he told her.

He frowned.

A pink slit ran across her neck. He leaned close to examine

it, parting the wound with thumb and forefinger. A thin stream of blood trickled out, but the bleeding was mostly done now. He leaned even closer, until he was inches from her face. The wound wasn't nearly deep enough to sever her windpipe.

Her hand lifted suddenly, and slender fingers grasped his wrist. Her eyes shot open. Her entire face went bright red and puffed up like a blowfish, until her lips popped and ejaculated water into his face. He blinked the salty sting from his eyes. She rolled onto her hands, her back heaving as she hacked water into the sand. Dillahunt fell onto his rear and stared at her in petrified astonishment. Another small wave rolled over the beach, sloshing past them. He barely noticed as the warm water cascaded over his legs. How could she possibly be alive? Was he imagining this? He was thirsty, but he hadn't yet gone a full day without water. Surely the hallucinations would not start so soon.

"You're alive," he stammered.

After a full minute of awful retching, which yielded little more than a small pool of murky water that quickly dissolved into the damp sand, she distantly replied, "Am I? I don't feel it."

He recovered himself and lightly patted her back. She sat in the sand, staring at the ocean and massaging her throat. Another wave washed past them, running over their feet and legs. "The ocean wouldn't let me die," she murmured wistfully.

She reached into her pocket and fished out something black and wrinkled, offering it to Dillahunt. Her lips twitched into a warped smile. "I saved your toe."

He swallowed a sudden urge to vomit. "Oh. Thank you. I'd wondered where that got off to."

Her smile vanished and her chin started to quiver. "I don't think it's lucky anymore."

"Maybe it is," he replied as he stared at her. He reached out to touch her shoulder, to make sure she was really there.

"I'll just hold onto it a while longer," she said. She stuffed the toe back in her pocket. Her lip continued to quiver. She was traumatized, as any sane woman should be. He would have been worried if she wasn't.

He took her hands in his. "Can you walk?"

Her laugh was so breathy it was nearly silent, and it threw her into another fit of coughing. "Walk? Why? Where?"

He had no answer to that. "I don't know. I suppose it doesn't matter."

She winced as she massaged her neck. "The ocean wouldn't let me die," she said again, whimsy replaced by certainty.

Dillahunt shook his head. "The wound wasn't deep enough to require any magical healing powers from the sea."

"That's because the water mended it."

"That's silly, Jacqueline."

"You weren't there." Her voice was soft, but her words were sure. "I felt the knife in my neck. There was so much blood."

"I'm sure there was. It's deep enough for bleeding." He looked at the wound again. She watched him placidly. "Whoever cut you was either an idiot or a weakling. Maybe both."

She lowered her head, and shadows fell over the hollows of her eyes, which were deeper than normal. "He is neither. He opened my throat, and the water closed it."

"Who did this?" he asked as gently as possible.

"Jenkins."

Dillahunt plunged a fist into the sand. "I should have removed that whelp's cock when I had the chance!"

"You're no less accountable," she replied evenly, with no lack of certainty.

He impulsively opened his mouth to defend himself, but there was nothing he could possibly say. Sending her away hadn't been difficult. It was clear to him now that he had never expected to see her alive again. He had never *wanted* to see her alive again. He was exhausted with solving puzzles, and she had proven insoluble.

"Vane's taken Kate to Mariposa," she murmured. "Probably wants her reward for himself."

Dillahunt grimaced as he considered their predicament for the hundredth time. "I suppose that's the least of our concerns now."

She let out a flighty little laugh. "It's all a game. We lost."

He watched the latest wave splash over his swollen foot, stinging as it seeped into the putrid stub. Soon the rot would creep up his leg and spread into his torso. Soon there would be nothing left of him but a black shell, drying in the sun. He wondered if Calloway would live long enough to see it. Maybe she would like that.

"We really should press on," he said. "Maybe we can find water. It must have rained sometime. Maybe we'll find a water hole." He looked up at the bright blue sky. Any other time he would have welcomed such gorgeous weather.

He forced himself to stand, leaning on the good foot, and offered her his hand. He was relieved when she took it. She was clearly too weak to get up on her own, and this wasn't the time for her to be stubborn. If there was any water to be found, they would have to find it fast.

They supported each other as they hobbled up the beach. There was no other way for them to go. In their condition they couldn't exactly scale the rocky hillside and move inland. Calloway complained of pains in her chest and constantly tried to scratch the wound at her throat. Dillahunt slapped her hand away every time. "That will never heal if you scratch."

"But it itches!"

"That's good. That means it's healing."

"I told you, it *already* healed."

He sighed. "The world is puzzling enough without mysticism."

The sun touched the horizon, casting a jagged yellow column along the waves, and for a while the sky and sea fell into deepening shades of amber and brown. And then the warm hues gradually faded, and the heat with it. A refreshingly cool breeze swept over the beach, and Dillahunt's shirt, which had been drenched in sweat, dried quickly.

"Why are we still walking?" Calloway wondered. Her words were slurred as though she was drunk. "I just want to sleep. Let's find a place to sleep."

Dillahunt barely heard her. "Do you see that?"

"See what?"

"That light?" Was he imagining the little orange flicker in the distance, maybe half a mile up the beach? It was too low to be a star, and it was a good deal larger.

"Is that . . . is that a fire?" Calloway murmured.

They continued in silence. If Dillahunt spoke of the fire again, he feared the illusion would dissipate. After another half hour of walking, it was obvious the fire was no mirage. The silhouette of a structure with a pointed roof was slightly blacker than the dark sky beyond it. As they neared, the flames cast flickering light across the front of a large tent. The fire was large, billowing from a shallow pit.

When they were within a hundred paces, Dillahunt dragged Calloway behind large rocks on the beach, near the water. Shallow waves slid in around them as they ducked low. "Vane left someone behind," he told her.

"Why would he do that?"

He shrugged. "Good question."

"I wonder if they have water?"

He licked his dry lips. "Better question."

The tent flap parted and the shadow of a large man stepped

outside. He moved to the fire, holding out his hands to warm them, but he remained a shadow that the light did nothing to illuminate.

"Stay here," he instructed Calloway.

She nodded groggily, setting her cheek against the rock. "Be quick. I'm so thirsty."

Dillahunt moved around the rock and shuffled up the beach, crouching low and trying to ignore the increasingly painful spasms that cramped his foot with every step. When he felt the heat of the fire, which was as tall as the man that stood beside it, he instinctively reached to his belt to draw his sword, but remembered he had lost it when he went overboard.

The big man moved behind the fire, and Dillahunt used that to his advantage, quickening his pace. The heat blasted his cheeks when he was within five paces of the flames. He quickly moved around the fire, glancing at the big tent. He hoped when he reached the other side of the fire, the man would be facing the ocean and would not see him coming.

But when he got there, he found no one.

Something cracked against the back of his skull. His legs turned to mush. He collapsed in the sand. Fingers gripped his shoulder and turned him over, and he looked into the fearsome face of . . .

"Dumaka!" Dillahunt exclaimed.

Dumaka pulled away, dropping the gnarled stick he had used to bash Dillahunt with. "Captain?"

Dillahunt propped himself up on one elbow and felt the back of his head. He looked at his hand and saw blood on the tips of his fingers. He felt faint. "Another gash," he muttered. "Another scar."

"Apologies, captain," Dumaka said. Nothing in his mild expression conveyed sorrow.

Dillahunt's arm gave out and he fell back into the sand. His head was spinning. Embers lifted from the fire beside him into the swirling stars above. He squeezed his eyes shut to stop the nausea, but he still saw stars behind his lids. "If I should pass out," he wearily instructed Dumaka, "Jacqueline is hiding behind the rocks over there. Go fetch her, would you?"

Dumaka nodded and departed Dillahunt's constricting field of vision.

After a while, even the stars faded.

He dreamed of his ship, sailing gentle waves under a vibrant blue sky. His crew went happily about their various tasks. He ran his hand along the starboard railing as he walked across the main deck. The smooth wood retained the heat of the sun, scalding his palm, but he did not pull away. It felt so real.

The tranquility didn't last. "Captain!" said Bastion, frantically pointing aft. When Dillahunt turned, a giant black cloud was in close pursuit, roiling toward the ship at alarming speed. The cloud rolled over the deck before he could think to order an evasion, not that there was anywhere to evade to. One by one his men were enveloped in darkness, and soon he was taken by the cloud as well, unable to see two feet in front of him. He stumbled through the black mist with his hands stretched out before him, shouting the names of his men:

"Bastion?"

Nothing.

"Early?"

Nothing.

"Dumaka?"

Nothing.

"Clemens?"

Nothing.

An icy wind slapped at his face in concussive beats, and the mist swirled about him but did not disperse. He walked for what felt like minutes, but he found nothing. He heard no one.

The sails did not clap and even the sea had quieted. Was he walking in circles?

His pace waned with every step. Lifting each foot became a maddening struggle, as though the heels of his boots were glued to the deck. He looked down, expecting to see planking, but instead realized that he was plodding through fine white sand. His feet sank to his ankles with every step. When he looked up, the black mist was gone, and an expansive white desert stretched out before him, with no mountains or hills. Other than low washboard ripples, it was flat and endless in every direction.

In the distance he glimpsed a figure moving hypnotically in the waves of heat that lifted from the sand. The figure seemed to be diminishing. Somehow, he knew it was Vane. He burst into a run, but after three bounds he crumpled in agony and clutched at his left foot. Except there was nothing to clutch. His foot was gone, with a shard of bone protruding from a red stump below his kneecap.

He shrieked at the top of his lungs, his chest shuddering in great waves, his lungs burning as all air abandoned them, but no sound escaped his mouth. He looked to the figure in the distance, which grew smaller and smaller, until it vanished below the horizon.

He woke.

Dumaka sat close, watching him while warming his hands. The sky was purple now. It must have been near dawn. He sat up, but he did not look at his foot. He didn't need to look to know it was in even worse shape than before he had fallen asleep. He swung his head around, but there was no sign of Calloway. "Where is she?"

"The girl has taken shelter in the tent. She drank too much."

"Drank too much?"

Dumaka handed him a jug of rum, half empty. Dillahunt regarded it skeptically. "What is that?"

"It is called rum."

"No need for sarcasm," Dillahunt said, taking the bottle. The rum burned his throat on the way down.

Dumaka watched him. "You should join her. Find what warmth you can before the end."

Dillahunt wiped his lips. "Her warmth is no longer mine to take."

"Then you are not only a poor captain, but a poor man."

"Yes, thank you for the words of wisdom," Dillahunt sighed.

"The girl is going to be alright," said Dumaka. "Cannot say the same for your foot."

"It doesn't matter."

Dumaka scoffed bitterly. "You are a fool of a captain."

A day earlier he might have had Dumaka flogged for his insolence, but so much had changed. "I am a captain no longer."

"On this we agree."

"How is it you escaped?" Dillahunt was unable to withhold accusation from his tone. His entire crew had died, but Dumaka had not only managed to survive, but find shelter and build a fire.

"Should I have perished with the rest?" Dumaka smirked at him. "How have *you* escaped, captain?"

Dillahunt looked into the fire. The blaze pained his eyes, but anything was better than looking at his foot, which was throbbing terribly. "Only because Vane willed it. He extends the inevitable. I have escaped nothing."

"You give up too easily."

"What would you have me do? Cling to hope?" Dillahunt spread his arms and looked around. "Let me know when you find it, as I must be blind."

Dumaka looked utterly disgusted.

Dillahunt didn't care. He fell back into the sand and rolled onto his side, facing the tent, picturing Calloway asleep inside. He prayed her dreams weren't as desolate as his had been, but he doubted there was room for any other kind.

Though he was no less exhausted, he could not get back to sleep. He tossed and turned in the sand for the better part of an hour, the belt of his pants digging into his hips. But that was the least of his pains. The fire gradually died down until there was nothing left but smoldering chunks of black wood, which Dillahunt thought resembled rotted limbs. Soon the sky was dark turquoise beyond the wisps of violet clouds.

A hand clutched Dillahunt's shoulder, giving him a fierce start. "I found it, captain!" Dumuka exclaimed.

"Found what?" Dillahunt grated, irritated with Dumaka's lack of tact.

Dumaka pointed frantically toward the sea. "Hope."

Dillahunt sat up. The silhouette of a single-masted sloop had appeared on the horizon, distant but closing fast on the beach. He didn't need a spyglass to recognize that ship. He knew it just from its outline. It was the very same ship that had led his crew to their doom.

The sloop dropped anchor, and a longboat with six men started for the shore as the sky grew brighter through gaps in the increasing cloud cover. It was going to be a grey day, but Dillahunt wasn't certain he would survive to see it.

When Dumaka seemed to realize "hope" was not approaching, he suggested they retreat to the tent. Dillahunt just laughed sardonically. "They would never think to look in there."

"So we just sit here and do nothing, *captain*?" He spat the word like a curse.

"You're welcome to ambush them, if you believe you can

kill six armed men. I'm afraid I won't be of much use."

"Were you ever?"

He shrugged. "Maybe they will end us sooner than thirst. That would be a kindness."

Dumaka looked appalled. "And what of the girl? They will not end her so quickly, I wager."

Dillahunt sighed. "I would spirit her very far away if only I had the means. Sadly, I possess no such magic."

Dumaka retrieved the gnarled stick he had used to clobber Dillahunt and held it defensively. His biceps trembled as he tensed. "I will not die so easily as you."

The longboat slid silently onto the beach, and Calico Jack rose to his full height and hopped off. Dillahunt had only glimpsed the man once before, in Pirate Town. He seemed to have misplaced his burgundy coat since then. The pirate captain started up the beach, smiling warmly beneath his red-feathered tricorn hat. His seedy-looking pirates followed close behind. There was no urgency to Calico Jack's movements, nothing to suggest he was looking for a fight. His men seemed less lax, hands resting on the hilts of their cutlasses. "Captain Dillahunt," he called in a deep, regal voice. "I am pleased to see you alive."

Not the sort of greeting Dillahunt had expected. He exchanged an uneasy glance with Dumaka, who wasn't about to drop his stick. "Come to watch me die, Rackham?" Dillahunt asked.

"Nay," Calico Jack replied with a little smile as he strolled up.

"Then how may I serve?" Dillahunt asked sarcastically.

"It's more what I might do for you." Calico Jack flinched when he saw Dillahunt's foot. "Oh, that looks ill."

"Isn't so bad," Dillahunt replied, but the pain lacing his voice was obvious.

Calico Jack turned to his pirates, waving them off. They took several steps back and waited at a distance. "No quarrel to be found here, men," he assured them.

"Are you certain Vane didn't send you back to finish me off?" Dillahunt wondered. "Seems a waste of time, otherwise."

"Nay." Calico Jack's eyes were lost beneath the brim of his hat for a moment, before he looked up again. "I'm afraid Charles has lost himself to madness. I do not believe I can claim him as friend any longer, nor would I wish it so even if he permitted it. I regret my part in what happened to your ship. I watched from afar, but there was naught I could do."

Dillahunt scoffed. "You could have come to our aid."

"And see my crew slaughtered alongside yours?" Rackham smiled sadly. "Late is better than never, wouldn't you agree?"

"I would not."

Calico Jack's eyes moved past Dillahunt. Dillahunt turned to see Calloway emerging from the flaps of the tent, setting one foot in the sand. She held a hand over the bandage around her throat while grimacing. Her eyelids were puffy and heavy, but they shot wide when she spotted Rackham. She froze in place.

"Nothing to fear, my dear," Calico Jack insisted, raising his hands.

Not convinced, Calloway lifted her foot and slid back into the tent, and the flaps closed.

Dillahunt resisted crying out as a severe jolt of pain shot up his leg out of nowhere. He masked the pain by shifting quickly in the sand, but he caught Calico Jack watching him dubiously. "Your foot needs attention," the pirate captain observed.

"It's infected," Dillahunt grunted. "Have to remove the leg, most like, or the infection will take me whole."

Calico Jack seemed to find that amusing. "The wound needs to be cleaned, but your foot is purple because you've been walking on it wrong."

Dillahunt looked at him squarely. "Why are you really here, Rackham?"

"I may be a pirate, but I am not a murderer when I can help it. My aim is fortune, not mindless slaughter. I do not approve of what Charles has done to you and your men, and I will do what I can to rectify my part in it."

"Then you will take me to Mariposa." Dillahunt could only hope that Vane hadn't lied to Calloway about his intended destination in order to deliberately throw him off his trail. Then again, how could Vane possibly know Calloway would survive, and that Dillahunt would find a way off the island? Vane had made him too paranoid.

Calico Jack hesitated. "Why would I do that?"

"Because that's where Vane has gone, and I think you know it." He studied Calico Jack's face for a reaction, but the pirate captain was adept at hiding his true thoughts. "There is nowhere else for me to go."

"What will you do when you find him?"

Dillahunt shrugged. "I will remove his cock and shove it somewhere unpleasant."

Calico Jack remained straight-faced. "I see."

"I will hunt that man to the ends of the world, if I must."

"If I may ask, with what ship will you hunt him, Captain Dillahunt?"

Rackham was missing the point. "I no longer claim the title of captain. I am just Dillahunt, now. I have one goal, and I will see it done, or my life ended."

"The latter, more like."

"That man destroyed everything I have and everything I am. There is nothing else."

Calico Jack looked at the tent. "Isn't there?"

Dillahunt offered no reply. Calloway was no longer his to claim. She had taken leave of her senses. Her lover was the ocean now.

"If you truly wish to follow Charles, catching up won't be a problem." Calico Jack gestured at his little ship, beaming proudly for an instant. "He has a day's head start, but *Swift* is much faster than his frigate."

"Then we've no time to lose," Dillahunt said, starting to his feet.

Calico Jack snapped his fingers at his men. "Help him up."

Dillahunt waved them away. "Dumaka can help."

Dumaka lowered his stick and glowered. "I do not take orders from you. You are no longer my captain."

"Fine, I'll do it myself." Dillahunt's arms quivered, and when the pain of pressing his foot into the sand for leverage became too unbearable, he fell. He sighed hopelessly. "Shit."

"So, you will face Vane with a limp," Calico Jack observed with a scathing chuckle. "I probably don't need to tell you how cunning he is, given that he scuttled your ship and wiped out your entire crew in the span of an hour."

"You think I will lose?"

"You've lost once already." Calico Jack's naturally authoritative voice gave import to every word. "I'm offering you a chance at life. I merely wish to absolve myself of guilt in this monstrous affair, so I might find a good night's rest and once more greet the dawn as a pirate without a care. I will take you as far as Mariposa if that is your wish. What you do when you get there is your choice. You may choose life, or you may choose to persist in your pursuit of Vane."

"I have but one goal," Dillahunt explained, since Rackham didn't seem to be getting it. "I will kill Charles Vane. What happens to me after is inconsequential."

21

VANE

"Frederick Lindsay? Him come here two days ago. Not see him since."

The constant noise of Keelhaul Tavern infiltrated Vane's ears, threatening to drive him mad. He set his elbows on the table and massaged both temples with his thumbs, while Trejean watched him from across the table with a curious look. "Are you ill, captain?" the Jamaican asked.

"This is not what I wanted to hear," Vane said.

Outside, the sky was a turquoise veil strewn with soft clouds that flared pink with the last of the sun's light. Night had yet to fall, but the tavern's occupants must have started their merrymaking very early that day. Atop the crates surrounding the mast, the ginger-haired flutist never seemed to need a breath as three fingers danced along his instrument. His tune gained in its hasty fervor, continuously building toward a crescendo that Vane feared would never arrive. Half-naked strumpets giggled stupidly in the laps of red-faced pirates as they sloshed ale all over themselves and made idiotic jokes and belted songs out of tune.

Vane would have happily given all of them over to Mr. Tanner, one after another, if only he had the time. They were fools, happy to drink away their lives until Woodes Rogers arrived to slip a noose around their necks. There was but one man who could lend aid, one man who could help Vane take back the Caribbean before it was lost to the crown, and that man was mysteriously absent.

"You wouldn't happen to know where I might find him?" Vane asked as politely as possible. It took every last thread of restraint not to bellow the question. He despised false courtesies, especially when he was forced to deliver them to scum such as Trejean, whose ribs he would gladly slip a dagger between.

Trejean glanced at the Jamaican twins that constantly flanked him, as if to remind himself that they had not left his side. Vane was not concerned with them, for he had two men of his own sitting on either side of him; Roman and Deter. *If I want you dead, Trejean, your bodyguards will present no obstacle.*

"I do not know," Trejean answered uncomfortably. "Mayhap I set you up with a beautiful woman to lick away your troubles? Me stock has increased."

Vane sighed and turned his gaze on a redheaded beauty he had been eyeing since he first entered the tavern. When she hiked up her dress to sit in a pirate's lap, he spied a T burned into her inner thigh. "I'll have that branded bitch after we've concluded our business." Her face didn't look anything like Kate's, but her body was similar, and that would be enough to satisfy Vane's as-yet unquenched thirst.

He hoped.

"She be a fiery wench," Trejean replied with a congenial

nod.

A far less pretty whore with long black hair sauntered up to Vane, opened her shirt, and stuck her big bouncy tits in his face. He fixed her with a dark glare that promised unfavorable deeds in the bedroom.

Trejean snapped his fingers angrily at her. "Did him call you over?"

Her stupid face went pale, and she covered herself up. "No, sir."

"Then go to someone who does. There be plenty of ugly pirates who fancy a woman uglier than them. Go make them feel good about themselves."

She nodded in shame and retreated back to more favorable company.

Trejean shook his head. "I throw that one out, but she always come back. I wouldn't grace her thigh with my brand."

"My query was simple," Vane pressed on, "yet you keenly deflect the subject with the ever reliable distraction of tits and arse. I'll ask again. Where is Frederick Lindsay? I did not see his ship in the harbor when I arrived. That worried me, but I told myself there was a logical reason for its absence."

"Most like," Trejean said with a shrug. "But I do not know nor do I care what it be. This is not my concern."

I could make it your concern, Vane wanted to say. "If you have any information as to his whereabouts, now would be the fucking proper time to inform me."

"Do I look like Lindsay's keeper?"

"No," Vane admitted with a dismal laugh. He glanced over the tavern's strumpets. "Unless poor Frederick has shed his clothes in favor of a new career. Some men have queer inclinations. I imagine a man of Frederick's stature would serve their needs well. He wouldn't even need to bruise his knees."

Trejean smiled knowingly. "I hear tales of *your* inclinations,

Charles Vane. You will find no babies or animals in here."

Vane raised a finger. "I never fucked a baby."

Roman and Deter snickered. Vane glared fiercely from one to the other, but only Deter was wise enough to restrain himself.

"Lindsay bruise up one of me girls," Trejean said with a defensive shrug. "Me customers don't fancy battered girls. Not the face, anyway. I bruise them where it don't show."

Vane closed his eyes and pinched the bridge of his nose. The flutist's increasingly playful tune was directly at odds with his darkening mood. He took a deep breath to prevent himself from flying into a rage, but he wasn't certain how much longer he could resist. He needed to reserve his temper for Frederick Lindsay, should he ever see the man again. He maintained a cool tone as he told Trejean, "I don't care if he stuck a cutlass up her cunny, I want to know where Lindsay has gone, and I want to know now."

Trejean bristled, standing and puffing up his great chest. The round table wobbled as his muscular legs nudged it. At full height, he was taller than his twin bodyguards. "You are no one to talk to me this way. I have not forgotten what you do to me ship last time you come."

Vane clenched his teeth and welcomed the pain that spiked through his jaw. The missing molar still nagged at him, as though an elusive shard of it remained in the gum and was poisoning his remaining teeth. Chewing his food had become agonizing in the last few days, and he had lost a good deal of weight. "Nay," he sighed, "but you seem to have conveniently forgotten what you did to deserve my wrath."

Trejean's chest deflated, the little bird skull at the end of his necklace withdrawing. "The little man come to me with an offer," he confessed.

Finally, thought Vane. "What offer?"

Trejean glanced at his bodyguards, whipping his straight white hair and dismissing each with a curt nod. He sat down again, leaning forward and setting his large hands on the table. The twins moved two separate directions and circled the table. Roman and Deter watched them closely, hands falling to their cutlasses. The bodyguards continued on, toward the bar. Roman and Deter relaxed.

"Lindsay wish you dead," Trejean explained.

Roman barked a laugh of surprise. "What?"

Vane angled an ear toward Trejean. "I didn't hear you?"

"Lindsay ask me to kill you. Him not happy with you."

Vane impulsively flung an arm in anger, and the back of his hand hit the tankard of ale before him, which he hadn't taken one sip of. Roman leaned out of the way as the tankard flew past him in a straight line, dousing a fat pirate at a nearby table. The man blinked as a sheen of golden liquid washed down his reddening face. "That's it! I'm going to fucking—" But then he saw who had soiled him. He smiled sheepishly, offered a pathetic little wave and looked away. "Accidents happen," he told the others at his table. Roman and Deter snickered like children making fun of a much smaller child.

"Frederick Lindsay wishes me dead?" Vane snarled.

"Warned you not to trust that little shit," Roman said. "Shoulda taken his head off when you had the chance and commandeered his ship. It's a big ship."

"Aye," agreed Deter. "Big ship."

Vane had heard just about enough out of Roman. "I already have a big ship. Or hadn't you noticed?"

Roman shrugged. "Two big ships is bigger than one big ship."

"Aye," said Deter again.

"Your grasp of arithmetic is impressive," Vane drawled.

"Better than yours, I wager," said Roman with a challenging

smirk.

Trejean glanced from Vane to Roman. "Should I leave you two alone?"

"My spirited new quartermaster speaks out of turn," Vane said.

"I thought every pirate's voice equal to him captain," said Trejean.

"So did I," Roman muttered bitterly.

"Within fucking reason," Vane replied. "I am here about Frederick Lindsay, not to openly discuss battle tactics in a crowded tavern."

"Then we will discuss it later," said Roman.

"Yes, we will." He would deal with his aggravating quartermaster later. Maybe he would make him disappear, just like Roman's parrot-haired friend. He suspected Kate Lindsay had something to do with Keet's absence, but she was beyond reproach. And, in truth, Vane was pleased to be rid of the little shit.

He returned his glower to Trejean. "About this bargain—"

Trejean raised a placating hand. "You should know, I turn him away."

"Is that supposed to impress me? I should gut you for waiting so long to tell me!"

Trejean looked down to contemplate his hands. His huge shoulders rose and fell as he seemed to wrestle with his thoughts. When he looked up again, a golden smile brightened his dark face. "I fear you will not get the chance."

Roman laughed hysterically and elbowed Vane's arm. "Fuck me, he's got a sense of humor! This half-a-slave sure talks—"

Roman's head jerked forward, his jaw dropped, and the tip of a dagger exploded from his mouth, splitting his tongue down the middle. Two of his front teeth popped out and skittered across the table. His head fell back as the dagger was retracted from his mouth, sliding out of the back of his neck. Vane looked up into the cold gaze of one of Trejean's bodyguards.

Deter tried to stand, reaching for his cutlass, but the second bodyguard was already behind him. The bodyguard slipped a dagger around Deter's neck and sliced his throat, dousing the table in his blood. Trejean stood and backed away to prevent his breeches from getting stained. Deter's eyes rolled desperately toward Vane as his life gurgled out of his throat in little red bubbles. He slumped forward, planting a cheek in his own blood.

The twins converged on Vane before he realized what had happened. They gripped his arms and held him down in his seat.

Vane looked at Trejean. "You treacherous fuck!"

The twin who had killed Roman balled his hand into a fist and smashed Vane in the jaw, where his molar had been removed. Vane nearly fainted from the pain. His vision blurred, and Trejean became a dark blob. Vane squinted until his vision cleared, but the throbbing pain remained, blossoming from his jaw in nauseating surges. "You said you turned down his offer!"

Trejean's golden teeth glinted with the fire of the hearth. "I did. But Lindsay struck bargain with a man who I cannot turn down."

"Oh, really? And who the fuck might that be?"

Trejean nodded to the entrance. Vane turned.

Frederick Lindsay entered, as small and dainty as Vane remembered. The pirates in the tavern paid him no heed as he strolled toward Vane. When he was within five paces, he stopped and folded his arms, unable to prevent a giddy grin from spreading. Boldness did not suit him. "Hello, Charles," he said. "You didn't truly think I would be fool enough to go through with your insane plan, did you?"

"You stunted shit!" Vane spat, wrestling against the embrace of his captors and blinking rapidly from the throbbing of his jaw. "Who have you consorted with? Say his name."

"It didn't take long to find him," Frederick replied. "In point of fact, he found me."

Vane seethed at Frederick's smug little face. "Tell your friend I'll be sure to gut him after I've ripped out your throat with my teeth. Or maybe I'll save you both for Mr. Tanner. He'll make it long and slow. Oh, yes."

"I don't think that's going to happen."

"Oh, you're going to kill me, are you?" Vane laughed. "You'll never get Katherine Lindsay."

"Won't I? As we speak, your ship is about to be boarded. Your men will die, and Katherine will be brought before me."

"Boarded? By who? Your pitiful crew of slavers? What will they attack my men with? Rusty chains? Buckets of shit?"

There was no trace of uncertainty in Frederick's eyes, and that worried Vane more than he was about to let on. "You've lost, Charles, and I'm the man who has beaten you. The sooner you accept that, the easier it will be."

"Fuck you! You've never done anything on your own, except fuck a perfectly good prospect up the arse. Trejean tells me you beat one of his whores."

Frederick looked to Trejean, and Trejean merely shrugged. "You did."

"What's the matter, Frederick?" Vane went on. "Do women frustrate you? Was she unable to please you? Did your cock fail? You shouldn't take it so hard. They say it happens to everyone, though I've been fortunate. Mine rises for anything with a soft wet hole. Others have more specific inclinations. Mayhap yours rises only for family? I'm sure your lovely mother would agree with me. What was her name? Martha. Yes, dear Martha. You feign to hate her so intensely, and you might have convinced yourself, but I wager a small part of you yearns for her. Do you think she'll let you inside her before she dies? She must be getting on in years now. If you bide your time, she'll be quite useless near the end, toothless and unable to squeal as you crawl naked on top of her. Her cunny might be a tad arid, but that won't stop you, will it?"

Frederick's lips twitched. "Enjoy your depraved abuses while you can, Charles. I've been to the eastern isle, and I've brought someone back with me."

"No one's been to the eastern isle and lived," Vane said with a snort.

"Then I am no one," Frederick replied.

"On that we agree," Vane laughed. "Show me the man you bargained with. Show me my true foe."

Frederick stepped aside, and a much taller man in a grey coat entered, old and bald and silver bearded. His milky white eyes seemed to lock with Vane's, even though they couldn't possibly see him. "Who the fuck are you?" Vane demanded.

"His name be Ash," Trejean offered helpfully.

"Aye," said Ash.

"Never heard of you," Vane said. What could he have done to wrong this old blind man? *Any number of things,* he decided. Maybe he scuttled his ship at sea. Maybe he killed his brother. Maybe he sullied his wife. Maybe his daughter. Who knew? He didn't really care. All that mattered now was getting out of here and returning with a vengeance.

"Oh, you wouldn't have," Ash said. "But the man I work for, you will know."

The flutist nearly toppled from his perch, his tune cut short with a horrendous screech. All heads turned toward the entrance, and after a series of startled gasps, the tavern fell deathly silent.

A towering shadow darkened the entrance, blotting out the

dimming turquoise sky beyond. Ash, who suddenly seemed much shorter, shuffled away. The heels of the impossibly tall man's boots thundered the deck. He wore a black tricorn hat and long black coat. The pirates and strumpets stared at him in awe as he walked through. He stopped before the hearth and looked up. The amber light revealed a chilling abomination. Shaggy dark hair spiraled from the right side of his singed head in wild, patchy tufts. The hair was missing entirely on the scorched left side, where the ear had been burnt to a crispy nub. His cheeks were a mess of blackened, flaking flesh, running with deep red fissures. Smoke sputtered from four glowing fuses clumsily fitted into what remained of an uneven beard, rolling up over the grotesque ruin of his face. The thin iris of a lone right eye gleamed sapphire beyond the haze. His left eyebrow had been burnt away, and there was nothing but a dark hollow beneath it, where an eye should have been.

Trejean's head fell in humble subjection.

"I trust you've met Edward Teach," Frederick said.

Blackbeard's guttural voice consumed the tavern, booming like the word of some ancient god. The fissures in his cheeks parted painfully when he spoke, revealing glistening raw muscle. "Charles Vane," he greeted. "Here I be expecting a pithy quip, and you leave me dangling. Have you nothing clever to say?"

Vane opened his mouth, but only one word emerged. "Fuck."

22

GABE

Something wasn't right. The ocean was too still and the night too quiet. No bonfires illuminated the beach, and most of the ships were dark in the harbor, with no suggestion of activity on their decks. Even Keelhaul Tavern had fallen silent.

Harry's boy lit two lanterns on *Advance's* main deck and made his way up to the quarterdeck, smiling at Gabe. He was twelve, with shaggy brown hair, a long skinny face, and twigs for arms and legs. He wore stained rags and carried a rusty dagger and very small pistol that Gabe wasn't sure even worked. There were a couple of Harrys aboard, but neither of them claimed to be the father. The boy refused to talk about it when asked. Some believed he was Vane's son, but Gabe didn't see any resemblance.

"Don't light this one," Gabe said as the boy approached the quarterdeck's darkened lantern with a slow match.

The boy stared at him, puzzled. "Why not?"

"I prefer it dark," Gabe replied.

Harry's boy glanced about conspiratorially. "Is something amiss?"

"I don't know," Gabe answered uneasily.

The boy shivered, even though there was no chill in the early night air. "I ain't never seen the island so dark. It's like they've all gone to sleep."

"Mariposa never sleeps," Gabe muttered grimly. "Go to your quarters. Keep a pistol at the ready."

The boy nodded and hurried off.

The half of the crew that remained on *Advance* were below decks, and muffled laughter wafted from the glowing hatch. They were having a party, enjoying a new batch of rum that several crewmen had brought back from Keelhaul Tavern shortly after their arrival in Mariposa earlier that day. The other half had gone to shore, and Gabe had expected to hear them dancing and singing and laughing along the beach, but there was no sign of them. Perhaps they had ventured deeper into the island. Keelhaul was not the only place of interest on Mariposa's western isle. There were a few more settlements inland, with more taverns and brothels, but it was unlike Vane's crew to stray far from the harbor.

Advance had dropped anchor further out than any other ship. Vane was a cautious man, even in friendly territory, but that did little to calm Gabe's nerves.

He walked to the stern and looked to the eastern isle, dark and mysterious. Atop the sharp cliff that jutted precariously over the ocean, a bonfire raged into the sky, and he thought he glimpsed figures moving around it. Beneath the cliff he saw a sloop that he was certain hadn't been there on his last visit. He wondered who it belonged to. He had never been to the eastern isle. The stories were enough to keep his curiosity at bay.

Gabe swept back his coat and twisted to scratch at his back.

The whip wounds Hennessey had dealt him were itching terribly, and he had to constantly remind himself not to scratch. They were healing, but that didn't make them any less of a hindrance. He strained to massage a particularly hard to reach laceration that ran down the center of his back, but eventually gave up.

He wondered what Kate was doing in the captain's cabin, just beneath his feet. Vane had appointed Mr. Tanner to guard the cabin door, with explicit instructions that no one was to enter. When Gabe asked for the duty, Vane had laughed in his face. "I think not, Mr. Jenkins. You fancy her. I doubt you could resist. I'm doing you a favor. She shields her cunny with violence."

Gabe wondered if she was thinking about him. She had not tried to kill him since he revealed the truth about Calloway's supposed death. Maybe she had taken him at his word after all. Unfortunately, there was no way to prove to her that he hadn't murdered Calloway. And even if the girl had survived the swim to shore, he had only bought her a few more days of life. She had probably died of thirst by now. Maybe a quick death would have been kinder.

I gave her a chance, he told himself. *That's something.*

He set his hands on the rail and sighed. Something struck dangerously close to his right hand, grinding into the wood, and he jerked away with a start. It was a hooked claw, one of three prongs.

A grapple?

He bent over the railing and peered downward. A rope dangled from the grapple, lined with knots that were each spread a foot apart for climbing. At the bottom of the rope, the slim outline of a longboat was barely visible against the calm water, huddled close to the stern. He saw three shapes, and one of them was ascending the rope toward the stern gallery.

They're coming for Kate.

As the figure reached the windows, he looked up suddenly, eyes gleaming in the dark, with a knife clamped between his teeth. Gabe pulled back and held his breath, hoping the interloper hadn't seen him. He reached for the grapple, but something stilled his hand. It would be easy to unhook it and let the man fall to the boat below, but the others would just find another way up.

He turned away from the rail and hurried down the stairs to the main deck. He approached the captain's cabin, where Mr. Tanner stood with his skinny arms folded. "No one goes in there, Mr. Jenkins."

"Lindsay is in trouble."

Tanner's buggy eyes rolled all about, looking at everything except Gabe. "That is impossible. Captain Vane instructed Mr. Tanner to stand watch, and standing watch is what Mr. Tanner is doing. No one has gotten past Mr. Tanner."

"Someone is about to get past Mr. Tanner," promised Gabe.

Tanner looked around. "Not possible. There is only one way in, and that is through Mr. Tanner. And, as you can see, no one has gone through Mr. Tanner."

Gabe sighed. He didn't have time for this. "I wonder, can Mr. Tanner be in two places at once?"

"Obviously he cannot," Tanner said with a snicker. "What other entrance could there be to the captain's quarters?"

"The stern gallery." Gabe reached into his sash and drew his curved dagger. "Mr. Tanner had best get out of my way."

Tanner's eyes widened at the sight of the blade, but not out of fear. "Such a pretty girl, that is. So shiny."

"It's not a girl, it's a dagger. Now move."

"Nay. Let Mr. Tanner touch it."

Gabe ground his teeth and looked around. "If I let you

touch it, will you move?"

"Aye."

"Fine."

Tanner gingerly set his index finger on the tip of the blade. His eyelids fluttered and he shuddered pleasurably. "You keep her so very sharp. You love her, I think."

Gabe frowned in disgust. "Alright, that's quite enough. Move."

Tanner slid out of the way, but his eyes remained on the blade. Gabe pushed through the cabin door and moved into utter darkness, save for a patch of stars showing through a shattered aft window. He kicked the door shut behind him.

Where is Kate?

His answer came in the form of cold ring pressing against his cheek. He heard the hammer of a pistol click into place. "Go on then," he said. "Do it."

"I like you better alive," replied a raspy female voice. "For now."

"Kate?"

"What are you doing here?"

"I saw a man climbing a rope." He pointed his dagger at the shattered window and lowered his voice. "The window's broken. Didn't you hear it? He must be just outside."

The cold ring fell away from his cheek. "He already got in."

He turned to stare at her, but he could only make out the vague silhouette of her hair. "And?"

"I don't think he found what he was looking for," she replied casually.

"Get behind me! Point me to him!"

"He's over by the desk. He had this pistol, but he wasn't inclined to use it. They must want me alive. Too bad for him."

As Gabe's eyes adapted, he found the desk. A dark shape lay beside it. "Is he dead?"

"I'm fairly certain he can't breathe with a quill buried in his gullet, but I'll get behind you if it makes you feel any better. Shall I cling to your backside and squeal as you jab at his corpse?"

"I prefer a damsel in distress clinging to my front."

She groaned. "There are two more in a boat below."

"I know." He started for the window, but he didn't hear her following alongside. He turned, squinting to make out her shape. "Are you coming?"

"Why, you scared to go all by your lonesome?"

"Are *you*?"

"No," she answered haughtily, "but I do happen to be barefoot, and there's broken glass over there. I've got enough scars, thank you. I'm confident you'll do fine without me."

He looked downward, though he couldn't see her feet in the dark. "You should really find a pair of boots."

"My toes like to breathe."

Gabe continued toward the window. His shins painfully knocked against something hard, which he quickly realized was the bed. He moved around it, ignoring the sting, and heard Kate snicker through her nose. When he was within five paces of the window, the heels of his boots crunched on glass. He walked as carefully as possible, but the noise was loud within the close quarters. He raised his dagger as he neared the window. Triangular shards of glass jutted dangerously from the frame on all sides, dripping blood. The intruder must have cut himself on his way in, before Kate plunged a quill into his throat.

"Do you see anything?" she called.

"Quiet!" he hissed over his shoulder.

A large hand shot up over the sill and grasped the cuff of his coat, jerking him forward. He thrust his dagger downward, and the blade sliced clean through the other man's wrist and wedged in the frame of the window. The shortened wrist spurted blood before it fell from view. The severed hand dropped to the deck, joining the many shards of glass. The intruder's spastic shrieks faded swiftly as he fell, concluding abruptly with a dull *thud* and a yelp of alarm from below.

Gabe stuck his head through the window and looked down. He saw two shapes in the boat now, which was rocking precariously in the water. Both men were laid flat, with one writhing underneath the motionless body of the man who had tumbled from the window.

Gabe reached out to yank on the rope fixed to the grapple that was hooked above. He turned to the darkness of the cabin.

"Not bad," he heard Kate say.

"Toss me the pistol."

"Use your own," she stubbornly replied.

"It's not on my person. I wasn't anticipating a battle."

After a moment's hesitation, the gun sailed toward him. He snatched it out of the air and turned to the window. He cleared away much of the glass lining the frame with several strokes of his dagger, and then stuck the gun out the window and pointed it downward. The final man had managed to worm his way out from under the man that had fallen on top of him. He was grabbing hold of the rope and getting ready to make his ascent. Gabe pulled the trigger. The top of the man's head burst into a sputtering red fountain. His body went stiff and he tumbled into the water like a wooden plank.

Another shot rang out. And then another. And another.

"Where's that coming from?" Kate asked with the mildest hint of concern.

Gabe thought he heard a scream. He ducked low and searched about for flashes, but saw none. The shots were not coming from any of the surrounding ships. He scanned the water, but didn't see any other boats. *Maybe the others aren't approaching from the stern.*

"It's coming from the main deck," Kate concluded. "We're being boarded."

Gabe tossed the pistol aside and hurried across the room. He collided with Kate on his way to the door, stepping on one of her toes. She let out a little squeal. "Sorry," he said.

"Maybe I *do* need boots," she decided.

He moved around her and opened the cabin door slightly, spying through the crack. Tanner was gone, and dozens of men were pouring over the starboard and port bulwarks and filing down the main hatch. Shots cracked in the hold and men shouted. One of the boarders stumbled over the rail, landing on his belly, and a granado slipped from his hand, its fuse a spiral of sparkling light as it rolled across the deck and down into the hatch. The other boarders scattered. A tremendous explosion sounded, and light beamed from the hatch for an instant, followed swiftly by a roiling cloud of smoke. Shouts turned to warbled shrieks as flames crept out of the hatch. A man ascended covered in fire, swinging his arms and wailing like a crazed banshee. Gabe couldn't tell if the poor man was one of *Advance's* crew or one of the enemy.

Kate leaned close from behind. "I don't understand," she whispered. "Why would anyone dare attack Vane?"

"I haven't the foggiest notion, but the whole island is against him, looks like. The ships have all gone dark. The beach is cleared out. Someone has leverage over this place."

"Who?"

He shrugged. "If discovering the truth means dying, I'm happy not knowing." He hoped Harry's boy would make it out unscathed, but there was no way to get to him now.

"So what do we do?" Kate asked. In the dark, he watched her slender figure move to the desk, where she retrieved her coat and put it on. "You can't use me for leverage. They'll just kill you after you hand me over."

"I know that." *Wise of you to remind me.*

Gabe carefully closed the door and latched it. He slid his dagger into the sheath concealed in his sash. He looked to the window and saw the thin line of rope that the intruders had used to climb up. "The longboat," he said. "It's our only chance. We just need to get to the jungle." Once they reached the jungle, no one would find them. "I know a place we can hide."

"I can't get to the window, remember? The glass." She sighed. "I suppose this is the part where you leave me behind and save your own—"

He felt around in the dark until his fingers grazed her thigh. She tried to pull away, but he snatched her to him by the waist of her breeches and scooped her off of her feet, with her back cradled in one arm and her legs dangling over the other. She threw an arm around his neck. "Speak of this to anyone," she rasped in his ear, "and I will murder you."

He chuckled as he carried her to the window. "You'd better make good on that promise sooner rather than later, or someone will beat you to it."

When he reached the open window, he set her on the sill. "Can I trust you to go first without taking the boat?"

She grabbed the rope and slid outside. "No promises." She started quickly down the rope, her wild hair and the tails of her coat tossing in the wind.

A loud *thump* sounded from the door. Gabe didn't bother looking over his shoulder. He crawled up onto the sill and grasped the rope. He swung outside and started down after Kate. She reached the boat quickly and waited below with her hands on her hips. When he was within ten feet of the boat, he let go of the rope. He landed on the body of the man with the severed arm and nearly twisted his ankle. The boat wobbled, and he took hold of Kate's shoulder to steady himself. She slapped his hand away. "You've done enough groping for one night," she said.

Gabe hefted the dead man by the shoulders and tossed him out of the boat. The corpse splashed into the black water and vanished from sight. "Grab an oar," he told Kate.

They sat side by side and rowed frantically away from the ship. The boat was small and easy for two people to maneuver, since its original company had intended to go unnoticed in the night. When they rowed out of the shadow of the stern, they saw six longboats piled alongside *Advance's* starboard side, with many more pirates scaling the hull.

They rowed with their backs to their destination: the beach on the far eastern side of the harbor, where the jungle was closest. It was the furthest point of the harbor from Keelhaul Tavern. Gabe had a feeling they didn't want to go anywhere near that place.

The ships remained dark all around. He pointed between a brigantine and a long sloop, which were anchored closely. "Row for that gap," he instructed. "We need as much cover as possible. They will have broken into the cabin by now and found you absent."

Kate stared placidly at *Advance* as she rowed. Her hair was deep red in the night, with only the distant glow of flames to highlight it. The death's head buttons gleamed silver along the lapel of the coat she had stolen from Jack Rackham. The wind tossed her hair aside, and he glimpsed the patch of garbled skin and small black hole. He was inclined to ask if it had hurt, but the question was rhetorical. *Of course it hurt.*

"It's hideous, I know," she said. She must have noticed him staring.

"Gives you character," he replied too hastily.

Her hoarse laugh was unmistakably cynical. "Oh, yes. I *was* dreadfully dull before my ear was bitten off. You would have hated me."

"I doubt that."

"Why did you help me?" she asked suddenly. "You could have let them have me and escaped on your own. No one would have followed."

Fire crept into the muscles of Gabe's arms, intensifying with every stroke of his oar. "Maybe I'm tired of watching women die."

"Then you think Calloway is dead?"

"I don't know," he admitted. "I hope not."

She lifted her sharp chin, and the soft light of the distant fire grazed her long neck. Her profile was a picture of defiance and pride. "Maybe you just want my reward for yourself."

He smiled wistfully and said, "A bit of shine sets every pirate out of his mind."

"What?"

"It's a song pirates sing," he explained. "I don't think I make for a very good pirate. I gave up my share so I could 'kill' Calloway, if you'll recall."

"Thank you for the reminder. I'd forgotten." She rapped her knuckles on her temple. "I've taken more than a few knocks to the head."

She'll never believe me, he realized despondently.

The little boat slipped between the bows of the sloop and the brigantine, and Gabe looked upward to make sure no one was watching. He didn't see any silhouettes looking over either ship's rail. When they were halfway through, he stopped oaring. His burning arms were instantly grateful for the respite. Kate took notice and stopped as well. They lingered in silence for a while, with the boat gently bobbing in the water. Occasionally, Gabe would stick out his oar to keep the boat from drifting into the hull of the sloop on his side. He shifted and looked to their intended destination. He didn't see any movement along the beach. "Our fortune holds," he said, breaking the silence.

Kate was fidgeting with her fingers, picking dirt out from under her nails. "So what happens when we get to shore? You take me to some secluded hideaway, seduce me, and turn me in after you've satisfied yourself?"

"You've been around pirates too long."

She inclined her head in acquiescence. "Any time amongst pirates is too long, I suppose."

"I don't care about your reward, Kate." To his surprise, he meant it.

She merely smirked. "What *do* you care about?"

He watched as flames took hold of *Advance's* mainmast, snaking toward the furled mainsail. If the fire wasn't extinguished soon, Vane's new prize would not last the night. "I won't let another woman die if I can help it."

"No one means to kill me. I'm a bargaining piece. I'm safer now than I've ever been."

"No one is safe out here," he reminded her. "Your worth may be vast, but you're also a great deal of trouble. If you prove more trouble than you're worth, one day you'll find yourself at the bottom of the ocean."

She sniffed dismissively. "I could have escaped on my own. You think a little glass on the floor would have stopped me?"

"I wager a wall of fire wouldn't have stopped you," he admitted. "The bottoms of your feet might be grateful, however."

Her chapped lips crept toward a smile, and Gabe's heart raced at the urge to moisten them with his own. Her eyes narrowed as though she suspected his sudden desire. And then she chortled derisively and curled her lip. "Do you honestly think I'd let you have me after what you did to Jaq?"

"I didn't kill—"

She gave her oar a fierce tug, stirring the boat into motion. "Spare me the extravagant lies, Gabe. I don't know how much of you is real, and I haven't the patience to sort it out."

He set his jaw and faced forward, fending off the impulse to stand up for himself. He wrenched his oar into motion and paddled extra fast to keep from tilting into the brigantine on Kate's side.

They emerged from between the two ships and rowed silently for the beach. When they reached the sand, Kate dropped her oar and hopped out first. Gabe held onto his oar and followed her over the side, into two feet of water. He sloshed forward a few paces, pivoted, and used his oar to prod the boat back to sea. When the boat was far enough away, he hurled the oar into the air. It sailed in a steady arc and landed perfectly in the boat. He turned to Kate and grinned, aiming a thumb over his shoulder. "You see that?"

Kate's lopsided scowl and folded arms suggested she was not impressed.

He sighed and continued onward, brushing her shoulder as he walked past. "It's not easy, is all I'm saying," he grumbled.

He led her into the jungle, which was not as dense as he would have liked. Trees were spaced too far apart, and plants and foliage were sparse. *We'll be too easy to spot from a distance,* Gabe realized. So they pushed onward, and the jungle grew thicker with every hundred paces.

The ground began to slope upward, and through breaks in the trees Gabe glimpsed dark hills ahead, ascending toward the main summit of the island. After a while the muscles in his legs stiffened and sweat trickled from his armpits. He checked often to make sure Kate was keeping up. She didn't seem fazed by the hike. "Don't worry, Gabe, your reward is still close behind you."

He swept a loose curl out of his vision in frustration. "How many times do I have to tell you, I don't care about all that?"

"Then where are you taking me?"

"A secluded hideaway where I might seduce you and then turn you in for the reward," he retorted before he could stop himself. His wit was always quicker than his wisdom.

"You're very funny," she replied flatly.

"It just happens."

They came to a big round boulder, half as tall as a man. It looked rather out of place in the middle of the jungle all by its lonesome, as though it had been dropped from the sky. It was covered in white bird droppings. Gabe knew he was on the right path, as this was the first of three landmarks he had memorized.

"I suppose I should be thanking you for aiding my escape," said Kate as they passed the boulder. She embellished a hopeless sigh. "I'm no good with gratitude."

He chuckled. "I wouldn't want you to drop dead from—"

Something struck the back of his head. He dropped to his knees. He threw out his palms and caught himself before his face could hit the sand. His vision crowded with colorful little dots that swirled about like crazed fireflies. His arms trembled as the muscles softened. He couldn't get back to his feet no matter how hard he strained. Sweat trickled from his hair, sliding down his cheeks . . . but when it dribbled into the sand, he saw that it was not sweat. Sweat was never so red.

"Thank you for aiding my escape," he heard her say, before another blow buckled his elbows and mashed his face into the red-spotted sand.

23

CALLOWAY

The twin mounds of Mariposa were dark and featureless in the indistinct predawn gloom. Smoke wafted from the harbor, the source of which was imperceptible from this distance. But it was not Mariposa that stole Calloway's gaze; it was the silky black water trailing past *Swift's* port bow. She wanted to strip off her clothes, leap in and swim the remainder of the way to the island, with nothing but the cool water to caress her skin. She was certain she could make the journey without drowning from exhaustion. And when she surfaced, any man watching from the shore would swear he saw a mermaid.

She gently ran a finger across her neck. The wound was healing fast. Some of the scab had flaked away, revealing a thin pink line underneath. There would forever be a faint scar to serve as a reminder of what the sea had given her. "The water mended me," she absently murmured.

"The salt may have helped a bit," Dillahunt objected.

"However, seawater cannot seal a severed neck. Jenkins let you live."

She had forgotten he was behind her, hunched on a barrel, struggling to fit his left foot in a boot that was a size too small. "The water mended me," she repeated. She didn't expect him to understand. She could never convey the rejuvenation she felt, as though her bones had been strengthened and her flesh renewed. She crossed her arms over her chest to grasp her broad shoulders, which had ached for two days after the long swim to shore, but now felt so taut and sturdy. Before Gabe Jenkins tossed her over *Advance's* rail, it had been too long since her last swim, and she had forgotten how strong it made her.

"I went in the water as well," Dillahunt sourly replied as he grappled with his boot. "Strange that I didn't sprout a fresh toe." Since Calico Jack rescued them, he had spent most of the last few days confined to a hammock below deck with his leg propped up. Rackham's confident young surgeon had restitched the wound, and his foot had returned to a healthy color, but Dillahunt claimed he could still sense the infection spreading up his leg.

Calloway turned to him and set her elbows against the rail. "I've always loved the water. My mother called me a fish."

He did not look up from his boot. "It *is* a wonder you were able to hold your breath for so long."

"I held it for five minutes once." She had spent so much of her childhood in the water, paddling against the waves that tried so hard to keep her from getting very far. But she had always outwitted the tide, diving below before each wave could carry her back to shore. She would stay under for as long as possible, opening her eyes and pushing forward as the waves rolled overhead.

"That is a talent," he granted, "but it isn't magic. I've

known many sailors who claimed the same, or longer."

She rolled her eyes. "Liars."

When Dillahunt's foot finally slipped into the boot, his face turned bright red, and he looked like he was going to pass out. His cheeks trembled, until a puff of air burst from his lips. "I am dying."

"You're being dramatic." When they first met, she had been charmed by his quirky bellyaching. Now it was an annoyance, no different than the noisy bird that once made its nest outside her window and woke her up with its chirping every morning.

He obstinately shook his head. "I can feel it. I have mere days before it claims me. A week, at most. I must finish my task before this rot spreads to my core."

Her hand found its way into her breeches to clutch the toe, hard as rock.

Dillahunt looked up, and then scowled with a sudden realization. "Jesus, it's not still in your pocket, is it?"

"It's lucky." She didn't really believe that anymore, but she hadn't the heart to tell him that it now served as a memento. As long as she held it, she would never again allow herself to fall for a man like him. If she ever came close to such folly again, she would take hold of the toe and remind herself that all things turned black in the end.

"Lucky?" He choked out what might have been a laugh. "It's the only part of me that is. I told you to cast that wretched thing over the side! Maybe the sea's magical powers will produce another me from my toe. That would be nice. I could use a new me. This one is spent."

She withdrew her hand and returned her arms to a tight self-embrace. "I would, if only the sea could grant a new personality. Sadly, I fear you would emerge the same."

He flicked his eyes at her in irritation. "And how would you have me emerge?"

"I would not have you emerge at all," she blurted. She immediately regretted it. There was no reason to be cross with a man she held no feelings for. It was a waste of energy.

"I see," he replied stiffly. "I suppose anger is reasonable. What I did was unforgiveable."

"Then do not expect forgiveness."

"Lover's quarrel?" said Calico Jack as he approached. He appeared more relaxed than usual, minus his hat with his long blonde hair flowing free of its usual ponytail. His white shirt was unlaced, exposing much of his chest, and he was beltless. He had even taken out his earring for the night. Calloway thought he looked much more dashing when he wasn't trying.

"We are not lovers," was her terse reply, to ensure no further misunderstanding. The thought of crawling back in a bed with Dillahunt sickened her.

"Then what are you? The men are curious." The captain offered a little smile. He had been flirting with her the entire journey, while Dillahunt pretended not to notice. "I might be curious as well."

She ground her fingernails into her shoulders. "You're very handsome, Jack Rackham."

Dillahunt started to react, and then looked away.

Calico Jack shrugged humbly. "They say every tenth man is born with fair features. I was fortunate."

She scowled. "It's not a compliment. I've learned not to trust handsome men."

"Then you've learned but one tenth of a lesson."

"Are you two quite finished?" Dillahunt snapped.

Calico Jack grinned knowingly. "Then you *are* together."

"I didn't say that," she huffed. "We are business partners, nothing more."

"No we are not!" Dillahunt objected with a sweep of his hand. "I will not be responsible for you any longer. Or anyone else, for that matter. I'll have no more blood on my hands, save for my own and Charles Vane's."

Calico Jack looked at Calloway, anticipating her response.

Calloway laughed. "I don't recall giving you a choice in the matter. Our goals are linked. When you find Vane, I'll find Kate."

Dillahunt stared at her. "What do you want with her?"

"Her reward, of course."

He snorted. "Somehow I think it's more personal than that."

Maybe a little, she admitted to herself. "May the best woman win," Kate had said. *She probably thinks she has,* Calloway realized. *As far as she's concerned, I'm dead.*

"That woman is far too dangerous," Dillahunt said. "The Caribbean will be better off when someone puts an end to her miserable life."

"I can handle Kate."

"Many men have tried," Calico Jack said with a wry smile. He thumbed his right eyebrow. The welt Kate had given him was almost gone.

Calloway smiled. "I am no man, as you seem fond of noticing."

An eerie silence fell over *Swift's* deck as Mariposa's harbor drew near. The source of the smoke soon became clear. Two sloops and several longboats had surrounded *Advance*. Pirates were dancing about a raging fire at the center of her main deck. Flames had crawled up the mainmast and claimed the furled sails, eating through the hemp and dispatching a thousand embers to confuse the stars. Squirming men were escorted toward the blaze. A few squirmed out of their captors' clutches and made a mad dash for the sea, but were shot down before they could leap over the bulwark. Most were not so lucky, and were tossed into the flames to die screaming. Charred corpses were deposited over the sides.

Neither of the two sloops moved to intercept *Swift* as she dropped anchor near the eastern beach.

"Your vengeance has been stolen from you," Calico Jack told Dillahunt.

Dillahunt was unmoved. "Charles Vane would never die so easily."

"That's true," Rackham agreed with an incisive glance. "And you hope to succeed where these men have failed?"

Calloway knew what Dillahunt's reply would be before he said it. "I will hate myself if I don't try."

Calico Jack laughed. "And if you're dead, you can't hate yourself. It's a fine plan, I'll grant you."

Dillahunt glared at him through the unkempt locks in front of his face. "I don't expect you to understand."

"Does it please you to watch his crew burn?" came a thick, resonant voice. Dumaka stood behind Dillahunt. Rackham had given him new breeches and a clean shirt, and offered him a position among his crew, which Dumaka had yet to accept. He had been very silent since their rescue, but frequent scowls directed at his former captain spoke loudly enough. He had lost all his friends, and he would never forgive Dillahunt for that.

Calloway couldn't blame him. She thought about Bastion often. She had been too afraid to ask Dillahunt how Bastion had died, and he hadn't offered.

"Death gives me no pleasure," Dillahunt replied, but Calloway knew him well enough to know he was lying; his right hand was rubbing thumb against forefinger. "I am not an animal. I am above base desires."

Calloway exchanged an amused glance with Dumaka.

"Neither do I feel sorrow," Dillahunt added with a raised finger. "This is justice."

"Whose justice, I wonder?" asked Calico Jack.

"Who cares?" said Dillahunt.

Calico Jack squinted into the blaze, and Calloway saw the face of a less confident man. "It used to be so much simpler," he said with a despondent shake of his head. "We're doing the governor's job for him."

Dillahunt stood and tested his new boots, wincing and hissing as he walked to the bulwark, filling the spot between Calloway and Calico Jack. "Are you sure we should be so close? Whoever these men are, they might be your enemy as well as Vane's."

Calico Jack was unconcerned. "You've seen how fast my ship can move. If you're still mad enough to pursue Charles, I'll see you ferried to shore."

"What about you?" Dillahunt asked.

The pirate captain shrugged. "I'll be on my way. I've no wish to get caught up in . . . whatever this is. I've heard bad things about Mariposa of late. Dark tales from the eastern isle."

Dillahunt laughed. "I will not be swayed."

Calloway pointed at one of the sloops. "What if they come about before we can get to shore?"

"That's your concern," said Calico Jack. "But I wouldn't fret. The shore is close, and something tells me if they had a mind to attack, they would have done so by now. Pirates are not a patient lot. Charles must have done something to cross them."

"Maybe they're after Kate," Calloway suggested. *Everyone's after Kate.*

"She's either dead or in their clutches by now," Dillahunt said. "You've no hope of retrieving her."

She didn't believe Kate was dead. Kate was too resourceful to die. "The odds are just as narrow as you catching Vane," she reminded him. "Yet that isn't going to stop either of us, is it?"

Calico Jack smirked at their bickering. "You're quite the pair."

"We're not a pair," Calloway snapped.

"Two makes a pair, my dear."

She backed away from the rail, away from Dillahunt. She didn't want to be associated with him anymore. Her back hit something rock solid. She turned and looked up into the hard eyes of Dumaka. "You should not go to that island," he warned. "That is no place for you. You should stay here with Captain Rackham. Dillahunt cannot protect you. He cannot protect anyone. You will die, just like everyone else who has followed him."

She touched his arm. "Not if you come with me."

He jerked his arm away. "I will not follow that man anywhere."

"Then follow *me*," she pressed.

He tightened his jaw and looked sideways, his great chest heaving with several deep breaths. "No."

She glanced over her shoulder to see if Dillahunt was watching, but his eyes were fixed on the burning ship. She lowered her voice to a whisper. "Guy may not be able to protect me, but you can."

He aimed a long index finger at the scar along her neck. "You died, and now you are alive."

"The water mended me," she told him.

His hard eyes softened, and she knew that he believed her. "You do not need my protection," he said. "You have the sea."

She gathered one of his massive hands in both of hers. Her fingers were so tiny compared to his. "I won't always be so near the water."

24

KATE

As always, she had no plan.

She made her way back through the jungle, winding through the trees. The sand grew softer under the soles of her feet as she neared the beach. But the sand was deceptive, and she was forced to pause and lean against a tree after slicing her heel on a jagged seashell concealed just beneath the surface. It wasn't terribly deep, and the bleeding ceased after holding her palm against it for a minute. She timidly moved on, trying not to put much pressure on that heel, but she would occasionally forget and feel the sting of sand grinding into the raw wound.

She wasn't sure of the time, but she guessed it to be nearing midnight. The sky was its blackest and the stars were their brightest. There was no moon, but her eyes had grown accustomed to the dark after spending so much time in dimly-lit cabins and a gloomy mansion.

Venturing inland didn't make much sense to her. She had

spotted a tavern on the far opposite edge of the harbor during the escape from *Advance*. There would likely be strumpets there, and maybe she could conceal herself among them until she could get away on a ship. Of course, her ruse would fall through the minute a pirate actually attempted to bed her and she buried Gabe's curved dagger in his head.

Gabe.

Had he really expected her to believe he wouldn't sell her to the Lindsays at the first opportunity? Why else would he risk his neck to save her? He was a cloud of lies, nothing more. He was lucky she hadn't killed him. *I should have,* she told herself again and again.

Gabe hadn't even the decency to admit to murdering Calloway. Instead he had invented an elaborate lie to gain Kate's trust, and not a very good lie at that. She clutched the hilt of his dagger, wishing she had drawn the impossibly sharp blade across his throat after knocking him unconscious with a rock. *Why didn't I finish him off?* She hoped it wasn't because of his pretty face. That certainly hadn't prevented her from putting a shot through Jonathan Griffith's skull when the time came.

I should have killed him. There was no chance of crossing paths with him again if he was dead. *I should have sliced his throat and never given him another thought.*

She wished she had followed her first instinct; the same instinct that had urged her to leave Nathan behind in Nassau. But Nathan's sudden death at the hands of Annabelle had affected her more than she had been willing to admit. His death had softened her.

I should have left Dillahunt in Vane's prison. She hadn't really needed Dillahunt to escape Pirate Town. Hornigold's crew would have been enough. Sure, Dillahunt's battle tactics proved useful, but she would have thought of another way. She always did.

I should have let Jaq die along with her father. Calloway never would have made it off *Queen Anne's Revenge* without her. Maybe the girl had never needed saving in the first place. Blackbeard must have realized she was his daughter, and that's why he hadn't killed her.

All of the people she had spared had betrayed her, and to what end? Most of them were dead now.

Friends are too hazardous, she told herself. *Hazardous to me and hazardous to themselves.*

She would have to start anew.

She would have to become someone else entirely.

She would have to change her name.

She might even have to shorten her hair, given that it was her most distinctive feature.

She shuddered. The notion of trimming it even a few inches frightened her more than death. *To Hell with that,* she decided. *I am not doing a thing to my goddamned hair.* Besides, shortening it would reveal her lost ear.

As always, she had no plan.

The trees thinned, and between the trunks she saw the glint of fire reflecting off of the water in the harbor. She arrived at the edge of the jungle just in time to see *Advance's* mainmast topple and splash into the water, where its flames were instantly extinguished. The rest of the ship seemed to have been spared. Maybe the enemy pirates had kept the fire at bay. It would have been foolish to sink a ship as fine as *Advance*.

She kept just behind the trees, scanning the shore. She soon realized how much she had been exerting herself. She ran her fingers through her hair, which was thick with sweat. She peeled her damp shirt from her chest and fanned herself with it. She wanted to take off her coat, but she didn't want to have to carry it, and she definitely didn't want to leave it behind. She had become almost as fond of Rackham's coat as she was of her hair. She tucked Gabe's dagger carefully into her belt and bent forward to set her hands on her thighs and catch her breath.

When she looked up again, she saw a longboat closing on the beach. She ducked behind the nearest tree, clutching the thin trunk. She watched as the boat came closer, five figures within, two of them in the rear rowing dutifully.

Beyond the longboat, the ship nearest the shore was a sloop. It was too dark to make out any details, but the sleek shape was distinctly familiar. "*Swift*," she muttered to herself. *What is Rackham doing here?* She glanced downward. *Maybe he wants his coat back.*

The boat slid ashore, and the three in the front jumped out while the rowers remained aboard. She couldn't see their features from here, only their shapes. One was huge and muscular, hulking above the other two. The second was hunched and limping on his left foot. The third was long and slender, with curved hips. Definitely a woman. The hulking man and the woman pushed the longboat back to sea while the other one limped onto the beach. The two that remained in the boat started rowing back to the sloop. The three figures started walking along the beach. The woman and the big man had to stop and wait for the hobbling man to catch up. "You should have brought a crutch," the woman said.

"Let me know when you find one," the man with the limp begrudgingly replied.

Kate knew those voices too well. Her breath caught in her throat and held there until her head threatened to swell from lack of oxygen. When she finally remembered to breathe, she gasped so sharply that the sound was nearly a squeal in her throat. The woman on the beach jerked her head toward the jungle, and Kate glimpsed the face of Jacqueline Calloway. Kate sheltered herself as best she could behind the tree.

That is not possible!

She drew Gabe's dagger. Her pained expression was reflected dimly in the polished blade.

When she looked up again, the silhouettes of Dillahunt, Calloway, and the tall man—judging by his build, that must have been Dumaka—were already much further up the beach. They were headed for the tavern on the other side. *They must be after Vane,* she thought. *Or me. Or the both of us.*

An irritating scraping sound prompted her to look up and see if a monkey or some other creature was picking away at the bark of the tree. After a moment, she realized the sound was coming from her mouth. She was grinding her teeth.

She knew what she had to do. It was the only choice left to her. She sighed. *If only I'd known before I cracked his skull.*

She watched until the three figures were tiny dots in the distance. She would have liked to run to Calloway and embrace her, but that would only end with Calloway betraying her yet again, with Dillahunt's aid. For two people who claimed apathy toward one another, they couldn't seem to stay apart for very long.

She tore her gaze from them, wondering if it was the last time she would ever see them. At least Jaq was alive. Kate prayed she would stay that way, but Calloway was not her concern anymore.

She turned to the jungle and burst into a sprint, refusing to let herself look again. She followed her own trail in the sand. She ran on her toes to avoid placing pressure on her injured heel. After a while the jungle grew too dense, and she was forced to slow down to keep from colliding with the trees. She came upon the large boulder covered in bird droppings and knew she was close. But when she found the spot where she'd left Gabe unconscious, all that remained was an indentation of his body in the sand and a set of tracks leading further into the jungle.

A flicker of light caught her eye.

Not a hundred paces off there was an orange glow dancing off of the trees. She retreated to the large boulder and crouched beside it. The voices of two men trailed from the direction of the light.

"I don't think no one came this way," said one.

"Keep your voice down," said the other, just as loud.

"Well there ain't no one out there to hear me voice, is there?"

"We don't know that, do we?"

"All I know is we've been out here for two hours and we ain't found no one. If there was someone to find, we would have done."

"The woman weren't on the ship, were she? If she weren't on the ship, it stands to reason she's out here somewheres lurking about."

"That's no standing reason! Might be she sunk like a rock soon as she hit the water and went straight to the bottom of the harbor."

"And killed three of our boys on her way down? I don't think so. I think she's out here, that's what I think. I think she's listening to us, and if you don't keep that flapping cunny of a mouth shut, she'll run off before we can find her."

"You're just as loud as I is."

"I'm raising my voice to make it heard over your voice, is all."

"I still don't know what we need her for."

"She's worth a fortune, says Ash. We mustn't kill her, says Ash. Well, a little rape never killed no one, says I."

"Aye!" said the other with renewed determination. "Why didn't you say nothing about rape earlier?"

"It goes without saying, don't it?"

A hand clasped Kate's mouth, clammy with sweat and large enough encompass her entire jaw. Her scream was muffled against a heated palm. She looked down and saw the oversized cuff of a black coat. A powerful arm snaked around her chest, fingers groping one of her breasts. Her feet left the ground as she was wrenched backwards. She landed on top of her attacker in the sand. He grunted beneath her as the wind was knocked out of him, but his grip did not falter. She grasped at the dagger in her belt.

When he spoke, she froze. "Nice of you to come back," Gabe breathed into her ear. His left hand released her mouth, but the right remained where it was. "Ill-timed, but nice."

She sighed in relief and relaxed against him, tilting her head sideways and letting her cheek mash his nose. "How's the headache?"

"I've had worse." The strain in his voice hinted otherwise, but he was hiding it well. "I can think of a few ways you might make it up to me."

She snickered. "Don't be silly. I didn't do anything. A hard fruit fell out of a tree. It's not my fault you never look up."

"*Two* hard fruits, apparently," he drawled. His lips grazed her cheek when he spoke. "What are the odds?"

"You're just unlucky." She glanced downward at his hand, which was still cupping her breast. "You have ten seconds to retract that hand." He didn't budge. "On an entirely unrelated note," she added casually, "I have your dagger."

"I was wondering where it got off to. Ten seconds, you say?"

"Eight seconds."

His fingers curled slightly, squeezing her. "You count slow."

"Five."

"Ten seconds is an awfully generous amount of time."

"Three."

"Why the sudden change of heart?" he wondered.

She tossed her head sharply, whipping his face with her hair. "Turns out you're less of a liar than I thought. Time's up."

He held her a second longer than she had permitted, and then he opened his fingers and lifted his hand. She rolled off of him onto her hands and knees. He remained on his back in the sand. His face was white as a sheet, his lips pale. She slid a hand around the back of his head and felt the wound. The tips of her fingers came away slick with blood. "Gabe . . . "

He curled forward and sat up, wincing. "It's not as bad as it looks," he groaned. "I've lost a little blood, is all."

She looked over her shoulder. The distant torchlight was fainter now. The two men had started in another direction.

"They'll come back," he said. He rubbed the back of his head and frowned. He looked so very tired. "We need to move."

She helped him to his feet, placing his arm over her shoulder and pushing upward. She maneuvered him through the ever thickening jungle as he pointed the way. She checked frequently to make sure no one was following. She saw no torchlight, heard no voices, but an eerie feeling continued to give her pause.

A hundred paces later, they came to a huge fallen tree trunk that had cut a line through the jungle where it landed. "Second landmark," Gabe said. "We're on the right path." The jungle was too thick at either end of the tree, so she had to help him over the trunk.

The ground increasingly inclined, and her legs started to protest. An hour later, they came to the third landmark. It was another fallen tree trunk, only this one was stretched across a ravine with a nauseating two hundred foot plummet to a little river at the bottom. Vines and gnarled roots jutted from the cliffs on either side. The river ran south, and through the V that cut through the jungle, Kate could see the white line of the beach a mile down, and the dark shapes of ships crowding the harbor beyond.

"Is this the only way?" she asked.

"'Fraid so," he replied.

She helped him across the trunk, which was barely wide enough for two people to cross side by side. He stumbled a few times, and she clutched him to make sure he wouldn't go over. "I need a rest," he groaned.

"Now wouldn't be the best time," she reminded him.

"Shouldn't have smashed me over the head then."

"Keep talking. I could just let you drop."

His laugh was faint. "Good luck finding my hideout on your own."

She placed her heel on a protruding piece of bark, forgetting her recent cut yet again. She hissed at the pain and twisted her ankle, wobbling in place until Gabe steadied her. She glanced sheepishly at him, dreading the inevitable snarky retort, but he offered none.

About forty paces after they made it across the trunk, the jungle opened to a big round lake that rested at the foot of a ninety foot waterfall streaming down a sheer cliff face. The thin white line broke on a protruding rocky ledge two thirds of the way down, spilling over the rim in a broad curtain that cascaded into the lake and saturated the air with a fine mist that was cool on Kate's cheeks. She bent forward and set her palms on her knees, catching her breath. "Dead end," she groaned. The lake looked so inviting, beckoning her to dive in. "At least we won't die of thirst."

"Up there," Gabe said, pointing at the ledge.

"That's your secret place? An outcropping?"

"Beyond the waterfall, in the rock."

"You sure this is right?"

"It's there," he assured her. "Trust me."

"You look ready to pass out. Can you even make that climb?"

He cast a wary glance into the jungle. "Don't wager I have a choice."

She followed him as he circumvented the bank of the lake toward the eastern edge, to the base of the crag where many boulders had piled over the years, forming a natural stairway toward the ledge far above. The size of the boulders gave Kate pause. They were blanketed in moss.

Gabe motioned for her to go first, and she stared at him questioningly. "In case you fall," he explained.

"You think you can catch me in your condition? If I fall, we're both going."

"Better you fall on me than the other way around, wouldn't you agree?"

She folded her arms. "Or maybe you just fancy another gander at my ass."

He was too weary to grin; instead his lips twisted into a lopsided leer. "It's a mutually beneficial arrangement."

It was a thirty foot climb, with more than a few uncomfortably thin footholds. The spray of the waterfall laced the mossy rock with a glistening sheen that was as beautiful to behold as it was slippery to grasp. When Kate was three feet from the top, she made the mistake of looking down. The stars twinkled in the ripples that swelled from the bottom of the waterfall, and for a nauseating instant she feared she would slip from her perch and tumble forever into a distorted night sky. She closed her eyes and pressed her cheek against the cold damp rock, until Gabe tapped her heel from below. "We have to move," he urged.

The ledge was four feet removed from the nearest foothold,

and Kate had to leap across the gap to reach it. Her arms slapped the flat rock of the ledge, which was slick with the water streaming over the sides. She grasped a vine sticking up out of a crack before she could slide off. She wrenched herself onto the ledge and collapsed onto her back. The constant stream of the waterfall touched down on the ledge just a few feet from her head. In only a few seconds her clothes were completely soaked, but she didn't mind that one bit. The climb had been exhausting.

Gabe leapt across. His face turned bright red as he struggled to crawl up. When he started to slide, Kate offered a hand. "Not a very safe place to hide," she informed him as she helped him up beside her.

He nodded at an old rusty hook that was embedded in the rock wall several feet above the gap they had leapt across. "There used to be a rope hanging from that. It made swinging across much easier. Must have rotted off."

"So what now?"

He pointed. Behind the waterfall she saw a dark crack cut into the cliff, just large enough for a person to slip through. It was perfectly concealed from the lake below by both the water and the angle of the ledge.

"After you," she said. She didn't like dark places.

He brushed past her and slipped into the crack, tilting sideways to fit through. And then he vanished. She hesitated, staring into the darkness. She took a deep breath and followed. The rocky walls were frighteningly close for several paces, and her heart thumped rapidly until the walls opened. But she was immersed in pitch darkness, and she was forced to slow her pace. The ground declined ever so slightly, and her heels briefly skidded on a slick patch of moss. "Gabe?" she called, trying not to sound as nervous as she was. The constant crashing of the waterfall on the flat rock of the ledge echoed deafeningly into the hollow, and she could scarcely hear her own voice. The air was musty and warm. She looked back and saw only a sliver of dull grey light.

"Gabe?" she called again into the darkness.

The distinctive clack of stone against metal was followed by a spark, illuminating Gabe for an instant, hunched low to the ground. A second spark cast his shadow large and ominous against rocky walls. The sparks burned sharp white streaks into her vision, and they would not fade no matter how hard she blinked. The third spark ignited fire, which blossomed swiftly upon a torch. He set the flint and steel aside and picked up the torch, standing in the center of the cavern.

It was the size of a small bedroom. Stalactites hung dangerously low from the ceiling. The uneven floor was slightly concave. On the right side of the room was a crude slab of a bed covered in dirty brown blankets, and on the left was a simple round table and a single chair. Three old pistols and two granados were scattered atop the table, and the stump of a candle sat lopsided in the center. Three small kegs rested on their sides against the wall opposite the entrance, stacked pyramidally with two on the bottom and one on top. Beside the kegs was a pile of rope, a shovel, and a grapple.

"What's in those?" she asked.

Gabe glanced apprehensively at the kegs as he set the torch in a rusty sconce on the wall above the table. "Best keep away from those. I've heard you like to blow things up."

Kate touched the rounded end of a stalactite as she circled it. The surface was so smooth, and it was low enough to bump her head on if she wasn't looking where she was going. "How'd you find this place?"

"I didn't," he said as he sat in the bed. The wood creaked under his weight. "Blackbeard did. This was one of his many stashes." He smiled weakly, rubbing the back of his head. "But we don't have to worry about him anymore."

Leaning vertically against the wall beside the bed was what looked like a short and stumpy flintlock musket, with a large caliber barrel and a muzzle that flared outward like a funnel. "That's a queer gun."

"It's a blunderbuss," he said. "It's shit for accuracy, but at short range it will knock a man off his feet."

She laughed. "What a silly name for something that kills."

"Nothing silly about what it does to a man's guts."

"I want one."

"You're welcome to it, just don't use it on me. I believe it's loaded. Powder is probably too damp. Mist from the waterfall gets in here, moistens everything. But the powder in the kegs should be dry, if you know how to prime a gun."

"Of course I know how to prime a gun."

He struggled to get out of his wet leather coat. He gave her a helpless look. "Would you mind?"

She hesitated. "The mighty Gabe Jenkins defeated by a coat."

"And a rock," he reminded her.

He gave up and fell back into the bed. She moved toward him and motioned for him to sit up. "Don't be a baby." He sat up and she helped him out of the coat.

"Should hang it outside," he suggested.

She tossed the coat to the floor, and he stared down at it in despair. "I like that coat."

"It's ruined," she said.

"It's got character."

"Gabe, you're twenty. You're too young to own anything with character."

He smirked sarcastically and nodded at *her* coat. "And you're not?"

She pinched one of the silver skull buttons. "It's Rackham's.

He is old enough to have character."

"You stole his character."

"Isn't that what pirates do?" She removed Rackham's coat, set it over the top of the three kegs, and gave it a tender pat. She turned, and Gabe's eyes plummeted. She looked down and realized that her shirt was completely soaked through, transparent and clinging to her breasts, with her nipples plain for him to see.

He averted his gaze. "Sorry."

"I'm sorry about your head," she said.

His eyes circled back around. "You were so keen on doing me in. What swayed you?"

"I saw Jaq."

His eyes narrowed. "What? Where?"

"On the beach. With Dillahunt. I think Rackham brought them here."

"Why would he do that?"

She shrugged and stepped toward the bed. "I don't know. It doesn't matter."

His brow pinched in confusion, maybe anger. "It mattered when you thought I killed her."

"But I was wrong. You didn't kill her."

She thrust out a foot, slipping it between his closed knees and prying them apart. She slid between his legs, setting her hands on his broad shoulders. His arms remained useless at his sides. "You may put your hands on me," she instructed him. The offer came out with more force than she intended, making it sound more like a request.

"What's gotten into you?"

"Jaq is alive because of you."

He looked at the floor. "And her mother is dead because of me. Have you forgotten that?"

She shook her head. "No."

"You'll crawl into bed with a murderer over a single good deed?"

She smiled. "No."

"Then why?"

She grabbed the plunging V of her shirt and tugged in two opposite directions, until the laces gave and the wet cloth peeled from her skin, baring her breasts. "Because I fancy you, and you fancy me. And who knows if we'll be alive tomorrow?"

His eyes scaled her body, widening as they reached her breasts. After a moment's hesitation, his hands shot forth, seizing the backs of her thighs and pulling her midsection close to his face. He buried his lips in her midriff, kissing her just below the belly button. The day-old gristle of his chin prickled her skin. His hands slid up her thighs and squeezed her rear. She tore at his shirt. He raised his arms so she could get the shirt up and over his head. She crawled into his lap, wrapping her legs around his waist. She pressed her breasts against his damp, warm chest and felt his heart beating rapidly. Their lips met, opening instantly so their tongues could entwine.

She ran her hands up his back. Her fingers grazed the crisscrossed scabs of the lash wounds he had endured before Rackham delivered him to Vane. Why Gabe hadn't revealed Vane's plan to Rackham and spared himself the agony, Kate did not know. Perhaps he thought he deserved the whip.

She spread her fingers into his thick, curly hair, careful to avoid the wound she had dealt. The muscles of his sculpted chest tightened against her. His large arms encased her. His fingers were so coarse against her back. She began to grind her hips against him, and she felt him hardening beneath her. She fumbled to untie his sash.

And then his tongue stopped working at hers. He suddenly clutched her shoulders and shoved her back a few inches. He fixed her with hard eyes. "This isn't right. I am undeserving of your affections."

The increasing bulge that she sat upon betrayed his earnest expression, which she managed not to giggle at. She took hold of his wrists and removed his hands from her shoulders, maneuvering them downward and mashing them against her breasts. She pushed forward. He was either too exhausted or no longer willing to resist. She didn't care which. His lips parted as she neared them again.

"I'll decide what you deserve," she whispered into his mouth.

25

CALLOWAY

"Hello again, my dear," said the towering man in black. He stood before the hearth, framed in its flaring golden glow. His face had been scalded so deeply that it revealed scant traces of the man he had once been, but what little Calloway could see was alarmingly familiar. And that guttural voice, which might have been amplified by supernatural means, could not possibly belong to anyone other than Edward Teach.

She shut her eyes and opened them again, expecting to wake. He had visited her in dreams, but none that felt so real. Waves of heat from the hearth constantly blasted her face, but Teach seemed immune, even though it must have been searing at his backside.

Teach had ordered everyone but his men from the tavern when Calloway, Dillahunt, and Dumaka were brought inside. Pirates hastily fled out the front and strumpets retreated to the back rooms. A score of seedy men remained, most of them possessing the same dull-eyed stare that Calloway had noted of the crew of *Queen Anne's Revenge.*

Behind Teach, beyond the hearth, three distinctly varied associates sat together at a table; a blind man in a grey coat, a very dark Jamaican with long white hair, and a short, cleanly-dressed blonde man who was visibly flustered. The blonde man seemed particularly out of place, fidgeting with his fingers and constantly glancing about.

"Found these three lurking on the beach," said the pirate clutching Calloway's left shoulder with a clammy hand. He smelled of dead fish. He had bright red cheeks and a cheery voice that might have charmed a child, so long as the child was wearing nose plugs. "We made sure not to kill any of them so you can pass your . . . uhh . . . judgment."

"Captain Dillahunt looks ill-handled," said Teach, looking over Calloway toward the entrance. Dillahunt had been deposited across the top of a table near the door, on his back with his legs hanging over the edge. Blood poured freely from a gash in his cheek. He moaned and kept trying to touch his face, while a skinny pirate with buckteeth continually slapped his hand away and tittered. Calloway had overheard someone call him "Skinny Benny."

"He's alive, Captain Teach," Skinny Benny said.

"Good."

Dumaka was being held by the two largest pirates, who were both shirtless and showing off their impressive muscles. Dumaka had not put up nearly as much of a fight as Dillahunt. In fact, when he saw blood gushing from Dillahunt's cheek, he had quickly tossed his cutlass into the sand and raised his hands. *Not the protector I had hoped for,* Calloway bitterly reflected.

"You've not sullied the girl, I trust?" asked Teach, swiveling his blue eye dangerously from one man to the next.

"Nay," answered the smelly pirate. "Recognized her, I did. This be the girl you took aboard *Queen Anne's Revenge* 'fore the ship went to the depths. Remembered what you told us, I did."

Teach hesitated. "I find myself at a loss. My mind be a vast hold brimming with memories, and more than a few have slipped through the cracks. What did I tell you?"

Calloway snorted, because Teach never forgot anything, despite frequent claims to the contrary. When they first met on Griffith's Isle, he had insisted he would not remember her, but he was proven wrong.

The smelly pirate stammered. He couldn't maintain eye contact with Teach for more than a second. "You told us what we should do if we sees the tall, manly-shouldered girl again. You said we should bring her straight to you, and she weren't to be sullied along the way."

Teach slowly moved forward, his boots thumping the deck beneath her knees with every ponderous step. He stopped within arm's-length of her and leaned forward for a closer look. Most would have chosen to look at the right side of his face, which wasn't quite as grotesque as the left, where he had received the majority of his burns. But Calloway's eyes were inexorably drawn toward the more hideous details. Much of his face was a distorted maze of scattered flesh, black and pink, with only a few scant patches of skin left untouched. His shriveled nose had gained an extra nostril where the fire had burned through. Along the left side of his head, where no hair remained, she could swear she saw the white of his skull within a deep fissure. "You do not shy from a monster's face?" he observed.

His breath was hot and foul, but she did not flinch. "You are no worse than before."

He made a deep-throated sound that might have been a laugh, but it was hard to be sure. "No less than I should expect of my own blood." He stared at her portentously, anticipating a reaction. When she offered none, he added, "You take your shoulders and height from me. Your mother was a dainty woman."

"Don't speak of my mother," she snarled.

Teach choked out a hideous cackle that made her flinch. A gob of saliva dribbled from one of the cracks in his lower lip. "What your mother lacked in stature she returned in temper. You claim the finest traits of both of us. You do not shy from my face, and neither do you shy from revelation of heritage. Or could it be you already knew? Aye, that must be the truth of it. Did Dillahunt tell you?"

"Gabe Jenkins told me."

Teach returned to his full height and picked at an extinguished fuse lodged in one of the spindly coils of his diminished beard. "And did the lad divulge his role in your mother's passing? I wager he did not."

"He told me everything."

"Did he, now?" Teach seemed shocked. "Then you know my hands be clean in that ill affair, however inclined I were to bloody them."

"It was your order."

He raised his hands innocently, but the gesture only made him larger and more terrifying. "I tried to halt Jenkins, but the boy be too swift in the dealing of foul deeds. My anger renders me hasty, on occasion."

Tears blurred her vision, spilling over and cooling her cheeks for an instant. The heat from the hearth swiftly dried them into the pores of her skin. "You were too cowardly to see it through yourself!"

He managed a proud smile. "My lone eye beholds a woman, when not so long ago two eyes gazed on but a child in a womanly form. Twice I nearly took your life. When you spoke of your mother, and the manner of her death, I knew why fate saw fit to stay my hand."

"Don't believe him!" barked Dillahunt, who was suddenly trying to sit up, while Skinny Benny shoved him back down. "That's not Edward Teach! It can't be! I watched him die!"

Teach nodded and closed his eye for a moment of reminiscence. The unsettling hollow of the opposite eye, which Calloway had burned away with one of the fuses from his own beard, remained open and ever observant. "Aye, you watched me plunge through fire. I would have ended you then and there, if only the deck hadn't given way beneath my heels. The flames gnawed at my flesh, and would have gladly eaten me whole if not quenched. My beloved *Revenge* opened up around me, but I never touched her deck again. Instead, she gave me straight to the sea, before the flames could claim my bones."

"Lies," Dillahunt shouted. "You're an imposter!"

"Do you recall my parting words to you, captain? Of course you do. Your mind does not readily relinquish a troublesome riddle, no matter how badly you wish it banished."

"I'm not playing this game!"

"Tis no game. I asked you if you yet realized who shared your bed, and your dumbfounded expression was reply enough. Even as the deck parted beneath my boots, I knew my work was done. I needed no blade to split you in two, when mere words would carry out the deed in my stead."

Dillahunt was still struggling to sit up, but he was severely weakened. Half his face was covered in blood. "Impossible. It was too great a swim back to Pirate Town."

"Aye, that it were," Teach allowed. "But you forget my other ship, *Adventure*. She came to my aid."

"I crippled *Adventure*!"

"A fine maneuver that were, Captain Dillahunt, but not enough to stop her from running out her sweeps. She was upon me within the hour." He swept an arm across the room. "The men you see here found me in the water. By rights, I should have drowned. The powers know I begged for it. The fire was gone, but still I felt the sting of its teeth all over my flesh. The agony was not of this world. But then I felt the salt latching to my skin, burrowing deep into open flesh, and I knew the truth at last. The sea would not permit my demise."

Calloway touched her throat. "What did you say?"

Dillahunt roared a laugh, then choked and spat blood. "Did you hear that, Jacqueline?" he croaked. "The water mended him too!"

Teach looked at Calloway. "What be his meaning?"

Calloway pulled her finger away from her neck too quickly. Teach reached out with a scorched-pink hand and placed a rubbery index finger under her chin, lifting her head. He scowled. "What does my eye see?"

"A wound mended," she answered.

"By the sea?"

She looked into his eye, the sapphire iris so very similar to hers. "Yes," she said at last.

Dillahunt kept laughing. Teach gestured lazily, and Skinny Benny jabbed Dillahunt in the ribs. He rolled on his side and groaned. "You're all mad!" he bellowed at the rafters. "You're maaaaaa—" Skinny Benny punched him again, shutting him up.

"Don't kill him," Teach instructed. "He'll not escape my wrath so easily."

The cleanly-dressed blonde man, who seemed so out of place, suddenly slammed a fist on the table he was seated at, and everyone turned to look at him. He stood and angrily ran his hands through his thinning hair. "This is a waste of time, Teach! Katherine Lindsay is a redheaded woman of twenty years! This freckled girl's hair is black, or are you as sightless as the corpse at my side?"

The blind man bristled. "Does he mean me?"

"Patience, Lindsay," Teach replied without looking. "She will not slip away. The harbor belongs to me."

Lindsay? Calloway studied the blonde man's face. Was this one of Kate's relatives, come to claim her?

The blonde man was unconvinced. "Assuming your men didn't roast her and toss her charred corpse to the sea. You promised me Katherine Lindsay, Teach. That was our deal. You wouldn't have known of Vane's arrival if not for me."

Teach slowly turned to face the man, grunting. "I would have known. You merely hastened Captain Vane's fate. Still, my days be shortened. The fire left me weak, and there be not enough souls in this world to sate me. The sea granted me time enough to conclude my affairs, and no more. You be as slight in years as you are in stature, and can afford the patience I cannot. You shall find reward for your aid in due time."

The blonde man sat down. "Good," he said, glancing around apprehensively. Calloway didn't have to know the man to read his body language. It was clear enough what he was thinking. He wanted out of here, away from all these pirates.

Teach turned to Calloway. It seemed to take great effort just to shift his weight. She wondered what the rest of his body looked like under his black clothes. "You spoke of Jenkins. Where did you uncover him? I'd fancy a word with the lad."

The smelly pirate laughed a little too loudly at that. Teach silenced him with his blue eye.

"Jenkins threw in with Charles Vane," Calloway answered haughtily. "He gave me this." She pointed to the line across her neck.

Teach started a chuckle, but it was overtaken by a hoarse, wheezing cough that resonated deep within his throat. It took him a full minute to recover himself, while everyone watched in silence. He hadn't moved from the spot he was standing when they brought her in.

He is dying, Calloway realized.

She glanced over the faces of the pirates as they looked at Teach with veneration, all them grasping their weapons of choice, eagerly anticipating their next violent order. They lived only to murder, whenever Teach released their leash. *What will they do without their master? Kill each other?*

"Do you need your crutch, captain?" asked the smelly pirate, removing his hand from Calloway's shoulder for a moment. She glanced at the rusty cutlass dangling from his hip, wondering if there was enough time to slide it from his belt and plunge it into Teach's chest. His body would topple into the fire of the hearth and burn. But he had survived fire before. Could he survive a blade through the heart?

The cutlass was within reach, but she didn't budge. Something was holding her back. They would surely kill her after she killed Teach, but that didn't frighten her. Death had made a pass at her once already, and she had emerged stronger. So what was stopping her?

Questions, she realized.

If Teach was dead, he couldn't answer any of her thousand questions. Questions about her mother, and how they had met. What had come between them? What had kept them from living out their lives together? She needed answers. So she would wait. If he meant to kill her, he would have done it by now. He'd had so many opportunities.

Teach hacked a few more times before he looked at his men. "Was Jenkins among the crew you killed on Captain Vane's ship?"

The pirates exchanged quizzical glances, shook their heads. "Didn't spot him," said Skinny Benny.

"Three of ours were killed at the stern," said another man.

This one was very tall, with long black hair bound in a thick braid, and he was wearing a necklace of shriveled ears.

"No need to trouble Captain Teach about that, Marcus," snapped the smelly pirate.

"Nay," Teach interjected. "Trouble me."

Marcus smirked defiantly at the smelly pirate. "We found their corpses, but not the boat they came in on."

"We *did* find the boat!" the smelly pirate insisted.

"Aye," said Marcus, "but not where it rightfully belonged, at the stern. We found it by the beach."

Teach nodded conclusively. "There be no mystery here. Jenkins fled with Katherine Lindsay into the jungle."

"We don't know that for a certainty," said the smelly pirate.

Teach's eye rolled toward him. "Your name be Smelly Joe, yes?"

"Aye."

"An apt name, as your stink be rivaled only by your ineptitude."

Smelly Joe blinked. "I don't know what that means."

"Give me your sword."

Smelly Joe drew his cutlass and handed it to Teach. Teach took the blade in one hand and seized Smelly Joe by the hair with the other. "Do you not wish to live?" he asked.

"Of course I do, Captain Teach!"

Calloway stood up and took three steps back, bracing herself for what was coming.

Teach raked the rusty blade across Smelly Joe's neck with three fierce jerks. A curtain of blood gushed down Smelly Joe's chest, and he dropped to his knees, then fell on his face. Teach tossed the cutlass away. He closed his eye and let his head fall back for a moment, inhaling deeply. His chest shuddered.

The prissy blonde man with the same surname as Kate stood again, appalled. The Jamaican clutched Lindsay's arm and pulled him back into his seat.

"Didn't have to do that," Skinny Benny muttered.

Teach's eye shot open. "I'll have you next, if you speak out of turn again."

Benny lowered his gaze. "Aye, captain."

Teach looked over the hearth to the Jamaican. "Trejean, position two chairs behind the hearth. One for me, and one for my daughter. Two thrones for a king and his princess. Captain Dillahunt and Captain Vane are going to offer us a contest."

Trejean nodded uncertainly, clearly unnerved by his guest but too afraid to do anything about it. "Aye, Captain Teach."

Dillahunt propped himself up on his elbows, his vigor instantly renewed. The skinny pirate reached out to force him down again, but Dillahunt snatched the man's wrist. "You have Vane?" he called to Teach.

Teach ignored Dillahunt. He set his gaze on Calloway. Scorched skin peeled from decaying teeth and mottled gums. His grin was a terrible thing. "My net be teeming with fish."

26

GABE

He was gently stirred into consciousness by the flow of the waterfall resonating into the cave through the long narrow tunnel. The torch was still burning furiously. Kate was gone from the bed. He sat up and rubbed the back of his head, which was still very sore. At least his headache had faded, forgotten in his passion with Kate. The crack of his knees echoed loudly off the walls as he stood. He lifted his arms, smiling at the pleasing burn of sore muscles stretched taut. He found his breeches crumpled on the floor and slipped into them. He didn't bother with his shirt.

He stepped on something long and cylindrical beside the bed. The blunderbuss. Kate must have been playing with it. He chuckled as he examined the priming pan, which was loaded with fresh powder. *She has a man's fascination with toys that kill.* He set it upright against the wall.

He slipped through the narrow passage and found Kate

standing outside on the ledge, with her back to the cave. She was naked beneath the waterfall, letting the water splash over her body. Gabe leaned against the rocky crag and folded his arms, watching her in awe for a full minute. The water must have stung her skin, but she stood tall and steady with her head back and her eyes closed. The water straightened the curls of her hair in a long line down the middle of her elegant back.

"How long do you plan on watching me?" she asked without so much as glancing over her shoulder.

"What?" He averted his gaze. "I wasn't watching. I was just getting some fresh air."

"Mmhmm."

She took a step toward the edge, and Gabe started forward in alarm, raising a hand. "Careful!"

She smirked back at him. "Afraid of heights?"

He scoffed. "Obviously not. I just don't want you to slip."

She leaned forward and peered over the edge. "It's not that far down."

"You'll crack your skull on a rock."

"Don't be a nag, Gabe Jenkins." She leapt off the ledge without warning, curling forward in midair. Gabe ran after her, his heart thumping, and crashed through the wall of water. He looked over the edge just in time to see her dive into the black lake below and vanish. He waited several seconds, but she did not emerge. He scanned the water, until finally he saw her head pop up near the far bank of the lake. "Water's warm," she hollered up at him. "Why don't you join me?"

He raised a finger and said, "Hold that thought."

He ran back into the cave and stripped out of his wet breeches as quickly as possible. He grabbed the coil of rope near the three kegs of powder and slung it over his shoulder. He emerged from the cave and tied a knot, fixing the rope to the rusty hook hanging above the gap between the ledge and the rocky steps they had climbed to reach the cave.

"Just dive in, you big baby!" she called.

"It's for the climb back up," he explained. He didn't feel like jumping the gap again.

He stepped timidly to the edge of the ledge once more and leaned forward. It was a long way down, and he felt more than a little dizzy. He took a deep breath and closed his eyes.

"Are you praying?" she teased.

"Shuttup." He leapt into the air, sailing downward without bothering to dive. For a moment, he seemed to be suspended above the black abyss, stars twinkling in the ripples. He aimed his toes downward just before he touched down. The water was bracingly cold at first, slapping his crotch and spreading a dull ache into his belly. When he opened his eyes, he was completely submerged in a black, cool shroud. He kicked his legs and propelled himself to the surface. When his head emerged, she was giggling. "A graceless leap," she said.

"Hurt my balls," he said, wincing.

"I'll do worse." She curled her finger, beckoning him to swim over.

He shivered. "You said it was warm!"

"It's warmer over here, I promise."

He swam over to her. When he was close, his toes grazed the pebbled lakebed, much shallower near the bank. He set his feet down and stood. The water was waist-deep. She sloshed forward and wrapped one arm around him. He lifted her by the rear, holding her just above his hips. She locked her legs around his waist and kissed him fiercely with wet lips.

"Your strength is back, I see," she said between kisses.

"I probably should be sleeping."

"You're supposed to stay awake after you hit your head, or you might never wake up."

She reached down into the water and eased him inside her.

He carried her out of the water and over to a long flat slab of rock on the shore of the lake, big enough for the two of them to lie upon. He set her on top of it and hunched over her. She held him close, grinding her nails into his hips as he gently thrust himself into her again and again. She let him do most of the work this time while moaning softly into his ear. Her moans grew to shuddering gasps.

When they were finished, he rolled off and collapsed on his back at her side, and the two of them stared up at the stars.

"I hope I didn't put a baby in you," he said, when he could think of nothing else.

She snickered. "You're quite the romantic, Gabe."

"Sorry," he chuckled.

"I can't get pregnant."

He looked at her. "No?"

"I tried with Thomas."

"Maybe the affliction was his," Gabe said, and then wanted to smack himself. He was saying all the wrong things. Sex had made him stupid. He wouldn't have cared with any other woman, but she was not any other woman.

A shadow passed over her face. "The affliction is mine, I'm afraid."

"I'm sorry."

She smiled an overly chipper smile that did not suit her. "Enough about that."

He wanted to stay here with her forever, staring up at the night sky. For once in his life, everything seemed exactly as it should. His past seemed a distant thing that had happened to someone else, someone far less fortunate. He felt sorry for that boy, whoever he was. This one had no wants or cares, except for the woman at his side.

And then, as if on cue, his stomach growled, and he realized how incredibly hungry he was.

Kate laughed. "I'm starving too."

He sighed. "I need to go back to the harbor, steal us some supplies."

"It's too dangerous."

"Starving's worse," he promised. He had once spent an unlucky stretch of three weeks at sea with nothing but a single hardtack biscuit to keep him from dying. He had made that biscuit last.

"I'll go with you," she said.

"No. Everyone's looking for you, and that hair of yours doesn't exactly blend in, unless you mean to chop it off."

"Never."

"Good." He couldn't imagine her without it.

"I used to hate it." She sounded amused. "I thought it was a curse. It took forever to get the tangles out. Didn't occur to me till later that I didn't *need* to get the tangles out." She thought about what she'd just said, then made a face and laughed at herself. "That was a metaphor, of course. I cannot live with tangles."

He was preoccupied by the little creases that formed at the edges when she spoke. "What are we going to do?" he wondered. "Stay out here forever?" A part of him hoped she would say "yes."

"I hadn't thought that far ahead," she admitted. "I'm shit with plans."

"You don't know what you want?"

"I know exactly what I want," she replied matter-of-factly.

"Tell me." He propped himself up on one elbow and looked down on her. Her sodden hair was scattered about her head, flattened against the rock. Her eyes were aimed at the sky, but occasionally they would shift his way, along with a coy smirk.

"I saw her in the harbor," she said, "when we were fleeing

Vane's ship. I was considering how best to dispatch you when she snared my eye. She's a brigantine, clean and new. Someone must have stolen her very recently. Probably from some poor merchant. Whoever her captain was, he must have been so proud of that ship, only to have her snatched from him. She is painted red along the bulwark. I would like to purchase her or steal her, whichever comes easier."

He gave her a dubious look. "Stealing from pirates is much harder than stealing from merchants, Kate."

"As I said, I haven't fussed over the details. All I know is I will christen her '*The Scarlet Devil*' and sail her around the globe, across every sea, until I grow tired of sailing and decide I want something else. Damned be anyone who gets in my way."

He liked the sound of that. "I knew you were a pirate the day I met you."

She laughed. "The day you met me, you were thinking of Annabelle. I decided it best not to know you."

"I was thinking of a friend Annabelle made me kill."

"No one can make you kill anyone, Gabe." The rasp of her voice put a sting in her words.

"I know that now."

She reached up to play with the stubborn lock of hair that always fell over his eyes, curling it around her finger. "And what do *you* want, Gabe Jenkins? Don't tell me you want 'this, right now.' That would be very sweet. And very boring."

He withered. "I'm not that soggy, I hope." Yet he might have said just that had she not warned him against it.

"Men say things like that when they're happy."

"Who says I'm happy?"

"Your smile."

He hadn't realized he'd been smiling.

She flicked his nose with the same finger that had been playing with his hair. "You haven't answered."

"I will, if you'll stop answering for me."

"Fine." She placed both hands on her stomach and interlocked her fingers. "Proceed."

He blinked, and for an instant Kate's hair was blood, and her face was no longer hers. Instead, she was Elise Calloway. Her dead eyes stared vacantly at the sky as they sunk into the darkening hollows of a gaunt face, shriveling away before him. He blinked again, and Kate had returned. She was frowning with mild concern. "Gabe? Are you alright?"

The answer came to him. "I want to forget."

"Everything?"

"Everything that came before this."

She was looking right at him, but her eyes seemed to be viewing some dreadful memory, just as he had not seconds before. "If you could forget the past," she said, "you'd make the same mistakes all over again."

They lingered there in silence for another few minutes, before Kate said, "I don't think this rock is good for my back."

He laughed and helped her up.

They climbed the stair of boulders back up to the ledge, but this time she made him go first, laughing all the way up. Climbing naked made him self-conscious, but there was no way she would have agreed to go first this time.

With the aid of the rope, the swing across the gap to the ledge was easy. They returned to the cave and both got dressed. "I won't be gone long," he said as he laced his shirt. He hoped she wouldn't put up a fight.

"You sure I can't come?" The question was just a formality, punctuated by a tremendous yawn. She was already reclining in the little bed. She would be asleep in minutes.

He shook his head. "Easier with one. I'll just steal a few things."

"Be careful. I don't like this island."

"Nothing to worry about," he assured her.

She hardly seemed worried. She pulled the blankets over herself and closed her eyes, turning her back to him. He chuckled to himself and turned to leave. In his haste, he didn't think to take his curved dagger.

He climbed down the rocks fast. His vigor had mostly returned, as if Kate had transferred her energy into him. He felt alive and strong, and his head didn't even hurt anymore.

When he reached the bottom, he ran around the lake and into the jungle. He kept running, his breath never increasing. He didn't stop until he reached the canyon with the tree trunk stretched across it. He carefully made his way across, staring down to make sure he didn't misplace his feet or catch his toes on a rut. After all he'd been through, stumbling off a tree and plummeting into a ravine would be a silly way to die.

When he reached the end, he looked up into the barrel of a pistol. A massive shirtless pirate whose face, chest, and arms were covered in dark tattoos grinned over the barrel. His face was riddled with black dots and swirling patterns. Inky black snakes spiraled down his arms. His ears were each lined with a dozen little gold rings. He wore bright red breeches. Gabe knew this man. He had served with him aboard *Queen Anne's Revenge*. Everyone called him "Tattoo."

"Hello, Jenkins," greeted Tattoo. "It's been too long."

"Not long enough," Gabe muttered.

27

DILLAHUNT

They dragged Vane from the back rooms and threw him down before the hearth. Blood was streaming down his forehead and into his eyes from a wound concealed somewhere in his auburn hair. *Good,* thought Dillahunt. *He is in no better condition than I.*

On the opposite side of the hearth, the monster who called himself Edward Teach grinned down from his tall chair, with Calloway at his side in a shorter chair. Her face was a mixture of confusion, horror, and curiosity. She had avoided looking at Dillahunt since Teach put her in the chair. It was as if she already considered him a dead man.

The Jamaican and the blonde man named Lindsay had moved their chairs to the right of Teach, at his behest, and the old blind man was seated beside Calloway. The five of them looked like some twisted mockery of a royal court, with a great black monstrosity for a king.

Chairs and tables were cleared from the center of the room and placed near the walls, leaving a nice big space between the hearth and entrance. Marcus climbed up on the crates that the flutist had been perched atop of, allowing him a bird's-eye view of the event.

The two largest pirates bound Dumaka's hands with thick rope, set him down in a chair, and moved to guard the entrance. Neither Dillahunt nor Vane was getting out that way.

The remaining pirates gathered about in a perimeter, licking their lips. "If either combatant draws near the wall, they will be cut," Blackbeard informed the room. The pirates drew their cutlasses and daggers.

Skinny Benny pulled Dillahunt off the table and ushered him toward Vane.

"Ghost!" Blackbeard called. "Bring forth the weapons best suited to these fine captains."

A ghostly-white albino teenager with large lips and short and curly golden hair stepped forth and tossed two plain wooden swords onto the floor, between Vane and Dillahunt. The pirates howled laughter.

Vane spat blood at the swords. "Child's toys. I'd kill him faster with my hands."

"I will not have you murder each other," boomed Blackbeard. "The victor will be set free. The loser will surrender his soul to me."

"More lies," Dillahunt said. "You'll kill us both, no matter who wins."

"Nay," said Blackbeard. "There be no subterfuge. The terms of justice be clear. I swear upon my word."

Dillahunt snorted. "This is not justice."

"It be the only justice you shall receive, Captain Dillahunt. You'd do well to heed my words. There be nothing else, so far as you're concerned. You are not in Nassau. The governor is leagues away, safe in his mansion. This be Isla de Mariposa."

Vane took off his green coat and tossed it at Ghost, who caught it instinctively and then cast it to the floor as if he feared it might bite him if he held it too long. "If you've stained my coat," Vane warned, "I will shove this toy up your arse, boy. I'm sure it's not the first shaft of wood you've taken in the arse." He kneeled to retrieve one of the swords, and then backed away quickly. He smirked at the weapon, if it could be called that. "I might as well fight with my cock."

"You're welcome to," called Marcus from above. "Haven't seen a good cockfight in months."

Everyone laughed.

"I will happily remove it for you," Dillahunt told Vane as he picked up the other sword. His wounded foot pained him when he bent down, but he managed not to show it. He didn't want Vane exploiting his weakness.

Vane raised an eyebrow. "What?"

"Your cock. I will see it removed before this is over."

"You're a sick fuck, Guy."

"At least I never sullied a baby."

Vane's shoulders sagged in exasperation. "Where do these gossips start? That never happened. And if I were prone to baby-fucking, I certainly wouldn't tell anybody about it."

"Then you admit it!"

"I admit nothing!" He paused. "It was a monkey."

"A *baby* monkey?"

"I don't know. Possibly. It didn't survive the fucking."

Dillahunt lowered his sword. He resisted an urge to vomit. "Why would you do that?"

Vane shrugged. "I was without a woman for months. I had been elected captain. My predecessor left behind a spider monkey in his cabin. The fuzzy little shit was fool enough to leap into my lap as I was pleasuring myself. It got what it deserved." Vane started to chuckle at the memory. "I gave its broken corpse to the crew. They were starved. The monkey wasn't the only one who ingested my seed that day."

"Jesus!" Marcus exclaimed from above.

Dillahunt was seething. "You are the vilest creature in the Caribbean, Charles Vane."

Vane beamed. "Thank you."

Blackbeard rose from his chair. "That be enough squabbling," he boomed. "Begin!"

Dillahunt clutched the pathetic weapon in both hands. The square grip was too bulky and jagged. His only comfort was that Vane had the same handicap. "It's time we finish this, Charles."

Vane wiped fresh blood from his eyes with his sleeve and pointed at Dillahunt with his wooden blade. "Before I put more splinters in that scarred face, just tell me one thing: How the fuck did you get off my island?"

"Thank your friend Jack Rackham for that."

"That traitorous shit. I should have killed him."

The two men moved in a circle, remaining five paces from each other, the tips of their swords far removed. Teach sat down and nudged Calloway with his elbow. She flinched at his touch. "Always a sluggish start," he told her. "But fret not, my dear. They'll be at each other soon enough."

Dillahunt glowered at Vane. His cheek burned where Skinny Benny had opened him up on the beach. He recited the names of his crew. "Bastion. Farley. Early. Clemens. Surley. Gerry. Terry Bell. Wincott."

Vane never lost his smirk. "Should I pretend to know what the fuck you're going on about?"

"Those are just a few of the men you murdered. Good men. "Bastion. Farley. Early. Clemens. Surley. Gerry. Terry Bell. Wincott."

The pirate captain rolled his eyes. "A few indeed. Nice of you to remember *some* of them. I wager there was at least one whose name slips your mind. Maybe two. Maybe ten. It's not your fault, of course. Some people just don't make an impression."

"I committed as many names to memory as my otherwise occupied mind would allow."

Vane struggled to keep his guard up through a heaving fit of laughter. "So occupied that it offered not a word of protest as you pursued a known mutineer toward certain death. I didn't even have to bait my hook with a nice juicy apple."

"You're not human," Dillahunt said.

"You're right," said Vane, flashing his teeth. "I am a shark. I do what I do. I devoured your crew, but it was *you* who led them into my jaws."

"Enough talk!" Marcus yelled down from atop the crates. "Start hitting each other!"

"Aye!" said another, and then another, and soon there was an uproarious chant of, "Fight, fight, fight, fight, fight!"

Dillahunt glanced sideways at Calloway. Her eyes flickered away from him, but he noted concern in the split-second that they met.

Vane struck the first blow, while Dillahunt's gaze was averted. The tip of Vane's wooden sword slapped him on the cheek, splitting the gash even wider. He hissed at the sting and felt blood quickly flowing down his face. "Just wanted to make sure you were taking this seriously," Vane said.

"Oh, I take you very seriously," Dillahunt growled, wiping his face on his sleeve.

Vane rolled his eyes. "Still mad about your men? Look, if it's any consolation, it wasn't personal. I had to send Woodes Rogers a message, and the only way to do that was to utterly decimate anyone he sent after me. The first was Lancaster, the second was you. Though, I must say, Lancaster was a real sport, unlike you."

"Does that include slitting a woman's throat and tossing her to the sea?" Dillahunt pointed at Calloway.

Vane frowned at the girl. "I did not slit her throat, but clearly I should have. Gabe Jenkins appears to have slighted me. And he seemed so reliable."

"The result would have been the same," said Blackbeard. "The sea mended my daughter, as it mended me."

Vane sputtered laughter until his face turned red. "I hate to be the one to tell you this, Edward, but the sea did shit work in mending you."

If Blackbeard was insulted, he didn't show it. Or perhaps his puzzle of a face simply wasn't capable.

"Too much talking!" someone shouted.

Dillahunt jabbed his wooden sword at Vane, poking his scalp. A fresh stream of blood ran down Vane's forehead. He blinked as it trickled into his left eye, and Dillahunt saw another opportunity. He lunged. Vane's eyes shot wide. He parried, slapped Dillahunt's sword aside, and punched him in the wounded cheek. Dillahunt's head snapped back. He swiveled on one foot, swinging his sword back around. Vane leaned out of the way as the wooden tip swept just inches from his nose.

In mid-swing, a cramp twisted Dillahunt's ankle, sending a jolt of bracing pain up his leg, and he realized his mistake too late. He was balancing on his wounded foot! He nearly toppled, but managed to catch himself on his good foot.

Vane looked downward, and realization brightened his eyes. He advanced quickly, lifting up and stomping a booted heel down on Dillahunt's left foot. Dillahunt wailed in pain and crumbled to one knee. He managed to thrust out his sword, but Vane whirled out of the way and smashed his sword across the side of Dillahunt's head. The upper half of Vane's sword snapped off. Dillahunt landed on his face and heard his nose crack on impact. Pain exploded through his skull. The floor was covered in a dried, crusty film of spilled ale and other unidentifiable liquids, with chunks of sick here and there. Dillahunt peeled his cheek out of the mess and rolled onto his back, gasping.

"What was that?" cried Marcus in outraged disbelief.

"He's done already?" shouted another.

"Boo!" chanted the others. "BOOOOOOOOOO!!!!"

Vane kicked the sword from Dillahunt's hand. It skittered away. The pirate captain spread his arms wide and shouted to the crowd, "This is no duel!"

Dillahunt grasped ineffectually at Vane's boots. "I'll kill you, Vane!"

Vane laughed and kicked his hand away. "Stop pawing at me. I just polished these boots."

Blackbeard stood again. "The victor is decided."

"I cannot claim victory over a weakling," Vane said. "Bring me a true opponent." He pointed with the splintered end of his sword. "How about you, Teach?"

"My dueling days be done," said Teach. "I expended the last of my youthful fervor on Captain Dillahunt. He used to present challenge. I must say, I be disenchanted."

"You and me both," Vane drawled.

Rage collected like rocks in Dillahunt's lungs, stifling his breath. He heard himself wheezing. Clouds of red swelled in his peripheral vision, closing in fast, until the entire tavern flushed a deep crimson. Suspended within the center of that murderous aura was Charles Vane, shaking his head in disappointment. "I expected more of you, Guy."

Vane whirled and aimed his sword at the blonde man. "Frederick Lindsay," he said. "Mayhap you would offer better contest."

Frederick Lindsay's jaw fell open. "The duel is over," he stammered. "You won, Charles."

"I've but licked a flea from my back. You are my true opponent, are you not? Of course you are, you little shit. Come, face me."

Frederick Lindsay was clearly mortified.

"The contest be ended," said Blackbeard, "satisfying or no."

"Fuck you, Edward. Do not take me for one of your many mindless minions. I challenge Frederick Lindsay to a duel."

"I fear that be a one-sided match."

Vane flung a hand at Dillahunt in disgust. "Could it be any worse than this?"

Teach shook his huge head. "Nay, I must not permit it. Justice has made—"

But Vane was already making his way around the hearth, circling toward Frederick with his sword pointed right at him. "Prepare to die, you little shit."

"Oh God," Frederick murmured in a high pitched voice.

The pirates merely laughed.

Teach stared placidly. "You'd best defend yourself, lad. There's naught I can do in my condition."

Dillahunt glanced over at his sword, which was a good ten feet away. It couldn't end like this. He couldn't fail Bastion, Farley, Early, Clemens, Surley, Gerry, Terry Bell, Wincott, and all the others. He rolled onto his belly and placed his palms flat on the sticky, stinking floor. He shoved himself to his feet, ignoring the pain that screamed up his left leg. He lunged at his wooden sword, scooping it up. One of the muscular pirates made a face and said, "Oy! You're not supposed to be doing that. Is he supposed to be doing that?"

Dillahunt limped toward the hearth. He used the pain to fuel him, to push him toward his goal. "Bastion, Farley, Early, Clemens, Surley, Gerry, Terry Bell, Wincott," he muttered through heavy breaths. "Bastion, Farley, Early, Clemens, Surley, Gerry, Terry Bell, Wincott."

He gained in speed with every step, until he was running. When he was within two paces of the hearth, he pushed off of his good foot, propelling himself into the air. He sailed over the hearth, and the heat from the orange coals seared at his legs. In that moment he knew what it was to be a bird soaring over a volcano, riding the updraft.

Vane did not turn to defend himself. The pirate captain's eyes were set on Frederick Lindsay, who was frozen stiff in his chair. Vane was inches from jamming his sword into Lindsay's gullet when Dillahunt landed on top of him. The two of them crashed into Frederick, toppling both him and his chair. Frederick squealed in terror. "Oh God! I am killed!"

But he wasn't killed, because Dillahunt had spread Vane flat on his back. Dillahunt straddled him and beat him brutally with his wooden sword. He bellowed a name with every blow. "Bastion! Farley! Early! Clemens! Surley! Gerry! Terry Bell! Wincott!" He beat Vane until the tip of his sword broke off, and then he gouged him with the splinters. Vane raised his hands in a feeble defense, and Dillahunt jammed splinters into his palms and wrists.

"S-stop," said Vane. His blood was everywhere, spurting all over everything. Dillahunt welcomed its spray upon his face, licking his lips. And when Vane's blood splattered his eyes, he didn't blink. "Stop! I yield! I yield, you mad fuck!"

"Bastion! Farley! Early! Clemens! Sur—"

"Enough!" cried Blackbeard.

The Jamaican had to wrench Dillahunt off of Vane, or he would have kept going until Vane had no hands left to shield himself with. Vane stared at him through a spattered face. His red arms fell limply to his sides. A hole in his right wrist poured blood.

The Jamaican stood Dillahunt before Blackbeard and gave him a clap on the back. Blackbeard was grinning with what few teeth he had left. "You've won the duel, Captain Dillahunt."

Dillahunt looked at Calloway. She offered an impulsive smile. It vanished quickly.

Frederick Lindsay scrambled to his feet and coughed, while staring warily in Vane's direction. But Vane was in no condition to hurt him now.

Blackbeard stepped forth to set a great hand on Dillahunt's shoulder. Dillahunt's knees buckled, but the Jamaican held him up. Blackbeard leaned in close with his one blue eye. He spoke low, his voice a heavy wheeze. "Gaze up, and tell me what you see."

The last of Dillahunt's energy had flooded out of him. He hadn't the strength to crane his neck. But he knew what was above him. He had viewed Keelhaul's roof from the outside when he was dragged in. "I see the upturned hull of a ship."

"Aye. And beneath you?"

"Planking."

"Aye. And stretching up through the hull?"

"A mast."

"Aye. A hull, a deck, and a mast." Blackbeard's hand fell from his shoulder. "Take comfort in these things. You will die within the confines of a ship, as any true captain should."

Calloway stood in alarm. "Father!"

Blackbeard gave his daughter a portentous look. "Justice must be served, my girl. This be my first lesson to you."

Dillahunt was dimly aware of uproarious laughter all around. He felt drunk, unable to comprehend the significance of what was happening. He tried to grasp Blackbeard's collar, but the monster had retreated just out of reach. "You said you'd let the victor go free," he heard himself lamely protest.

"Aye. I said I would set you free, and set you free I shall.

The only true freedom from this world be found in death. I be a man of my word, but rare be the man who listens to my words." He looked at the Jamaican. "Stretch Captain Dillahunt over the hearth."

28

CALLOWAY

Dillahunt didn't scream right away.

The two big shirtless pirates held his arms while Trejean and Skinny Benny held his feet. The four of them—two on either side of the hearth—stretched him out and lowered him facedown toward the searing coals. He jerked violently in their unyielding grips, twitching his scarred face from side to side. He hissed and grunted, squeezing one eye shut while the other darted about, as if he thought there might yet be a way out of this. When at last he seemed to fathom that there was no escape, he opened both eyes and looked at Calloway. Rippling waves of heat swiftly dried the translucent sheen from the whites of his eyes.

"Father," she pleaded in a soft voice, clutching the sleeve of Teach's coat. She hated calling him that, but she didn't know how else to move him. "Don't do this."

"You care for him still?" Teach wheezed, not removing his

blue eye from Dillahunt.

"I . . . " She hadn't considered that. She had thought herself indifferent to Dillahunt's fate, but no one deserved to die like this, least of all the man she had loved. She had hated him for a time, but she never wanted anything like this. "He is not an evil man." *Not like you,* she wanted to augment.

"Nay," Teach agreed. "Dillahunt is but a stubborn fool."

Yet he did not order his men to remove Dillahunt from the hearth.

Calloway struggled to think of something to say. "He is not Benjamin Hornigold," she blurted. Surely there was nothing worse than Hornigold's betrayal.

"Hornigold's demise was much longer," he informed her in an ominous tone. "This death be kinder by far, I assure you."

"I see no kindness here," she replied firmly. She was surprised that her voice did not shake.

Teach let out a raspy sigh. "You have the heart of your mother. This will be over soon. Fire will expunge Captain Dillahunt of his corporeal form. His soul will be free to venture where it pleases. Mayhap he will choose to linger at your side."

I doubt it, she thought.

Dillahunt must have heard Teach's words, because he made a sound that was almost a laugh, and then he pulled his gaze from Calloway. He did not look at her again.

Her hand was in her pocket, gripping the dried prune that had been Dillahunt's toe. *I would stop this if I could,* she desperately yearned to tell him, but she knew it wouldn't matter. He wouldn't believe her. He had never trusted her. She blamed Teach for that as much as she blamed Dillahunt.

When his skin started to smoke, he loosed a wail that she would never forget. It began as a mournful moan and ascended into a warbled howl of dismay. His nose turned black first, cracking and dripping blood upon the coals, where it sizzled and dried. His chin and cheeks went next, bubbling and steaming. His many scars opened like tiny mouths all over his face. Blisters popped and flaked away from pink muscle. His lips split and peeled from the gums. He spasmed violently, saliva and blood drooling from his mouth. The front of his shirt caught fire and quickly burned into his skin. Blackened tufts of hair fell from his scalp. His cries reached a maddening pitch, until he sounded like a child squealing in its crib. The muscles of his cheeks dried and pulled apart, revealing bone. His face caught fire in a sudden wave, and the pirates collectively loosed an orgasmic gasp.

The big pirate holding Dillahunt's right arm released him in surprise, and Dillahunt slumped against the orange coals. When the pirate lifted him back up, the entire right half of Dillahunt's face came off, stuck to the coals.

Several seconds passed before Calloway realized Dillahunt had stopped screaming. The only sound that remained was the crackling and popping of his skin.

He's gone.

Her lips and cheeks were numb from the heat. She had to remind herself to blink. She knew she should cry, but she could not muster the emotion. What did it matter? There was nothing she could do. There was nothing *anybody* could have done to save Dillahunt except Dillahunt. Rackham had warned him, but he had pigheadedly persisted.

The flames curled up his torso and crept down his limbs, toward the men that were holding him. The two shirtless pirates started to sweat. Skinny Benny looked nervously to Blackbeard. "Captain?"

Blackbeard nodded. "Unhand him. He be finished."

They dropped Dillahunt onto the coals. Embers billowed from beneath him and scattered across the floor. All of his clothes burned away, and before long he was nothing but an unrecognizable black and red husk, sputtering and crackling. The tavern quickly filled with the sweet aroma of cooking flesh.

Calloway heard a low rumble. At first she thought the tavern was shaking, maybe from a strong wave crashing against the stilts that the pier was suspended upon. When she realized her stomach was growling, she heaved over the side of her chair. Nothing emerged from her mouth except a thin stream of saliva. It had been too long since her last meal. After tonight, she wasn't sure she would ever be able to eat any kind of cooked meat again.

Vane, who was huddled on the floor with his bloodied arms tucked together, tilted his head toward her. He looked rather sickly. But he was alive, and Dillahunt was dead. He had survived Dillahunt's unexpected onslaught just long enough. "It should be *you* in that fire," she told him.

As poorly as he looked, his smirk was easily recovered. "It seems Guy wanted the fire more than I."

Teach gestured at Trejean. "Set Captain Vane in Frederick's chair and tend to his wounds, before he has no blood left to bleed."

"As you wish," Trejean grumbled, clearly unhappy with all of this.

Frederick Lindsay whirled on his heels, jaw gaping in outrage. "You aren't going to kill him?" Calloway had forgotten all about this small man who didn't belong. He was very easy to forget.

"I'd advise a silent tongue for the remainder of the night, Lindsay," Blackbeard wheezed impatiently, "if you'd prefer to see the dawn."

Frederick glowered at Vane for a split-second, and then turned away with his fists clenched at his sides. *How is this little fool still alive?* Calloway wondered.

Trejean helped Vane to his feet, careful not to touch his wounds.

"Bind Vane's wounds as best you can," Teach said. "But do not deny him use of his fingers. He'll be needing them."

"For what?" Vane asked as he collapsed into Frederick's chair.

"I yet have use for you," Blackbeard answered.

Calloway stood, outrage overwhelming her trepidation. "He tried to kill me. He tried to kill your *daughter*." The word tasted so foul, but she didn't know how else to influence him.

Teach sighed portentously. "Death may have freed Dillahunt, my dear, but take comfort knowing that Vane will never be free. He will forever serve me, and when I am gone, he will serve you, my daughter."

Her knees gave out, and her rear hit the edge of the chair as she fell back into it. "What?"

"You will be my successor, and all that is mine will be yours." He turned to his men. "Isn't that right, lads?"

Every man in the tavern, save for Vane and Frederick, exclaimed "AYE!" in unison.

She felt the blood draining from her face. She clamped a hand over the outside of her pocket, grasping the thing within.

"I am not your servant, Teach," Vane spat.

Blackbeard's steely blue eye swiveled toward him. "You are if you wish to live. Do you *not* wish to live?"

"Fuck that question," Vane returned. His facial muscles softened as he gradually forfeited his indignation. "How long must I serve?"

"Till you be dead."

Vane lowered his head. It was strange to see him looking so humble. "What do you wish of me?"

"I will see your wounds tended to. You and Marcus will retrieve Katherine Lindsay for Frederick. I know exactly where she be cowering." Teach looked at Frederick. "I do not slight those who aid me."

A smug grin lit Frederick's face, and he threw a spiteful glance at Vane.

Two men won't be enough to retrieve Kate, Calloway thought. Not even a ship full of pirates could contain that woman.

Teach faced Frederick. "Return to your ship until I send word."

Frederick nodded anxiously. He hastily fled the tavern.

Vane's face turned red as he worked his jaw. "I suppose that means the deal is off."

"Frederick Lindsay deals with *me* now," Teach said.

On the opposite side of the room, by the entrance, Dumaka was already conversing with one of Teach's men. He almost smiled at whatever the man was telling him, but he seemed to sense Calloway's eyes upon him, and stiffened his lips instead.

She was appalled. How could he be so cavalier after what had just happened? Did he really hate Dillahunt so much? *Crusader's* only survivor was a coward.

Something popped and sizzled. Calloway didn't have to look to know the sound had come from the corpse in the hearth. Dillahunt's flesh was starting to smell very much like a pig on a spit.

Marcus hopped off the crates. His long ponytail swayed as he sauntered up to the hearth. His nostrils were flaring. "Seems a shame to let good meat go to waste," he said as he gave his belly a little pat.

At first, Calloway dismissed the comment as a tasteless jest. But then she looked over the faces of the other pirates. All of them were leering hungrily at the burning corpse. The strange albino boy with shiny blonde hair licked his fat lips.

Comprehension must have shown in her eyes, because Teach looked concerned. "Not in front of my daughter," he said. "She be new to our ways."

"Oh God," she murmured, looking at her father. "You're not going to let them—"

He raised a scorched hand to calm her. "We will let Captain Dillahunt burn until his bones be naught but ash."

The pirates made their disappointment clear, sighing loudly and turning away from the hearth. "I'm starved," she heard one of them mutter sullenly.

"Me mouth be watering," groaned another.

She looked to the open doorway and wondered if she could make it out of the tavern before any of these beasts could snatch her up and drag her kicking and screaming back to Teach. If she could dive into the black water and vanish from their sight, she might be able to swim to safety. But where would she go? She'd just lost her last ally.

There is no safety, she concluded.

Blackbeard's cracked lips distorted into a frown. He nearly looked ashamed, but Calloway knew it was only for her benefit. "Aye, it be true. The flesh of a man heals the soul. It be only after I died that I discovered it for myself. These good men returned me to life with the flesh of our own. I did not take pleasure in it at first, but beggars must not be choosers."

Vane hissed in disgust as he looked at what remained of Dillahunt. "Still think I'm the vilest creature in the Caribbean, Guy?"

Calloway touched her neck. "I required only water."

Blackbeard reached for her, and she did not flinch from his touch. He drew a rubbery finger tenderly across her neck. "My wounds be greater than yours," he said. "I would not wish my anguish upon you. You have already endured so much for one so few in years. I would see you shielded from the terrors of this world."

She couldn't prevent a mad laugh from bursting from her

lips. *You are the terror of this world,* she might have said. Instead, she gestured at Dillahunt's corpse, though she could no longer look at it. "This is a fine start."

"Captain Dillahunt had no love for anyone but himself. He was poorly suited to protect you." He narrowed his one eye. "You know it be true."

She could not deny it. She could only turn from his unflinching eye. "Dillahunt couldn't protect *anyone.*"

"Will you mourn him?" he wondered.

"I already mourned him."

A burly man covered in tattoos entered the tavern. When he saw the burning corpse in the hearth, he stopped in his tracks. "That smells fine," he said.

"Did you find Katherine Lindsay?" Teach asked.

The tattooed man recovered his wits, blinking and looking at Teach. "Nay, but I found another."

Teach turned to Calloway. "Ash will show you to a room in the back. I will visit you shortly. Shed tears for Dillahunt if you must."

She clutched her belly, which was twisting with both hunger and nausea. "I told you—"

"Naught but words," he said, cutting her off. "Words are too easily dwarfed by unforeseen sentiment, dallying beneath a black tide."

Ash took her by the hand. His grip was firm but gentle. He urged her out of her chair and led her toward the back rooms. He seemed more aware of his surroundings than a man with full use of his eyes, moving without hesitation. She followed him through a dark hallway, with the hull on her right side and doors on the other. Through the seams in hemp drapes she glimpsed strumpets crammed in each little room, looking very anxious. They entertained no patrons tonight.

The hallway curved along with the hull, and then bent

sharply to the left toward a door that had been painted red, lit by a flickering torch hanging in a golden sconce. Ash opened the door, and Calloway walked into a luxurious room that spanned half the width of the building. There were no windows. Over a dozen large paintings depicted beautiful women in various stages of undress, most of them baring their breasts, and a few of them baring everything else. The longest painting stretched over the bed, with a beautiful red-haired woman reclining on an opulent couch, with perfect breasts and long legs. *What is it about men and redheads?* Calloway wondered.

The big bed in the center of the room was covered in expensive looking pillows, which rested against a dark oak headboard. Chestnut blankets ran with swirling golden patterns that glimmered in the light of the candles set atop the round tables on either side of the bed. A large oak desk on the right side of the room was covered with rolled parchments.

"This be Trejean's quarters," said Ash, "but he's given it over to your father while he conducts his business."

"Conducts his business?" Holding duels and burning men alive was not her idea of business.

Ash nodded slowly. "Aye. This be his first trip to the western side of Mariposa since we brought him here."

"Who are you people?"

"Everyone you see here served under Captain Teach at some time or another. We owe him our lives, we do. He stationed many of us on the eastern isle, and there we remained until he had need of us."

"Were you always . . . " she hesitated " . . . cannibals?"

"Nay. Our taste for flesh be born of necessity. We were starving, and we turned to the dead and dying for sustenance."

She shuddered. "That's awful."

He shrugged. "It weren't so bad. Mayhap you'll get a taste for—"

She stopped him with a stiff hand. "Never. You are animals. Do not mistake me for my father."

"Of course not," he said in quick, humble agreement. "You be something entirely different. You be exactly what we need."

"What do you mean by that?"

Ash looked over his shoulder, as though he had said too much but couldn't resist. "He's been looking for you, Miss Calloway. I've never seen him so happy."

"You've never 'seen' him at all."

His aged cheeks wrinkled as he smiled. "Seeing and knowing be two different things."

She peered into his milky eyes, unable to discern any hint of an iris or pupil. "Were you born like this?"

"Aye," he said.

"Then you have no idea what the ocean looks like?"

He tapped his nose, and then he tapped both ears. He smiled. "I've seen more of the ocean than a man with eyes."

He took his leave, closing the door behind him.

She walked toward the bed, staring down. Through slits in the planking she could see the water glistening beneath the pier.

She sat on the bed and fished Dillahunt's toe out of her pocket. The hard, shriveled black thing didn't resemble anything that belonged on a human body. She turned it over and over and over, until it slipped out of her fingers. It landed on the floor, and she dropped to her knees to scoop it up, but she was too slow. The toe rolled toward a crack between the planking. She panicked, thrusting out a hand. She succeeded only in nudging it along with the tips of her fingers. It dropped through the hole, vanishing. A second later, she heard it plop in the water below.

"Maybe the sea's magical powers will produce another me from my toe," she remembered him saying, stubbornly refusing to believe her. "That would be nice. I could use a new me. This one is spent."

When she realized she was on her hands and knees, scrambling after a decrepit body part, she almost laughed at her silliness, but the laugh caught in her throat. Her belly restricted, collapsing on itself. She couldn't breathe. Her cheeks were wet before she realized she had started crying. Wracking, silent sobs followed soon after. She couldn't stop. The harder she tried to gain control of herself, the worse it got. She collapsed to her side and coiled into a fetal position, digging her nails into her stomach as she convulsed.

She wasn't sure how long she writhed on the floor, with more water flowing out of her eyes than seemed possible. The planking was dark with her tears by the time she stopped sobbing.

When she finally recovered herself and stood up, the great shadow of Edward Teach loomed in the doorway, still as some ancient tree that had always been there and would remain forever rooted. The light of the many candles in the room was unable to illuminate him. A sapphire orb gleamed in the void. "Are you through with sorrow?" he asked as gently as his guttural voice would allow.

"I have no sorrow left," she answered. "For Guy or anyone else." Her sorrow had streamed through the planking and into the sea. What were tears compared to an ocean?

"That be what I longed to hear." He sounded proud.

She glared at him. "I live only to please you, Father."

"There be a fire in you, my dear."

She shook her head. "You mistake me for another."

"You speak of Katherine Lindsay," he said. "Her fire will soon be extinguished. I have dispatched Captain Vane to fetch her. She will soon be on her way back home."

Calloway tried to laugh, but her voice was nearly gone. Her

words came out as a light rasp. "Vane will fail."

"We shall see," he replied. "I have a gift for you."

Oh god, she thought. *What horrors will you show me now?*

"You need not be fearful, my dear," said the terrible scorched monster. "It be a fine gift, sure to please. What you do with this gift be the quandary."

29

GABE

He awoke submerged to his neck in black water. The top of his head smacked a sturdy bamboo cage. He hacked water out of his lungs. The back of his skull was pulsating. Tattoo had knocked him out at some point, he wasn't sure when. The last thing he remembered was emerging from the jungle onto the beach and seeing Keelhaul Tavern in the distance. He had asked Tattoo if that's where he was taking him. It was the second time he'd been knocked out tonight, and he doubted he would survive a third.

He had no idea where he was. Jungle surrounded the water pit on all sides. A tiny frog watched him from atop one of the bars, its neck continuously expanding into a massive green bubble. Something slithered along his leg. He was careful not to jerk away from whatever it was. His heels were set on a bed of smooth round pebbles that moved around whenever he shuffled his feet.

The stars were still shining brightly through the jungle canopy. It must have been nearing dawn by now. He was shivering terribly. He didn't know if it was cold or if he had simply lost too much blood. He touched the back of his head. His fingers ran over a large lump, which hurt when he pressed it.

He tensed his muscles as the whatever-it-was slithered around his waist and then up his belly.

He waited for what felt like an hour. The sky only seemed to get darker. Monkeys screamed in the distance. Sometimes they sounded like people. It occurred to him he didn't much care for monkeys.

And then he heard the cracking of twigs underfoot, and he smashed the top of his head against the bamboo cage as he tried to see through the bars. "Who's there?" he called, blinking through the blistering pain.

A tall and slender silhouette came into view. It was not a man. The little frog hopped through the bars to get away, plopping into the water somewhere behind Gabe. The girl knelt before the cage, set her fingers on the bars, and leaned in close. Short black hair caressed her cheeks. "Hello, Gabriel," she said. "I did what I promised. I carried your face into the abyss."

"Jacqueline," he gasped.

"Yes," she hissed. "You didn't expect to see me again, did you? The water thwarted you." She traced a finger along the little scar in her neck. "See?"

"What are you talking about? I saved you!"

"Saved me?" She slammed her hands against the cage. "What did you save me from, precisely? Guy is dead, murdered in front of me by my . . . by Blackbeard."

"Teach? Have you lost your senses? The man is dead."

"He's not dead!" She furiously rattled the bars. "He lives! Just as I live!"

Gabe found this incredibly hard to believe, but it did explain why Vane's ship had been attacked in the harbor. Only Teach could have commanded a force that large.

"I spared you, Jacqueline. I took the deed for myself so Vane couldn't do it. It was the only way."

"Why?" she demanded. Her eyes were huge. Veins jutted from her long neck. "Why would you do that?"

"Why do you think?"

Her lips twitched. "You expect me to believe you felt bad?"

"It's the truth."

The little frog swam in front of his face, kicking out its long shiny legs with every stroke. It bumped into his chin and swam the opposite way.

"I don't believe you. The water did this."

"Maybe it helped," he granted, though he didn't really believe it. "But the wound was never grave. You are alive because of me, whether you want to believe it or not."

"And my mother is dead because of you."

He let his chin sink into the water. The frog swam in circles before him. "Yes."

She pressed her face between the bamboo bars, showing him her teeth. Her blue eyes were piercing even in the dark. "Even if you did spare me, it changes nothing. You took away everything I held dear." He expected tears to follow next, but they did not. "You owe me."

"My life," he agreed. "It is yours to take."

"Or I could just leave you here." She stuck a hand through the bars, dipping a finger. "The water doesn't agree with everyone."

The whatever-it-was slithered against his back. He decided it was an eel. He wondered what else was lurking in the water. "I'll accept whatever you decide."

"I don't care what you accept. Death is not enough."

"I would die five times over if it would bring your mother back to you."

"Only five?" Her laugh was hollow. "Death is too easily conquered. How many times has Blackbeard died?"

"I am not Blackbeard."

"No, you were just one of his minions."

"No longer. I wouldn't carry out his will even if it meant my death."

She cocked her head like a bird, and suddenly he worried he'd said the wrong thing. "What about *my* will?"

He wasn't sure what he was supposed to say. This wasn't much easier than dealing with Teach, and her eyes were no less blue. "I am yours to command."

"Are you?"

"That's what I said." He was growing tired of this. He was aching all over. His head was killing him. He just wanted to sleep. "Tell me what you want."

She licked her lips and smiled. "I'm more concerned with what *you* want. Where have you been, Gabe?"

"What do you mean?"

"It's a simple question. What have you been doing all night?"

She wants Kate, he realized. "I've been evading pirates. They swarmed on Vane's ship, killed everybody."

"They were looking for Kate, and you already know that. You took her with you. Don't lie."

He didn't say anything.

"Why would you protect her unless . . . " Her face bloomed with sudden comprehension. "You love her."

He tried to laugh, but only sputtered water. "I don't love that woman." He struggled to think of something to say, something she expected to hear. "She's a means to an end. I hid her so I could turn her in and claim the reward for myself."

She narrowed her eyes and smiled, and he felt like a very small mouse caught under the paws of a hungry cat. "Then you won't mind fetching her for me."

He chuckled as if he didn't care. "And I suppose you'll take the reward after all my hard work"

She shook her head. "I don't care about the reward, Gabe. Not anymore. It's yours, for all the good it will do you. All I care about right now is getting Kate out of this place, far removed from all of this madness."

"You expect me to believe you actually care what happens to her?"

"I *do* care. Kate is a danger to herself and everyone around her. She saved me, and I'm going to save her in turn. And if I can hurt you in the bargain, so much the better. I don't believe she is nothing to you. I think she's *everything* to you. You might not even know it yet, but you'll know it soon, when you have no one left but yourself."

He looked at the frog, swimming and swimming, its bulbous eyes always above the water. "You honestly think I won't run the opposite direction as soon as you open this cage?"

"I have Blackbeard at my back now. He will find you eventually. Unless I convince him otherwise."

"I don't care what happens to me."

She thrust out a hand, snatching the little frog out of the water and drawing it through the bars. "Then you won't run." She stood and examined her new pet in a cupped hand. "You'll do this because you know it's what's best for Kate. And because you owe me."

"And then what? You'll kill me?"

"I am not Blackbeard." She stroked the frog lovingly with her index finger. "Bring me Kate and your debt will be paid."

He reached up and clutched the bars. "All will be forgiven?" He laughed at how stupid that sounded, given what he had done.

She set the frog in the dirt and watched as it bounded into the brush. "There are greater evils than you, Gabe Jenkins. Make your choice, but make it fast. Vane is already on his way to collect Kate. I suspect he'll die in the attempt. He's never been able to get the better of her, but something tells me she won't see *you* coming."

30

VANE

"Did you like watching him burn?" Marcus asked as he watched Vane slowly and clumsily crawl over a fallen tree trunk that cut through the thick jungle.

"The man was a fool," Vane grunted. It was hard to push Dillahunt's final moments from his mind. He could still see him tossing his head about, looking for a way out right down to the very last instant, until the fire swept over his face and burned the life right out of him. Vane had personally overseen the slow deaths of countless men, and he had noted that same mad hope in all their faces. They all expected some miracle to spare them. It never came. "If he had just allowed me to kill Frederick Lindsay, he'd be alive, and I'd be ashes."

But at least I would have taken Frederick with me.

"Aye," said Marcus. "But no one survives Teach's games in the end."

Vane needed no reminder. He knew this reprieve was only

temporary.

"You don't look so good, Charles," Marcus taunted. "Sure you don't need a hand?"

"Call me Charles again, and I'll gut you."

Marcus chuckled. "You're welcome to try, Charles."

"Fuck you." Vane hopped off the trunk. He allowed his legs to give out from under him, and he spilled onto his hands and knees. He groaned and cursed, pretending it was a great struggle to get back on his feet. In truth, he didn't feel as bad as he should have. A lightheaded euphoria made the trek through the jungle much easier than he was willing to let Marcus believe. He had lost a lot of blood while fending off Dillahunt's attack. His hands and arms were wrapped in thick bandages, with bruised fingers sticking out the ends. He looked ridiculous. Though some of the wounds were very deep, there was no pain other than faint prickles. He knew he would feel it later.

Not that I'll live that long, he reminded himself.

There was only one thing left to do. Frederick Lindsay had taken everything from him. He would not let that betrayal go unanswered, even if it meant hastening his own fate.

He took a breath and moved past Marcus. The ground was unsteady, covered in vines and rocks, and Vane teetered all over the place, exaggerating his drunken movements and colliding with trees. Marcus laughed behind him. "Haven't the foggiest notion why Teach made you come along. You're quite useless."

Teach's motives were no mystery. "He wants to shame me."

"He's going to kill you," Marcus pointlessly informed him.

"He kills everyone when their use runs out," Vane grated over his shoulder. He saw a tree directly ahead, and he made no attempt to move out of the way. He lightly smacked his head, while kicking his boot against the base of the trunk so it would make a very loud noise. Marcus howled laughter. "I am drunk on blood-loss," Vane moaned pathetically.

"You're going to end yourself before Teach gets the chance."

Vane pretended to shake away the pain he didn't feel.

"There's no winning," Marcus went on. "He likes his games, but in the end, it's always the same."

Vane halted to set his hands on his knees and catch his breath, even though he wasn't winded. "Why the loyalty?" he asked, hoping to keep Marcus talking. Not that it was hard. *This twit loves the sound of his own voice.*

Marcus stopped beside him and played with one of the ears hanging from his necklace. Vane stared into the man's fully dilated pupils. Those endless black pools offered no comfort. There was nothing beyond, as with all Teach's followers. "Blackbeard cannot die," Marcus answered. "You've seen that for yourself."

Vane snickered. "The thing I saw in that tavern was barely alive, clinging to a thread. He will be dead in a fortnight."

"His shell will decay, but his soul will endure through the ages, long after the rest of us are dead and gone."

"Feasting on human flesh has addled your brain."

Marcus ignored the insult. "At first we feared his mind was lost. He spoke nonsense in the dark. We fed him. He took thirteen lives. The thirteenth was a man you were acquainted with. We found him down in the deep dark of Pirate Town."

"I don't know who you're talking about." That wasn't entirely true. He remembered leaving two men down in the dungeon, one of his own, and a man named—

"Ogle," said Marcus. "You tortured him, I believe."

"I tortured a lot of men."

"You left this one alive."

"I was in a rush," said Vane. "It seems your lot finished the job for me."

"Ogle's soul returned Teach to us."

"You're all truly mad."

Marcus waved a hand dismissively. "I wouldn't expect you to understand, but how can you deny what you've seen with your own eyes?"

"What precisely have my eyes seen?"

His great pupils shrunk for a split-second. "A lost daughter returned to her father when the man is but a few breaths from death. Is that not a miracle?"

Vane clasped bandaged palms to his temples, feigning a battle with wooziness. "Is that bitch to be your leader when Teach dies? A girl who trades her cunny for coin?" He almost felt sorry for Calloway. He didn't want to think about whatever dark fate her loving father intended for her. *Better she had perished by my hand.*

Marcus sighed. "No point explaining it to a dead man. Let's get moving."

"I'll need a weapon."

Marcus grinned shrewdly. "What for? She's only a woman."

"Kate Lindsay is not to be underestimated. If you send me in there without a weapon, she will kill me."

"Afraid of a woman, Charles?"

"You don't know her."

"We both know the minute I hand you a pistol, you'll shoot me between the eyes and flee into the jungle."

The nausea made it easier to repress his usually irrepressible smirk. "A fool's errand. Blackbeard's forces are too mighty. Mariposa is teeming with his men. I'd never escape."

Marcus gave Vane's shoulder a hard slap. "I'm glad I don't have to remind you of that."

"Good," said Vane. "My trust is established."

"I'll give you my spare pistol when we get to the lake, not before. I'll unload it first, but at least you'll have something to threaten her with."

They continued on, with Vane in front. Whenever Marcus wasn't looking, he picked away at the bandage around his right hand, until his hand was completely exposed and he could freely wriggle his fingers.

They came to a fallen trunk that stretched across a ravine. Vane leaned forward to look over the edge, and then he cast a wary glance at Marcus. "I can't do this."

Marcus stepped up onto the huge trunk, tapping his heel against it to test its weight. It didn't budge. "It's sturdy, Charles."

"I don't give a shit. I'm done."

Marcus drew a pistol from his sash and held it at his side. "You'll go, or I'll shoot you in the belly and leave you to bleed out."

Vane stepped to the foot of the trunk, a mere two paces from Marcus, and folded his arms. "Then shoot."

"Never figured you for the cowardly type, Charles."

"This is not cowardice." *Aim that pistol at me, and you'll find out what this is.*

Marcus did exactly what Vane hoped he would do, and stuck the pistol in Vane's face. The barrel pressed his forehead. "Thank you," said Vane. His right hand shot up to grasp the barrel, angling it away from his head while he thrust out his left palm and caught Marcus square in the chest. Vane leaned into the blow and fell on top of Marcus, whose back hit the trunk. Marcus wriggled beneath him, but Vane straddled him as he would a lover, clinching him with his legs. He realized with delight that he was holding the pistol. Marcus immediately stopped struggling when Vane pointed it at him.

"You bloody fool!" Marcus howled. "My mates are just behind us! Do you really think Teach would send only two men? They'll kill you for this!"

"No they won't," Vane said. "They'll take me before Teach, and *he'll* kill me. But he was going to do that anyway."

Marcus calmed himself. He seemed to think he still had the upper hand. "So what's your plan, Charles? Kill me and capture the woman all by yourself? Didn't you hear what Teach said? She's hiding in a cave halfway up a waterfall. You'll never make the climb."

Vane gripped the necklace of shriveled ears. "Firstly, I'm going to paint this bridge with your brains." He did exactly that, shoving the barrel into Marcus's gaping maw and smiling with satisfaction as the back of his skull exploded, dousing the bark. The hemp of the necklace snapped, and over two dozen ears scattered everywhere, rolling down either side of the trunk.

Vane chucked the smoking pistol over the edge, watching as it sailed down to the little river below. He drew the spare from Marcus's sash. It was already loaded. "Secondly, I'm going to scale that waterfall, and I'm going to deliver Katherine's severed head to her loving brother-in-law."

Dillahunt had deprived Vane of his only chance to kill Frederick, but he could still take the one thing Frederick coveted most.

31

KATE

The constant flow of the waterfall crashing upon the rocky ledge outside had surely influenced her dreams, because she found herself riding an exquisitely turbulent sea. She was clutching the wheel of the helm as her ship crested dangerously tall waves. There was no one else aboard, but the ship maneuvered as though it had a full crew. She didn't even need to issue commands; the ship obeyed her thoughts. Seawater sprayed her face and salt stung her eyes. The sky was grey and frightening, and bolts of lightning struck the top of the mast. On the third strike, the black flag caught fire, and the skull and crossbones quickly burned away. The ship plunged down a long wave and scaled the next. The wave lifted up and up, stretching away from the bow. The clouds parted at the top, and a shaft of sunlight nearly blinded her. She knew she would never reach the top of that wave. The ship would tumble back down into the sea and carry her straight to the bottom. The wave came crashing down over the deck and washed over her like a warm blanket, shrouding her in darkness.

It was a good dream.

When she opened her eyes, a dark shape filled the crack that led out of the cave. "Gabe?" she called.

The man stepped into the cavern.

It was not Gabe.

Not even the soft light of the torch could ease Vane's alarming pallor. All the blood had drained from his face, which was beaded with water and sweat. His auburn hair draped straight and limp, forgoing its curls. His arms were covered in bandages, which were hanging in shreds from his hands and dripping blood on the ground. "That's a murderous climb," he gasped.

"Charles," she replied in a daze as she fought to sit up in the bed. One of her arms was numb and tingling. It was a struggle just to keep her eyes open. She wondered how long she had been asleep. "This is a pleasant surprise. I wish I could say you're looking well."

"I'm not at my best." He drew his pistol.

She rubbed her eyes. Distantly, a warning was sounding, but she was too tired to give it credence. For all she knew she was still dreaming. "What are you doing?"

He sighed apologetically. "Though your tits give me inclination to believe in a higher power, I'm afraid I must slice your head off and present it to Frederick Lindsay as a final gesture of defiance. I apologize in advance." He aimed the pistol. His arm shook, until he gripped his wrist with his other hand. "I would prefer to make this quick. As a courtesy, I will shoot you before I take your head. Hold still please."

"Would you give me a moment?" she murmured groggily. *At least let me figure out if this is a dream.*

"I can't spare the time."

"I'd prefer to keep my head attached, is all."

He sighed again. "Look on the sunny side, Kate. You will never be more beautiful than you are now. Would you prefer to wither into an old maid, cunny all dried out like an apricot left in the heat too long? That's a slow torture. I'm doing you a kindness. I promise not to muss your hair."

"How thoughtful."

"You're welcome. Now hold still."

Before she could offer further protest, he pulled the trigger. The *clack* of the hammer gave her a fierce start, jarring her into full consciousness. She examined her chest for a few seconds before she realized there had been no shot.

Vane frowned and looked at the gun. "Well this is fucking embarrassing."

"It's the spray of the waterfall," she realized. She slipped a hand beneath the blanket to grip the blunderbuss she had tucked beside her hip. Fortunately she had not kicked it off the bed in her sleep. "Dampens the powder on the way up."

His smirk twitched into a sheepish smile. "Would you give me a moment?"

"I can't spare the time," she recited with a smile, and pulled the trigger. The blast tore a great hole in the blanket and opened up Vane's left shoulder, kicking him up off his feet and propelling him sideways toward a wall. He crashed through a stalactite, and the shattered pieces pattered the ground. He hit the wall and slid down with smoke pouring out of the crater in his shoulder. The left side of his face was painted in a thousand tiny red dots.

"Y-you f-fucking b-bitch," he choked. "You k-killed me. I'm k-killed by a woman. The g-great Charles V-Vane. Me!"

She tossed the ruined blanket aside and stepped out of the bed. Thankfully, she had dressed before going to sleep. "How many more men do I have to kill before they stop being surprised when I kill them?" She found her maroon coat atop the keg of powder and slipped it on. She fitted Gabe's curved dagger into her belt.

Vane raised his right hand. The left was useless at his side, with blood gushing from the smoking hole in his shoulder. "B-Black . . ."

Kate turned slowly. "What?"

"B . . . Black . . ."

She kneeled beside him. She couldn't see how bad his shoulder was through the smoke that wafted out of it, but she could smell it burning. "What are you trying to say, Charles?"

"Blackbeard."

Her gut filled with dread. Why would he say that? A trick? "What about him?"

"He lives."

"You're lying." But what if he wasn't? She never saw Blackbeard die. She had only taken Dillahunt's word for it. And Dillahunt's word wasn't worth much.

"No," Vane said. "He's alive. He killed D-Dillahunt."

"Dillahunt's dead?"

"Deader than d-dead," he answered with his customary smirk, which not even his impending doom could rob from him. "T-Teach made me come h-here, to f-fetch you for F-Frederick f-fucking Lindsay. More of his m-men are on their w-way."

"My husband's brother is here?" She tried to think back. She might have met Frederick once, but she could not recall his face.

He nodded.

"You were forced here against your will?" It was a flat question, devoid of emotion. She would not feel sympathy for the man who had murdered so many of her friends.

Another nod.

"Did you see Gabe Jenkins?" She was afraid to ask, but she

had to know.

"He was c-captured."

"Of course he was," she heard herself murmur. She wanted to scream. She had finally found someone who wanted her instead of her reward, and already he was gone. She was alone. She had always been alone, ever since losing Thomas. For the briefest of moments she had convinced herself it would not always be that way. She had allowed herself a glimmer of hope. *I should have known better.*

But she would not let Vane see her despair. His last image would be that of a fierce woman who needed no one.

She gave his leg a pat. "You should have fled, Charles."

Vane's eyes were starting to glaze over. "Nowhere to f-flee to. Teach is e-everywhere."

She stood and shrugged. "That's not my problem."

"It's everyone's p-problem."

"Yet it's not Teach who killed you," she reminded him. "Men like you and Dillahunt are so very much alike. The goal is all that matters. You'll sacrifice everything to reach it, until there's nothing left to sacrifice but yourself."

His smirk grew, even as his head sank into his shoulders. The smoke thinned, and she could see the white of his collarbone in the black and red hole. He was fading.

There was no time to waste. She had to think fast. She frantically looked around the little cavern. Everything she needed was right here at her disposal. She moved to the three kegs of powder and popped the cork of the topmost keg. She hefted the keg and angled the opening downward, trailing powder in swirls along the floor.

"What are you d-doing, b-b-bitch?" Vane demanded as she poured powder over his legs. "I'm already f-fucking d-dying."

When the floor was covered in powder, she set the keg down and plucked the torch out of its sconce. She returned to

Vane. She lifted his right hand and placed the torch in it, closing his fingers around it. "You want to hurt Teach?" she asked. "Make the most of this."

She left him there.

She slipped through the narrow passage as fast as she could, just in case Vane opted to drop the torch early and take her with him. But there was no explosion. When she reached the waterfall, she saw three pinpoints of torchlight in the jungle. They were coming.

She leapt through the waterfall and dove into the lake below. She swam back to the surface and popped her head up. She swam under the wide arc of the waterfall, directly beneath the ledge. She found some boulders piled up above the water, and she crawled atop them and waited in the dark, behind the curtain of water. It was the perfect hiding spot.

She waited there for minutes, and still she heard no explosion above. Either Vane was holding on for dear life, or the torch had gone out. Her thoughts inevitably turned to Gabe. His handsome face smiled at her through the sheets of water. *I shouldn't have let him go,* she told herself. *I should have made him stay.* Instead, she had gone to sleep, because she didn't want him to see how much she fancied him. Not yet. She would save that for later, after she confirmed the feeling was real. But there would be no later. She had missed her chance.

The men Vane spoke of arrived in pairs. There were six of them total. Big pirates, all in black. She didn't recognize any of them. They had indistinct faces, and the dull-eyed stare that she recalled from the crew of *Queen Anne's Revenge*. They remained silent. They doused their torches in the lake and immediately started for the stair of boulders on the eastern bank. She watched through seams in the curtaining water as they scaled the boulders without a word, until they reached the top, where the ledge blocked them from her view. She slid off of the boulders and back into the water. She swam to the far bank of the lake, keeping her head low.

When she was near the shore, and her toes brushed the pebbles below, the water trembled. She spun around and looked up. The entire mountainside rumbled. The waterfall suddenly ballooned from the ledge, like a giant bubble bursting, and a massive fireball erupted from the thin mouth of the cave, sending a roiling black cloud up the crag. Three flaming bodies were projected from the ledge, flying three separate directions. Two of them touched down in the lake, fiery corpses sizzling as they were extinguished, and the third landed in one of the trees on the far eastern bank, where he continued to burn. The ledge broke free, and the long slab of rock tilted downward. Water and fire rolled down it. It crumbled as it fell, until it broke on the boulders Kate had been hiding atop of not a moment before. A tremendous wave rushed toward her. She raced for the shore, but the wave caught her and carried her forward, washing her over the rough rocks.

She scrambled to her feet and retreated to the trees, brushing off dirt and gravel as she ran. Her elbows were scraped up pretty bad, but it could have been worse. She spared a look back. Fire continued to spill from the little cave above, even as the waterfall washed over it.

"Good work, Charles," she whispered.

She turned to run before she looked where she was headed, and she promptly slammed into a muscular chest. She fell back, landing on her ass in a patch of vines. Her eyes scaled a long black coat.

She gasped when she saw his face.

Gabe's curly hair was slick with sweat, as if he'd been running, and he looked utterly exhausted, but he was smiling that pretty smile. Exhaustion only made him more handsome, and the thickening grizzle enhanced his already stout jaw. "I leave you alone for a few hours," he said, "and you blow everything to Hell."

She couldn't restrain herself. She didn't want to. She didn't care if she looked like a silly girl. She sprang to her feet and pounced on him, throwing her arms around him and kissing him fiercely on the lips. He clutched her waist, kissing her back. "You're alive," she murmured between sloppy kisses.

"Why wouldn't I be?"

"I think Blackbeard survived." She released his lips only briefly. "And I think he's in Mariposa."

"I know," he said as his hands slid up her sides.

She spread her fingers into the thick wet tendrils of his hair. "I thought maybe he got you."

"He didn't." His tongue grazed hers.

"We have to go," she insisted, but she couldn't stop kissing him. He reeked of sweat and dirt, and it was the best thing she had ever smelled. She never wanted to stop. "When those men don't return—"

"I know," he said, but he kept kissing her.

They might have gone on like that for the remainder of the night had she not fended him off. She pulled back and clasped a hand over his mouth. He kissed her palm, and she laughed. "We have to go, Gabe."

His voice was muffled behind her hand. "Ready when you are."

She took his hand and guided him into the jungle. "We have to find a ship. We have to get away from this island. If Teach is alive and running things, who knows who we can trust. We'll have to be careful. We'll have to—"

He snatched her other hand and pulled her back toward him. He gathered both hands behind her back. Her stomach fluttered. She wanted to, but now was hardly the time. "Gabe, we can't—"

Something foreign snaked around her wrists and tightly constricted, too coarse and ragged to be his fingers. The rope was secure before she could think to react. The tip of a boot kicked the back of her leg, and she went down on her knees in a soft patch of brush. "NO!" she cried. She struggled against the rope, but he had secured it too tightly. She tried to stand, but a firm hand held her shoulder down. She tried to look back. If she could make eye contact, maybe she could reason with him. He seized her by the hair, holding her head in place. "NOOOO!!"

"Don't fight it."

He released her shoulder and retrieved the dagger from her belt. He gave the hilt a sharp whip, and the sheath flew off. He brought the sharp blade to her neck.

"Gabe, don't do this!" she pleaded desperately.

"I'm not going to kill you," he promised, "but I will cut you if you don't hold still."

"You *are* killing me!" She writhed in her restraints, burning her wrists on the rope. The skin would be raw tomorrow, but that would be the least of her worries.

"Don't be so dramatic."

"It's Calloway, isn't it," she sneered. "I just can't escape that girl."

"She's going to sell you to your brother-in-law. You're going to live out the rest of your days in London. Safe. Away from all of this madness. So stop tossing about, because it won't do any good. You can't stop this. At least you'll be alive. Maybe one day you'll thank me."

She barked a hoarse laugh that pained her throat on the way out. "I'll curse your name long after you're dead. She's going to kill you, you know. She despises you."

"That's her choice."

She wished she could see if his eyes betrayed the peaceful

resignation in his voice, but he would not relinquish his stiff grip on her hair. "You think you owe her something? You don't. It was her own father who made you kill her mother. You don't owe her anything, Gabe. You saved her life, remember?"

Hot breath seethed into her ear. "It was my hand that did the deed! I owe her everything!"

"You were a young fool. You were scared."

"Maybe so, but that doesn't earn me any sleep at night."

"And what will this accomplish? Even if she forgives you, what then? You think you'll never again see her mother's face when you're alone in your hammock on the deck of some ship?"

"It doesn't matter," he sighed. "I have to do this for her. I don't expect you to understand."

"You may as well slice my throat right now."

"That's not going to happen. You keep pretending you're something you're not. This is no place for you."

She felt her muscles softening, and she cursed her body for giving up. "I thought you knew me."

"No one can ever truly know anyone but themselves."

"This isn't you."

He laughed bitterly. "See? You don't know me at all."

She stopped struggling. It was useless. Gabe was lost, just like all the others. There was nothing she could say to change his mind, and she had no way to overpower him.

But she could still hurt him. "I might have loved you someday."

"I know." He took hold of her wrists, lifted her to her feet, and spurred her into movement. "Let's go."

Her feet felt heavy. The vines and brush and patches of sand were suddenly cumbersome to tread. After a while, she gave up looking for an escape. There was no point. "What will you do now?" she wondered.

"Now?" He hesitated. "Now, I'm going to find me a nice strumpet."

She wished he could see her contemptuous scowl. "You disgust me."

"You're not the only fish in the sea, Kate."

32

CALLOWAY

Calloway's wrist began to strain under the weight of the heavy hemp drape as she pressed it to the doorframe. She wasn't sure why she'd come here.

Kate was sitting at the foot of a tiny slab of a bed in a narrow little room that had belonged to one of Trejean's many strumpets. Her face was cloaked somewhere beneath her hair as she gazed down at the fat iron shackles secured around her ankles. She was bound to the frame of the bed by huge rusty chains. "These restraints are absurd," she complained in a ragged voice that was barely audible. "I'm not a rhinoceros. I'd have an easier time gnawing through the bed."

Calloway made herself laugh. "I suppose they were meant for a very big pirate."

Kate looked up. Her eyes were lined with water and shot with blood. She might have aged five years. "Are you here to mock me?"

Calloway shied from Kate's glower. Why was it still so hard to look at her, after all the horrors she had been privy to? "I just wanted to say goodbye. I don't suppose we'll ever see each other again."

Kate's lips twisted. "I wouldn't be so sure."

Calloway's laugh was genuine this time. "Even if you could make it all the way back here, I won't last the month."

"Your father," Kate realized.

"I have no idea what he wants with me."

"You should flee." Her words were edged with concern, but Calloway wasn't convinced.

She took a step forward, letting the hemp drape swing closed behind her. Her aching wrist was instantly grateful. "And I suppose you want to help me escape?"

Kate nodded. "Unless you'd rather wait here for Blackbeard to kill you?"

Calloway shook her head. "There's nowhere for me to go."

Kate threw her hands up in frustration. "Anywhere is better than here. He killed your mother, Jaq."

Calloway felt the pressure of her tightening jaw. She'd barely had a single night to process her father being alive. He hadn't tortured her or locked her up. She was free to leave the tavern if she wished. She didn't know what she was supposed to do.

"Better the devil you know," she answered finally.

Kate hissed a scathing laugh. "There's only one devil, Jaq, and you've thrown in with him."

Calloway aimed an accusatory finger. "And you threw in with the man who carried out his orders. The man who killed my mother! Did you forget?"

For once, Kate offered no reply, confirming what Calloway already knew. Kate and Gabe had been lovers, if only for a brief time. "How could you do that, knowing what he is?

Knowing what he'd done?"

Kate fidgeted with her fingernails. "I saw you on the beach earlier, and I knew then that he hadn't killed you."

"And that was enough for you?" Calloway slapped a palm to her forehead. "I shouldn't be surprised. You slept with the man who murdered your husband."

Kate threw up her hands and let them slap her thighs. "What do you want me to say? Life is short."

The air was dense with the smoke of the candle on the bedside table, which was burning at an angle. Calloway was just about to leave when Kate spoke again. "We should have been great friends, you and I. You could have been my sister. That's all I ever wanted."

"So did I." The words flowed on impulse, before she could consider what she was saying. It wasn't true. She didn't want a sister. She didn't need a sister. She needed a mother.

Kate's piercing eyes seemed to pass right through her. Despite her present circumstance, she had surrendered none of her infuriating confidence. "No, you didn't. I've never been anything more than a thing for you to absorb and toss away." Her words were gentle yet poised.

"That's not true!" But the protest was feeble.

"Maybe not," Kate granted. "Maybe you'll keep a piece of me in your pocket." She held up a hand, and Calloway flinched from the sudden gesture. "Would you like a finger? I won't be needing all ten."

"I only ever wanted to save you," Calloway insisted. "The way you saved me."

May the best woman win.

Kate beckoned her closer. Calloway swallowed her timidity and stepped forward. Kate gently took Calloway's hands in hers, drawing her down to her knees. Kate framed Calloway's face with her hands, softly caressing her cheeks. Her palms were warm and calloused. She leaned forward, wetting Calloway's dry lips with a tender kiss. It was nothing like kissing a man. Her lips were so much thinner, so much kinder. Kate pulled back and smiled the sweetest of smiles, and Calloway wished she could take everything back.

"If fortune sets you in my path again," Kate said, "I will open your belly and strangle you with your own entrails."

Her fingernails dug painfully into Calloway's cheeks, but that sweet smile did not falter. Calloway clasped her hands over Kate's, prying them away before her fingernails could shear the skin. She shoved Kate off and stood in the same motion. "You're mad, Kate!"

Kate's smile grew. Wild strands of hair had tumbled over her face, shading her eyes.

Calloway wiped her lips with the back of her hand and fled from the room, out into the corridor. She did not look back, but she would never forget that sweet smile, and the promise that accompanied it.

Gabe Jenkins was waiting for her in the tavern.

It was an hour before dawn's first light, and there was nothing but black beyond the always open entrance. None of the patrons had returned. Dumaka had vanished. Three of Blackbeard's men were drinking silently at the bar, and the two large shirtless men stood watch at the entrance. Several strumpets were lazing about. Some of them were awake, gossiping with one another. They glanced apprehensively at Calloway when she entered, and promptly stifled their gossip.

Dillahunt's corpse had been cleared out of the hearth. She didn't want to know what they had done with him. The room still smelled faintly of burnt flesh.

Gabe was alone and halfway through his latest tankard of ale, cheeks flushed red and eyelids drooping low. A pewter plate with a succulent red crab was untouched. He sat up straight when he saw her and gestured slackly at his meal. "It's yours, if you want it.

"I'm not hungry." That was a lie. She was so hungry that her belly felt like it was going to cave in, but she could not eat. Not tonight, anyway.

She slid a chair out. It was surprisingly heavy. Or maybe she was just too exhausted to move a wooden chair. She hadn't slept in over a day, now that she thought about it. Teach had offered her one of the nicer rooms, with a big bed with soft sheets, blankets of fur, and plush pillows. Before Gabe returned with Kate, she had tried to fall asleep, but when she closed her eyes she saw flesh catching fire and blackening.

She sat beside Gabe. It was much easier to meet his sad eyes than Kate's. She found her confidence returning. "You'll be delivering Kate to Frederick Lindsay," she informed him. She'd been looking forward to this.

Gabe smirked, pretending he didn't care. "Of course I will."

"It's not a problem, I trust?"

He lifted his tankard in a lazy toast, bowing his head. "A bit of shine sets every pirate out of his mind."

"What does that mean?"

"It means I'll do it."

Between their chairs, his pretty dagger was embedded in the edge of the table. He had probably struck it there in a fit of anger. She touched one of the three vibrant turquoise stones set in the silver-mounted hilt. In the torchlight it almost resembled her father's eye. "You're not doing this for shine," she said.

He shrugged. "It won't hurt."

She clutched the hilt of the dagger and jerked it free, leaving a deep wedge in the wood. She studied herself in the shiny blade. "It will hurt you plenty."

Gabe looked down into his tankard and worked his jaw.

"She's not the only fish."

"What?"

"Nothing."

Her fingers tightened around the dagger's hilt as she looked at his face. She knew she should put the dagger in his skull. But he looked so tired and pathetic. "I'm keeping your knife," she said. She stood and tucked the dagger through her belt.

"It's yours," he said, "along with everything else."

"You know where to find Kate." She stuck a thumb over her shoulder toward the back rooms. "You will meet Frederick Lindsay on the beach just after dawn."

"Fine."

"Don't fall asleep," she warned.

"Couldn't sleep if I wanted to."

"No less than you deserve." She pushed the chair into the table. It slid in easily. Just like that, her energy was renewed. She involuntarily touched the raw line along her throat. It had become a habit. "Tell me the truth. Did you really spare my life?"

He pushed a loose curl out of his face in order to look her in the eyes. "If you really thought I tried to kill you, you wouldn't be relying on me right now."

She knew he was right, and she hated him all the more intensely for it. "After tomorrow, I don't ever want to see you again."

"You won't," he assured her.

She walked back down the corridor, passing the strumpet's little rooms. She quickened her pace as she passed by Kate's room. She didn't want to see her face again. Fortunately, everything had fallen so perfectly into place with Gabe Jenkins. *Not so fortunate for Kate,* she reminded herself with a smile.

There was only one thing left to do now.

Her fingers found the hilt of her new dagger as she rounded

the sharp corner toward the red door that led into Trejean's quarters. Trejean stood before the door, hunched with his ear to the wood. His long white hair was disheveled. He gasped when he noticed Calloway behind him. He slapped his palms together as if in prayer. "Please, do not tell your father."

"Were you spying?"

Her question struck horror in his dark face. "That is an evil word. I do not 'spy.'"

"No one would blame you," she said, hoping to soothe him. She hadn't meant to alarm him, she was merely curious. "Did you hear anything in there?"

He grasped the bird skull hanging from the end of his necklace. "I should not say."

"You *should* say." She took a confident step forward, making her posture as straight as Kate's, which was always so perfect. Kate always seemed tall even though she was shorter than Calloway. "Or would you like me to tell my father you were spying?"

Trejean's face twisted in fear. "You wouldn't!"

She smiled. "Wouldn't I? I am Blackbeard's daughter. Who knows what I'm capable of?" *I certainly don't.*

He shook his head in distress, knuckles whitening as he squeezed the bird skull. "Him talk to a woman."

"There's a woman in there?" She was stunned, and a little horrified. She didn't think Teach held such desires anymore. She imagined that part of him had burned away, emotionally and physically. And what strumpet could pretend not to be utterly revolted by him, let alone touch him?

"No *real* woman in there," said Trejean. "Him talk to a woman, but she's not there."

"That doesn't make any sense."

"Him talk to a ghost."

She frowned. "How do you know this ghost is a woman?"

"Because him talk to her as a man talks to a lover."

Calloway shivered. Was Teach delusional enough to think her mother would visit him?

Trejean started to back away. "I leave you to your father."

She grabbed his wrist, and he stared at her hand in shock. She tried to soothe him with a reassuring smile. "This is your tavern, yes?"

He nodded solemnly. "Aye."

"I imagine this is all quite maddening for you. You have every right to know what goes on here."

"Teach do not see things this way." He clutched her shoulders with massive hands. His eyes were desperate with fear. "Promise you do not tell him."

"Why should I tell him?"

"You make fine point," he said. He released her shoulders and hurried around her, disappearing around the bend.

When she was sure he was gone, she opened the door and stepped in. The room was swathed in a murderous red. Most of the candles had burned out, and those few that still flickered were burning low. The wicks would extinguish themselves in their own wax within the hour. The strumpets in the paintings along the walls were dark and devilish, naked skin bathed in shades of crimson. Their eyes followed Calloway as she crossed the room. Their vivacious smiles seemed to broaden with her approach.

Teach was propped up against the many pillows of the bed, resting atop the blankets. He wore a robe that was as black as his beard. His boots were off. His huge hairy feet seemed to be the only part of him that had not been touched by fire. His chest rose and fell with shallow breaths. Within the mottled ruin of his hideous face, his blue eye tracked her as she rounded the bed. "My daughter, you've come to me at last." His voice was a low wheeze.

"I couldn't sleep."

"Nor I," he said.

"I have questions, Father."

He looked downward, and she remembered the dagger in her belt. Did that make him nervous? She hoped so.

"I knew you would." He patted the bed. "Come, sit beside me."

She turned her back to him for a moment as she sat on the bed. She folded one leg beneath her to appear casual and relaxed, but she let the other hang over the edge, with her heel planted on the floor. He took her hand in his, stroking her with fractured, seared fingers. "Your skin be so soft," he said.

"What are you going to do with me?"

"You needn't fret, my dear. It is precisely as I've said. You will lead my men after I be gone."

"Why would your men follow me?"

He gave her hand a squeeze. "You be of my own blood. That be more than enough for them."

"That means nothing. When you die, they'll rape and murder me."

His cracked lips formed a smile. "You cannot understand the depth of their loyalty. Not yet. I be too weak to travel to the eastern isle, but when my soul has left this rotting shell, Ash will take you there, and there you will learn the truth."

The hairs prickled along the back of her neck. "What truth?"

He closed his eye, wheezing softly. "That be for you to uncover."

She looked away so he wouldn't see her frustration. These riddles were maddening. When she looked back at him, his eye was open again, but he was looking past her. Within the puzzle of ruined flesh, she glimpsed reverence.

"Who do you see?" She already knew who it was.

"My eye beholds your mother." He pointed to a dark corner. "A glorious sight she be, even through vision halved by a stubborn daughter."

Calloway didn't bother to look. "I can't see her."

"Aye," Teach nodded. "She doesn't want you to see her. Not yet. You be young, with long years ahead. I be old and near to dying. She beckons me."

"You think you'll join her?"

There was no trace of doubt in his terrible face. "I know she does."

She smiled, because she knew better. "But Father, my mother is not in Hell."

Fractured skin bunched as he frowned. "You be cross with me still?"

"You killed her."

He released her hand and showed her his palms. "Not with these hands."

"No," she admitted, pushing his hands back down into his lap. "Your tongue is far deadlier."

He grinned proudly. "You are truly my daughter."

If her stomach held any food, she would have vomited. "Stop calling me that."

He closed his eye for a moment of reminiscence. His wheezing grew heavier with every word. "Even now I can see the brothel in Port Bayou St. Jean where first I met your mother. Sixteen years ago, it were. A seedy place, if ever I saw one. She didn't belong there. No woman belonged there. How long did she keep you in that place before she moved you to yet another brothel in Nassau? How long before she vended your body? How young were you when you first had a man betwixt your nethers? Did your mother beg your leave before she offered you to that first suitor?"

She knew what he was trying to do, but it would not work.

Her mother had never forced anything on her. "The first was my choice. I did the deed under her nose. She was so angry with me."

"I'd wager you were too young to make choices of your own, my dear." He revealed his horrible teeth. "If I had the energy, I would scour the seas for the man who claimed your maidenhood. I would strangle the life from him with these hands and piss on his corpse. I would live that much longer just to perform the deed."

His promise made her smile, but her smile was born of impassive amusement rather than love. He was trying so very hard to stir her affections, even at the expense of her mother's memory, who he claimed to love so dearly. She knew then what she had to do. All doubt was lifted.

She leaned forward to distract him with a kiss on the cheek, while she gripped the dagger in her belt. His flaked skin tasted foul, but it might as well have been as sweet as candy. She slipped the dagger free while his eye was locked on hers. "It pleases me beyond words to have you here, so near the end," he said.

She smiled warmly at him. "Oh Father, you talk of looming death, but I do not think you will pass in your sleep. You are stronger than you want anyone to know."

He nodded. "Aye. You know that better than anyone, Jacqueline. The water healed us both."

She could not resist divulging the malice behind her smile. "I will bury you a thousand leagues from the sea, Father. You will never again feel the sun on your cheeks or taste salt on your lips."

He didn't seem to feel the blade until it bit half an inch into his neck as she drew it across. His eye widened with sudden comprehension, and then honed on her with lethal intent. He gripped her wrist and sat up. He continued to rise out of the bed, picking her up with strength she hadn't anticipated. She struggled to press the blade deeper into his flesh, but he clutched her wrist in place. She heard his feet hit the floor as he stepped out of the bed. He ascended to his full height, holding her aloft. She clung to him, one hand on the back of his head while the other urged the dagger forward. He embraced her tightly with one arm while twisting her wrist painfully with the other. She heard the bones in her wrist snap a split-second before a fierce jolt of pain clinched her arm. Her fingers opened involuntarily, releasing the hilt. The dagger slipped from his neck, clanging at his feet. The wound was not as grievous as she had hoped. He lifted her up until her head hit a beam in the ceiling. All sound faded. He hurtled her across the room with impossible force. She was splayed flat across the opposite wall, and she fell along with one of the paintings. The frame splintered as it landed on top of her.

"I meant to give you everything, and you dare betray me?" His wheezes grew to a frantic chorus. "It seems you must join your mother before I do."

He marched forward with no trace of his former weakness. In the dim red light, he was no longer Edward Teach. He was Blackbeard, the monster she had first met on the beach. She had tried to kill him then too, and failed.

"Twice I spared your life against my better judgment," he reminded her. "It pains me that you make me do this."

He ascended in height as he approached, taller and taller. The knot in his belt came loose, and his robe opened as he reached for her, dimly revealing every inch of his horribly charred body. His eye glowed blue, brighter than any light in the room could have allowed.

Calloway opened her mouth to scream.

Something silver flashed in front of Blackbeard's face, before it vanished into his throat. His ravaged cheeks puffed up like a blowfish, until his lips popped and blood burst from his mouth and flowed down his chin, black as tar in the deep red light, mingling with the spirals of his half-beard. The dagger was wrenched from his neck, and glistening black sheets washed out of his severed throat and down his robe. He clutched his throat and fell to his knees. Calloway was doused in the warm torrent of his blood. She blinked until she could see again.

Gabe Jenkins stood behind Blackbeard, dagger in hand. "No abundance of seawater will mend this wound," he said.

Blackbeard gagged, face bloating so terribly that even the fissures in his cheeks seeped blood. His shoulders sagged, his arms dropped to his sides, and he choked a final word. "Elise."

Gabe looked to Calloway. "Shall I continue? He might come back."

"Not even a monster can live without his head," she answered without delay.

Gabe seized a tuft of Blackbeard's hair and held his head in place as he hacked away at his neck. Blood flowed in arching sheets with every stroke, like the seawater spraying from the bow of a ship. On the third stroke, Blackbeard's eyelid fell over his blue eye, but the other remained an empty void. With a fourth and final hack, the body fell away.

Calloway pushed the splintered pieces of the picture frame off of her as she sat up. She wasn't sure she could stand just yet. "I was supposed to do this," she lamented in a quivering voice.

Gabe placed the severed head upright on Blackbeard's back, turning the hideous face toward Calloway. "Well, now you have another reason to hate me. Don't suppose this makes us even?"

She glared at him. "You didn't come here for that. You came here to snip a loose thread."

He scowled at her choice of words as he used the end of

Blackbeard's robe to wipe blood off of his blade. He stuck the dagger in his sash and walked over to her, offering her his hand. "If I were so terribly concerned with loose threads, I wouldn't have stopped with your father."

33

FREDERICK

Dawn heralded a gloomy day devoid of sun, but Frederick's mood was no less jovial. He dressed early that morning. He wore the crispest white shirt he could find and a new pair of dark brown breeches. He polished his boots until he could see his reflection in the shine. He scrubbed his face with a sponge and pulled his thin hair into a taut ponytail. He donned a dark blue coat with gold buttons, and then regarded himself in a little hand mirror. He was pleased with what he saw.

When he emerged on deck, he ordered Thomas Hobbs to clear all glass and any other potentially lethal objects from his cabin. A big and scary tattooed messenger had arrived on a little boat just before dawn, calling up to *Rampart's* deck with instructions for Frederick to meet a man named Jenkins on the beach in one hour. The messenger warned him that Katherine was dangerous, and to take proper precaution in securing her. Frederick was skeptical, but he wasn't about to leave anything to chance, not when his entire future was at stake.

Desmond and Harrison rowed him to shore under a grey sky. He had been too excited to eat that morning, and his stomach rumbled as the boat bobbed up and down. A cool breeze washed over the gentle waves. He was glad to be spared of the heat.

The many galleons and brigantines and sloops were quiet in the harbor, their crews still sleeping. The beach was empty. The pirates would likely return to their singing and dancing and debauchery later in the day, as though nothing had happened, but Frederick would be long gone by then, and he would never need to return to this cursed place.

His two men rowed around Vane's former ship, *Advance*, which was silent and dark in the harbor, like an immense black coffin. It was Teach's ship now, and would probably be put to some horrible use that Frederick would rather not think about. He wondered what had become of Vane. He supposed he needn't worry. If Vane was alive, he had bigger concerns than revenge. Still, until Frederick knew for sure, he would never feel truly secure.

He tried to push the uncertainty from his mind as he looked on the beach ahead. It didn't work. Vane's snakelike voice returned, like a whisper in his ear. *Do you think she'll let you inside her before she dies?* Frederick shuddered at the vile words. If only Captain Dillahunt hadn't been so keen on winning that duel, Vane would have been executed. Then again, if Dillahunt hadn't won, Frederick would likely be dead as well. He would never forget the fury in Vane's eyes as he bore down on him with his blunted wooden sword.

The boat slid ashore, and Frederick's men helped him out. There was no avoiding the water, and all the hard work he had put into polishing his boots proved to be a wasted effort. He flashed irritated glances at Harrison and Desmond, but they didn't acknowledge him.

Not long after, Jenkins emerged from Keelhaul Tavern with Katherine Lindsay in tow. He had to spur her into movement several times, while she flashed him angry looks.

As the two of them neared, Frederick's heartbeat increased. Her hair was just as red as he remembered, but her face was considerably darker than the pale girl he had met so many years ago. She had changed so much, he might not have recognized her even if he'd known her well.

Jenkins marched her up, gripping her arms from behind. Her hands were bound behind her back.

"Hello, Katherine," Frederick greeted in his most pleasant tone.

She tossed her hair out of her face and smirked down at Frederick. Her straightened posture was the epitome of confidence. Her features were more exotic than he remembered. It was difficult to look into her hardened eyes for too long, so he lowered his gaze to her breasts. She was no longer thin as a rail. Her hips were thicker and her breasts fuller. Her darkened cleavage showed plainly through the V of a dirty white shirt. She wore no boots.

He forced himself to lift his eyes. "It stirs the heart to see you again."

"Something's stirring, I'm sure," she quipped, glancing downward. It was obvious that she didn't know who he was, although his resemblance to Thomas probably accounted for her vaguely uncertain frown.

"I must say, the Caribbean agrees with you. Martha will not recognize you."

She angled her head inquisitively. "Should I know you?"

"Frederick. We met once, before you married my brother. I am the youngest."

She looked skyward to allow herself a moment of reminiscence. She shook her head. "Strange. You didn't leave a mark."

Gabe nudged her. "That's enough, Kate."

"It's fine," Frederick told Jenkins. He met Katherine's challenging glare. "You didn't leave much an impression on me either. Had you looked the way you do now, I can assure you I would never have forgotten. If only Thomas had lived to see the beauty you have become."

She rolled her eyes.

She does not like me, he realized. He hoped his kind smile did not betray his thoughts. It would be a long journey across the Atlantic. She would warm to him eventually. When she grew bored, her curiosity would quite naturally drive her into his arms.

Jenkins moved around Katherine. "You're not getting her without the reward. Don't think I can't kill you and your men if you try to slight me."

Frederick had no trouble believing the young man. "No need for threats, Mr. Jenkins."

"Let's hope not. I don't fancy this kind of bargaining."

Katherine's laugh was short and sharp. "You love it, Gabe."

Frederick snapped his fingers at Harrison and Desmond. They hoisted the first of two chests out of the boat and into the water, carrying it onto the beach. Their muscles strained under the weight. Jenkins left Katherine's side to inspect the contents, while Harrison and Desmond went back to the boat for the second chest.

"What is this?" Jenkins balked.

"I assure you," said Frederick, "the contents of these chests are worth more than the reward my family offered."

The young pirate swept a loose curl of hair out of his face. "I've seen these chests before."

"Katherine should recognize them as well," Frederick said. "They belonged to her former captor, Jonathan Griffith." He studied her for a reaction, but she merely looked to the sea. That was probably the last name she wanted to hear.

"It'll do," Jenkins said, closing the lid of the first chest and clapping his hands. "She's yours."

"Just like that," Katherine murmured distantly, and shook her head.

Frederick pointed at Keelhaul Tavern. "Tell Teach we are even." He never wanted to look into that horrible blue eye again.

Jenkins smiled. "Blackbeard is dead."

That was too good to be true. "You lie."

"His body is spread out on a table in Keelhaul, while his subjects pay their respects." Jenkins pointed. "Go have a look for yourself, if you've time to spare."

I don't, thought Frederick. "How did he die?"

"Jacqueline Calloway found him with his head in his lap, swiped clean off. Seems Trejean got tired of sharing his tavern. The Jamaican vanished in the night." The handsome young man's expression turned solemn. "The girl has inherited her father's men, for as long as she can hope to manage them."

Frederick was inclined to leap for joy, but he reserved himself. He didn't know anything about Teach's daughter. What if she proved to be just as sadistic as her father? "And does she require my services?"

Jenkins shook his head. "Calloway wants this woman as far from the Caribbean as possible. Beyond that, she has no further business with the likes of you."

Thank God, thought Frederick with an irrepressible shiver of elation that made Jenkins smirk. Frederick thrust out a hand. "Shall we shake on it?"

Jenkins regarded Frederick's hand suspiciously. The pinch in his brow grew longer. "I'd rather not. I don't trust clean hands."

Frederick wanted to smack the young man, but the hilt of the dagger sticking out of Jenkins' blue sash gave him pause. "You have a rather poor attitude toward negotiation, Mr. Jenkins."

Jenkins shrugged. "I'm a pirate."

Katherine threw a fierce glare his way. "Yes, you are."

"Never claimed otherwise," he defensively retorted. "Safe journey, Kate."

She looked away. "Good riddance, Gabe Jenkins. If we ever meet again, I'll be sure to repay you."

"You had your chance," he shot back.

"And you yours. You won't get another."

The young pirate cast his gaze to the sand, hair falling over his face. The air between them was thick with tension. Frederick wasn't surprised. Jenkins was the sort of man who could have any woman he wanted. *Except this one,* Frederick thought with a smile of satisfaction.

He turned from Jenkins without another word.

Harrison and Desmond helped Katherine into the boat. Frederick followed. This time he didn't care that his boots got wet. They were just boots.

They started rowing for *Rampart*. When they were a third of the way across the harbor, Frederick looked back and saw Jenkins alone on the beach, sitting atop one of his chests, with one arm resting casually across a bent knee. His curly black hair fluttered in the breeze.

"Should have let me kill him," Harrison remarked despondently. "Would have been so easy."

"I wish you had," Katherine grumbled.

Desmond shook his head. "That one isn't easy to kill."

"How would you know?" said Harrison. "He didn't even bring friends. Could have slit his throat and taken the chests *and* the girl. That's what pirates would do."

"We're not pirates," Frederick reminded him. "Who knows what a man like Jenkins is capable of? Double-crossing Vane nearly got me killed. You'll all be well compensated for your services when we return to London, I assure you. My mother will be exquisitely pleased."

Harrison shrugged. "It was a lot of treasure, is all."

Frederick looked at Katherine, who was staring over the side and into the water. "That was nothing," he said. *She is everything.*

Katherine remained silent as she climbed aboard *Rampart*. She glanced about the deck, and Frederick wondered if she was impressed. She was probably used to dirty ships, but *Rampart* was clean and large . . . at least on the outside. Below decks were horrors best left unseen. Claw marks, chains, and the rank stench of piss and shit, which never quite fled no matter how hard his crew scrubbed the decks. Sometimes, when slaves were stashed below, the smell seeped into Frederick's cabin and prevented him from sleeping. Thankfully, he would never have to transport slaves again.

"You will stay in my cabin," he informed her. To his immediate disappointment, she didn't appear relieved by the news.

She ran her finger along the shaft of a cannon. "Do you have any books for the journey?"

"Books? No. But you'll find plenty of books in London. My mother has a grand library. You remember Martha? Lovely woman. For reasons beyond me, she misses you terribly. She probably wants to know how my brother died." He chuckled. "I wonder if your stories will ease his loss? Perhaps you should soften the grisly bits."

"Martha," she murmured. She seemed dazed. "Is she well?"

"I have no idea."

Vane's silky voice returned, easing into his ear. *She must be getting on in years.*

Katherine wrinkled her nose distastefully. "She's your mother. How could you not know?"

If you bide your time, she'll be quite useless near the end, toothless and unable to squeal as you crawl naked on top of her.

"Martha's wellbeing is not my concern, so long as she lives long enough to see you delivered safely to her."

Her cunny might be a tad arid, but that won't stop you.

"Cast off at once," Frederick curtly instructed Clarence, who was yelling at a couple of deckhands over something trivial. Clarence loved to yell at deckhands, though his faint voice was far from intimidating.

"Aye, captain," Clarence replied, eyeing Katherine. "Shall I secure the prisoner?"

"She is not a prisoner." He would not treat her as Jonathan Griffith and his savages surely had. He wondered how many times had she been raped before she had submitted to Griffith's charms. A dozen? Two dozen?

Frederick would win her over with kindness, something that was almost certainly alien to her after so much time spent amongst villainous scoundrels who were familiar only with seedy women in seedy ports. And when he presented her to Martha in London, Martha would see not only her beloved Katherine returned, but a woman who had fallen desperately in love with Frederick.

Frederick seized his lower lip between his teeth, biting away a sly smile.

"She is our guest," he informed Clarence.

Katherine looked at him suddenly. "So I'm free to leave, am I?"

"I'm afraid that's the one thing I cannot allow."

Her eyes softened, and a smile brightened her pretty face. She was even more stunning when she smiled. "I'm only playing, Frederick. If you want the truth, I'm sick of the Caribbean."

"Of course you are." He knew a lie when he saw one. She was too quick to change emotions. Maybe she had been able to fool pirates, but he was no pirate.

"Clarence, show Katherine to my cabin."

Clarence leaned in close to Frederick, lowering his already breathy voice. "I don't trust this woman, captain. She survived pirates. Who knows what she's capable of? Are you certain keeping her in your cabin is wise?"

"I have taken precautions," Frederick assured him, patting one of Clarence's bony shoulders. He was in too fine a mood to let nagging get him down.

"Aye, captain," Clarence replied uncertainly. "But don't say I didn't warn you when you wake up dead tomorrow."

Clarence escorted Katherine to Frederick's cabin. Frederick watched as *Rampart's* crew went to work, weighing anchor. The ship's great sails unfurled, and she was off within the hour. Frederick turned from Isla de Mariposa, happy to never look on those twin islands again, and faced the murky horizon ahead.

Soon they were speeding across a silver ocean, with a grey canvas of clouds close overhead. It was an ugly day, but the wind was on their side. That was all that mattered.

By early afternoon, Frederick's curiosity got the better of him. He hurried to his cabin. When he reached the door, he stopped to compose himself, smoothing out his coat and straightening his hair. He cleared his throat and entered.

She was right where he hoped she'd be, on the bed. One leg was folded over the other. She sat up as he entered, throwing her legs over the side.

"Don't get up," he said.

"Just glad to see you," she said. "I've been bored out of my skull in here."

He looked around. The room had been cleared of anything dangerous, per his instruction. The wine had been removed from the cupboard. Quills and a letter opener were absent from the desk.

She offered him a little smile. "Why don't you come join me?"

He stayed right where he was. This was too easy. "Show me your hands."

She raised two fists, tightly clenched.

"Open them," he instructed.

She opened her fingers. Her palms were empty. "Nothing dangerous here," she promised.

"We're half a day from the closest isle. There is nowhere for you to swim, should you do me harm. And my crew are fine men, not pirates, so don't think you can corrupt them. The charms of women are wasted on my first mate. He won't hesitate to whip you severely and have you chained up below, where you'll endure the stink of slaves for the remainder of your journey. Don't think he wouldn't do it. He's done worse to slave women."

She made a face. "You worry too much, Frederick."

"I am a cautious man. I've heard you are quite dangerous."

"Only when I'm bored." She set a hand on her leg and curled a finger.

That did it. He couldn't resist any longer. He tore off his coat, stripping off two of the buttons in his haste. Her smile increased into a grin as he rushed into her arms. He seized her by the legs and splayed her flat across the bed. She giggled. He started to unlace her breeches. She opened her mouth in shock. "You're a fast one. No kisses?"

"After," he assured her.

She shrugged and let her head rest in her nest of thick red

hair.

He slid off her breeches. Something jingled in the pocket when the breeches hit the deck, but he dismissed it. Maybe she had stolen a couple of coins from his desk. She was welcome to them. It was the least of his concerns. He buried his face between her legs, slipping his tongue inside her. She clenched his head with her thighs and made all the right sounds. As he worked his tongue, he marveled at his fortune. This was all happening so fast. He had expected her to hold out for a week at least. Was this a dream? It couldn't be. It felt too real.

His cheek brushed against something rubbery along her inner thigh. At first he dismissed it, but then he pulled back to have a look. It was a scar—no, a burn.

She lifted her head. "Why did you stop?"

The burn was in the shape of a T. It was a brand.

Frederick fell away from her. The breath left his lungs as his rear smacked the deck. He clutched his chest, digging his fingernails into his own flesh. "You . . . " he tried to gasp, "you're . . . "

She sat up. "I'm what?"

"You're . . . "

"Yes?"

"You're not . . . "

"Spit it out, Frederick."

"You're not Katherine Lindsay!"

The woman's eyes went as wide as a child caught in the act of stealing. She looked down at the brand in her thigh. Her face loosened, as though a veil had fallen away. She blinked, sighed, and retrieved her smile. "I'm not sure how much longer I could keep that up, playing all haughty and fancy."

He struggled to breathe. "Who are you?"

"My name's Anne, but you can go on calling me Katherine if you like. I don't mind."

Frederick knew what he had to do, but he couldn't find the strength. He knew he had to get to his feet and run to Clarence and order him to turn about and make for Isla de Mariposa at once. But he also knew that it wouldn't make any difference. It was already too late. Gabe Jenkins and Katherine Lindsay would be long gone. "You're just one of Trejean's whores."

She wrinkled her nose. "That's an ugly word. I'm a strumpet. I *was* a strumpet. Gabe told me what I should say and how I should say it. I'm good at playing a part when I'm told to, if you get my meaning. He told me to pretend like me and him were lovers and I was cross with him. He said it would be like acting in a play." She reached down over the bed and fished a little red purse out of a pocket in her breeches. It jingled of coins as she shook it. "He paid me handsomely. Spending money for when I get to London. He said a pretty girl like me would have no trouble finding work."

Frederick barely heard her. He buried his face in his hands, staring through the slits of his fingers at the wavy blue patterns embroidered in the blanket hanging off the bed. He wondered how long it would take him to drown if he leapt off the stern of the ship. If he did it at night, no one would notice his absence until dawn.

"The bitch claimed her own bounty," he said, laughing hysterically into his hands. His fingers slid from his face, fingernails grinding painfully into his cheeks on their way down. He looked at the pretty whore before him, who was oblivious to his immeasurable torment. "Why? Why would you . . . why would you pretend to be her? Surely not just for a bag of coin?"

She mussed her red hair with her fingers and flashed a whimsical grin. "We've all heard stories about her. What girl doesn't want to be Kate Lindsay for a little while?"

EPILOGUE

June, 1719

With only two days left in the journey to Virginia, Terrence Baldwin watched with mounting dread as a brigantine rode the rippled column of fire that stretched from the horizon, where the swollen golden sun was suspended above the sea in a blood-red sky.

He had just settled down after an exhaustive day aboard the merchantman that had once been named *Lady Katherine*. He reclined in a hammock on the main deck and opened his favorite book. He had collected over a dozen in his travels, but this one meant more to him than any of the others. It was well worn, and some of the pages were starting to fall out. Its previous owner had kept it in far better shape. He loved the musty scent of yellowing paper and aged ink. He was about to continue where he left off, at his favorite part. Odysseus had just ordered his crew to bind him to the mainmast of his ship so he would not fall prey to the temptation of the sirens, whose beautiful song had lured so many sailors to their dooms.

That was when something caught Terrence's eye over the port bulwark. He closed the book and sat up. The brigantine was closing fast, and atop her mainmast fluttered a vibrant British flag. Terrence rolled out of the hammock, tossing his book inside the net.

He found Captain Shelby peering at the approaching ship through a golden spyglass. Stuart Shelby was only five years older than Terrence, with flowing blonde hair and a broad chin. He was tall and extremely handsome. He shaved twice a day, early in the morning and again in the middle of the afternoon, ensuring that his jaw never betrayed a hint of shadow. He wore a frilled white shirt, blue breeches, and white stockings. It was too hot for a coat.

"They are closing fast, captain," said the first mate, Garrett, who was ten years older than Shelby. He dressed similarly, but his demeanor was far less relaxed, and his hair was striped with silver.

"A few are smartly dressed," said Shelby, "but they are hiding most of their numbers. And that is as clean a flag as I've ever seen." Shelby slapped the spyglass closed and handed it to Garrett. "Pirates."

Garrett reopened the spyglass and had a look for himself. He grimly set his jaw. "They outgun us, captain."

"Aye," said Shelby.

Terrence couldn't restrain himself. "So what do we do?" he blurted.

Garrett's face spasmed with outrage. "You speak out of turn, Baldwin!"

Shelby set a hand on his first mate's shoulder and cooled him with a smile. "Mr. Baldwin is nervous around pirates, and with good reason."

"I'm sorry, captain," Terrence said, bowing his head. He

closed his eyes for only a moment, but that was long enough to see the corpse of Thomas Lindsay, and the blood seeping into the planking around him. He had not forgotten that day. He would never forget.

"No apology required," Shelby assured him. "But you need not fret."

Shelby had good reason to be confident. He was renowned for slaying a pirate captain who had made the mistake of boarding his ship. Shelby and his men fended off the remaining pirates, whose bravado fled when they saw their captain killed, and Shelby safeguarded the ship's goods before they reached the New World. Terrence knew this because Shelby's men recounted the tale night after night. Because of Shelby's heroism, the Lindsays were quick to employ him and offer him *Lady Katherine*, half a year after its former captain's death. Shelby was undaunted by the ship's misfortune, and renamed her "*Providence*."

Shelby turned to the deckhands that had gathered on the main deck, anxiously awaiting his orders. "We'll make them work for our cargo, but I cannot guarantee our speed over theirs. Once boarded, I'll entertain no acts of heroism without my initiative."

The deckhands nodded their understanding.

The pursuit didn't last long. As soon as *Providence* moved to evade, the enemy brigantine lowered its false flag and raised a giant black one embroidered with a red rose crossing over a white cutlass.

Booms sounded from chase guns. The first shot splintered the aft railing on *Providence's* quarterdeck. The second split the mizzenmast, toppling it. Three crewmen scattered before the mast could claim them.

Several more blasts sounded, thumping the hull in rapid succession.

The base of the sun dipped into the sea as the brigantine pulled alongside *Providence's* port. The wispy clouds that had gathered along the horizon caught fire. The silhouettes of over a hundred men crowded the brigantine's deck, framed in a canvas of ever-deepening reds permeated by wisps of orange flame. They raised their cutlasses and axes and pistols, and they roared in a thunderous unison. They fired into the sky, shots echoing off of *Providence's* sails. Trails of smoke dissipated swiftly in the strong wind.

The pirates laid planks across the two ships while Shelby and his men watched. Terrence's heartbeat escalated with every passing second. He looked at Shelby, who was just standing there, hand resting atop the hilt of his sword. His face was calm, his smooth chin held high.

A handsome young man dressed all in black, save for a blue sash, crossed over first. He stepped onto *Providence's* deck without a care, sweeping a hand through a thicket of curly black hair. His long black coat flapped in the wind. In his sash was sheathed a dangerous-looking curved dagger. He looked around. "Where is your captain?"

Shelby stepped forth. If he was afraid, he didn't show it. "I am Captain Shelby."

"I'm Gabe Jenkins." His smile was amicable. "Thank you for surrendering so quickly."

Twenty-two pirates crossed over the planks and spread out behind Jenkins. They varied greatly in age and appearance. Some were cleanly dressed, while others looked as though they hadn't bathed in years.

"How might I help you gentlemen?" Shelby asked.

"We are short on supplies," Jenkins answered. "We will take only enough to keep ourselves from starving, but not your entire stock. And we might help ourselves to some of your cargo. I'm sure your employer will understand. The Atlantic is a treacherous crossing."

"That will not do," Shelby replied. "We have only enough food to get us to port."

"Your crew is well fed, captain, and you are only two days from port. They'll survive with half their normal provisions."

Shelby's hand fell upon the hilt of his sword. "And if I refuse, captain?"

Jenkins seemed amused. "You've mistaken me for someone else."

"You're not the captain?"

"Nay."

"Then let me speak to him! Or is he too cowardly to come out of his cabin?"

Jenkins laughed heartily, and the rest of the pirate crew joined in his merriment. "You don't know my captain."

Jenkins stepped aside, and across the planking strolled a slender young woman in a long maroon coat with death's head buttons that gleamed of polished silver. Her wild hair echoed the crimson sky, interspersed with fiery streaks of orange. She wore slim black breeches and tall leather boots. A white shirt was provocatively loose across her chest. A golden hoop weighted her left ear. When the wind tossed her hair away from her right ear, Terrence saw that she had no right ear at all. She clutched a long cutlass in one hand, letting the blade rest on her shoulder, and a flintlock pistol in the other. She cast a long shadow that ended at Terrence's feet. She looked directly at him, narrowing her eyes.

It can't be, he thought. Her face distantly recalled that of the girl who had been taken from this very ship a year and a half prior, but Katherine Lindsay had never been so full and so confident and so beautiful.

She shifted her gaze about the ship, from mast to mast, while a wistful smile played at her lips. "What is this ship's name?"

"*Providence*," Shelby proudly declared.

She smirked skeptically. "Are you certain?"

"What does it matter? I will not surrender her to you."

She tapped the blade of her cutlass against her shoulder. "She's not yours to surrender."

"I beg to differ."

"Do you know who I am?" The question was too casual to sound conceited.

Shelby shrugged carelessly. "A whore who mistook herself for a pirate?"

Gabe Jenkins groaned.

The woman's shoulders shook as she laughed. "Well now I *have* to take this ship."

Shelby's sword screeched as he unsheathed it. "Then we shall resolve this like men." He raised the sword high above his head and charged at her.

"An unfortunate choice of words," she quipped. Her cutlass never left her shoulder. Instead, she aimed her pistol and squeezed the trigger. The shot caught Shelby in the center of the chest, flinging him off of his feet. He landed hard on his back, and his skull smacked the deck near Terrence's feet.

The crew gasped and scattered, including Garrett. Some fled down the main hatch, while others retreated to the quarterdeck and forecastle. Terrence thought he heard a splash, but he was too petrified to move his head. He remained where he was, feet cemented to the deck.

Smoke trailed from a small black hole in Shelby's chest as he gaped in horror at his killer. His eyes rolled upward to lock with Terrence's. The captain opened his mouth. "This can't be hap—"

Shelby died.

The woman who could not possibly be Katherine Lindsay

tossed the smoking pistol aside. A furious gust of wind kicked up as she stepped forward, and her untamable crimson curls smoldered in the radiance of the setting sun, burning with the frenzied wrath of the devil's fire.

"This ship is mine."

ACKNOWLEDGEMENTS

Once again, a big fat heaping "THANK YOU" to my editors, Claire Edwards and Mark Baumgartner. I couldn't do this without you two.

And to anyone who made it this far, I am beyond humbled that you read three of my novels. Kate's journey would not have continued without reader demand!

**DON'T MISS THE FIRST
TWO ADVENTURES!**

Available at Amazon
and other stores

facebook.com/thedevilsfire

TheDevilsFire.com

ABOUT THE AUTHOR

Matt Tomerlin awoke one morning with an inexplicable urge to dispel the romantic notion of pirates. He began work on a screenplay titled, "The Devil's Fire." After extensive research on piracy, the screenplay became a novel. He published the novel several years later, and followed it with two sequels.

Tomerlin currently resides in Southern California.

Printed in Great Britain
by Amazon.co.uk, Ltd.,
Marston Gate.